A NOVEL

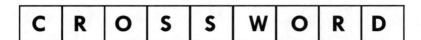

CROSSWORD

William Rawlings, Jr.

A NOVEL

HH
HARBOR HOUSE

AUGUSTA

CROSSWORD
By William Rawlings, Jr.
A Harbor House Book/2006

Copyright © 2006 by William Rawlings, Jr.

Harbor House
111 Tenth St.
Augusta, GA 30901
www.harborhousebooks.com

Jacket and book design by Nathan Elliott

Library of Congress Cataloging-in-Publication Data
Rawlings, William, 1948-
  Crossword / William Rawlings Jr.
    p. cm.
  ISBN 1-891799-50-9
  1. Crossword puzzles--Fiction. I. Title.
  PS3618.A96C76 2006
  813'.6--dc22
                              2006022290

Printed in the U.S.A.

10 9 8 7 6 5 4 3 2 1

For Beth

A C K N O W L E D G E M E N T S

WHEN ASKED about what goes into the writing of a work of fiction, I am fond of saying that I like the product but not the process. Briefly put, it's hard work. Without the support of friends and the forbearance of family, I'd probably still be pecking away on the first chapter. There are many to whom I owe a debt of gratitude.

My special thanks to Will Shortz, games editor of *The New York Times*, who was most generous with his time and input as I tossed about ways to integrate crossword puzzles into a mystery. Tommye Cashin, who has appointed herself head of my local fan club on Georgia's Golden Isles, gave me invaluable support.

Every writer hopes for a perfect manuscript, as error-free as humanly possible. My "readers" and reviewers have been most helpful in working toward that goal. Thanks to (in no special order) John Diaz, Elane Lewis, Johnny Warren, Anne Nevin, Clyde Wright, Charlie Rinkevich, Ran Shaffner, Jack Markley, Leigh Baumann, Larry Walker, and Jessica Heldreth, to name a few.

I appreciate the thoughtful daily support of my Senior Administrative Assistant, Brandi Thigpen, and the many others whose words of encouragement have kept me going.

My wife Beth, and my two children Elizabeth and Sarah, make it all worthwhile.

And of course, were it not for the talented, innovative, and at times quirky Laura Ann Ashley, my muse, none of this would have happened at all.

1

THE FIRST AND ONLY TIME I looked into the eyes of Raphael Caldera they stared back at me sightless from his severed head resting in a bed of yellow zinnias in the neatly manicured front yard of Miss Callie Walker. It was not a good way to start my day.

The call came just as I was leaving. I'd locked the house and was about to climb into my pickup when I heard the distant jangling of the phone. I glanced at my watch—8:26 a.m. I debated going back in to answer it, but figured that if it was that important they'd leave a message or call back later. Few things in my life—or in Walkerville for that matter—required great urgency. The ringing stopped for a moment and then began again. I backed the truck up and turned toward the driveway and Main Street.

I was about to pull out into the deserted Sunday morning boulevard when I heard the wail of a police siren in the distance followed rapidly by the appearance of flashing blue lights from the north heading my way. I waited for the patrol car to pass, but instead it slowed and came to a screeching halt directly in front of my truck. I recognized the sheriff's deputy but couldn't remember his name. He rolled down his window and yelled, "Hey, Mr. Rutherford. We've been trying to get a hold of you. Have you seen or heard from Stewart Jarrard in the last twenty-four hours?" Stewart Jarrard was an attorney who had recently rented office space from me.

"No. Is there a problem?"

"There may be. We don't know right now." He hesitated and then picked up the mike of his radio. "Hold on a minute." I didn't have much choice. He was blocking my exit.

After a brief exchange with an unseen voice he said, "Can you follow me? We'd like to see if you can help us identify someone." Flashing blue lights early on a Sunday morning and an unidentified person. There was no way that this could have a good outcome. He made a quick u-turn and headed back in the direction from which he'd come. I followed.

It's the uncertainty that eats at you. Dozens of scenarios played through my mind as I drove, trying to imagine what connection I might have to the assumed victim. He'd asked about Steward Jarrard. Why? Had there been an accident? A murder? Was someone in my family involved?

About a mile from the city limits we rounded a curve and the answer became obvious. There'd been a wreck at an intersection of the highway and a small, secondary crossroad. I could see an eighteen-wheeler half-off the pavement, its trailer tilted slightly toward the ditch. The trunk of a blue sedan extended from beneath the trailer, above which rose an ugly irregular patch of black soot and melted aluminum side panels. Small wisps of grey smoke drifted toward the clear blue sky as two firemen stood guard with bulky red extinguishers. A fire truck, an ambulance, and half a dozen haphazardly parked patrol cars played out an irregular visual staccato of red and blue lights. Through the open window, I caught a whiff of burned oil, and with it, an ominous hint of burned flesh. Someone was dead.

The patrolman who'd been turning back traffic from our direction waved us through. I parked behind the deputy and followed him past the debris toward a small well-maintained white frame house facing the road. The smell grew stronger. With morbid curiosity I glanced at the unburned rear of the blue car protruding from under the trailer. The top had been peeled back by the force of the impact. The driver's door was open, but the interior had been thoroughly charred. The trunk lid was ajar. The license plates were from Fulton County, Georgia. The victim was from Atlanta. I breathed a little sigh of relief, but wondered why the cops wanted to talk to me.

We approached a small knot of EMTs and police officers from both Walkerville and Adams County huddled next to the porch of the house. A bright blue tarp covered a flower bed on one side of it. I recognized Sheriff Arnett just as he saw me. "Matt, thanks for coming. I'm sorry to drag you out on something like this, but it looks like we've got a problem here. I'd welcome any help you could give us."

"What happened?"

"Obviously, there was a wreck. We have a fatality and—as I guess you can see—there was a fire. Thank God we stopped it before the gas tank went up. The vehicle's from Atlanta. We ran the plates and found out it was reported stolen sometime late yesterday afternoon. The body's pretty well burned up—I don't think we're going to have much to work with in terms of finger prints. And if the guy had a wallet or a driver's license, we couldn't find it—probably burned up, too."

"So, what do I have to with this? And what about Stewart Jarrard? You're not thinking he was the driver, are you?"

"Ah, no." The sheriff shifted his chewing tobacco in his mouth, clearly trying to decide how much he wanted to tell me. He continued, "We have some reason to believe that there may be a connection between Attorney Jarrard and the victim—whoever he is. Once we realized that, the first thing we did was try to call Jarrard, but all we got was a recording saying that his phone was out of order. I sent one of my men out to his house—looks like there's been a break-in. The phone lines are cut and the place is pretty well trashed. I reckon some things are missing, but I don't have any way of telling what until we talk with him. You probably know Jarrard better than anyone else in town. You don't have any idea where he might be?"

"No, but how do you..."

He cut me off. "Then how about telling me if you recognize the victim?"

He walked over to the flower bed and lifted up a corner of the blue tarp. The dark-haired, olive-complected head of a young, Hispanic male stared with glazed eyes toward the smoldering wreckage. I flinched involuntarily.

"I've never seen him before. But again, what's his connection to Jarrard?"

"We think he was going to kill him. Or maybe he already has."

2

THE WHOLE EPISODE RESULTED from a random event, two people with diametrically opposed goals whose paths happened to cross on a bright Sunday morning. To understand how it ended, you have to know how it began.

Walkerville's City Square was laid out in its current form after the Great Fire of 1855. It's rectangular, with the long axis lying in an east-west direction. Dominating the center is an ornate Victorian courthouse, built on the ruins of the one General Sherman and his troops burned in 1864. At one time, the Square was the hub of commerce for the county and surrounding communities, lined with general stores, haberdashers, a bakery, and the like, or so I've been told. By the time I grew up there, most retail businesses had moved to one of several shopping centers near the outskirts of town, abandoning the Square to an odd collection of attorney's offices, small gift and antique shops, two competing buffet-style restaurants serving unlimited amounts of fried food for a fixed price, a Korean-run sundry store catering to the black community, plus several city and county departments housed in renovated buildings.

Main Street, a broad tree-lined boulevard, forms the eastern edge of the Square, but the other three sides are marked by smaller lanes that never anticipated any traffic more demanding than horses and wagons. A number of years ago, the City Council solved the problem—more or less—by making these streets one-way. This works fine for locals who know how the system works, and totally confuses visitors who inevitably take the wrong way as they turn off Main Street into the Square.

Cpl. Millard Buck, a two-year veteran of the Walkerville Police Department, was just beginning his patrol shortly after 7:00 a.m. when he noted a blue sedan with Fulton County plates cruising slowly the wrong way down Gilmore Street on the north side of the Square. The driver seemed to be looking for an address.

"Hell, I started not to say anything," Buck explained. "It's Sunday morning and the place was deserted anyway. But I figured, well, I ought to let the guy know he's going the wrong way—I wasn't about to pull him over or give him a ticket or anything. So I flashed my lights at him and gave him a little whoop of the siren.

"That's when things started. He'd sorta pulled over and it looked like he was studying the front of Attorney Jarrard's office. When he heard the whoop, he looked up kinda wide-eyed and hit the gas. I just thought I'd scared him, and even then I wasn't in a mood to chase after him. He went tearing around the Square the wrong way and then runs the red light at Main Street heading east. Didn't leave me much choice, so I turned on my blues 'n' the siren and went after him.

"I guess he thought he could outrun me, or maybe lose me out in the county on one of the dirt roads. I stayed pretty much on his tail. He was heading north, so I radioed for back-up from the sheriff—I figured they might have a man out that way. Anyway, he was flying down Jenkins Road right where it hits Highway 15. Must not have seen the stop sign. I wasn't a hundred yards behind him when he plows up under the truck.

"He had to see it coming. He hit his brakes, but there was no way he could stop. Runs right up under the trailer—took the roof off his car like the lid of a sardine can. I saw this thing go flying out of the car and roll up here in Miss Callie's flower bed. Turns out it's his head. Shoulder belt probably came back and cut it off clean.

"I checked on the truck driver—he was okay. About that time the fire started. We both tried to put it out with our extinguishers, but it was about to get away from us when the fire department got here and got it under control. He…"

I interrupted him, "But how did you connect all this to

Jarrard?"

The sheriff answered, pointing at a bulky plastic bag. "We found this in the trunk." Donning a pair of latex gloves, he reached in and brought out a singed briefcase, its faux-leather plastic cover melted by the heat of the fire. Setting it on the edge of the porch, he flicked open the catches. A stubby black machine pistol with a long cylinder attached to its barrel lay on top of a folder of papers.

Looping his gloved finger in the trigger guard, the sheriff picked up the weapon.

"Silenced Mac-10. Forty shot clip. Six hundred rounds a minute. Not your average hunting rifle. And this," he continued, gingerly extracting the folder and opening it on top of the briefcase. Inside were a series of photos of Stewart Jarrard and a single typewritten page with his name, home and office addresses, and phone numbers.

"I guess you can see why we might be a little concerned..." His voice trailed off, waiting for my reply.

"Yeah." I couldn't think of anything else to say.

3

IT'S POSSIBLE THAT I did know Stewart Jarrard better than anyone else. I'd been back in town myself for less than a year, but I had the advantage of having grown up in Walkerville. It's the sort of small Southern town that doesn't really consider you a native until your family has lived there for at least four generations. I'd inherited a building on the City Square, a former lawyer's office. It was vacant. Jarrard called me out of the blue and said he was considering moving to town to open a practice. He said something about just having gotten through "a bad divorce" and that he wanted to start over somewhere quiet where life was a bit slower. He couldn't have picked a better place.

Jarrard was living in the suburbs of New York City at the time. He'd flown down on a miserable day in January and raved about the weather. I guess everything is relative. I asked him how he knew about Walkerville and the vacant office. He'd seen a note in his law school bulletin about the untimely death of Nicolas Morgan, the attorney who'd occupied the office before him and an older alumnus of his law school.

Jarrard already had a Georgia law license. His firm kept an office in Atlanta and he'd spent several years there as an associate before making partner and moving to New York. The divorce had hit him pretty hard, he said. He needed a change. I had an empty building. From my perspective, it was an ideal match. He asked about a long-term lease and wrote me a check for the first three months of rent. Who was I to argue?

It was now May, and Jarrard had become a regular member of the community. He purchased a comfortable older home on the outskirts of town and hired a maid to do housekeeping three days a week.

He joined the Rotary Club, played golf most weekends at the local country club, and seemed quite happy to be ensnared in the routine banalities of a small town law practice. He called me on occasion for advice about this or that, and we occasionally shared a cup of coffee and conversation in one of the restaurants on the Square.

But I couldn't say I knew Stewart Jarrard well. He was friendly to the point of being gregarious, but consistently and politely declined most invitations to parties and other social events. Except for joining an occasional golf foursome, he mostly kept to himself.

I guessed his age to be about fifty. He always dressed neatly, preferring dark suits cut generously to hide his middle-age paunch. As an unattached male with high income potential, he naturally became an object of interest among single, divorced, and widowed females, ranging in age from thirty to sixty. After a few months of trying, most of them seemed to give up, the word floating around the gossip circles being that he wasn't ready for another relationship so soon. He never talked about his marriage or his ex-wife. No one seemed to know whether or not he had children still living "up North."

I drove slowly back to the house, turning all this over in my mind. Jarrard had never come across as an obvious target for murder, but the fact was that I knew very little about him. I figured the truth would come out eventually; it usually does.

□□□

TEN HOURS LATER, I was just finishing my supper of tuna on rye with mayonnaise when the back door bell rang. I walked out in the center hall of the house to see the silhouette of a police officer standing on my back porch, accompanied by a shorter, heavier figure whose head swiveled constantly back and forth as if looking for something in the yard. I opened the door to see the sheriff himself accompanied by a very jittery Stewart Jarrard.

"Matt," the sheriff began somewhat awkwardly, "I hate to

trouble you, but I was wondering if we could come in and speak with you for a moment?"

"Sure," I said, trying to hide my reluctance. I opened the door wider. Jarrard scurried in past the sheriff into the relative safety of the dim hall. I led them to the front parlor and motioned for them to sit down. Jarrard nervously eyed the yard through the open curtains. He hadn't said a word.

"I really appreciate you talking with us," the sheriff began, "and to get right to the point, I want to ask you for a little favor. You were awful kind to give us some help this morning, and as I guess you can see, Mr. Jarrard is alive and quite well…"

"I've been at a continuing education course," Jarrard spoke for the first time. "Up in Atlanta. They're required, you know. To keep your law license."

What does that have to do with anything? I thought.

The sheriff continued, "I don't have to tell you what happened this morning and, of course, our concern that Attorney Jarrard here might be in serious danger."

"I can't imagine what…" Jarrard interjected.

"Please let me finish," the sheriff said.

Jarrard nodded acknowledgement.

"What we know thus far is that there was a break-in at his house. Someone—we think it was one person, but it could have been more—tore the place up. Could be burglary, or vandalism, or they could have been looking for something. We think what happened is that when I sent the deputy out to the house to check on things, the intruder was still inside. He must have heard him drive up and hightailed it out the back door before our man saw him.

"We found a single set of tracks leading east into the woods, after which we lost the trail. The interesting thing is that I just got a call about an hour ago from a farmer who lives about a mile and a half down the road. He went to his barn this afternoon and discovered that his old pickup truck was missing. He'd seen it last night and thinks someone stole it while he and his wife were at church."

Jarrard continued to fidget nervously, shifting back and forth on the embroidered silk settee. He opened his mouth as if he wanted to say something, but thinking better of it waited for the

18

sheriff to continue.

"Anyway," the sheriff said, "this is an unstable situation to say the least. We've obviously got to assume that the dead man and the burglar were working together, and that somewhere out there someone may be interested in doing some harm to Mr. Jarrard."

Jarrard bit his lip and raised his eyebrows as if to say the whole thing was beyond his control. I simply said, "Yes."

"Things are certainly in flux, and until we have a better handle on what's going on, I think we're obligated to offer him protection." I didn't like the way the sheriff used the word "we." He looked at Jarrard and paused.

Before he could continue, Jarrard blurted out, "Matt, it was my idea. I suggested to them that you'd probably let me stay over here for a few days. Just until I get the house repaired. They kicked in the back door and dumped out all the drawers and cabinets. And I fully intend to get back home as soon as possible but I think I need to get a good alarm system installed before I do…" His voice trailed off as if the short outburst had relieved the pressure inside.

"After I thought about it, it does make sense," the sheriff said. "I know you installed a good alarm system last year after those break-ins that followed your Aunt Lillie's death. And you're right here in town on Main Street. Hell, if I tried to post a guard at Mr. Jarrard's place, I'd need at least two men for each of three shifts— I just don't have the manpower. Same thing would apply to one of the motels. Here at Rutherford Hall, there's no way a person could sneak up on you without somebody seeing him. The Walkerville Police station is just around the corner, and my men pass by here every half an hour or so. Won't be any trouble to stop by for a little look-see when we do."

"I don't have any real family, you know, since the divorce," Jarrard said. "I feel like you know me better than anyone else in town. You've always been willing to help me out when I needed it."

His round face gave me a look that reminded me of a lost puppy about to be condemned to the pound.

"I know it may be a slight imposition, but I surely would appreciate it if you could help us on this one," the sheriff said. "It'd only be for a few days, a week at most, until we can get a handle on the situation and make some other arrangements."

They had put me in a position where I really couldn't say no. I smiled grimly, trying to hide the annoyance. "Uh, sure. I think that'd be fine. I've got plenty of room and it won't be a bother at all," I lied.

I was annoyed and felt put-upon, but the sheriff did have a point. I did have an extra bedroom, a good alarm system, and the location of Rutherford Hall made it unlikely that anyone would try to break in, especially if they knew the area was being watched.

"Great!" Jarrard smiled, easing his bulk up from the settee. "I packed a few things, and I'll just get them out of the car."

4

I PUT JARRARD IN ONE of the upstairs bedrooms overlooking the gardens and the old stables. He set his bags down and pulled the curtains shut before looking around the room. "I don't want to interrupt my schedule, you know," he said. "I'm sure this is all a case of mistaken identity or the like. I intend to carry on as usual. I'm going to work every day. I'm going to see clients and I'm not going to let myself be intimidated by…" He didn't finish the sentence, instead reaching up to close a little crack in one of the curtains facing the side yard.

"I promise I won't be a bother," he continued. "I usually get up early and eat breakfast at the Country Buffet on the Square. And most evenings I'll spend working on my crosswords. They've gotten to be a bit of an obsession."

I handed him a spare key to the back door and scribbled the alarm code on a scrap of paper. "Crosswords?" I said, trying to make conversation and change the subject at once. "Really? You mean like newspaper crossword puzzles?"

He nodded, still checking out the room.

"Which ones do you like? I take the Macon *Telegraph*, the *Atlanta Journal-Constitution* and the *Wall Street Journal*. I'll be glad to save them for you."

"The *New York Times* usually. Especially near the end of the week when they get more difficult. The easy puzzles run on Monday and Tuesday and Wednesday. By Friday or Saturday they're usually rather challenging. But I spend most of my time

21

writing them."

"You write them?" I was surprised.

"Well, it started off as a hobby, you know." He seemed relieved to be talking about something other than the day's events. "Back when I was a federal prosecutor. Something to do to calm my nerves while the jury was out. And after a while, you get pretty good at it. It's a game. You've got to think like the fellow that wrote the puzzle, you know. I finally decided I wanted to try writing one on my own. Most of the big newspaper editors will take unsolicited submissions. Sort of like writing a book and sending it to a publisher, hoping he'll want to print it, but on a smaller scale. About ten years ago, the *Times* took one for their Tuesday edition. Since then I've had about a hundred published, mainly in the *Times*, but also in several puzzle magazines. Sometimes I write under the byline 'Flavius Silva.' A Roman commander, you know." Jarrard liked to say "You know." I made a few more polite comments and wished him well. He was starting to unpack his things as I headed back down the stairs. I was not at all pleased with the situation.

The sheriff was true to his word. A steady stream of patrol cars eased in and out of my driveway at all hours of the day and night. Uniformed patrolmen strolled by at odd times, shining bright lights into the dark recesses of my yard.

As for Jarrard, I saw little of him for the next couple of days. On Monday morning, I heard his alarm clock go off at 5:30 and the beeping of the security system as he slipped out the door shortly after 6:00.

That evening, he returned at dusk, parking his Cadillac in the back yard next to my Ford pickup. I offered him dinner, but he said he'd just eaten before returning to the house. He told me that he'd met with the sheriff and several state investigators, and that "they're making progress on things," whatever that was supposed to mean. He'd lined up some repairmen for the house and ordered an alarm system, but work couldn't start until the police were totally finished with "the crime scene."

I found his choice of words odd, but remembered that he'd been a prosecutor sometime in the past. We exchanged a few sentences before he excused himself to his room for the night.

Tuesday was the same, with Jarrard leaving at first light. I was drinking coffee and reading the newspaper in the kitchen when Eula Mae arrived at 8:00. She'd worked for my Aunt Lillie two or three days a week for nearly twenty years, and—to use her words—had "come with the house" when I inherited it. Normally she was the embodiment of sunshine. This time she let herself quietly in the back door and threw her bag in the pantry. I said good morning. She muttered an inaudible reply. I was surprised.

"You all right this morning?" I asked.

"Well, I'd say I got a bit more sense than you do, Mr. Matt." She noisily shuffled the dishes in the sink, not looking at me. I figured that I'd done something to make her mad.

"Okay, whatever I did, I'm sorry."

She didn't reply and continued rinsing the dishes and stuffing them in the dishwasher. After a moment she said, "Look, I ain't the boss here, and I ain't the one to tell you what to do, but why come you lettin' that lawyer fella Jarrard stay here? He ain't gon' be nothing but bad news."

"How'd you know about that?"

"Us maids talk. My first cousin's wife's sister's working for him. Say he be real peculiar. Secretive, kinda. Always working on them computers and them puzzles of his."

"It's his hobby. He enjoys it. What's wrong with that?" I didn't like having to defend myself. Or Jarrard.

"Well," she said, folding her dishrag and turning around to face me with arms crossed, "I hate to say it, but there ain't no good gonna come outta him being here. Somebody's done tried to kill him, tore his house up, and you be the fool that takes him in. You gonna get splashed with the same mud what dirties him."

"Eula Mae, it's not like that. I don't like having him here any more than you apparently do, but the sheriff came to me and asked."

"Yeah, but ain't you got no sense? You don't half know the man. Ain't nobody here that do, so near as I can tell. Most of the folks you hang out with around here I knows. I knows them, and I knows they family, and I may know they daddy or they granddaddy, but this Jarrard fella, he move down here from New York." She gave a firm nod of her head, as if that fact alone were evidence enough that he couldn't be trusted.

"Look, it's just for a few days, okay? Just till he gets the repairs at his house finished."

Eula Mae turned back to the sink, resuming her rinsing. Glancing over her shoulder she said, "You mark my words."

I worried she might be right.

5

JARRARD ARRIVED BACK at the house Tuesday evening shortly before sunset. In contrast to the night before, he seemed more relaxed and accepted my offer of a drink. I had just handed him a glass of Maker's Mark and water when his cell phone rang. He grabbed it from his pocket as if he'd been expecting a call. He spoke for a moment, nodding frequently, saying "Good," and "Great!" and "I'm glad to hear that." Finally, he said, "Let me ask if he'd mind," and held the phone down at his side.

"Matt, that's the sheriff on the line. They've made some progress in the investigation and he'd like to fill me in. Would it be all right if he came over for a few minutes?"

I said that would be fine, and that they could talk in the library. He spoke into the phone again, flipped it shut, and stuffed it back in his pocket. He gulped down the remaining bourbon in one long swallow and eyed the bottle sitting on the sideboard.

We sat in the kitchen and talked while we waited. Jarrard seemed upbeat. Two drinks later the sheriff arrived, parking his plain black Ford Crown Victoria in the back yard. He bounded up the steps clutching a manila folder. I pointed them toward the library, but Jarrard, inappropriately jovial after three quick drinks, suggested that we all sit down in the glassed-in dogtrot overlooking the boxwood garden. "Matt's been a part of this from the start," he said, "and I think he needs to be brought up to speed." He had made himself at home.

Rutherford Hall was built around 1870. Like many homes of

the day the kitchen was separated from the main part of the house by a long narrow porch, the dogtrot. Years ago, my grandfather had it enlarged and enclosed by huge windows for use as an informal sitting room. On one side it looked out on the back yard and old stables, on the other to a geometric maze of finely pruned boxwoods more than a century old. Jarrard led the way and flopped down on an overstuffed couch, waving his arm toward two armchairs for the sheriff and me. I sat down quietly; there wasn't much I could say.

"So, give us the good news," Jarrard said.

"I think we're making progress," the sheriff began. "I said on the phone that we'd had some breaks, and it looks like we've got IDs on both the dead man and his partner. There were apparently just two of them. Remember, I told you that the vehicle involved in the wreck had been reported stolen from a shopping mall parking deck in south Atlanta. Well, the pickup that went missing Sunday from near your house was found in another section of the same mall, obviously stolen by the second man.

"Now, the good thing is that they've got a closed circuit TV system that records all the cars entering and leaving the area. Mall security was able to identify the stolen truck as it pulled in, and they could pick up the driver on various cameras as he walked back to the parking deck and got into another car. We got the tag number for *that* vehicle as it exited the mall and traced it to a rental car agency near the airport. It was rented this past Saturday morning by two Hispanic males, both of whom registered as drivers. They were due to return it Sunday afternoon, but didn't show up. They found the car late this afternoon in one of the long-term parking lots at the Atlanta airport.

"That's the basics," the sheriff continued, "and the good news is…"

"Can we offer you a drink?" Jarrard, the consummate host, interrupted him.

The sheriff shot me a who-is-this-guy look and said, "No. Thanks. I'm on duty." Jarrard smiled and leaned back, waiting for him to continue.

"Where was I? Oh, yeah. Turns out the rental car company got photocopies of both of their driver's licenses, not to mention the fact that they paid for the rental with a credit card. Both had Virginia licenses listing Richmond addresses. One of my investigators called the Virginia DMV this afternoon and they e-mailed us blow-ups of the licenses, which I've got here."

He took two sheets of paper out of his folder and laid them on the table facing Jarrard. The attorney rattled the ice in his glass and peered cautiously at the photos on the licenses as if he half expected them to bite him.

"Nope. Never seen either one of them." He seemed a little relieved.

"The names on the licenses are Raphael Jésus Caldera—that's the dead man—and Eduardo Fernando Rojas. The licenses are legit, but according to the Richmond PD, Caldera's address is a laundromat and Rojas's an empty lot. They're looking into that. And the credit card was a clone—a stolen number for a real account—and of course worthless."

"How about the car—and the pick-up?" Jarrard asked, shifting back and forth. "Prints or the like."

"The crime lab's processing them. And we've got in a request to the Feds for help in identifying any flight bookings coming or going."

"Oh." Jarrard rattled the ice in his glass.

"Take a couple of days, minimum."

"Oh."

"I think we'll eventually come up with something—or somebody—but right now, any more thoughts on who might want to see you," the sheriff hesitated, "injured?"

Jarrard sucked at an ice cube from the bottom of his glass and glanced at me as if he'd like another drink. I ignored the hint. "Well," he said, "like I told you yesterday, it's probably going to be somebody I put behind bars when I was doing federal violent crimes prosecution. Probably someone who just got out of the pen. Did the U.S. Attorney's office in Atlanta talk with you?"

"They did, and they're working on a list. Reviewing your old cases and the like."

"So maybe we should just sit tight for the moment."

"Don't have much choice," the sheriff said, carefully laying the license photos back in his folder. He hesitated a moment and said, "Again, you're pretty certain it couldn't be something else? Another client, business deal gone bad, someone you sued, that sort of thing?"

"Oh, heavens, no! I was a partner at Dewey, Naughton, Pierce, Williams, Young and Eaton. The ultimate white-shoe law firm. We did a little securities work and some civil litigation, but mainly real estate, trusts, estate planning, tax law and the like. Pretty boring stuff, really." Jarrard rattled the ice in his empty glass and headed for the kitchen to pour his own drink.

6

I WAS AT MY OFFICE Wednesday morning when Sheriff Arnett called.

"Matt, mind if I come over?"

I told him that I wasn't busy. He said that he'd be there in fifteen minutes.

Aunt Lillie had managed her estate from Rutherford Hall. My late father's estate was managed by Nick Morgan before his death. With both Lillie and Morgan dead, the job fell to me. I rented a quiet second-floor office overlooking the City Square and moved everything there. I had inherited well. There was a lot to manage, but not a lot that needed to be done on any given day. I hired a part-time secretary who worked a couple of half days a week and who could show up and look efficient on those rare occasions when I met with someone on business. The former tenant in my new office had been an insurance agency.

The sheriff entered without knocking. "When are you going to put your name on the door?" he asked. "You probably get people in here wanting to buy auto insurance."

"I do, actually. I'll get around to it one of these days. I still haven't made up my mind on whether I'll spend the rest of my life in Walkerville."

"Hmm," Arnett said, gazing around the room. He walked over and peered out the window. "Nice view of the Square."

"Yeah, a regular floating opera. The on-going pageantry of life in a small Georgia town."

"Don't knock it, Matt. This town's been good to your family. I, for one, am glad you're here and hope you'll stay. You could do a lot for the community."

Jesus! I thought. *He's going to ask me to join the Rotary Club.*

I said, "You said you wanted to talk with me. What can I do for you?"

"Nothing, really." Arnett stared out at the Square for a moment. "I guess I just wanted to apologize to you. And I didn't think I should do it over the phone."

"Thanks, but…"

"No. Let me finish. I'm sorry that I put you in that position the other night. I realize that you couldn't exactly say no to Jarrard. I was just up to my ass in alligators trying to get the investigation rolling. He said you were a friend and that you'd probably let him stay with you for a few days. It sounded like a quick and easy solution to one of about fifty problems I had to deal with that day. I can't say I really knew the man before now, but I must have spent five hours talking with him this week. He's a strange bird, to say the least. And after last night… well, I realized that I'd really stuck you. What I want to say is that I'm sorry, and that I owe you one."

"Thanks, but you don't need to apologize. He's not been much of a bother."

"Yeah, but he came across as a total asshole last night. You'd think he owned the place."

"He was about half drunk," I said. "Probably scared out of his wits and afraid to admit it."

I realized that I was defending Jarrard again.

"Whatever. But I won't put you in that position again. The good news, though, is that we've about wrapped up things at his house. The GBI will be finishing up today, and I understand from Jarrard that the carpenters and alarm system people are getting started first thing tomorrow morning. He should be back home by Saturday. He's arranged with a private security firm out of Atlanta to provide round-the-clock coverage for the next few weeks."

"How's the investigation coming?" I asked.

"Pretty good. The Feds say Rojas flew back to Miami after he dropped off the rental car at the airport. They've got an APB out for him, but I suspect that he's laying real low. No word yet from the U.S. Attorney's office, but they're bringing in the FBI. I'm supposed to meet with an agent from the Atlanta office today at 11:00. What I really want to do is turn this entire investigation over to the state and federal boys. It's gotten too big for me. I'll keep you informed, though. Probably meet again with Jarrard tomorrow or Friday, depending on what I hear." The sheriff glanced at his watch. "Gotta go. Again, my apologies."

"No problem," I said and walked him to the door. "I can take a house guest for three more days."

I kept busy for the rest of the day. I checked on some timber that I was harvesting on some land I'd inherited from my father. I got home by 4:00, took a shower and was reading a book when Jarrard arrived at 5:30. "I finished early. Got some take-out. Fried chicken. Mashed potatoes. Green beans. God, I love this food you eat down here. Want some?"

It was early, but I was hungry. "Sure," I said and followed him to the kitchen.

He dumped the chicken on a plate and pried open the container of potatoes, slathering gobs of thick brown gravy on top of them from another container.

"You know," he said between bites, "I feel a little better about things. Arnett's a sharp guy. GBI's on the case. The FBI was here today. It's all going to work out just fine."

I spooned some potatoes on my plate and grabbed a thigh. The chicken was still hot and dripping with grease. "Anything new?" I asked.

"Yes and no. The FBI's convinced that someone I prosecuted years ago is behind it. They don't know who, but they're gathering up a list. Bad cases, folks that have gotten out of prison in the last couple of years—that sort of thing."

I started not to say anything. I didn't want to upset him. But my curiosity got the better of me. "But where does it end, Stewart? Right now all you know is that there's somebody out there who wants you dead. What if you don't find him? What if the police and FBI can't stop him?"

I realized immediately that I'd said the wrong thing. Jarrard crammed a huge spoonful of potatoes in his mouth which was still half full of chicken. He mumbled something, and then pointing at his mouth, chewed rapidly and swallowed. He eyed the plate of chicken and said, "They will. They have to. If they don't..." He tore into a breast and the rest of what he was trying to say emerged as a slurred medley of chewing sounds and words. I nodded sympathetically, having no idea what he was talking about.

I tried to change the subject. "How are the repairs to your house coming?"

Jarrard shoveled a mound of green beans on his plate and dug into them with a fork. "Good, I think. They're going to start tomorrow, but I've gone over everything we need to do with the repairmen and the alarm system people. They should be finished by Saturday." He seemed relieved to be talking about something other than the threat to his life. "And I've hired a security firm to watch the house for a while."

"Yeah, Sheriff Arnett told me."

Jarrard's head jerked up. "You talked with Arnett?"

I nodded.

"What did he tell you about the investigation?"

"Nothing, really. He mentioned that the U.S. Attorney's office wanted the FBI on the case." I paused. "Oh, and that the guy named Rojas flew back to Miami from Atlanta."

"No word on any motives? Anything like that?"

"He just mentioned what he said in passing. I'm sure you know more than I do." I wasn't about to tell Jarrard the real reason I'd been talking with the sheriff. "As far as motives go, the only thing I've heard is that whoever's behind it is probably someone you put in jail while you were a prosecutor."

"Good," Jarrard said, and reached for another piece of chicken.

7

THURSDAY PASSED QUIETLY. Again, Jarrard left early and returned near dark, exchanging a few pleasantries before disappearing upstairs to his room. I spent most of the day doing paperwork downtown. From my vantage point on the Square, I noticed several official-looking vehicles parked in front of his law office. Investigators, I assumed.

Around 8:30 that evening, Jarrard came downstairs to ask if he could borrow my computer to send an e-mail. "I've got it right here on this USB flash drive," he said, holding up a small object. "All I need to do is plug it in and launch it."

"Sure," I said, and took him into Aunt Lillie's old office.

While the computer was booting up he explained, "It's a crossword, you know. I'm submitting it to the *New York Times*. Finally finished it. I've been working on it for a month. I hope they'll take it, but you never know."

I called up the e-mail program and left him alone to send his message. It vaguely occurred to me that this could have waited until the morning, but at the time I thought little of it.

Friday was the same. It was Eula Mae's day to work; she was still miffed and didn't hesitate to let me know it.

"What you need in this house is a good woman, Mr. Matt. Not some old, fat, broken down Yankee lawyer that somebody wants dead. You need Miss Lisa back. You still ain't heard from her, is you?"

"No, and I don't know that I will." I still missed her terribly.

"How long's it been now—six months?"

"More than seven."

"Didn't she say she was gonna call? Or write? Or something?"

"Yes, but maybe she can't. Maybe she…"

"Well, maybe you just ran her off. Did you ever think of that?

"Perhaps. But somehow I doubt it." I couldn't tell Eula Mae that the agreement I'd signed forbade me from any contact with her for six months. Not that I cared. I would have broken it in a minute if I knew where to find her. But she seemed to have disappeared off the face of the earth. All I had was the gold coin and the unsigned note that said, "I love you."

"…and so I think you need to start seeing other women." I had zoned out for a minute while Eula Mae was talking. She was probably right. I should get over Lisa and get on with my life. But a part of me said she was still out there somewhere and that she'd call.

"You listening to me?" Eula Mae questioned.

"Sorry. I was thinking about something else."

"Well, you better think about this. You need to get that lawyer man outta this house, and then you need to find you a decent woman to be here with you. You ain't getting any younger, Mr. Matt. This big old house needs some children in it, and it ain't gon' happen with that tub of lard sleepin' in your upstairs bedroom."

"I think he'll be leaving Saturday morning. Why are you so down on him?"

"Just a feeling. I just got a feeling. He eats too much."

Eula Mae had been gone for several hours when Jarrard returned. It was nearly dark. He said that the work at his house was mostly finished and that he'd be leaving in the morning. He said that he needed to talk with me but wanted to clean up and change into something more comfortable first. I told him that I'd wait for him on the dogtrot.

Half an hour later he sauntered in, dressed in baggy pants and a Hawaiian shirt that hung loosely over his ample midriff. He flopped down in one of the wing chairs. I sat opposite him on the sofa.

"Got a quick shower. I feel better now."

I offered him a drink. He declined. "I drank too much the other night. I think I made a fool of myself, and" he paused, "I guess I want to say I'm sorry. You've been a great host, Matt. I know this has been an imposition. I'd like to find some way to repay you for all..."

"You don't need to do that, Stewart. I just hope things work out for you."

"You've been a good Samaritan. You've taken a stranger in and showed me every courtesy. This wouldn't have happened in New York."

"Walkerville is not New York."

"Yes, I know." He shifted uncomfortably in the chair. "In addition to everything else, you've been a friend to me when you didn't have to be. I guess I don't have many real friends. You get to be my age and your whole life is built around your career and your marriage, then you do something really stupid and your world falls apart. I mean, I've some acquaintances—people I know through the crossword puzzle community—but no one I'm close to. No real friends."

I couldn't figure where all this was leading. I said, "I'm glad I could be of help to you."

"You could have said no, and you didn't. That's what counts. I was born and raised in New Jersey. My father used to say that you always need one good friend. Someone you can trust. I realize now, after all that's happened this week, that I don't even have that one friend.

"It's not that I'm worried about anything. But there are some things that happened in the past. Some things I know about—found out about actually—that might be important. Not that I was directly involved, mind you. I just made some discoveries that would hurt a lot of people if they were ever made public. Some things that should never see the light of day."

Again, he shifted back and forth in the chair, apparently uncomfortable with his own words.

"I think the sheriff, the FBI, and everyone else is in agreement that what happened last Sunday is connected to my days as a prosecutor. But somewhere in the back of my mind, I just can't be too sure. There's a possibility—a remote one, of course—that..."

"I take it you haven't said anything to the FBI."

"Oh, Lord, no! They'd want to investigate. It would open Pandora's Box, and might hurt a lot of people I've already hurt enough. And really, nothing of consequence has happened. And won't. I know that. I've made sure of that. It's just that if something happens to me, then…"

"Stewart, you don't need to be telling me all this. I don't want to know it. You need to talk with the cops, the FBI, whoever. If…"

"No, you don't understand. As long as they don't know about it, everything will be fine. I've taken care of it. Sleeping dogs and all that. If they were to start an investigation, well…" He stared out into the darkness for a moment. "I've got a wife—I mean an ex-wife—and two kids. Girl's at Princeton. The boy's finishing up at a private school in New York City. It would hurt them beyond words."

It was the first time I'd heard him mention his family.

"As if what I did hadn't already hurt them enough. You know, my son, Stewart, Jr., won't even speak to me. And my daughter…" He looked down and dabbed at his eyes.

"I can't tell you what to do"

He looked back up. "I don't want you to. I don't think you'll have to. It's just that if anything ever happens to me, I want to be sure that certain people know that this information will be taken to the authorities. I hadn't planned on this situation. There are some others…" He stopped. "Can I take you up on that drink?"

"Yes, if you'll quit talking in circles and get to the point." I was annoyed.

"I'm sorry. It's just something I've never discussed with anyone. I need to start at the beginning and explain the whole thing to you. Let me get a drink in me first."

Jarrard rose and started toward the kitchen. The window glass on the garden side exploded with a sharp crack. The bullet hit him squarely over the heart, the force of it lifting his body up and flinging him over a small side table that splintered into a dozen pieces. I hit the floor and rolled toward the relative protection of the sofa. The silence was broken only by three short raspy breaths from Jarrard's motionless body, followed shortly by the wail of police sirens.

8

THE BULLET THAT ENDED Stewart Jarrard's life was fired at 9:18. By 10:00, the yard was full of police vehicles and the entire house surrounded by yellow crime scene tape. The murder took place within the city limits, so this time primary jurisdiction fell to the Walkerville Police Department and Chief Roger Mathis, the one man in Walkerville who had it in for me.

We were standing with Sheriff Arnett in the dining room next to the dogtrot. "So, how long's it been Matt?" Mathis was saying. "Nine months, or something like that? In fact the last time I was in this house it was to investigate your cousin Lance's murder. Ever since you came back to..."

"Lay off it, Roger," the sheriff said. "Matt had nothing to do with this. Jarrard was here only because I brought him here and asked Matt if he could stay for a few days. He was doing me a favor, dammit."

"I don't doubt that, but Walkerville's had a total of two murders in the last two years, and somehow both of them have taken place in this house. Matt may not have had anything to do with either one of them, but when I smell shit I look for the flies."

I watched the exchange in silence. There wasn't much I could say. I thought Arnett was about to slug Mathis when they were interrupted by the arrival of an FBI agent. Arnett introduced me to Special Agent Kight who said, "It's just luck that I decided to stay here in Walkerville tonight. We interviewed Jarrard on Wednesday and again for a second time on Thursday. After I spoke with my people in Atlanta and Washington yesterday I made an appointment to see him tomorrow morning at eight. I drove down this evening so I could get an early start and be home for the weekend. You never know…" Turning to Arnett, he said, "Any idea about the shooter? Any evidence?"

"This one's Walkerville PD's case." He nodded at Chief Mathis. "Happened in the city limits."

Mathis gestured toward the high-intensity lights flooding the boxwood garden.

"Looks like the gunman hid between the hedges just below the window. Had an easy twenty-five-foot shot. We found a spent .223 shell casing. Judging from the exit wound, I'd suspect he was using a soft-point hunting round."

"Footprints or the like?"

"Not that we've found, but we're going to put off any more searching until light. The boxwood maze has gravel paths. Ground's too hard for prints."

"Any witnesses?" Kight asked.

"One, but probably not a good one. We got a call about 9:30 from an old lady who lives directly behind Rutherford Hall. Says she heard what she thought was a car backfiring. It was unusual enough to make her look out the window. She thinks she saw someone or something run across her back yard. She volunteered first thing that she's got cataracts, so you don't know whether she's trustworthy. One of my men is over talking with her now. We'll check her yard in the morning. It might explain how the shooter got away, though. He could have parked on one of the residential streets two or three blocks over, worked his way through several yards to the back of this house, and then lay in wait for Jarrard, hidden by the boxwoods."

Kight said, "I appreciate all you're doing and all that you've done, but I've talked with my people in Atlanta and we're going to assume jurisdiction for the investigation of this case. It's clearly an interstate case; it involves a murder that possibly traces its motives to Jarrard's service as an officer of the court, and, most importantly to you, I'm sure, it's going to require federal resources to properly investigate it."

I could see the look of relief on Arnett's face. Mathis scowled. "So the FBI's taking over?"

"Just let me say that we want to work *with* you, but we also want to assume primary investigative control." Kight tried to sound diplomatic.

Mathis wanted to be argumentative. "So you don't think we can handle it, eh? Small town cops and all that?"

Kight glanced around the room. All other conversation had quieted while half a dozen pairs of eyes waited for the next volley in the exchange. He looked down at the floor for a moment, then said, "Chief Mathis, Sheriff Arnett, may I speak with you privately for a moment?"

I waved them in the direction of the parlor and they disappeared off up the hall. I hadn't been officially interviewed, so they knew nothing about my conversation with Jarrard just before he was killed.

What he said didn't make sense. I'd heard only what sounded like the orchestra tuning up before the main performance. He talked about making "some discoveries" of things that "should never see the light of day." He referred to "sleeping dogs" and "Pandora's Box." For a moment it sounded like he was hiding some great personal embarrassment, but it had to be more than that. Whatever it was must have involved him in some way—he spoke about how it would hurt his family. But then he also said that he wasn't directly involved and that a lot of people would be hurt if the information became public. I had no real choice. I had to let someone know, presumably the FBI if they were going to take charge of the case.

Fifteen minutes passed. The Crime Lab van arrived and technicians began unpacking their gear. Jarrard's body lay in a pool of blood, his eyes half shut and a trickle of now dried blood running out of the corner of his mouth. A deep red blotch over his heart coordinated nicely with the colors of bougainvillea on his bright Hawaiian shirt.

Kight and the two Adams County lawmen returned from the parlor. Arnett had a smug look on his face. Mathis appeared cowed.

"Okay, boys," he announced loudly, "the FBI's taking charge of the case. We're going to handle the local investigation, Sheriff Arnett and me, but if you have any questions about anything else, I want you to direct them to Agent Kight or one of his men. They'll be wanting to personally interview any witnesses and will need a daily update on anything we find here." He turned to one of the city patrolmen.

"Stone, you're in charge here. I want you to be sure that Agent Kight gets all the cooperation and resources that he needs. I'll be back at the station." With that, he walked out of the room.

Kight and an agent named Rentz from the Georgia Bureau of Investigation grilled me for more than two hours. The questioning wasn't hostile, and I didn't get the impression they thought I might be in any way connected with Jarrard's killer. The GBI agent, who was in charge of the crime scene, had me walk him through exactly what happened from the moment Jarrard arrived at the house until the moment of his death. He appeared interested in the most minute details, stopping me every now and then to say, "Now exactly what was the victim doing when…"

The FBI agent, on the other hand, seemed far more interested in what had gone on in the months before the murder. How well had I known Jarrard? Did he ever mention anything to indicate that he might be running from something in his past? I don't think I was very helpful to either one of them.

Near 1:00 a.m., the forensic team packed up and left, taking Jarrard's body with them to the State Crime Lab for an autopsy. As they were leaving, they gave me the name and phone number of a firm specializing in crime scene clean-up. I stood in the doorway leading to the dogtrot and surveyed the damage. A huge purple lake of congealed blood surrounded small islands of broken table pieces. The smell of the night mingled with the sound of frogs chirping in the distance drifted through the shattered windows. I suddenly felt cold and began to shiver. Deliberately leaving the lights on, I set the alarm and climbed the stairs to bed. I felt numb. It still hadn't all sunk in.

9

I SHOULDN'T HAVE SLEPT well, but I did. I dreamt, remembering only snatches of the imagery. Stewart Jarrard and I were in a noisy crowd of people—I think it was a circus or a county fair. He wore the same bright Hawaiian shirt and was trying to explain something very complicated to me. I couldn't quite understand what he was saying. His words didn't seem to make sense.

Jarrard pointed at a door, saying, "You can hear me better if we go in here where it's quiet."

A sign above the door read "Fun House," and beyond it he led me through a long series of mirror-lined halls. We came to what appeared to be a dead end.

He stopped and said, "I know this looks like a wall, but it's really a door. You just have to understand how to get through it."

He turned and walked deliberately into the mirrored surface. The wall exploded loudly into a mass of broken glass, the shards slicing into his flesh as he forced his way through. I awoke with a start, my pulse racing. A flash of lightning illuminated the room, followed rapidly by rumbling thunder that rattled the windows. Windblown rain beat against the panes.

The clock read 4:02 a.m. For a moment I couldn't decide if the whole thing had been a very bad dream. I eased down the stairs into the big central hall. The lights in the dining room and the dogtrot were still on. The pool of blood, now darker, glistened with moisture from the rain that had blown in through the smashed windows. I turned out the lights and went back up to bed.

At 7:22, I was awakened again, this time by someone persistently punching the doorbell and beating on the back door. The storm had blown over and bright sunlight streamed through the bedroom windows.

Throwing on a pair of jeans and a T-shirt, I ran downstairs to find my Uncle Jack pacing back and forth on the stoop. When he saw me, he looked relieved.

"Thank God you're okay, Matt," he began. "I tried to phone but I got a recording that your line was out of order. Why didn't you call me?"

It hadn't occurred to me that I should, but I didn't want to tell him that. I've never been especially close to my family.

"The phone was working last night. The lightning must have knocked it out. But I..."

"But you *are* all right?" he asked, interrupting me.

"Yes, how did you..." I started to ask as he pointed toward the front yard. The answer was obvious. Two mobile TV vans from stations in Augusta and Macon were parked on Main Street, their telescopic antennae topped with satellite dishes pointed toward the sky. A City of Walkerville police cruiser was parked in my driveway, blue lights flashing. I could see Chief Mathis giving an interview to a shapely female reporter with a serious look on her face.

"Turn on the TV," Jack said. "That looks like the Augusta station. I just caught the interview with him from the other one."

I flipped on the small TV in the kitchen. The screen filled with the concerned face of Chief Roger Mathis speaking into a microphone held by a female hand. "...been a real tragedy, as you said, Mary," he was saying. "I pride myself on Walkerville's low crime rate. But now this—clearly a brutal assassination of a prominent local attorney."

The view pulled back to include the over-coiffed newscaster. "Any leads that you can share with us at this point, Chief Mathis?"

"No, but I will say that this is the second murder to occur in this house in less than a year. The previous victim appeared to have lost his life in drug-related violence."

"This is quite a beautiful old home, Chief," she replied. The

42

camera pulled back further to show the front of Rutherford Hall. "Who does it belong to?"

"One of Walkerville's oldest families, the Rutherfords. The current owner of record is Matt Rutherford, the fifth. He moved back here from California just about the time of the first murder. Of course, this current tragedy..."

"That son of a bitch!" I said and headed for the front door. Jack grabbed me by the arm and pulled me back.

"Hang on, Matt. You'll do nothing but make a fool of yourself. Mathis would like nothing more than to have you do that in front of a camera, which is just what you're going to do if you walk out that door. Just take it easy. Why don't we have a cup of coffee and you tell me what happened? Things can only get better."

□□□

THINGS GOT WORSE. Perhaps it was a slow weekend for news. Perhaps the bizarre nature of the whole chain of events propelled the story up news directors' interest list. By 8:30 a.m., phone service was restored, allowing a deluge of phone calls from press and wire service reporters from as far away as New York. A total of four camera crews showed up on my doorstep by the end of the day. Following my uncle's advice instead of my natural instincts, I politely referred them all to Sheriff Arnett, who in turn issued a series of high-sounding and essentially meaningless progress reports on the "investigation."

While this was going on, a team of half a dozen officers swarmed over the boxwood maze and rear yard of the house, searching on their hands and knees for clues under the watchful eyes of multiple TV cameras.

As if this were not bad enough, Kight and three other FBI agents appeared at mid-morning with a search warrant that allowed them to "search, secure, and retrieve any and all evidence, physical or otherwise, pertaining to the investigation of the death of William Stewart Jarrard, as authorized under Federal Code..." They collected and hauled away all of Jarrard's effects, including his clothes, laptop computer, several thick files, and what appeared to be a bag of dirty laundry. Video footage of the agents sporting "FBI" labeled windbreakers removing several bulky loads of evidence was played over and over on local news shows and

CNN.

Not counting a host of distant cousins, I have three close relatives in Walkerville: Jack and his wife Margie, and my mother. I'd debated about calling her earlier, but she tends to sleep until the late morning most days, recovering from her "cocktails" of the night before. She called shortly after noon.

"Matt, what is going on? What have you gotten yourself into now? I just got a call from Gladys Pinkston who says you're all over the news—something about a murder of that lawyer fellow, Jarrett. If you've gotten…"

"Jarrard." I corrected her. "He was here at the house and someone shot him."

There was silence on the other end of the line, then, "You not involved in this are you, Matt? I'm your mother. You can tell me the truth."

"No, not at all. He…" I stopped in mid sentence. Jack was mouthing *Let me talk with her* and holding out his hand. "Here, talk with Uncle Jack." I handed him the phone. I wandered off while he tried to explain the situation.

After surveying the murder scene I broke down and called the crime scene clean-up firm. They agreed to come in an unmarked van and promised—for an extra 25 percent of their regular hourly fee—that they could complete the job overnight and out of sight of the TV cameras. The woman on the phone, who made the whole thing sound rather routine, said "We get that sort of request all the time. No problem."

Right, I thought.

Repairing the physical damage to the house was easy. Jack and I made a quick trip to the hardware store for replacement panes and caulk and finished the job in less than an hour. The crew searching the yard for clues announced that they had finished. We went out and removed the yellow crime scene tape from around the house and gardens.

The clean-up crew arrived shortly after dark in a black van discretely labeled "CSCU, Inc." on the door. After giving me a glossy brochure and offering to let me watch a video on the value of professionalism in this important task of "bio-environmental mitigation," they presented me with a contract that equaled roughly three months of Eula Mae's wages. I signed it and gave them a credit card number. They finished and left rapidly enough to allow me to calculate that I'd paid them in excess of a thousand dollars an hour. At that point I didn't care. I simply wanted the whole thing over with.

Aunt Margie came over around 9:00, bringing some homemade spaghetti and a large bottle of red wine. They stayed with me until nearly midnight, fielding the few phone calls that continued to come in and generally lending me some support by their presence. Again, I slept well. I dreamed but remembered nothing on awakening Sunday morning.

Sunday passed quietly. The number of phone calls had fallen to a trickle, and most were from friends around the country who'd seen the coverage on TV. Waiting until after 11:00 when most of Walkerville's citizens would be at church, I left in my truck and spent the remainder of the afternoon riding around, looking at timber, and listening to the radio. It had just been one of those bad episodes, I reasoned, but now it was over and I could concentrate on other things. I couldn't have been any more wrong.

10

MONDAY DAWNED BRIGHT and peaceful. Eula Mae arrived as usual at 8:00, smiling smugly and delivering a terse string of I-told-you-sos. The traffic on Main Street surged to its 9:00 peak before settling down to a leisurely midday stream of cars and pickups. Rutherford Hall, for all that had gone on over the weekend, seemed unchanged. The causal observer wouldn't have noted the few extra ruts in the centipede lawn or the fresh caulking around two windowpanes overlooking the backyard and boxwood maze. Other than the missing table on the dogtrot and the slight smell of disinfectant lingering in the air, the interior was as it was before.

I ate an early breakfast at home, then walked a couple of hundred yards for coffee at one of the restaurants on the Square. The regular crowd was its usual friendly self, and other than a few cordial nods and brief inquiries about the weekend, it was almost as if nothing had really happened. Stewart Jarrard seemed fast on his way to becoming a strange but minor footnote in Walkerville's undistinguished history.

I sauntered over to my office about 10:00, arriving to find my part-time secretary Beverly sifting through the last few days' mail.

She said, "Good morning," and, trying to look somewhat disinterested, stated, "I hear you had big goings-on over at your house Friday night."

"Yeah, kinda scary," I said, not volunteering any more.

"You weren't hurt, were you?"

"No," I replied, making it clear that it was none of her business. She went back to sorting the bills in silence while I checked my e-mail.

Around 10:30, Agent Kight called wanting to come over to "clarify a few things." He and another FBI agent named Davis arrived fifteen minutes later. "We've been going over your statement from Friday night and had a question about one thing. You said that Jarrard e-mailed something from your computer on Thursday evening. Is that correct?"

I said that it was.

"It was supposedly a crossword puzzle that he was submitting to the *New York Times*?"

"That's what I think he said. Of course, I really don't know. I saw that he brought down a USB flash drive with whatever he was going to send already on it. I got him online and left him alone. I suppose he could have been e-mailing anything to anybody. Wasn't there anything on his laptop?"

"Do you mind if we check your computer to verify that?" Kight said. I noticed that he didn't answer my question.

"Not at all. Unless you intend to take it somewhere. I use it fairly often and don't want to be without it."

"Oh, no. We can take it in, but if you don't mind, we can just copy your hard drive to a back-up and have our people in Atlanta look at it."

It seemed like a strange request, but I had nothing to hide. "Sure. Let's do it now and get it out of the way." Forty-five minutes later I was back in the office. I really didn't expect to hear from Kight again.

The weekly *Adams County Sentinel* hit the local newsstands Tuesday afternoon with the sensationalized headline of "Local Attorney Gunned Down In Drive-By Shooting," accompanied by a photo of Jarrard blown up from a group shot taken at a Rotary Club picnic in April. The article was full of speculation and various misstatements of fact, but I was pleased to see that my name was not mentioned. The writer stated only that the murder occurred at "a private residence," and that local, state, and federal authorities were cooperating in the investigation. No mention was made of the apparent first attempt on his life less than a week earlier.

Sheriff Arnett called Thursday to say there was nothing new

in the investigation. By the weekend, talk in the cafes had turned to the upcoming end of the turkey hunting season as the murder of Stewart Jarrard faded rapidly from the town's collective memory.

□□□

IN THIS, THE THIRTIETH YEAR of my life, about the last situation I would have expected to find myself in was the one I currently occupied—unemployed, living in the same small town where I'd grown up, and with no particular direction for my future. It wasn't supposed to work out this way. I'm well-educated, with a master's degree in linguistic anthropology. I was at one time a member of the management team of a very successful high-tech firm in California. At age twenty-seven, I was pulling down a mid-six figure salary, living in a posh condo in Palo Alto with a beautiful blond girlfriend named Brandi, driving a Jag, and anticipating retirement to a life of leisure in my mid-thirties.

But just when things couldn't be any better, life has a way of slapping you in the face with a harsh dose of reality. Even now, a couple of years later, it's hard to decide if the series of events that brought me home were merely random happenings, or the fiendish punishment of the gods for some unknown slight on my part. My family has lived in Walkerville for more than a century and a half. My very name, Matthew Rutherford *the fifth*, seemed to imply that I, too, would end up living out my days here like my father, and his father, and his father, and so on. I left at age seventeen, intending to return home only for occasional holidays and family funerals.

But fate intervened. I found myself the sole occupant of Rutherford Hall and somewhat unwilling—if not ungrateful— heir to the family wealth. The condo was traded for a huge, old rambling house on Main Street; the Jag for a Ford F-250 pickup. Days formerly spent extolling the versatility of software products were now spent hiking through pine plantations with a forester making decisions on when to harvest trees that had been planted by my grandfather decades before. Evenings at the clubs were now evenings at home, reading. The pace of my life had slowed to a mere crawl.

The one thing missing, as Eula Mae liked to remind me,

was Lisa Li. She's brilliant, with a Ph.D. in mathematical games theory. She was living in San Francisco when I hired her, sight unseen, to come to Walkerville to help me unravel an old family secret that eventually solved the mystery of my father's murder that took place when I was a child.

The daughter of a Taiwanese mathematician and an Irish-American flower child, the first time I laid eyes on her I thought she was the most beautiful woman that I had ever seen. We fell in love—or so I thought—and then she was gone. Somewhere in the back of my mind I still believed that she'd call, but days turned into weeks and the winter became the spring. I'd heard nothing from her for nearly eight months.

With the strange episode of Stewart Jarrard behind me, and no word from Lisa, it struck me that it was time to get on with my life.

11

ON MONDAY MORNING, more than ten days after Jarrard's murder, Beverly rang my cell phone with a message. "They called and want you to call Davis Funeral Home," she said.

Beverly was naturally obtuse, and not usually by design.

"Who called?"

"The funeral home."

"What did they want?"

"They wanted you to call them."

"Why?"

"That's why they called you. So you could call them and tell them why you're supposed to…" She paused. "Oh, just call them," she finished and the line went dead. In a small town, everyone assumes that you've got most of the local phone numbers memorized. I didn't, but dialed directory assistance and got the number for the mortuary.

"Davis Funeral Establishment," the somber female voice on the other end of the line answered.

"This is Matt Rutherford. I had a message to call you."

"Mr. Davis wanted you to know that Mr. Jarrard's service is being held at 11:00 this coming Friday, the thirtieth, and that you and the other honorary pallbearers need to be here by 10:45. They want you all to sit together."

I was caught off guard. "Er… what service?" I honestly had no idea what she was talking about.

"His memorial service."

"Oh." I tried to think quickly. "I didn't realize that he was going to have a service." To be honest, I hadn't really thought about it.

"Yes. He requested that his remains be cremated and a small ceremony be held in his memory."

"And who are the pallbearers?"

"Only honorary pallbearers," she corrected me. "His ashes are to be scattered." I could hear her shuffling papers. "Let's see, there are the members of the Walkerville Rotary Club, the Adams County Bar Association, and you. That's all."

That was one way to get a decent crowd at one's funeral, I thought, but I had no intention of being there. "Tell Mr. Davis that I greatly appreciate the request, but I've got to be out of town that day."

"Thank you, Mr. Rutherford. I'll deliver your regrets," she said and hung up.

An hour later, Sheriff Arnett called. "Matt, we're still working on the Jarrard case. Can you spare a few minutes to meet with Agent Kight and me?" An hour later we were drinking coffee in the sheriff's conference room.

"I got the message that you said you couldn't make it for Jarrard's service. We'd really like for you to be there," Arnett said.

I couldn't hide my displeasure. "I really don't want to, okay? This whole thing has been pretty traumatic, and at this point I want to stay just as far away as possible. Does that sound unreasonable?"

They didn't say anything as they waited for me to continue. After a moment I said, "Why is he having a memorial service here, anyway? He'd lived in Walkerville for only for a few months. It's not like he's put down roots in the community."

Arnett glanced at Kight, who nodded, then said, "It's not him who's having the service. We are."

"What do you mean?"

"Let me explain. Jarrard did leave a will, and he named Rachel King, our local probate judge, as his executor. From what we've found out, he was fairly well off, but before his divorce, he was nothing short of downright rich. The ex-wife came pretty close to cleaning him out. Except for her and their kids, there's no real family. He's an only child, both parents dead, no close cousins. The will's a real simple one. Directs his executor to have his body cremated and his ashes scattered. The rest of his estate is to be placed in trust for the benefit of his two children, administered by a bank in New York. That's it. But to be precise, the exact wording is that after the cremation, the executor is to 'dispose of my remains in a fitting and proper manner.' Well, we interpret that to mean that there is to be a memorial service."

"Why? What are you getting at?"

"There's one other thing. The day after the first attempt on his life, he added a codicil to his will. It didn't change anything, but was interesting. It was a list of people that he wanted notified in the event of his death. Have a look at it."

Arnett handed me a photocopy of a two-page list of names and addresses. I perused it quickly and handed it back. "What's unusual about that? He was worried, naturally, being here and away from most of the people he's known and worked with over the last twenty years—why wouldn't he want them notified?"

"You may be right," Kight replied, "but in some respects, we're not making a lot of headway on the investigation. So, we're following the victim's wishes—more or less. We've—or, I should say, the executor—has sent out invitations to the service. You never know who will show up."

"Let me see that list again," I said. "Who are these people?"

There were twenty-six names on the list. Kight went down them one by one. "No major surprises, really. I don't see the ex-wife on here, but here are half a dozen names from his old firm. These three here are bankers, and here," he said, pointing at one name, "is his ex-father-in-law."

"Pendleton Brewster Habersham? Habersham's, LLC. Who and what is that?"

"A well known auction house in New York City. You must not be into art and antiques?"

"No," I replied simply.

"These two, though," Kight continued, "have us stumped. One of them is a warehouse manager in Greensboro, North Carolina, and the other is a proctologist in Nashville. We have no idea what the connection is. We're probably going to get around to interviewing them, but if there's any connection between them and Jarrard's murder, we'd rather develop some leads and theories first. Have some information in hand before we approach them."

"So, why do a memorial service?"

"Kinda like hunting rabbits, Matt," Arnett said. "You stand in one spot and send the dogs out. No telling what they'll flush up. It was our initial assumption that Jarrard was killed for revenge, but we haven't developed good evidence to support that. And, too, that theory doesn't explain why Caldera and Rojas trashed his house. They could have been looking for something. Most importantly, you said he was about to tell you something before he was shot. Could be a lot more to it than we know. A calculated professional hit like this one could very well mean someone wanted him silenced. So we're gonna hold a little party of sorts and see who shows up."

Arnett grinned.

□□□

ON FRIDAY MORNING at 11:00, I filed into the chapel of Davis Funeral Home accompanied by the twenty-four members of the Rotary Club who couldn't find an excuse not to attend, plus two retired members of the Adams County Bar Association. The lack of lawyers was explained by the fact that Superior Court was in session and most of the other half dozen or so had active cases on the docket that day. I dressed conservatively in a blue blazer and khakis with a muted print tie.

The crowd was surprisingly large. I'd expected half a handful of curiosity seekers to turn up, but in total, almost seventy-five people filled the small space to near capacity. The chapel was laid out with a central aisle and church-style pews on either side leading to a small elevated stage with a lectern-*cum*-pulpit. Dozens of oversized flower arrangements covered the platform. In front of it, where the casket would normally be placed, stood a small table covered with a plain, white, linen cloth. A bronze urn occupied its center, illuminated by a single, bright spotlight from the ceiling. It occurred to me that the place would double nicely as a venue for small weddings.

Two Adams County deputies dressed in nondescript black suits stood by the entryway, greeting each mourner and quietly insisting that everyone sign the guest register. Neither the Rotarians nor either of the elderly lawyers seemed to find this unusual. The honorary pallbearers entered in after the crowd had been seated. I noticed an unmarked van with tinted windows positioned in the parking lot near the mortuary entrance. I presumed that someone was inside taking pictures. My instructions from Arnett and Kight were simple: "Keep your eyes open for anything out of the ordinary, and introduce yourself to as many out-of-town people as you can."

The service lasted about twenty minutes. A minister spoke briefly and then turned the podium over to the president of the Rotary Club, a retired Human Relations manager for one of the local plants. He said a few words about how in the short time that Jarrard had lived in Walkerville, he'd exemplified the Rotary Four-Way Test in all of his actions. The minister then said a long benediction, working into it the elements of the Four-Way Test, praying for the soul of one who'd told the Truth, been Fair to all concerned, strove to build Goodwill and Better Friendships, and whose presence on this earth had been Beneficial to all. I doubt if he'd ever met Jarrard. I wanted to gag.

With the service over and the pianist playing something solemn, the honorary pallbearers were escorted out to stand in the foyer and greet the mourners as they exited. Most of them I knew, or had at least seen around town; some I didn't. Only one person stood out. He introduced himself as Conan McKenna. Late-forties, average height, neatly dressed in a dark business suit with a white shirt and bright red tie. He spoke with an accent—Irish, I'd guess, but wasn't certain—and said that he'd come to deliver the condolences of Habersham's. I mentioned that I understood that Mr. Habersham had been Jarrard's father-in-law. For an instant I thought I saw something flash across his face, then nothing. He said, "Yes, a real tragedy about that," and moved on down the line.

By 12:15, the parking lot was once again empty except for a few retired Rotarians standing in a knot and laughing over some unheard joke. I went back in the chapel looking for Arnett or Kight. The owner, Will Davis, was directing a small crew removing the flower arrangements to a large trash bin behind the building. "Save all the cards, boys. Somebody's gotta write acknowledgements, you know? Write on the back of them what the arrangement is—

like a spray of roses, or white flowers, or whatever—so t.
know what to thank 'em for."

He saw me coming and stepped down from the stage.
Matt. You were pretty close to him, eh?"

"Not really, no. Have you seen the sheriff?"

"They left a few minutes ago. Said he'd be back in a while to
pick up the cards from the flowers. Don't know why—guess he's
gonna take it on himself to write notes."

"Maybe, I don't know." I turned to leave. Jarrard's urn was
still sitting, glowing in its pool of light on the linen-covered table.
I asked, "What are you going to do with the…," I struggled for the
proper word, "ashes?"

"The cremains? They asked me to scatter them. I'll probably
put 'em out back on my hydrangeas. Gives the flowers more of a
pinkish hue." He smiled. I left.

12

I INTENDED TO FIND Kight and Arnett to report in, but hunger got the better of me and I headed instead for The County Buffet on the Square. It's one of those typical restaurants that you can find in any small, southern town. Everyone looks about the same, dressed in jeans and work shirts. About the only difference between those with college degrees and those without is that the latter group tends to wear their caps while they eat, while the former group takes them off. I ditched the tie and sport coat and stepped up to the buffet line to fill my plate with fried chicken, creamed corn, and butterbeans.

I was digging into a second helping of banana cream pie when I looked up to see two conservatively-dressed middle-aged men heading across the dining room toward me. They waved. I nodded my head, having no idea who they were. The taller of the two, in his fifties and looking somewhat uncomfortable in a suit that clearly had been purchased when he weighed twenty pounds less, said, "Mr. Rutherford?"

"Yes." I stood up and extended my hand. "Have we met?"

"No, and we are so sorry to bother you. I'm Phil Bonifay and this is Dr. Lawrence Cordy."

Dr. Cordy extended his hand and mumbled something that sounded like, "Pleased to meet you." He was short and balding and kept looking around the room, evidently ill at ease in an unfamiliar environment. I invited them to sit down.

"Mr. Rutherford," Bonifay began apologetically, "we're

friends—or I should say we *were* friends—of Stewart Jarrard. We had no idea he had passed until we got the announcement about the memorial service. We thought we should be here since we've known him so long, but we got lost on the way down from Atlanta. It looks like we missed paying our respects."

"You're from Atlanta?" I asked. I didn't recall seeing any Atlanta addresses on the list that Arnett showed me.

"Oh, no. I'm from Greensboro…" Bonifay began.

"And I'm from Nashville. In Tennessee," Cordy finished.

"Yes, of course, I saw your names on the list. You're the proctologist," I said to Cordy.

"Yes." He appeared embarrassed and looked around to see if anyone had overheard me.

Bonifay seemed to be the spokesman. "We've been friends—the three of us—for years. We're all ardent cruciverbalists,"

"You're what?" An image popped into my mind of Cordy lashed to a cross while being verbally abused by Bonifay.

"Cruciverbalists. Serious crossword puzzle fans."

"Sorry. New word for me." So much for my degree in linguistic anthropology.

Cordy spoke. "When I got the note, I called Phil. He'd just gotten his that day. We decided to fly into Atlanta and share a car driving down. We got lost. Took a wrong turn in some depressing little town half way between here and I-20. You really live far out from the city, you know?"

"I know." I decided not to say more. "So, how did you know my name?"

"Stewart e-mailed us both just before his death. The same note," Bonifay replied. "Said he'd had a problem at his house and was staying at your place."

"He said his friend Matt Rutherford had been good enough to take him in while he had some repairs done," Cordy chimed in. "He really appreciated that, he said. Yours was the only name we knew in Walkerville so when we missed the service we figured we'd try to look you up. Say how sorry we were to hear about Stewart. We asked someone on the street and they said that they'd seen you eating lunch in here. The lady at the cash register over there pointed you out."

One of the disadvantages of small town life, I thought. No

privacy. I reasoned that I'd try to make a little conversation, then get rid of them so I could finish my lunch. "So, you both are into crosswords?"

"Much more than that. We write them. We're both regular contributors to the *New York Times* weekly puzzles. In fact, that's what he said he was sending us from your house, a puzzle he wanted us to look at."

I was suddenly interested. "You said he sent you a crossword puzzle from my house?"

"Yes, he e-mailed the same note to both of us. It was a cover note with a puzzle attached to it. Stewart was evidently thinking of submitting it to the *Times*," Cordy said. "I believe that he wanted our opinion, but he said in his note that he was going to call both of us by phone that weekend and fill us in on some details."

"Sort of sounded mysterious really," Bonifay said.

"We knew he'd not been himself, though," Cordy continued. "Ever since he moved to Georgia, well, he just seemed—how do I put it?—preoccupied."

"And the quality of his work had suffered for it," Bonifay picked up. "Stewart always was a loner, but he did great puzzles. First time we met, it was at a regional tournament, he won the prize for best off-color clue. 'Bestiality.' Stumped me, and I'm good. Can you guess the answer?"

"Uh...no," I said. I'd about decided these guys were total nuts.

"Screw ewe." Bonifay grinned.

"What?"

"Screw ewe," Bonifay repeated and kept grinning. I decided this must be some sort of a joke.

"I'm not sure that I get it."

I could read disappointment on both of their faces. Bonifay explained, "'Bestiality' is the clue, right? The answer is 'screw ewe.' As in a female sheep, E-W-E. Got it now?"

"Oh, yeah. Clever. Stewart must have been quite a guy." I forced a smile.

"We knew he was sick, though," Cordy picked up. "The quality of this last puzzle he sent was, well..."

"Just say it, Larry," Bonifay said, "It was bad. Amateur stuff. I can't believe that he'd even think of submitting it to the *Times*. It was not just bad. Embarrassingly bad. He was slipping. We were talking about this on the way down here from the airport. But that was Stewart. Still trying to carry on despite whatever it was that was going to take his life."

"You know how Stewart died, don't you?" I asked.

"No," Cordy said, more confident now in his role as a physician. "Illness for some people is a very private thing. They try to keep up appearances to the last. I'd have thought cancer or something like that. He was past fifty."

"He was shot and killed."

They stared at me in shock. Cordy mumbled something. Bonifay tried to speak but couldn't seem to find his words.

"I think it would be a good idea if you spoke with the investigators."

13

I TOOK THE CRUCIVERBALISTS by the sheriff's office, leaving them in the waiting area while I went back to explain the situation. I found Arnett, one of his deputies, and Agents Kight and Davis studying a flat-screen monitor while a slide show of photos taken at the memorial service flashed on the screen. I explained as best I could about Bonifay and Cordy, and told them about the man named McKenna. Kight said the two men might help answer a few questions, and that he was "already aware of McKenna," whatever that meant. I told him I'd be around if they needed me, but I thought I'd done my part to help with the investigation. He told me they still had some questions for me, but they could wait until later.

I was walking out of the sheriff's office just as the courthouse clock chimed twice. It was a beautiful spring afternoon. The sky was a perfect shade of cerulean blue. The sound of a mower and the smell of fresh cut grass drifted across from the courthouse lawn. I was tired of hearing about Stewart Jarrard. It had been two weeks since his murder, and the whole time the incident had been hovering over me like a cloud blocking the sunshine. For an instant, I had an intense desire to see Lisa. The world could live without me for a couple of days. I drove back to Rutherford Hall, threw some clothes in a gym bag and headed to Atlanta for the weekend.

□□□

ON MONDAY MORNING I was at my office preparing a bid for a timber tract when Sheriff Arnett called. "How was your weekend?" he asked casually.

"Fine." I didn't volunteer more, hoping against reality that this was a social call. I knew that it wasn't.

"Got a few minutes?"

"When?"

"Now's fine with me," he said.

"What's up?"

"Not much. Just want to go over where we stand in the Jarrard case."

My first reaction was to slam the phone down, but I said, "Listen, Sheriff, I appreciate your calling, but I'll leave those details to you guys. That's your job. I'm out of the loop."

"I know. But there are some things that might be important. Things you need to know."

I looked at the clock. I didn't have time for this. "Why don't you come on over? I've got a project I'm working on right now, but I can spare you half an hour." Within ten minutes he was knocking on my door.

We exchanged a few pleasantries before Arnett said, "I wanted to give you some follow-up on Cordy and Bonifay. We appreciate you sending 'em our way. Apparently they knew Jarrard through 'the crossword puzzle community,' to use their term. I had no idea there were so many of them."

"Cruciverbalists," I said smiling.

"Yeah, didn't quite catch that word."

"As for Jarrard, they paint a picture of a man who was worried about something, but they have no idea what."

"So they told me."

"And the puzzle he sent to them. That confirms what you said about him sending something by e-mail the night before he was killed. Nothing that's clearly connected to his murder, though."

"So it would seem." I wondered why the hell he was here. He wasn't telling me anything I didn't already know.

"Oh, and the FBI lab said that they couldn't find anything unusual on your computer hard drive. They figure Jarrard went directly to the internet, called up one of those e-mail programs, and sent the files directly from the flash drive. Nothing suspicious about that, and Bonifay and Cordy confirm it. So… guess that's it."

"Anything else?"

"No. Wait, yes, there is. They found Rojas—our headless friend's partner—in Miami. He…"

"Why didn't you say so," I interrupted him. "Find out who hired…"

"Let me finish," Arnett said. "They found Rojas in Miami. He was floating in a canal. Looks like he was killed shortly after he arrived there."

"I see." I wasn't sure what to say. After a pause I asked, "What are you *really* here for, Sheriff? You drop in on short notice on a Monday morning ostensibly to tell me things I already know. If you're fishing for something, you're not doing a real good job of it."

"I'll give you credit, Matt. You're right." Arnett looked relieved. "Or maybe I'm not a good liar. I need to find out something for sure—you *have* told us all you know? There's nothing else? No hint from Jarrard about possible other motives? No mention of money? Or blackmail?"

"No, goddammit." I slammed my fist on the table. "I was as far from him as I am from you right now when he was shot. If you're such a fool as to believe *that* wouldn't scare the truth out of me, what more do you want?"

"I've got to be honest with you. Roger Mathis, our esteemed local police chief, thinks you're hiding something. And he's about got the FBI convinced, too. Somewhere in the back of his mind he's still got it that you were involved with your cousin's death last year. I know that's bullshit. But that was one of the reasons they wanted to see what was on your computer. To see if you were holding back on something Jarrard told you. They didn't find any clues in Jarrard's effects, including the things they took from your place or in the files at his office. They were talking about bringing you in for questioning again. I finally talked them into letting me come over here and see what I could find out.

"Matt, they know something we don't. Jarrard's murder is turning out to be more than some ex-con putting out a contract on the prosecutor who put him behind bars. I believe you, and I still feel guilty for dragging you into this in the first place. I'll tell 'em I've talked with you, and I'm convinced that you don't know any more than you've told us. I think that will be the end of it."

"I hope so. I'm getting tired of this shit."

□□□

THE REMAINDER OF THE WEEK passed quietly as the town slid into summer. One of the local lawyers agreed to take over Jarrard's clients and cases, and cleaned out his files. I put up a sign in the window advertising the office for rent and placed a small ad in the *Sentinel*. I passed the sheriff several times on the highway. He waved; I waved back. School was out for the summer and a steady stream of families packed into SUVs passed back and forth on Main Street in front of Rutherford Hall on their way to and from Florida and the delights of Disney World. Eula Mae settled down to her usual easy-going self, being especially pleased to find that I'd had a couple of dates with the neighbors' daughter who was home for the summer from graduate school. The biggest item on Walkerville's agenda appeared to be the annual Fourth of July Parade, the street dance that followed, and the fireworks that evening.

Saturday, June 14 was Flag Day. The only reason I remember it was that the evening before a dozen members of the local Veterans of Foreign Wars Post spent three hours lining both sides of Main Street with American flags posted every forty feet in the narrow strip of grass between the sidewalk and street. I'd noticed them when I drove out to pick up Laura, the graduate student, for dinner and a movie in Augusta. We ate sushi, suffered through a really bad film that had gotten rave reviews, and got home shortly before midnight. I invited her in for a glass of wine, but she asked for a rain check saying that she had to drive to Atlanta the next day to meet with her major professor. I wasn't sure if she was serious or finding a convenient excuse. She kissed me goodnight and asked me to call her on Sunday. I got to bed shortly before 1:00 a.m.

I woke up at 8:00 to the sound of someone pounding on my back door. Annoyed and still half asleep, I disarmed the alarm system, opened the upstairs window, and stuck my head out to see who was so stupid as not to be able to find the doorbell.

Charlie Poole stood on my back stoop peering up and flashing a semi-toothless smile.

"Hey, Mr. Rutherford, how you doing?"

"Fine," I said. "What do you need, Charlie?"

"I wanna wash yo' truck."

Charlie is one of those unique individuals who make up the indelible fabric of most small towns. If he lived in a city, he'd be shuffled away to some group home, hovered over by well-meaning counselors, and put on display by advocates for the homeless as just another example of the heartlessness of American society. I couldn't guess how old he was—in his forties probably—and at one time I understand he'd had a job and family. Too much alcohol over the years had taken its toll, neuron by neuron, such that now he held the dubious distinction of being the town pet, subsisting on handouts and back-door charity. He lived with his elderly grandmother much of the time, but every couple of months he'd go on a bender and she'd kick him out. He'd wander around, half stoned, until either he ran out of money and was forced to sober up, or was picked up by the local police for a few days of steady meals as a guest of the City of Walkerville. Most of the time, however, he was a pleasant distraction, always willing to do odd jobs or yard work for a meal or a little cash.

Charlie pointed at my truck. "I was walking along the sidewalk there," he pointed, as if I didn't know where the sidewalk was, "and I seen yo' truck was awful dirty, Mr. Rutherford." (He pronounced my name "Rufford.") "I know you needs it washed, so I'm here to help you."

I looked out at the truck. It could have used a wash job. "Sure, Charlie. How much?"

"Fifty dollars."

"A little steep. I'll give you ten and a plate of some of Eula Mae's leftovers. Deal?"

"I'll get right on it, Mr. Matt. Where's your hose bib?"

"Over there near the stable. I'll need to come down and move the truck for you."

I pulled on a pair of jeans, grabbed my keys, and padded down the stairs. Charlie eagerly shifted back and forth on his haunches as I unlocked the door. I stepped out on the stoop. "You ain't got no shoes on, Mr. Matt. If you goes out in that yard barefoot you gon' get sandworms. Lemme see them keys. I know I'm a drunk, and I ain't got no license, but I ain't drinking this time o' day and you don't need no license to drive a truck 'cross a yard."

He was right. I handed him the keys. "Pull it over there toward the right side of the stable. There's a faucet and hose right inside, and a bucket there in the back if you need one." I watched as he climbed up into the big green Ford F-250.

"This got four-wheel drive?" he yelled, again flashing his few remaining teeth.

"Yeah, but you don't need it."

I thought I'd better watch just to make sure that he didn't have any trouble. Charlie slammed the door. I could see him fiddling with the keys. He leaned forward and turned the ignition. As if pulled apart by unseen forces, the truck appeared to disintegrate inside a massive ball of flame. The blast made a noise, I'm sure, but I don't remember hearing it. Just the world flying apart as I raised my arms and tried to turn away. The last image I have in my mind is of the flags fluttering in the breeze on Main Street.

14

MY HEAD HURT. I was sure of that. And I had to pee. I had to tell them. Otherwise... But the words wouldn't come. I couldn't remember how to say them. I made a noise. Not words, a noise, something like, "Unh." I tried to move my hand. Something held it in place. I pulled at it. Nothing.

Then a voice, speaking to me said, "It's okay, Matt. Hang in there."

I tried again, this time my tongue and lips seemed to work. "I've got to pee, dammit."

The voice again. A woman, speaking to someone else: "He's coming out of it. Let's up the phenobarb a couple of mics." Then, to me: "You've got a tube in your bladder. It's okay. Just hang in there."

□□□

LIGHT AND DARK. Voices again, fading in and out. I caught snatches of big words: "dysrhythmia," "hyperalimentation," "intracranial." Sometimes I could understand small phrases: "...potassium is four. That's stable," or "...CT shows the sulci less flattened than initially."

What are sulci? I wondered, and drifted back off.

□□□

JOHN PHILLIP SOUZA. I remembered the name now. They called it "Stars and Stripes Forever," and the words we used to sing when we were kids: "Be kind to your friends in the swamp, for a duck may be somebody's mother" or did I make that up? I couldn't remember. Lisa was laughing, or was she crying? Or both? I couldn't tell which. Then a male voice saying, "His renal function is back to normal. We cut the drip off about six hours ago. He should be lightening up soon. I'm not sure he can hear you just yet."

Lisa again. "I know it's crazy, but he likes music. Something to help him celebrate the Fourth."

I opened my eyes. I couldn't focus. A shape. Female. Long black hair. Lisa. She screamed and I felt her hugging me in the bed. "Matt. I'm here. It's me, Lisa. Oh, God, I'm here. Can you hear me, Matt? Do you understand? I'm here for you."

I'm not sure, but I think I smiled.

□□□

JULY 9. They had moved me from the trauma unit at the medical college hospitlato a long term facility for "rehabilitation." I was sitting in the cafeteria, wearing my hospital-issued pajamas, slippers, and a fuzzy white bathrobe stamped "University Hospital Health Care Systems." Lisa was massaging my right hand.

"You know," she said, "if they had been more careful with their IVs, you wouldn't have these places on your hands."

"They'll heal." I said. I was sipping on my first cup of coffee. It smelled and tasted strangely exotic, as if I were drinking it for the very first time. "I'd forgotten how much I like this stuff."

"You were in a coma for nearly three weeks. The neurosurgeon said they were keeping you sedated until the swelling in your brain subsided. They all keep telling me that you've made some sort of miracle recovery."

I looked at the cast on my left arm and felt the scars on my face. "I'm alive at least." I had never really known the meaning of the word "weak" until now.

"Well, you've lost some weight, and…"

"How much?" I'd been afraid to look at myself in the mirror.

Lisa hesitated, "About twenty pounds—But you've gained a lot of it back since you've been eating."

I was still foggy-headed. I tried counting backwards from a hundred by sevens. "One hundred, ninety-three, eighty-four—no, eighty-six, seventy-nine…"

"Matt, what are you doing," Lisa asked.

"Trying to make my brain work right."

□□□

JULY 16. I had been in the hospital more than a month now. They said I could go home in the next few days. Or somewhere. I was almost back to my previous weight. The physical therapists called me their star patient. I could do nine minutes on the treadmill without giving out. "Pretty good, given the size of the lung contusion that you suffered," the pulmonologist said. I couldn't lift weights until the cast came off, but the orthopedist said I had "good callus" and that they'd get it off before I left the hospital. "Of course, with the metal plate on your ulna, you're going to be setting off metal detectors for the rest of your life," he added.

Thanks for small things.

Lisa slept in the chair in my room. She'd wait until I was asleep and go to her motel room to shower and change clothes. I was told that my mother visited often when I was first hospitalized, but I hadn't seen or heard from her since I regained consciousness. I suspected that she was drinking again. Uncle Jack and Aunt Margie visited daily. I'd been out of my coma for more than a week when I asked, "How are things at home?"

"Not bad," Jack said. "The damage to the house was minimal, really. I'll have the repairs finished long before you're ready for discharge. The FBI spent a few days there. You're going to need a new truck, obviously."

"Charlie? I take it…"

"He didn't suffer, Matt."

"The bomb was intended for me."

"That's what they're telling me." Jack looked grim.

We didn't speak of it again.

□□□

ON THE MORNING OF JULY 17, I returned from my morning PT session to find Special Agents Kight and Davis in my room speaking with Lisa. They smiled as I was wheeled through the door.

Kight held out his hand. "Good to see you, Matt. You were

68

lucky."

"So I hear."

"I know you've been through a lot, but the docs tell me that you're well enough now to discuss some things. We were here last month right after the bombing, but they weren't too sure about your prognosis at the time. Looks like you're making a good recovery."

"I'm not a hundred percent, but I'm getting there." The old feeling of annoyance began to creep into me.

"I guess you understand what happened," Kight said, half asking.

"More or less. Someone planted a bomb in my truck. That's all I know." I paused. "But I bet you're going to tell me that it had something to do with Stewart Jarrard's murder, right?"

"Unfortunately, you're right. Why don't you get comfortable? This is going to take a few minutes." He leaned against the dresser while I eased myself onto the bed. Lisa sat in the armchair. Davis pushed the door shut and stood in front of it.

"I've been with the bureau now for nearly fifteen years, and this has been one of the most bizarre cases that I've worked. It started off as a local case—the attempted murder of a small town lawyer. Unfortunate, of course, but not uncommon. And then it got bigger, and bigger, and bigger. What was it that Jarrard said about Pandora's Box?

"I'll spare you the details, but let me tell you briefly what we know. First, Jarrard was no saint—or maybe he was, depending on which side of the fence you're on. We suspect, but we honestly don't have any real evidence, that there are some missing funds. I use the word 'missing' because it's unclear if they were stolen, or misappropriated, or misdirected, or even existed in the first place. Whatever the case, Jarrard appears to have been at the center of it. I think he made some people mad. Some very mean people. We reason…"

"Mr. Kight," I said, "I hate to admit it, but I'm having trouble following you. They said I had a pretty bad lick on the head. I realize that I'm maybe a little slow on the uptake, but I have no idea what you're talking about."

"Me, either," Lisa said. "And I'm thinking pretty clearly. What do you mean by 'depending on which side of the fence you're on?' Or that you can't decide whether the money's 'stolen, misappropriated or misdirected?'"

Kight seemed a bit taken aback. He thought for a moment and said, "Suffice it to say that the Jarrard murder was just the tip of an iceberg, and the attempt on your life and the death of Charlie Poole are directly related."

"You've already told us that," Lisa snapped.

"Then let me get to the bottom line. We're working on things, but the case is still wide open. The threat to your life is real and continuing. I understand from your doctors that you're about ready for discharge. We don't think you should go home just yet."

"Why? Why would someone want me dead?"

"We're not sure, but our theory is that Jarrard knew something—'knew too much,' as they say in the gangster movies. If the missing funds exist, we think he knew where they were. More importantly, he knew where they came from and where they were going. We believe that whoever's behind this has two goals. First, they want to recover the money. Second, they wanted to silence any outsider who might know about it. If they are unable to accomplish the first goal, they'll settle for the second."

"I still don't understand it all," I said.

"You don't really need to," Davis spoke. "The only thing that you need to understand, Mr. Rutherford, is that your life is not worth a plugged nickel if we don't apprehend whoever is behind this. And short of that, you're living on borrowed time."

I wasn't sure how to respond. I looked at Lisa. I could read both fear and anger on her face. I said, "So I take it you have suggestions as to how to proceed?"

"That's why we're here, Mr. Rutherford," Davis continued. "This is a federal investigation. You are an important material witness. We want you off the streets and hidden away until we can make some arrests."

"Meaning?"

"Meaning that—in our best estimate—we'll have a break in this case in the next sixty to ninety days. We've spoken with your doctors. You've still got some recovering to do before you're back up to speed. We want to offer you a secure location to stay while you fully recover and we work on the case."

"You said 'witness,'" Lisa said. "Are you talking about the

Witness Protection Program?"

"Oh, no. Nothing like that," Kight replied. That's a permanent, or at least a very long-term, relocation with changes in identity and a whole new life. We want to provide protection for you, but with the idea that you'll be returning home in two or three months, maybe less if we get some breaks."

"Where did you have in mind?"

"The mountains of North Carolina," Davis answered. "A cabin of sorts, but a very private and secure one. You'll be very comfortable there."

"And very safe," Kight added.

"So you're talking about my leaving here and going there instead of back to Walkerville?"

"Right," Kight said. "And of course Ms. Li is welcome to join you. There'll be some low profile security, but you'll be left alone to do as you please."

"What is this?" Lisa asked. "A prison farm for white-collar criminals?"

"No, not at all. It's a single house that sits on the side of a mountain in the middle of a hundred acres of woodland surrounded on three sides by the Nantahala National Forest. You'll just have to see it. It's about four years old and was built as a private residence for one of the southeast's largest importers of cocaine. Unfortunately, he only lived there for about two months before moving to his current digs in the Federal Prison System. He plea-bargained a thirty-year sentence, part of which required him to turn over his assets to the government. The house is extremely well-protected by location, with the only vehicle access being a half-mile driveway beyond a closed gate. There's a killer view from the deck—you can see fifty miles on a clear day. It's got satellite TV and broadband internet."

I looked at Lisa again. My brain was still foggy. I needed her input. "What do you think?"

"I take it we'll be sharing the place with one of your men?"

"Of course not. You can take your own vehicle and come and go as you please. It's near Highlands, in North Carolina, just over the Georgia state line. This time of year the mountains are full of folks vacationing or spending a few weeks at their mountain place. Lots of snowbirds and retirees. You'll just blend into the crowd."

"What do you think?" I asked Lisa.

"As long as I can be with you, I don't care. Let's do it."

15

AFTER MORE THAN FIVE WEEKS in the hospital and two days filled with "pre-discharge conferences," I walked out the door to freedom on Tuesday morning, July 22. Well, not exactly. To be more precise, they insisted on rolling me out in a wheelchair and making me sit and watch while they loaded my things into the back of Lisa's blue BMW convertible.

The preceding two days had been hectic. Sunday, July 20 brought a parade of visits from the various doctors who'd taken care of me during my stay. My trauma surgeon breezed through, checked the chest tube scar on the left side of my thorax, and marveled at how quickly my ribs had healed. The neurosurgeon told me that they had considered a craniotomy, but decided against it. The orthopedist wanted mainly to talk about NASCAR racing, but did take a cursory look at my left arm after his assistant removed the cast. The neurologist asked a few open-ended questions and pretended to make conversation while actually assessing my short- and long-term memory. I told her that I still felt "foggy." It seemed to be my new favorite word. She suggested crossword puzzles as mental exercise and couldn't understand why I burst out laughing at the thought.

Monday was devoted mainly to the rehab staff. They made well-meaning practical suggestions for my "continuing recovery," and talked about "aftercare" and "post-traumatic stress disorder." I tolerated this as long as I could before running them off. They left me with a stack of brochures and a 24-hour toll-free number to call should I feel the need. I abandoned them in the drawer of the bedside table.

Uncle Jack was there both days. He arrived Tuesday morning lugging two huge duffle bags of clothes, plus "your wallet, toothbrush, razor, and that kind of stuff." He said that things were back to normal at the house, and that everyone was still asking about me. The cover story was going to be that I'd been more severely injured than I actually had—I wondered how that was possible—and that I was being sent to a special rehabilitation hospital in south Florida for long-term care.

"We've put out the word that you had a significant brain injury and that you have trouble speaking, writing, and walking. If you can't communicate, you'll be less of a target." He said he had everything under control with the farms and that he'd handle my business informally until I could get back home "for good."

"And I brought you this," he said, handing me a thick envelope. "There's ten thousand cash in hundred dollar bills, and a credit card from the bank in your name. Don't worry about anything. I'll cover it all and you can pay me back later." I hugged him and started to cry. They'd warned me about that, saying after a head injury like mine I might be "more emotional" than usual for a while. Lisa had giggled and muttered something that sounded like, "Finally, a sensitive man!" Now she just smiled and hugged Jack, too.

Our instructions were to drive to Highlands, North Carolina, where we were to meet Agent Davis at 3:00 p.m. in the parking lot of the Post Office. We had five hours to get there. We stopped by a convenience store and bought me a cheap pair of sunglasses. Lisa put the top down and we headed west on I-20 into the sultry heat of the dog day morning.

I said, "You know, no one has ever told me exactly what happened. I remember the explosion and then waking up in the ICU. You were the first thing I saw."

Lisa kept her eyes on the road and waited a moment before answering. "All I know is what they told me. You must have raised your left arm to protect yourself and turned to your right just as the truck exploded. Something—a big piece of metal probably—hit your arm and side. It broke a few ribs, collapsed your left lung, smashed your arm, left you with an assortment of cuts—that sort of thing. They think the head injury was the result of the blast tossing you into the side of the house. You're lucky to be alive."

"Yes," I said. For some reason I wanted to cry again. Emotional lability, I remembered. "How long have you been..." I paused, uncertain as to what to say. "When did you get there?"

"On the Tuesday after it happened. You were still on the ventilator. Everyone thought that you were going to die."

"You've been here more than a month, then." I couldn't seem to get the concept of time straight in my mind.

"Yes," Lisa said. We rode for a while in silence and then, "You haven't asked the one thing that I thought you'd ask, though."

"What's that?"

"You haven't asked where I've been."

It wasn't that I hadn't thought about it. Or that I didn't want to know. It was more that at some point in my life Lisa suddenly disappeared and now, when I truly needed her, she reappeared as if missing months had not existed.

I said, carefully, "I didn't want to know. When I thought about it, I asked myself, Why is it important? The only thing that matters is that you're here. That's all I really care about."

"Matt, it wasn't that I..."

"You don't need to explain."

"I do, but now's not the time. Later, we'll talk."

We rode silently for an hour, turning north across the rolling Georgia piedmont through the village of Washington toward the university city of Athens.

Every now and then, Lisa would reach out and squeeze my hand. The only thing she said was, "I am so sorry that I missed your birthday in October. I meant what I said in the note."

□□□

WE ARRIVED IN HIGHLANDS at 2:30, half an hour early. It's a small resort village tucked in a high mountain valley at the intersection of several narrow, twisting two-lane roads. We parked the BMW and strolled up and down Main Street, window shopping and breathing in the cool mountain air. Lisa scoped out a souvenir shop while I felt strangely out of place away from my hospital home of the past month. Just before three we drove to the Post Office and waited for Special Agent Davis.

We'd not been there five minutes when he arrived driving a ten-year-old pickup with North Carolina tags. He smiled and asked, "Ready for a little R and R? I think you'll really like the house." He asked us to follow him, driving off to the south toward a town named Walhalla. The road narrowed and twisted back and forth through fir and hemlock forest for a mile, then began to descend toward a valley below in the distance. A short way down the hill, Davis slowed and turned onto an unmarked paved drive that was suddenly blocked by an imposing set of iron gates set in posts of grey granite. Through his rear window I could see him hold up what appeared to be a garage door opener. The gates swung open. The driveway continued for another half a mile, zigzagging its way back and forth up a steep mountain through dense stands of rhododendron and mountain laurel before emerging into a gently rolling meadow on the rounded summit. Two hundred yards before us the edge seemed to drop off into infinity, and on it sat a huge wood and stone house, its grey and brown finishes stolen from the surrounding forest. We parked under a portico supported by massive hewn chestnut beams and floored with cobblestones. Lisa said, "Wow." I just stared.

"Impressive, eh?" Davis said. "I know you'll be comfortable."

"Are you kidding?" Lisa said. "This damned thing is big enough to be a hotel. I'd expected the bellman to be unloading our bags while the valet waits to park our car."

"I wish," Davis said. "But we run it on a government budget. The cleaning service comes by once a week, and the grounds get mowed several times during the summer. Other than that, you're on your own, except for the housekeeper. She'll check in most days and make sure that you've got what you need. She was supposed to meet us here at 3:30." He glanced at his watch. "We're a little early, though. Come on in and let me show you around." He unlocked the front door, swinging it open for us to enter. It was the one of the most incredible sights I'd ever seen.

16

TO DESCRIBE THE HOUSE as merely huge would have been an understatement. The entry door led into a cavernous room lined on the opposite side by a row of six French doors opening onto a deck that stretched across the back of the house. The cathedral ceiling was supported by chestnut logs matching the ones under the portico. To our right, a stacked stone fireplace dominated one wall. To our left, a kitchen and dining area overlooked the forest to the east.

"Something, hey?" Davis gestured with his open hand. "All this, paid for by neatly wrapped packages of white powder imported from South America." He pointed at the ceiling. "See those beams there? Something around 150 years old. Rescued from old barns. Only the best."

"Prison has probably been an adjustment for him," Lisa said sarcastically.

"Yep," Davis said. "Drug smuggler or not, you have to admit the guy thought big. The house has three stories. It's built on the side of the mountain, so you actually enter on the top floor. The master bedroom suite is over there beyond the fireplace. Below us there's another sitting area and four smaller bedroom suites. On the ground floor there's a full gym, a hot tub, and access to a small lawn that overlooks the valley. Let me show you the view."

Lisa's head swiveled back and forth, taking in the space. A moose head with a full set of antlers was mounted above the fireplace.

"You know, if you replaced that stuffed animal with a basketball goal, you'd probably have enough room for a..." I nudged her in the ribs and turned, grinning broadly.

Davis opened one of the French doors and we stepped out onto a wide, covered deck. The world seemed to plunge away before us into a blue-green vista of forests and gently rolling hills as far as the eye could see. "This house is built on the last tall mountain range before you start to drop off toward the foothills. Down there, just below us, is what the folks here call a 'bald,' an exposed patch of rock that drops off almost five hundred feet straight down. And out there," he said, gesturing toward the distance, "is North Carolina, a piece of northeast Georgia, and in the far distance, South Carolina."

The view was joltingly beautiful.

"In that direction right there," Davis pointed in front of us, "you can see the lights of Clemson stadium in football season — more than thirty miles away. And over here to your left the glow that you see on a clear night will be the lights of Greenville—that's even further. Toward the southwest, there, you can..." We were interrupted by footsteps behind us. A severe-looking red-headed woman stood quietly in the doorway.

"Ah, Cornelia, good to see you again," Davis smiled.

"Lisa, Matt, I'd like you to meet Mrs. Williams. She's our housekeeper and general den mother. Her job is to make sure that you two are comfortable."

I extended my hand. "Pleased to meet you, Mrs. Williams. I'm Matt Ruther—"

"No last names, Matt." Davis cut me off. "Mrs. Williams doesn't really need to know. Just Matt and Lisa will do."

Lisa extended her hand politely. I caught a look of annoyance on her face.

The housekeeper smiled broadly, revealing crooked teeth. "Jes' call me Cornelia. Don't need no 'Mrs.' or the like. Mr. Williams walked out on me fifteen-odd years ago and I been on my own ever since." Her words were shaped with an east Tennessee-Appalachian twang, a countrified version of Dolly Parton. Under slightly frizzy red hair, her fair-skinned face was weathered from years of sun exposure. I couldn't tell her age. She could have been thirty-five or fifty-five. "I'm gon' be in and out checkin' on ya.

I won't get in yer way, now. Jes' here when you need me." She stepped back as if she'd spoken her lines and was waiting for the play to continue.

"Well, good," Davis said. "Let's see the rest of the house."

I couldn't help but wonder what the place had cost to construct. The house was built into the side of the mountain. Viewed from the drive, it appeared to be a large one-story structure. It was only from the valley side that one could appreciate its true size. The upper and middle floors opened onto large decks with stunning views. The ground floor opened onto a partially covered patio and small patch of manicured lawn that ended abruptly at the steep drop of the rock face. "Don't wander out here at night," Davis warned. "One misstep and they'll be scraping you off the rocks down there."

A full-sized gym and workout room with mirrored walls took up about half the ground floor. The rest was a reproduction of an English pub, complete with a formal bar and dark oak furniture. The doors could be opened to make it an indoor-outdoor space for parties. A gigantic hot tub capable of holding at least ten steamed quietly on one end of the patio.

We rode a small elevator back up to the middle floor. It was divided into four private bedroom suites surrounding a common sitting area and another fireplace that mimicked the one on the entry level. A dark bearskin rug stretched across the wall over the mantle. "I'm going to call my friends in PETA," Lisa said to Davis, sounding very serious. He frowned and pretended not to hear. She winked at me and smiled.

Using the stairs this time, we returned to the entry level. "I've been saving the best for last," Davis said. "The master suite." He swung open a set of double doors next to the fireplace. Muted fabrics in shades of green and gold covered an antique bed and overstuffed armchairs that faced a smaller and more intimate fireplace. A single pair of French doors opened onto a private patio shielded from outside view by a hewn granite wall.

"There're separate his and hers bathrooms and dressing rooms," Davis said. "Off to the side there is a small office with a computer, a printer, and the like. And watch this." He picked up a device that looked like an oversized TV remote control. Studying it for a moment, he aimed it at what appeared to be an antique chest and pressed a button. The top of the chest began to rise silently to reveal a plasma-screen television concealed inside. He pressed another button and a news program appeared. "You've got a couple of hundred channels of satellite TV and—I know you'll like this, Lisa—broadband internet via a wireless network. The access codes are there on the desk in the office if you want to use it. Sit in the hot tub and check your e-mail, eh?"

"All the comforts of home," she replied, again with a shade of sarcasm.

"So, I guess that does it for us. I'm going to leave you here with Cornelia to go over any thing I've missed. I'll check in with you every several days, but if you need me, call." He handed Lisa his card. "Don't hesitate to use the phone for any long distance-calls, or order anything you want on pay-per-view. You're on Uncle Sam's tab for the time being. Cornelia will keep the kitchen stocked with staples, but if you want something more, there're a couple of good grocery stores in town, and lots of restaurants. Just be sure that you carry one of the gate openers with you if you leave. There're several in the table drawer by the front door. Can't get in or out without 'em."

Davis paused, waiting for us to say something. Cornelia stood silently in the background.

"Thanks. We'll let you know if we need anything," Lisa said.

"Matt, you haven't had much to say. Everything all right with you?"

Davis was right. I still was not myself. It wasn't that I couldn't think—it was more that my mind seemed to work in slow motion. Little subtleties, a smell here, a taste there, a different turn of phrase in speech, they all seemed somehow different, or foreign, or new, even in the most familiar situations. It was like my mind was slowly reprogramming itself.

I replied, "Sure, things are fine. I'm just getting used to being out of the hospital. Give me a few days and I'll find something to complain about."

Lisa smiled, reached out and squeezed my hand.

Davis left, and Cornelia seemed to come alive. "I do hope you folks are gonna enjoy being here. I grew up over near Sevierville, in Tennessee. Came over here with my husband and just stayed on after he left me. Too embarrassed to go home, I reckon. All this house here, I ain't exactly used to this kind of finery, but it's a good job and they pay me well. I should be grateful. Let me show you around."

She and Lisa disappeared in the direction of the kitchen. I sat down in a cushiony armchair facing the fireplace and moose head. I wondered if things would ever be back to normal.

17

CORNELIA LEFT AFTER PLACING our bags in the bedroom. Lisa watched her drive away and then came over and hugged me.

"It's nearly five. Are you hungry? Cornelia made some chicken salad for us. She seems so sweet. And there's stuff for sandwiches if you'd like me to make you one."

I felt like I wanted to cry again. It was so strange. I had always been the guy who didn't care. The one who never showed emotion. Now.... I blinked and broke away, avoiding her eyes. "Yeah. Sounds good. Maybe some chicken salad, but..."

"Matt," Lisa said. "You don't need to be embarrassed. You've been though a lot. I know how hard this has been on you, but I'm here. For you. It's going to be all right. Everything is going to be all right. I promise." She held me while I sobbed.

□□□

WE ATE CHICKEN SALAD on the deck and watched as the sun dropped lower in the sky, painting the ever-changing vista before us in from a palette of blues, reds and golds. We said only a few words, letting the scene before us do the talking. In a small utility room, Lisa found a wine cooler stocked with a good collection of reds and whites. She chose a côte du Rhône and poured me a glass.

"My first alcohol in more than a month. You're not trying to get me drunk and take advantage of me, are you?"

"No. I've had you before. A little something to replace the

Ambien they've been slipping you in the hospital."

I took a sip cautiously. I held it in my mouth a moment and then swallowed slowly, drawing in a short sip of air through my lips. The flat acidity of the tannins mixed with flashes of raspberry and blackcurrant followed by a spicy hint of pepper.

"It's so weird," I said. "It's like every taste, every sensation—even familiar ones—are somehow new and more intense."

"They fed you with IVs for nearly a month. Your taste buds are waking up."

"Perhaps, but it's not just taste. It's smells and sounds."

"And touch?" She smiled and took my hand.

"Yes. And touch."

"Gentle soft touches, too?"

"I think so. It's been a long time."

"Too long, I think." The golden rays of the sunset bathed her eyes.

"Then come with me," Lisa said, softly tugging on my hand.

We made love. Slowly and gently. Afterwards, I cried for a long time before I sank into a dreamless sleep.

The smell of coffee and bacon aroused me. For a moment I was still in the hospital, half expecting to hear the clang of food carts in the corridor. I opened my eyes. The room glowed with the soft illumination of morning light filtering through the patio doors. I could hear the sounds of a radio playing in the distance. There was a little ache in my chest, but I felt alive and more alert than I had since I woke up from my drug-induced sleep. I stumbled naked toward the bathroom, looking for a robe.

I found my toothbrush and razor laid out on the granite counter next to the sink. I could see that Lisa had unpacked my bags and arranged my clothes on hangers and shelves in the adjacent closet-dressing room. I spied a white terry-cloth robe hanging on a rod, and stepped in to put it on. On the opposite wall, a huge mirror stretched from floor to ceiling. A naked man, late twenties or early thirties, stared back at me from it. He looked somehow familiar with the same sandy blond hair, but pale and thinner with dark circles under his eyes. I stood before the mirror facing him, duplicating his every move and staring back with equal interest. I fingered the ugly purple scar on the left side of my chest. He touched his matching one. I turned my head to show him the scars of the healed lacerations on my cheek below my left eye. He turned his head to show me his.

Behind my new acquaintance in the mirror I could see a doorway in which Lisa suddenly appeared in a silk nightgown, watching me watch him. She stepped forward and put her arms around my waist. Her doppelgänger in the mirror did the same.

"You're beautiful, you know. A little worse for wear lately, but still beautiful," she said.

"Perhaps. I was just looking at that guy in the mirror, and…" I paused.

"And…" She squeezed me.

"He really needs a haircut."

"All in good time." The couple in the mirror stared back at us. "You want some breakfast?" she asked.

I watched her finely sculpted lips move, and noticed how she brushed her long hair out of her face. "In a few minutes, but first…" Over my shoulder I watched as my new friend turned to kiss her, then headed back toward the bedroom. This time I didn't cry.

□□□

"OKAY," LISA ANNOUNCED after we'd showered and dressed. "This is Day One of your rehabilitation regimen. You've proved to me that some parts of you still work, but we've got to get you back to where you were on June 13. We're taking a walk."

With Lisa in the lead, we headed out at a leisurely pace across the meadow and down the long drive. After a few minutes I was totally winded. I stopped, leaned over, and propped my arms on my knees. "I'm really out of shape."

"I know," she said, "and the altitude probably doesn't help. I got up early for a run this morning. The thin air makes a difference."

"You did what?"

"I went jogging. Down to the gate and back a couple of times. But I haven't been tied to a hospital bed for more than a month. I'm your new personal fitness trainer, spiritual guide and cheerleader rolled into one. We've got a lot to do, so just get ready."

I laughed and surprised myself that I did. I was feeling less emotional. "Why don't we ease back up the hill, then?"

"Great idea, but first let me mark the spot." She pulled a piece of chalk from her pocket and wrote "July 23" on the blacktop. "This afternoon, we'll stop here, but tomorrow, we go farther. And the day after that, even farther. We're walking now, but when you can make it to the bottom and back in fifteen minutes without stopping, I'll give you a break. Until then…" She smiled and started back up the hill at an easy pace without waiting for me to follow.

Over the next week, we settled into a regular regimen of early morning and late evening walks up and down the steep driveway broken by a one-hour workout in the basement gym before lunch. Between, in the afternoons, we napped, or sat on the deck taking in the mountain breezes. Cornelia arrived every morning about eleven, bringing a newspaper and the local mountain gossip while she zipped around the house straightening and dusting.

We'd been there three days before Davis called. He said he was in Atlanta at a meeting about the case and that they thought they were "making progress." Agent Kight got on the phone and asked if our accommodations were adequate and told me that he'd keep us informed. I called Jack and Margie to let them know that things were going well. They said that my mother was doing better and seemed to have cut back on her drinking. I told them to tell her that we were all right.

Lisa made a couple of trips into town for groceries, bringing me back a big tin of some nutritional supplement protein powder that she insisted I drink for breakfast. "The man in the health food store said it would help you rebuild your muscles."

"You didn't tell him anything about what happened or why we're here, did you?"

"No, of course not. Don't be silly. I went in to find some vitamins for you and told him that you'd been recovering from major surgery. He said this might help." She busied herself placing groceries in the cabinets. "Look, Matt, Highlands is a small, vacation village. I saw a brochure that said the wintertime population is only three or four thousand, but this time of year the place is so crowded that I had trouble finding a parking space. I honestly don't think we need to be worried about someone recognizing us. We're just two more strangers in the crowd. You'll see. When you get tired of my cooking we'll get reservations and eat in a real restaurant."

By the thirtieth, I could make it to the driveway gates and back in less than an hour, taking it very slowly on the uphill climb. According to the scales in my dressing room, I had gained eight pounds. Lisa found a pair of scissors and trimmed my hair, which by that time had begun to lap over my ears and curl up on my neck. The figure in the mirror began to look almost normal, as color returned to his face and the red stripes of his scars began to fade.

On Saturday, August 2, after our morning walk down and back up the mountain, Lisa announced, "You've been at training camp now for eleven days. You've earned a break. Why don't we go into town this afternoon and do a little shopping? We can pick up some groceries and maybe have an early dinner. Interested?"

I was ready for a change. "Sure. Do we need to make reservations somewhere?"

"I already have. Paoletti's at six. It's an Italian place on Main Street. The menu in the window looked good. I kind of thought you'd want to get out, but I wanted to give you a chance to say no."

We left at three. Lisa grabbed one of the oversized gate openers on the way out the door. "These things are huge," she commented. "I guess that's so you won't lose one."

"It's strange that there's not a keypad, or some other backup way to get in or out," I said. "What if the battery goes dead? Or what if you have a visitor? There's not even an intercom."

"Don't know," she replied from behind her Wayfarers. "The guy must have liked privacy. Or security. Guess you'd need it if you were in the drug trade."

"Yeah, but I still find it strange." I realized that my mind was beginning to work again.

18

THE GROCERY STORE, if one wanted to stretch the definition, was named Mountain Fresh. In any other city it would have been considered a large convenience store, but here it passed for the local version of Kroger or Publix. Lisa parked in front next to the self-service laundry. I watched her as she grabbed a cart and reviewed her shopping list like a traveler about to embark on a complicated journey. I followed her meekly down the first aisle while she compared prices and read labels until she said, "Why don't you go pick out some wine or something? I'm shopping and this requires precision and energy. You're going to get bored." I agreed gladly.

I wandered around, randomly surveying the goods. The store reminded me of a few I'd seen in California resort towns. Small, but overstocked with a vast collection of wine, a chilled selection of cheeses with unpronounceable names like asaigo, cotija, gorgonzola, and pouligny, plus a generous selection of overpriced snack crackers. The patrons were, for the most part middle-aged, affluent and—judging from the parking lot—driving either Suburbans or Mercedes with Atlanta-area license plates. A little older than Lisa and me, but I could see how we'd blend right in. She was right. I shouldn't worry about being seen in public.

Lisa finished her shopping and checked out while I stood idly by just inside the front door flipping through a real estate brochure that I'd picked up from a rack. I marveled at the prices. Even the most dilapidated single-wide was more than a hundred thousand;

I figured that the house we were staying in would be priced well into the millions.

I was studying the floor plans of a group of new condos when I sensed someone staring at me. I looked up to see a gaunt, disheveled-looking old man jerk his head down and rapidly push his cart down an aisle out of view. I tossed the brochure back in the rack and walked over to peer around the corner. He was at the far end of the aisle, hunched over the meat cooler, intently studying the roasts. I'd only gotten a glimpse of his face. From his back, I could see that he was dressed in worn, wool pants that looked like they might have belonged to a suit at one time. His shoes were scuffed with heels nearly worn off in the rear. I couldn't guess his age from what I'd seen, but he had to be in his seventies. I decided that I was being paranoid and went to help Lisa push the cart of groceries out to the car.

We loaded the bags in the trunk. A clock in the distance chimed the half-hour. "It's 4:30," Lisa said. "We've got an hour and a half. Want to ride over toward Cashiers? There's supposed to be a great view from one of the overlooks."

"Sure," I said. I was thrilled just to be out and about.

We drove north and east on Highway 64. Just beyond a sharp curve, the road hugged the side of the mountain overlooking a spectacular panorama with sheer-sided mountain and a valley below. Lisa pulled the BMW to the side of the road and we got out to take in the view. Consulting a guide book that she'd bought in town, she pointed to the mountain and said, "That is Whiteside. We can go hiking there next week if you'd like. And the valley down there," she pointed off to the southeast, "is the Chattooga River basin. The Chattooga is where they filmed the movie *Deliverance*."

"Really?" I said.

"Yes, and over there..."

"Lisa." She stopped and looked up at me.

"Yes?"

"Where were you?"

"When?" I could see alarm in her eyes.

"When you left. Last fall. I thought we..."

She dropped the guidebook to the ground and hugged me, burying her head against my chest. "Hush. Not now."

"No. I want to know. Now. I've been afraid to ask, but I've got to know. Why didn't you call me?"

Tears welled up in her eyes. "I... I couldn't call you. I wanted to but..."

"Why? Why couldn't your call me? You promised..."

"Matt, please. Please don't ask. I don't... I can't..."

I gently pushed her away and looked into her eyes. "Lisa," I stumbled, trying to find the words. "I need to know. What happened?"

She looked up at me, her expression a mixture of fear and sorrow.

"Tell me," I said.

"I wanted to, but I was afraid. I..."

"Afraid of what?" I demanded.

"Of you," she murmured. "Of us." She backed away a step, rubbing her eyes with her hands. "Let me talk for a minute. Then you can ask all the questions you'd like."

I nodded. She took a deep breath and began, "Last year, remember how they made us promise not to contact each other for six months? Didn't you think it was strange?"

"Yes."

"They took me away that morning before you woke up. They told you I was going back to San Francisco, but instead I ended up at Fort Meade, near Washington, DC. They'd seen what I could do cracking codes and knew that I spoke fluent Mandarin Chinese. They made me an ugly little proposition. Either I spent six months working for them on what they referred to as a 'special project,' or they'd find a way to charge you with Nick Morgan's death. They used our relationship, Matt..." A tear ran down her cheek.

"Who is 'they?' What did they make you do?"

"I'm not exactly sure 'who.' Oh, I know names and places and dates, not that I could ever use them. Basically it was a joint espionage operation conducted by the CIA with the backing of the NSA. They flew me to Tokyo, where I posed as an employee of the U.S. Embassy. One of the clerks in the Japanese Defense Agency was passing messages to the Chinese military attaché. They'd been intercepting them but couldn't break the code. So they put me to work. They watched my every move. I wanted to call you but I was afraid to. And then I realized that it wasn't my fear of the government or getting caught, it was you that I was afraid of..."

"What are you talking about?"

"I realized that I'd fallen in love with you, and I didn't know how to handle it. There was one part of me that ached to be with you, and another part that told me I'd only get burned. So I lied to myself. I tried to pretend that you'd used me, that you didn't care about me. That you'd only needed me to help you find..."

"Lisa, how could you..."

"I don't know." She turned and looked out toward the mountain, her eyes wet. "I don't know what I was thinking. I was on some crazy assignment in a foreign country. I tried to push you out of my mind, but you kept coming back. I picked up the phone a dozen times to call you, but every time I'd get halfway through dialing your number and hang up. It went on like that, week after week, until one day I realized that I had to quit lying to myself. I needed to be with you. I needed to know where things were going to go from there. With us."

"So what did you do?"

"I finished the assignment. I cracked their code—I got them what *they* wanted, and came back to find what *I* wanted. They paid me well for my time and got me home. The first thing I did when I got to the States was to call you. Of course, I heard what happened. I flew to Atlanta, bought a car, and I've been with you ever since. And by telling you all that I've just violated all sorts of national security laws."

"Then we've said all we need to say. Let's go have dinner."

Lisa couldn't see it, but I could feel myself smiling on the inside.

□□□

PAOLETTI'S WAS CROWDED with early evening diners. We waited ten minutes for our table, making idle conversation with a couple from Atlanta who'd just bought a house in Inverness Glen, one of the many cookie-cutter gated golf course developments that were sprouting from the surrounding mountains. I ordered veal, Lisa had the lobster ravioli. We split a bottle of Veuve Clicquot and shared tiramisu for dessert. Walking back to the car, I thought for a moment I saw a figure watching us from the shadows of a nearby building. When I stopped and looked, though, no one was there.

"Did you see something?" Lisa asked.

"No," I replied, but I wasn't sure.

19

WE SLEPT LATE Sunday morning. Cornelia had the day off, so we ate a leisurely brunch on the deck off the kitchen, sipping coffee and munching on smoked salmon and bagels with cream cheese. "You know," Lisa remarked, "it's strange that we haven't heard any more from Kight or Davis, or anyone for that matter. We've been here for nearly two weeks now, and the only soul that's been through those gates is Cornelia. I thought Davis said something about a caretaker."

"Maybe they're just leaving us alone while they work on the case. I can't imagine what more I could tell them that they don't already know."

Lisa sliced off a dollop of cheese, spreading it carefully on a scrap of bagel before popping it in her mouth.

"You know more about what happened than I do," she said. "In fact, I never really heard all the details. Guess I didn't want to ask. Your Uncle Jack gave me a broad outline, and the sheriff told me..."

"Arnett was there?" I asked. I had no memory of seeing him."

"Oh, yes." She looked up, surprised. "You don't remember? But then you were just coming off whatever sedative they were pumping in you through that IV. He told me that he felt horribly guilty, like a lot of what happened was his fault. He said that if he'd never asked you to let Jarrard stay at your house in the first place..."

"Did I talk with him?"

"Yes, briefly. I think once he got the word that you were going to make a full recovery he felt better. He called a couple of times, but didn't come back after they moved you to rehab."

"I have no recollection of seeing him." I could remember everything that happened up until the morning of June 14. I could remember my last week or two in the hospital. The time in between seemed to drift in and out of my memory like snatches of a television program playing in another room.

"It has to be the drugs they were giving you. I think they can induce short-term memory loss."

"You said that my mother was there…"

"She was."

"But I don't remember seeing her. Did anyone else visit?"

"God, yes! You'd been in the ICU less than a week when I arrived. The waiting room was always full of people coming in and out, asking about you. And the flowers and cards…"

"I don't remember any of that."

"Well, of course not. At first, when you were still on the ventilator, they kept you sedated. The neurologist and critical care docs kept talking about 'closed head trauma' and 'cerebral edema.' They wouldn't let anyone in."

"But how did you…"

"Your uncle. He told the doctors I was your fiancée or closest friend—or something like that—I didn't hear the details. After that, they let me stay with you twenty-four hours a day."

"Oh." I thought a moment. "You didn't have to do that."

"Yes, I did," she said, and kissed me lightly on the cheek.

□□□

I WAS HUFFING AND PUFFING my way back up the driveway on Monday morning when Cornelia arrived. Lisa was fifty yards ahead of me, looking over her shoulder occasionally to yell out a word of encouragement. Cornelia slowed her battered Chevy Malibu and rolled down the window. "Y'all have a good weekend?"

I nodded, taking a deep breath. "Great," I said. "We went for a ride, had dinner in town."

"Well, I thought you might be wanting for some decent food.

I brought you a little country ham and some other goodies from home. If you gonna visit here for a while, you might as well eat something local. I'll set it out for you to have for lunch." She rolled up the window and headed up the drive toward the house.

Lisa was disappearing in the front door of the house just as I stumbled into the mowed meadow. I half-jogged the last hundred yards, fighting to keep up the pace. By the time I lurched through the front door, she and Cornelia were setting a spread of covered dishes on the patio table.

"Lunch is coming up," she said. "Hope you're hungry."

I mumbled a few words of acknowledgment between deep breaths while waiting for my pulse rate to drop. Cornelia said, "We got ham and biscuits, potato salad, fried cornbread, fresh string beans, rice and gravy, and a nice peach pie that I made from some fresh peaches I got down at the Farmers' Market in Dillard. Put some meat on ya bones." She set out two plates and headed back to the kitchen to get some silverware.

"You've only set two plates," Lisa said. "You're not going to eat?"

"No, I'll eat here in the kitchen."

"For God's sake, Cornelia, sit down and have lunch with us. You can't just…"

"Well," she hesitated. "They told me I'm not 'sposed to mingle with the 'guests.' 'Gainst gov'ment policy."

"That's crazy," Lisa said, grabbing another plate from the cabinet. "You sit down right here and help us eat all this food you've brought."

Cornelia smiled and agreed without hesitation.

Half an hour and multiple helpings later, she said, "It's been a real pleasure working up here with you two. Most of the folks that stay here ain't nearly as nice."

"How so?" I asked.

"Yankees, mainly. From New York or Chicago or somewhere like that. Ain't genteel people like you two. And usually a lot older—in their fifties or sixties and used to being waited on. Some of 'em order me around like I was some sorta maid." Cornelia clearly had her pride.

"How long have you been working here?" Lisa asked.

"Since right shortly after the gov'ment got the place. About three years, I reckon. It pays pretty good, and gives me time to clean people's houses on the side. Being on my own like I am, it takes a good bit just to live."

"Keeping up this house is a pretty big job. Don't they give you any help?"

"Oh, yes. The lawn people come about every two or three weeks, depending on the rain. They should be here this week."

"What if something breaks, or the sink gets stopped up? Do they expect you to fix that?" Lisa seemed a bit miffed.

"Well, there used to be a caretaker, an old retired FBI agent, but he had to quit work about a year and a half ago. Problems with his nerves. He didn't do much anyway—I think it was one of them political jobs where they pay you for just being there. He used to just show up about once a week, walk around the house and say, 'Looks okay to me,' and then go down and check on the stuff in the basement room and leave. Usually wouldn't stay half an hour. And then, after they put in the extra satellite dish, he didn't hardly ever show up. I just got used to taking care of things m'self."

"What satellite dish?" Lisa asked.

"Them two out there on the far side of the yard. You can't hardly see 'em, but they're just above the bald. For satellite TV and internet."

"So…" Lisa began.

Cornelia, at last having someone to listen to her complaints, continued, "He was a strange duck, let me tell you. Toward the end there, he got down right spooky. Paranoid, I think they call it. He still lives around here, somewhere. Down toward Sky Valley, I think. I see him every now and again sorta wandering down the street, looking all lost."

"What happened?" Lisa asked, determined to get in her question this time.

"One day, Agent Davis came around and told me that Mr. Nesselrode—that was his name, Horace Nesselrode—wouldn't be coming back, and that if I needed anything I was to call a number in Asheville and they'd send someone out right away."

"They told us the fellow who had this house built was a drug dealer," I said. "Did anyone around here know where the money to build it came from?"

"That's what they told me. It was before I went to work here, but honestly, there's a whole lot of peculiar folk up here."

"Speaking of paranoid, he must have been worried about security. You can't even get in the gate without one of those huge garage door opener things. At least you don't have to worry about door-to-door sales…"

"There's the keypad," Cornelia said.

Lisa and I both sat up. "What keypad?" we asked simultaneously.

"The one on the right side of the gate. You can't see it from the driveway, but you just look around on the side and there it is, with an intercom. It's about five feet off the ground—same level as the TV camera."

"Camera?" we both again said simultaneously.

"Oh, that drug man was paranoid all right. Had all kinds of security stuff here, but I think the gov'ment mostly took it out after they got the house. There used to be a camera at the gate down there that looked through a little peephole. You can't see it unless you look for it. When I first went to work here, there was a little TV screen here in the kitchen and a telephone-like thing where you could talk to somebody at the gate through the intercom. They got rid of all that and started using those big opener things. But the keypad still works. I let myself in and out with it every day."

"That's strange," Lisa said. "I wonder why they didn't tell us about that?"

20

AS CORNELIA PREDICTED, the yard service crew showed up shortly after dawn Tuesday morning, waking us from a sound sleep with the sound of lawnmowers and leaf blowers. I pulled on my jeans and a T-shirt and strolled out the front door to have a look. A white, heavy-duty pick-up pulling a trailer was parked under the portico. Leaning on its hood, a beefy man dressed in work clothes idly watched half a dozen Hispanic laborers, two of whom were mowing while the others attended to the shrubbery and lawn debris. He saw me and nodded, "Morning."

"G'morning," I replied, watching the workers scamper about the yard. The drivers finished mowing and started to load their machines back on the trailer. "You guys work fast."

He smiled. "Got to. Time is money." He reached in his pocket for a cigarette and said, "Pretty place you got here."

"It's not mine. We're just guests."

"Summer rental, eh? Lot of people up here this time of year."

I nodded, not feeling it necessary to explain otherwise.

"How long have you been doing the grounds here?" I asked.

"This year and last. They pay us by the year—cheaper that way."

"You have any trouble getting that truck and trailer up that long winding driveway?"

"Nah. Years of driving in the mountains. Piece of cake."

"Tell me, how do you get through the gate?"

"It's plenty wide. No problem there."

"No, I mean how do you get the gate to open?"

"I use the entry code, of course. With the keypad. Why do you ask?"

"Just curious."

□□□

THE DRUG LORD WHO'D BUILT the house apparently liked to entertain. Just off the patio on the lower level, an elaborate stone grill and outdoor fireplace overlooked the valley below. On Wednesday morning after my slow run down and up the mountain, I emerged from the shower to find Lisa examining it carefully, poking at the grate and looking in the stainless steel firebox. Sensing my gaze from the deck above, she looked up and said, "I think we need to cook something out here. How about some thick steaks, a little late summer corn, a good bottle of California merlot, that sort of thing?"

Fifteen minutes later, we were headed down the driveway toward town, shopping list in hand. Lisa was driving. I pointed the opener at the gate and pressed the button. The gate began to swing open as she lifted her foot off the brake to drive through. "Stop," I said. She gave me a puzzled look. "I want to see the keypad."

I got out of the car and walked over to the stone and masonry column supporting the gate. As Cornelia described, an all-weather keypad with a small speaker grate above it was recessed in the side. Moving to the front of the pillar, I found a slit no more than a half inch wide between two stones. I could barely make out a tiny digital camera sensor tucked inside.

"What do you see?" Lisa yelled.

"Just what you'd expect. A keypad, and what appears to be a hidden camera."

"Why are you interested?"

"I don't know. Something's strange. Why didn't they give us the code to get in? Or better, why didn't they tell us that there was a keypad entry system to begin with?"

Lisa looked at me with a slight frown. "Don't you think you're being a little paranoid yourself? If they don't tell whoever stays here the code, they don't have to change it every time some 'guest' or another comes and goes."

"But it's no secret. Cornelia has it. The yard people have it. Why not us?" I looked at the bulky opener.

"I think there are other things we can worry about," Lisa said as we drove onto the highway to town.

There are two grocery stores in Highlands-Bryson's and Mountain Fresh. Lisa had been buying the provisions and seemed to have familiarized herself with both. We started off at Bryson's. She headed straight for the meat counter but couldn't find the exact cut she wanted and decreed that we should go back to Mountain Fresh. We parked again in front of the laundry; I handed her a hundred dollar bill and volunteered to watch the car. Like most men, I hate shopping.

It was a beautiful day, a little hot even. I got out and propped myself against the side of the car. The white wood clapboards of the Episcopal Church across the street gleamed brightly in the sunlight. I leaned back in the car and was fumbling in the glove box for my sunglasses when I heard a voice behind me say, "You're staying in the house, aren't you?"

I raised my head to see the figure of a thin old man silhouetted against the sky. "I beg your pardon?"

"I said, you're staying in the house, aren't you?"

"What house?" I asked, looking him over. It was the same man that I'd sensed staring at me on my last visit to Mountain Fresh.

"The government's house. Out on Walhalla Road." He appeared younger than I'd thought when I first saw him, probably in his early sixties. He was wearing the same jacket and charcoal grey pants that I'd seen before. His faded blue dress shirt was frayed at the collar. Wisps of white hair hung down over his ears.

"No," I said, thinking as quickly as I could. "We're from Atlanta. We just bought a condo out in Inverness Glen."

"No, you're not. I don't know *who* you are, but I know *what* you are. But it's all right…"

"What do you mean, you know what I am?"

"A witness, I'd guess. You don't have the look of a hit man who's decided to squeal. And you're too young to have worked your way up in one of the mob families. Drug dealer? Maybe. You could be that, now? How far off am I?"

"Who are you?"

"Name's Nesselrode. Used to be FBI. The bad guys used to call me 'Ness,' like Eliot Ness, but he was not FBI. Treasury Department. Bureau of Prohibition. Taken down by the way he handled the Cleveland Torso Murderer Case. Bad guys don't know that though. I let 'em call me Agent Ness."

So this is Cornelia's Horace Nesselrode, I thought. "Mr. Nesselrode, or Mr. Ness if you prefer, I really think you've got the wrong guy this time. I'm sure that…"

"No, no, no, *no*! I do *not* have the wrong guy." He appeared agitated. "You don't need to lie to me. I know what goes on. I may be 'out of the loop,' as they used to say back at the Hoover Building on Pennsylvania Avenue, but I will *not* allow my years of training and expertise to be wasted. Once an FBI agent, always an FBI agent. *Fidelity, Bravery, and Integrity*—that's the Bureau's motto. No, no, no. Your secret is safe with me, and I will keep an eye on you. Or should I say that I'll keep an eye out for you? One of those. And just to prove it…"

Over his shoulder I saw a local police car cruising down the street. "Look, Mr. Nesselrode," I said, pointing at the cop. "If you don't back off, I'm going to flag down him down and tell him you're harassing me."

Nesselrode's eyes widened, and he took a step back. "Ah…" he started, then squinted, seemingly processing the options. He wrinkled his brow and moved one step closer. "You just do that then. Call him. Look, he's checking out the parking lot."

I raised my arm as if to wave, peering into Nesselrode's eyes. He glared back. I lowered my hand.

"See," he said, gloating. "I knew you wouldn't do it. I know your type. Running from the law all your life. You want to keep a low profile—blend in with the crowd. Just another pretty face, eh? Am I right?"

"No, you're not…" I started, suddenly aware that Nesselrode's head was jerking to the left, staring across the parking lot in alarm. The police cruiser had turned in and was slowly approaching us.

"Okay," he said, his speech pressured. "So now I leave, but just remember this. They see what Mr. Moose sees and they hear what Mr. Bear hears, so you…" He turned suddenly in mid-sentence and scurried away, his head held down.

The cruiser pulled up and stopped. The tinted electric window whirred down to reveal a smiling, middle-aged patrolman. "Old man wasn't bothering you, was he?"

"No, not at all, officer."

The cop smiled benignly. "Just wanted to be sure. He's one of those locals who give small towns what they call 'character.' He's a little crazy, but harmless. Likes to talk to people on the street. Tells 'em he used to be an FBI agent, or the like. We just put up with him."

"No problem. I'm from a small town myself. I know how it is."

"Well, enjoy your vacation," the cop said as the tinted window whirred back up.

For some strange reason, the face of Charlie Poole popped into my mind.

21

"SO YOU THINK the guy's a nut?" Lisa said, emptying the last of the merlot into my glass. The remains of our steak dinner were scattered on the table in front of us as the last rays of the setting sun painted the treetops red. We were both feeling the effects of the wine.

"Yes or no. I don't know. Cornelia said that a retired FBI agent whose name was Nesselrode used to be the caretaker here. He said that his name was Nesselrode, and he seemed to know that this house is owned by the government and that we're staying here. I guess that's it. The whole conversation didn't last three minutes."

"Hmm," she said, pulling her sweater around her shoulders. "Let's go sit inside. It's getting chilly."

We grabbed our glasses and flopped down on the overstuffed leather couch in front of the fireplace. I lay at one end, she at the other facing me. She picked up my foot and began massaging it. "And what was it he said about moose and bear?"

"Something like, 'They see what Mr. Moose sees and hear what Mr. Bear hears.' I think he's just crazy."

Lisa began to stroke my thigh with her foot. She nodded toward the moose head hung over the fireplace. "A little more wine, and Mr. Moose is going to get an eyeful." She raised up to crawl toward my end of the sofa.

I sat bolt upright. "You don't think…"

Lisa pushed me back and laid her head on my chest. "I don't

need to think. It comes naturally. All I've got to…"

"No, I'm serious." I pushed her away, suddenly very sober. "Have you seen a ladder anywhere?"

"In the utility room closet, but…" She stopped, frowning. I found the ladder and unfolded it in front of the fireplace. "What the hell are you doing, Matt? Can't this wait until later?"

"You'll be glad it didn't if what I'm thinking turns out to be right." I climbed up the ladder and began to examine the huge head.

Lisa watched from the couch, her arms crossed. "What do you see?"

I couldn't see anything unusual. "Nothing yet. Help me get this thing off the wall." The moose head was mounted on the exposed stacked-stone chimney that rose to the ceiling above the mantelpiece. I assumed that it hung from some kind of a hook.

"It must weigh a ton. Be careful."

Using both hands to grab the furry neck, I pushed the head up slowly. It didn't move at first. I pushed harder. The wooden plaque behind the mounted head began to scrape across the stone. I gave it a little shove. The entire head came away from the chimney and began to fall down toward the floor. I lost my balance and reached out with both hands to steady myself on the mantelpiece.

With a grating and then a thud, the head slipped out of my grip, dropping and then suddenly stopping as if hung on something. It twisted back and forth just above the mantle. "What the…"

I swung the antlers to one side and peered behind the dangling wooden plaque. I could see the hook where the head had been attached, and below it, a thin blue wire emerging from the stonework and disappearing inside the stuffed neck through the back of the plaque. I could just make out the lettering on the wire: "Category 5."

"I guess I was wrong," I said. "Help me get this thing back up here on the wall." Lisa steadied the ladder while I eased the head with its massive rack back in place.

"What was that all about?" Lisa asked as I put the ladder up.

"Nothing. Just some craziness." I smiled. "Why don't we do some stargazing?"

"Matt, are you…" I shut her up by putting my arms around her and kissing her, then half-pushed her toward the front door.

I tugged her fifty yards to the middle of the meadow. The sky was still a faint shade of purple. A quarter moon hung over the trees just above a brightly shining planet. Lisa tried to speak but I shushed her. I stopped and looked around. Nothing. No one watching.

"There was a wire coming out of the back of the head. It was labeled 'Category 5.' That's what they refer to in the electronics business as 'Cat-5.' It's used for a lot of low-voltage electronic systems like computer networks."

"So? That doesn't…"

"It's also used for alarm systems and video monitoring. Remember the camera at the gate? We know that there was a video system here at one time."

"Cornelia said they took it out."

"Did they? Think about what Nesselrode said: 'They see what Mr. Moose sees and hear what Mr. Bear hears.' You don't suppose…"

I could barely make out Lisa's expression in the twilight. She backed away, wrapping her arms around her chest and giving a little shiver. She seemed to be thinking.

"What did Cornelia say the old guy did? That he'd show up about once a week, walk around and 'check the stuff in the basement room.' And that after they put in the satellite dish system he didn't work very much at all." She was silent for a moment. "Talk about paranoia. Now you've got me worried."

"I think we need to take a closer look at a few things," I said.

22

The mechanical room was in the basement. When we first arrived, I'd stuck my head in for a look, but really hadn't paid it much attention. I remembered seeing a couple of hot water heaters, two air handlers for the heat pumps, and an emergency diesel-fired generator to keep the electrical and heating systems running during power blackouts.

Rather than go back through the house, we walked down a set of outside stone steps that led to the lawn overlooking the valley. The grill was still warm, a wisp of smoke from its dying embers drifting slowly toward the south. The patio door leading to the stairway foyer between the gym and British pub room was unlocked. Cautious now, we stepped inside. I noted a small sensor on the hinge side of the door. Routine alarm system stuff. A motion detector mounted high in one corner space flashed a bright red light. We stood very still. The light went off. I waved my hands. The light came back on. Nothing unusual. No cameras.

The door to the mechanical room opened off the back of the foyer. I turned on the light switch next to the door and surveyed the room. It was about twelve feet wide and ran the length of the house from one side to the other. The structure had been partially built into the side of the mountain; the back wall of the space was monolithically poured reinforced concrete. Exposed pine joists with white-backed insulation between them lined the ceiling. Various pipes and drains disappeared and reappeared in and out of the spaces between the joists. The air handlers hummed noisily.

The diesel generator and its control panel sat silently at the far end. The faint smell of damp permeated the air.

We shut the door and stood inside, both taking in the details of the room. Lisa pointed silently at what appeared to be a smoke detector mounted on one of the floor joists above us. "Let's start at that end and work our way back," I whispered, pointing toward the generator. We found two rolls of construction felt and a box of rusty nails. A moldy wooden cabinet held twelve boxes of cellophane-wrapped party napkins with balloons and shooting stars, plus several sheets of gift wrap, tape, and a clear plastic bag full of pre-tied package bows.

There was nothing out of the ordinary until we reached the area behind the English pub room. The partition framing of this section was covered with unpainted plywood instead of drywall. Two spare four-by-eight-foot pieces, apparently left over from construction, leaned against the wall. I looked into the crack behind them and couldn't see anything. With a bit of effort I slid one to the side, uncovering a solid-looking wooden door with a deadbolt lock.

"Wonder where this goes?" I whispered to Lisa.

She shrugged. "Looks like it would open behind the bar area, I'd think."

We walked back out to the base of the stairs and peered into the pub area. A high counter ran across the back of the room, above which a mirrored wall lay behind a series of shelves stocked with a selection of liquors. A dark oak bar running the length of the room was in front of this, served by a dozen high-backed bar stools and a brass rail below on which the drinkers could prop their feet. Three oak tables with chairs were scattered around the room. An out-of-place 1950s-style neon-encrusted juke box glowed against one wall. "There's not a door behind the bar that I can see," Lisa observed.

I walked to the end of the bar and paced off the room. I then walked back to the door to the mechanical room and observed the distance to the front of the bar. "About three feet missing, I'd estimate."

"You wouldn't think there was a space there, though. The mirror behind the bar gives the illusion of depth."

"We need a flashlight," I said, and bounded up the stairs to the upper level to find one. My energy seemed to have returned.

The locked door was in a poorly lit corner of the basement room. I played the flashlight on the lock and handle, studying them closely. "Looks well-oiled, but there's dust on the knob. I don't think anyone's been in here recently."

I moved the light slowly around the door frame. It opened outward into the mechanical room. There would not be enough clearance for it to swing inward. In the crack on the hinge side between the door and the jamb, I could see a small white protrusion from the wall side. "Look at this." I pointed it out to Lisa. "What do you think?"

"Mechanical trip switch, probably. Open the door and the alarm goes off. Do you see a keypad anywhere nearby?" We searched the adjacent area. Nothing. "Probably on the inside with a delay of thirty seconds or so to disarm it once you open the door." She paused briefly and continued. "Matt, we've got to see what's in there. If it turns out that…" She didn't finish the sentence.

I tried thinking of a way to bypass the alarm. My mind was still not working right. "I don't know…"

"Give me your wallet and take off your shoe," Lisa said over her shoulder as she headed toward the other end of the room. I did as she asked. She opened my wallet and pulled out an American Express Card. "Never leave home without it," she murmured while studying the hidden alarm switch closely with the flashlight. Making her mind up, she handed me the light and said, "Focus the beam right here."

I held the light while she eased the credit card in the space. "Good," she pronounced. "I think I can make this work. Go get me a few nails and a roll of tape out of that cabinet down there." I got what she wanted and held them out to her. She tore off four long strips of tape and hung them loosely on the wall next to the door jamb.

"What we're going to do is this: I'm going to wedge the trip button in with the credit card. Then, I'm going to knock the pins out of the hinges. I'll hold the card while you lift and pull the door back from the hinges toward you. As soon as I've got enough clearance, I'll tape the card over the button to keep it from popping out and setting off the alarm. Once that's done, we're inside."

"Are you sure the tape will hold—and are you going to have

enough clearance to hold the credit card in place while I lift the door out?"

"We'll just have to see," Lisa said. She slipped one of the nails into the lower end of the middle hinge. Using the heel of my shoe as a hammer, she tapped on it gently, forcing the hinge pin out of the top. With her third sharp blow it flew out and landed with a noisy clink on the bare concrete floor.

"This is going to be easier than I thought," she said smiling. She removed the lower pin the same way. "Now, when I do the top one, the door might fall back on you. I want you to keep some pressure on it to keep that from happening. I'm going to wedge your wallet in the crack under the door so it won't drop down suddenly." She unfolded my wallet and slipped one side into the narrow crack. "Here goes." The top pin came out with two taps and fell to the floor next to the first one.

"You ready?" she asked.

"I hope so."

"Then get ready to grab the door as I pull it out from the hinges."

Holding the credit card in place with her right hand, Lisa slipped the fingers of her left into the crack between the bottom of the door and the floor on the hinge side. She gave a gentle tug. With a sharp bump, the door slipped off the hinges and came to rest on my wallet. Lisa held the card firmly in place. I could see a trickle of perspiration run down her forehead. She slipped her left hand out from the space beneath the door and grabbed a strip of tape. "Now ease the door toward you, hinge side first, about two inches."

I did as I was instructed. Lisa held onto the card. "Now pull it straight out away from the lock side to slip the deadbolt out. Do it real easy." Again I followed her instructions and the door came free, falling back into my grip. "Lean it over against the wall while I get this card secured." She strapped the rest of the tape over the credit card to hold the alarm button in place.

We both breathed a sigh of relief. A faint hum emanated from the dark interior. Multiple small red and green lights glowed in the blackness. Lisa reached inside and felt for a light switch. "Got it," she said and flipped it on. Two long ceiling-mounted fluorescent tubes poured out light.

It was a narrow space, less than three feet deep and at least twenty feet long, running the entire length of the rear wall of the pub room. Immediately in front of us was a stack of electronic gear sat on wooden shelves, connected to a maze of wires. An alarm keypad, its red light blinking to show that it remained armed, was mounted just above the light switch. Lisa eased in and sidled carefully down the cramped room. I followed. Just behind the middle of the bar area, the "wall" glowed with the dark green light of a two-way mirror looking into the pub space. Two small cameras pointed at the empty bar stools. At one end of the closet, dozens of blue Cat-5 cables streamed out of conduits and attached themselves to a thick black instrument box. From it, more cables, black this time, snaked to a series of five stacked instruments, each with solid green and blinking red lights visible from the front. Digital video recorders—DVRs.

While I studied the boxes and wiring, Lisa examined a small flat-panel monitor. She pressed a button and it came to life, flicking every five seconds from one scene to the next. She found a keyboard and a mouse on the shelf below. I could see her move the mouse, type a few letters, and then click on the screen several times silently cursing with a grim look on her face. Because of the narrowness of the space, I couldn't get a clear view of what she was seeing.

"Unbelievable," she said. "Absolutely unbelievable." She twisted the monitor so I could see the screen. At the top was the date, July 23—the day after we'd arrived—and the time, 8:14 a.m. Over the small speaker I could hear Lisa's voice, tinny, but unmistakable, saying, "Yes, yes!" On the screen I could see our naked bodies as we writhed on the bed in the master bedroom.

23

THE HOUSE WAS INFESTED with cameras, thirty-two by our count, each with an audio track recorded along with the video. Their placement seemed to follow a rough pattern. Whoever installed these was less interested in security, and more excited about recording the goings-on of the guests. There was the camera at the gate, and another hidden under the portico pointed at the front door. The rest of them all appeared to be focused on places where people were likely to have conversations, both public and private.

In addition to the cameras in the bar and in the moose head, there were others that covered the gathering spot in front of the second floor fireplace, the kitchen table, the chairs on the decks, and so on. Several were cleverly concealed behind bedroom mirrors. "So the drug lord was a voyeur, too?" Lisa observed.

"You're assuming the video surveillance system came with the house," I said. "How do we know that?"

"We don't, but this system is just too elaborate to be a retrofit," she replied. She had been fiddling with the playback from the DVRs. "It looks like it was set up to maintain a record of the last thirty days." She paused, clicking a screen menu with the mouse. "I think—no, I'm sure—that a video record is logged only if there's motion. Look at this here, for example."

She twisted the screen around for me to see. A view of the upstairs sitting area appeared with a date and time stamp for the day we arrived. The room was empty for about fifteen seconds, then Agent Davis, Lisa, and I walked into view. I could hear Davis say, "Something, hey? All this, paid for by neatly wrapped packages…"

"Today's the sixth," Lisa continued. "The video goes back to the seventh of last month. It appears the system erases more than thirty days old. The question is, who sees it?"

"No one's been here, obviously, but why would they keep it up and running if they weren't using it? Remember what Cornelia said about Nesselrode not coming around much after they put the extra satellite dish in? You don't suppose…"

Lisa was already following the cables. "Okay, there's output from the DVRs to this," she said, pointing at a nondescript black box, "then there's a shielded coaxial cable linked to the port labeled 'Output' that disappears back into the wall. You may be right. Let's put all this back like we found it and go for a walk. We need to talk."

With considerably less effort than it'd taken us to get into the room, we reinstalled the door and hinge pins, removed the credit card blocking the alarm, and propped the plywood back over the area. To the casual observer, nothing appeared to have been disturbed.

We exited on the lower patio and took the steps back up to the front lawn. Once we were sure that we were out of range of the camera and microphone under the portico, I said, "First of all, let's assume that the system was in place when the government got the house. They probably just left it there—if for no other reason than it would be too much trouble to rip out. There might be times when they want to record—or secretly observe, anyway—what's going on. Say they had someone in the Witness Protection Program, and they were debriefing him. Say the guy was nervous about cameras and notes, but they needed an exact record of what…"

"Yeah, yeah, yeah," Lisa interrupted me. "All that's obvious. The real question is whether or not you and I are being watched, and if so, why?"

"So how do we find out?"

"We're way out in the middle of nowhere. We haven't seen anybody come to download the video, so we can assume if it's being watched, they have to transmit it out electronically. The phone line connection goes through miles and miles of copper wire—that wouldn't work. The only practical way that they would have enough bandwidth to send even a rudimentary video and audio feed would be by satellite. And that ties in with what Cornelia said."

"What are you thinking?"

"I'll show you in the morning. Let's go back to the house."

□□□

LATER THAT NIGHT, before we went to bed, I threw my terry cloth robe over the mirror.

□□□

WE GOT UP BEFORE BREAKFAST and dressed for our now routine morning run. We left by the front door, as usual. Then, avoiding the field of vision of any of the outside cameras, we circled back around to the satellite dishes perched on the edge of the bald. There were two of them, about eighteen inches in diameter and pointed toward the south. They were mounted on a sturdy metal post driven into the ground at the base of a large fir tree.

Lisa produced an adjustable wrench that she'd found in the utility room. Being careful not to scratch the metal, she loosened the support bracket that held the dishes in alignment, gave it a firm bump to move them about three inches away from their previous angle, and then retightened the nut. Meanwhile, I dragged a six-foot long, three-inch wide fir limb that had fallen out of the tree and draped it over the dishes as if it had landed there as a natural occurrence. We looked to make sure that we'd left no footprints, and crept away to complete our exercise.

The phone was ringing as we opened the front door forty-five minutes later. It was Agent Davis. "Matt, how's it going?"

"Good, thanks. I think I'm slowly getting back to normal."

"Well, you've been though a lot."

"I have."

There as an awkward pause. "How's Miss Li?" Davis asked.

"Fine. She's being a real taskmaster. We just got in from our morning exercise run."

"Any plans for today?"

"No."

"I thought I might come up and visit with you—see how things are going. Give you an update on the investigation."

About time, I thought. "Sure, we'll be here all day…"

Out of the corner of my eye, I saw Lisa signaling me. She mouthed silently, "He wants to come up?"

I nodded.

"Tell him late this afternoon. We need to go to town," she whispered.

"Uh, wait a sec…Lisa says we need to go to town. How about this afternoon, say after three?"

"That's good. It'll take a couple of hours to drive up from Atlanta anyway. See you then."

Lisa headed for the bathroom and motioned for me to follow. She shut the door and turned on the shower. I told her what Davis said.

"The lying bastard. We disable the satellite dish and within an hour he wants to pay us a visit. The first attention he's given us in three weeks. We need to get to town. There's one more thing we've got to do."

An hour later we were in the tiny local Radio Shack store. Lisa pulled one of the gate openers out of her pocket and laid it on the counter. The clerk, a pimply faced teenager, stared at it for a moment and said, "MP3?"

"No, garage door opener. It's not working just right. You see, we're from Atlanta, and I think there's a problem with our transmitter—sometimes it works and sometimes it doesn't. I was wondering if you do repairs?"

The kid reached in his pocket and pulled out a piece of bubble gum in a worn wrapper. He opened it and popped it in his mouth. "You checked the batteries?"

"They're new."

"Well, the owner's not here right now. We do some repairs, but we send a lot of stuff out. I can change the batteries for you," he said, reaching for the opener.

Lisa placed her hand over it. "I said the batteries are new. Let me put this another way: Do you have any instruments that you use to make repairs?"

"Dunno," the kid mumbled, trying to form a bubble. "Like I said, the owner's not here. He does alarm system work on the side and I don't know how to use all that stuff back there."

"Back where?"

"In the back. Where he does repairs."

"How about if I look and see what's there?" Lisa placed her hand on his and flashed a seductive smile.

"Uh… dunno. I'm not sure if the boss would want me to…"

I laid a twenty on the counter. "What he doesn't know won't hurt him."

"You not gonna break anything, are you?"

"Oh, no," Lisa said, still gripping his hand. "I've done some repair work before and I just need to see if you've got a spectrum analyzer."

"A what?"

"Why don't we just look?" she said, still smiling.

The clerk blushed and seemed to swallow his bubble gum, "Well, I guess if…"

"Good," Lisa said. "You're kinda cute, you know."

Ten minutes later, she was holding a probe over the opener while she watched a line move slowly across a small grey LCD display. The clerk was busy with a customer in the front. A spike erupted from the line and scrolled across the screen. Lisa looked at her watch. "Every three seconds it emits a fairly strong radio-frequency signal."

"Meaning…"

"Meaning the reason that we weren't given a code for the gate keypad is that they have been tracking us whenever we leave the house. Let's go. I'm curious to see what Davis does when he gets here."

The customer was just leaving as we emerged from the repair area. The kid looked moon-eyed at Lisa. "Get it fixed?" he asked.

"You are *so* smart. You were right all along. The batteries were in backwards." She leaned over and gave him a peck on the cheek.

"Come again," he said as we walked out the door. "I mean, like, really. Like, you can come back here whenever you…"

I could see him still talking as we walked to the car.

24

DAVIS ARRIVED AT 3:15, this time driving a government-issue Ford. A thirty-something-year old, dressed casually in jeans and a twill work shirt, accompanied him. They parked under the portico and knocked at the door, smiling. "Matt, Lisa. How are you? Gosh, Matt, you look great. You must've gained ten pounds. You look just like you did before..." He stopped, remembering his guest.

"Oh, let me introduce Larry Hill. He's one of the caretakers here. Things have been going so well with Cornelia in charge that we haven't had much need for him to check in. I just thought that as long as I was up, I'd bring him by for a look-see."

Hill extended his hand and said, "Pleased to meet you." I noticed a small canvas tool kit on his belt. "I'll just check things out while you talk. Make sure there's nothing that needs attention." He headed off down the stairs without further explanation.

Davis said, "Why don't we sit down and let me fill you in on where we are with things?"

We sat on the sofa in front of the moose head. Lisa was attentive but kept finding excuses to be up, first to serve coffee, then crackers, then cheese. I noticed each time she went to the kitchen she glanced out toward the satellite dishes. After her third trip, I saw her smile and nod almost imperceptibly.

Davis rambled, not really saying anything new. There had been no luck with any of the forensic evidence from the bombing.

They'd used dynamite, he said, and it was traced to a batch stolen from a road construction company in Tennessee two years earlier. All the leads about Caldera and Rojas had been dead ends. None of Jarrard's cases from his days as a Federal prosecutor seemed to have any connection to his murder. He summarized by saying, "In essence, we've hit a bunch of cold trails that lead to stone walls. No one's tried to contact you, have they?"

It seemed like a strange question, given the fact that we were supposedly in a secure hideaway. I was unsure if I should mention Nesselrode. "Only some crazy old guy in town. Said he was ex-FBI. Name was Ness or something like that." I tried to be vague.

"Sure. Nesselrode. Horace Nesselrode. How's he doing? I haven't talked with him in a good while. He was with the Bureau for years. Good agent, but he had some problems… I guess I'm not supposed to say that. How about I say he had some 'issues' and decided to take early retirement. Actually, he worked here for a short while when we first acquired the house. I felt sorry for him. Gave him a part time job as caretaker, but even the stress of that…" Davis's eyes narrowed ever so slightly. "What did he say to you?"

"Nothing really. Said he was a former agent. He seemed to know that we were staying here." I didn't mention Mr. Moose.

Davis looked a little relieved. "He's pitiful, really. Paranoid delusions. If you run into him again, I'd just ignore him. Don't let him bother you."

Larry Hill appeared at the top of the stairs. "Did you know that a limb had fallen on your satellite dish?"

Lisa and I tried to look surprised. I said, "No. Should we have?"

"Only if you want to watch TV or use the internet."

Lisa said, "We haven't turned on the television in a week, and I don't think either of us has used the computer since we got here." She paused. "How'd you find that?"

"Just routine checking. That's the caretaker's job. I noticed that the dishes had been knocked out of alignment. Couldn't get a signal in or out. I fixed it."

"Thanks," I said. "I guess we'd have noticed it eventually. Good thing you came. It probably saved you a trip up later." Lisa just smiled.

Davis rose to leave. "I'm glad you've been improving so quickly, Matt. And Lisa, it's awful good of you to stay here with him. I'm sure that you're eager to get home, but we don't think the time is right just yet. We need to get a better handle on the case. Until then, you're safe here. And remember, you're free to come and go as you please. Use the internet, make calls, whatever. Just don't divulge your location."

"We really appreciate your concern," I said. Lisa continued to smile.

Davis and Hill left. We stood under the portico waving for the hidden camera.

"What a liar," Lisa murmured under her breath, knowing full well that our every move was being watched somewhere.

□□□

WE WENT INTO HIGHLANDS for dinner, this time eating at a small, rustically furnished restaurant beside a lake. Suddenly, every minor event seemed to be part of a bigger plan. The waiter gave us a good table next to the window with a view of the sunset over the mountains. I picked up the salt and pepper shakers, half-seriously looking for hidden microphones. The maitre d' seated a middle-aged couple at a table beside us. The man, who saw me looking in his direction, smiled and nodded. I asked the waiter to move us to a noisy little table next to the kitchen door. We needed to talk.

"I feel like a rat in a maze," I said. "I don't know what the hell is going on."

"Neither do I, but quite obviously someone—presumably the FBI—is very interested in what you and I say and do."

"But why?"

"For the same reason that someone tried to kill you. That someone—assuming it's one person—thinks Jarrard passed on information to you before he was shot. If you die, the secret dies with you. On the other side, the government wants you alive so they can find out what you know."

"But that doesn't make sense. If this 'someone' tried to kill me and failed, doesn't it seem logical that I'd sing like a bird to the FBI?"

"Maybe. But what if the information was the key to something

117

very valuable? Stolen millions or the like? What if the FBI thinks you'll lay low until the heat is off and then cash in?"

"Why would they think that?" The face of Chief Roger Mathis flashed into my mind as I spoke. The waiter arrived and stood over us until we ordered. I had the trout, Lisa the prime rib. We settled on a California blanc de noirs.

He left and she replied, "I don't know…"

"Neither do I, but I think I know who may have given them the idea."

"It puts us in a very bad position. Someone wants you dead for what you might know; someone wants you alive for the same reason. We're damned if we do and damned if we don't."

"Lisa, you keep saying 'we.' This is not your fight. I care about you, and I want you here with me, but you've got to leave. We can't hide here forever, watched like bugs under a microscope. If we leave, and if you stay with me, I'm afraid someone will track us down and…"

"You fool," she began. "If you…"

The waiter arrived with the wine. She quietly watched him present the bottle, open it with a flourish, present the cork for my inspection, and then stand impatiently while I tasted the wine. I signaled my approval with a nod. He filled Lisa's glass and then mine before leaving. I waited for her to finish her sentence. She sipped the wine, silent in her thoughts, and then said, "Why don't we just enjoy our dinner? We can talk about all this tomorrow. It's been a long day."

25

WE LEFT EARLY THE NEXT MORNING, forgetting our usual exercise routine. It was Lisa's idea. I was now in fairly good shape, she decided, and we could try something more than the up and down the driveway of the preceding weeks.

"We need to talk," she said over the noise of the shower, "as far away as possible from this velvet prison and its microphones and cameras."

The sun was peeking over the mountains to the east as we pulled out of the long drive onto the main highway. I'd left the gate opener with its hidden transponder propped neatly against the stone pillar just under the keypad.

We drove toward Cashiers under a clear blue sky. "The guidebook says that Whiteside Mountain is an easy hike," Lisa said. "Shouldn't be crowded this time of day." She was wrong. The parking area at the trail head was full of SUVs and jeeps. Small knots of people—families with children, preadolescents and teenagers in groups from nearby summer camps, older couples, and single hikers—all seemed to have had the same idea. We managed to find a parking spot and joined the throng up the gentle incline toward the top.

We walked slowly, Lisa reading from the guidebook. "The trail's about two miles long. Says here we're on the Eastern Continental Divide and that we're supposed to see peregrine falcons and look for wildflowers." I could tell she was preoccupied. "The hike is described as 'moderate' and..."

"Lisa," I said. "Cut it out. We can't ignore what's going on. We've got to talk—there's got to be a way out of this situation."

"But how?" We hiked in silence, thinking. A noisy throng of children ran past us, their harried parents huffing behind in an effort to keep up. At the top of the mountain, the trail narrowed, following a winding course along the edge of an exposed granite bald. Sheer drops of hundreds of feet fell away sharply, overlooking a green valley nearly half a mile below. A rusty metal railing lined the trail's edge, more of a warning than a true barrier. We walked for several hundred yards, passing other hikers stopped to take photographs or marvel at the view.

A gently sloping dome of exposed rock appeared to our right. Patches of dark green moss basked in the morning sunlight while bright clumps of tiny yellow flowers poked out from crevasses in the stone. "Why don't we sit up there?" I said. "We can be far enough from the crowd to have a little privacy." We scrambled up the side and stretched out on a smooth patch of stone in the morning sunlight.

"It's so beautiful here," Lisa said after a moment. "It wouldn't take much effort to make the world and all our worries just disappear."

"I wish," I said, "but we've got some hard decisions to make. We..."

I was interrupted by a scream and the sound of clattering on the rocks below us. Then, "Eric! Kyle! You get back down here this minute!"

Two boys, perhaps seven or eight years old, ran screaming across the lower portion of the exposed rock near the trail. The one in the lead was wearing a black cape and eye mask, and wielding a toy sword.

"You'll never catch Zorro!" he yelled and disappeared into the bushes.

His companion ran after him, yelling back, "No fair! You're the bandit, not Zorro."

A harried-looking mother in her mid-thirties emerged from the direction the boys had come. Looking around, she saw us and yelled, "Have you seen two little boys come this way?"

Lisa grinned and pointed toward the direction they'd taken. The woman sprinted off after them.

"That's just the sort of thing that makes you wonder about having kids," she said. Then, her face turning serious, "Let's list our options. It seems to me that we've got our choice of two. We can stay here or we can leave. If we stay, we're protected and safe, but only at the price of losing our privacy. If we leave..."

"Why don't I just tell them that we found the camera system and demand an explanation?"

"What kind of answer do you think you'd get? Of course, they can't deny it. They'll say it was there when the government acquired the house, which it probably was, and that you're here for your protection and that they were not spying on you and so forth. You wouldn't expect them to show their hand, would you?"

"I guess not." I thought for a moment. "We could demand that they disable the cameras. Shut the surveillance system down."

"What are they going to do then? Tell us that they think that maybe if we leave you just *might* be okay, but they make no guarantees because they still don't have an inkling about who wants you dead? Right! I suspect that we wouldn't be here if they didn't think we knew something. Kicking us out is probably their Plan B, anyway. Put a little more pressure on you."

"Okay. Say we leave on our own. Tell 'em or not tell 'em that we've found the cameras. Just say that I'm better now and want to hide out somewhere else."

"A possibility, sure, but who's to say that without the government's protection we'd be able to hide out until the case is solved? And what if it's never solved? Are we going to have to...?" Lisa stopped, looking down the rock toward the trail. The kid in the Zorro outfit was sprinting toward us, his sword waving.

He ran up to me and said, "Is your name Matt?"

I nodded, alarmed. "Yes. Why?"

"Then I'm supposed to give you this." He reached inside his shirt and pulled out a white envelope.

I took it. It was blank. No name or return address. The flap was sealed. "Who is this from?" I asked.

"I don't know. The man down there," he gestured with his sword toward the bushes, "told me to give it to you."

"Who? What man?" I couldn't see anyone.

"I don't know, but he called me 'Don Diego.' That's the real name of Zorro. He's not like Kyle. He knows who I am."

"What does he look like?"

"I don't remember. He's old, like you. And wearing a green or blue T-shirt. And he gave me $5."

Zorro's head jerked up at the sound of hoarse female cry from below. "Eric, where are you? Get down here this minute!"

"Gotta go," he said. Zipping his sword through the air in the sign of a "Z," he scampered down the rock in the opposite direction.

We watched him disappear. Lisa looked at me wide-eyed and speechless. My pulse racing, I examined the envelope. It appeared to have a letter inside. I put my finger under the flap and pressed up. The cheap paper tore open, sending a folded object fluttering to the ground. I picked it up and unfolded it. Inside were three photographs: one of my mother in her bathrobe apparently walking out to get the morning paper, another of my uncle Jack and his wife Margie sitting on the veranda of their cabin at the lake, and a third of Lisa emerging from the front door of Mountain Fresh carrying an armful of groceries.

The paper wrapped around the photographs was a note consisting of three short paragraphs:

These were taken with a telephoto lens. They could just have easily have been the view through a rifle scope.

Be at the Wine Garden at The Old Edwards Inn tomorrow at 3:00 PM. Miss Li is welcome to accompany you. Do not tell your hosts where you are going. In case you are not aware, the gate openers contain a tracking device.

This is your one opportunity. We want your cooperation. If you choose not to offer it, we will eliminate one of the individuals in the photographs to demonstrate that we are serious.

26

A COLD FRONT BLEW in overnight. The following day, a Saturday, dawned slowly. I set the alarm for 7:00 but awoke in a cold sweat at 5:30, lying in bed and thinking while the light from the patio door painted the room a somber grey. Lisa slept soundly, stirring with a start as I eased out of bed to start breakfast.

We spent most of the morning on the small lawn overlooking the valley and away from the cameras and microphones. We tried to plot strategy. We passed the note back and forth, trying to divine some hidden meaning in the words. Neither of us were hungry at lunch, but managed to force down a sandwich of cold cuts and tomatoes. We left the house at 2:15, again hiding the gate opener propped against the stone pillar.

The Old Edwards Inn is one of several vintage hotels on Main Street in Highlands. Built in the mid-1930s, at one time it would have been described as "homey." Now, joined with a nineteenth-century boarding house next door and completely refurbished at a price of tens of millions of dollars, it had become another venue for Atlanta's nouveau riche to conspicuously spend their surplus cash by lounging in rooms boasting of period antiques or sleeping on European bedding fitted with thousand-count Frette linens. Next to the attached restaurant, an outdoor wine garden peeked out at Main Street from behind a shrubbery hedge.

We arrived promptly at 3:00, just as the sun began to break through high-scattered clouds. A liveried waiter greeted us at the gate. I gave him my name and he replied, "Ah, yes, Mr. Rutherford.

We were expecting you. We've been holding a place." He showed us to a small table under the shade of a tree and held Lisa's chair while she sat down. I sat in the only other chair.

"I think we were meeting someone," I said.

The waiter looked puzzled. "Think?" he asked.

I realized that my words didn't make sense. "I'm sorry, let me rephrase that. A friend of ours said that he'd be here at three. We were looking forward to talking with him."

I had no idea whom we were supposed to meet. There might be a dozen of them for all I knew, but I didn't expect to arrive and find that a two-person table had been reserved for us.

"Of course," the waited smiled. "It's a surprise, then. I'll be right back." He disappeared inside the restaurant. I had no idea what he was talking about.

We looked around at the other customers. Several couples were laughing loudly at the table next to us. A twenty-something woman with a shiny, new wedding band stared longingly at the man seated across from her as they sipped champagne. A mixed assortment of couples and groups all seem absorbed in their wine and conversation. No one paid us any attention.

Our waiter emerged from the building carrying a silver tray with a bottle, two glasses, and a wrapped gift. He set it on the table between us and said, "Happy Birthday, Mr. Rutherford. Welcome to the Old Edwards Inn."

"But..." I started.

Lisa gave me a sharp look and I held my tongue.

"I must say that your friend thinks highly of you," the waiter said as he uncorked the bottle.

"How so?"

Rather than replying, he held the wine label for me to see: Château Margaux. "A 1999. Quite a vintage year."

"He's not going to be here?"

"No, didn't he tell you? He said that something had come up at the last minute, but that he wanted you to enjoy yourself. It's all paid for, of course. Oh, and I was supposed to say that he'd ordered such a great wine because you never know when your next meal may be your last." He poured the wine for me to taste, then filled our glasses and set the brightly wrapped package in front of me.

I looked at the package and then back at the waiter. "Enjoy," he commanded and left.

I looked at Lisa and raised my eyebrows in a "What do I do now?" expression. She said, "I guess we open it."

I picked up the package, half expecting to hear a ticking clock. It was light. I shook it. Nothing rattled inside. Cautiously, I slipped the ribbon off the box and tore open the wrapping paper revealing an unlabeled white gift box. I opened the top to see that it was stuffed with pastel pink tissue paper. I slipped my hand inside to feel a small firm object. Carefully, I folded back the paper to reveal a cell phone. I stared at it, tilting the box for Lisa to see. It began to ring softly. I looked at Lisa.

"Answer it," she said.

I flipped the phone open and said, "Hello."

A mechanical-sounding voice on the other end replied, "For God's sake, Mr. Rutherford, it's not going to bite you."

"Who are you?" I demanded.

"I don't think the time is right just yet for you to have that information. Suffice it to say that I am the only person who can offer you the hope of a long and prosperous life. You notice that I said 'hope,' Mr. Rutherford, because I can assure you that your lack of cooperation will certainly insure your premature demise." He was speaking through a device that disguised his voice.

"What do you want from me?"

"At this point, I want you to enjoy the wine."

"Who are you?" I demanded again. "Where are you?" My eyes scanned the crowd.

"Please, please. All in good time. Call me Victor if you must. I should say that if things work out as planned, you'll not need to know my real name, or have to admit that this contact ever took place. As to where I am, let me reveal only that Miss Li is wearing a lovely pair of jade earrings, and that in your rush to get dressed this morning, you missed a belt loop on the back of your trousers."

I stood up and surveyed the other tables. No one seemed to notice. I looked up. Dozens of windows from surrounding buildings had a clear view of our table.

The mechanical voice on the phone said, "Don't make a fool of yourself. You'll not be able to see me. Why don't you sit back down so that we can have a brief conversation?"

I sat down.

"Good," the voice said.

"What do you want from me?" I repeated.

"As I said in the note, we want your cooperation. We want to recover something that was stolen from us. The FBI seems convinced that you know more than you've been willing to tell them. You *are* aware that the house you've been occupying offers you as much privacy as a fish in a glass bowl? Your every move has been filmed. Your every conversation recorded. Once we found where you were hiding, we considered your elimination. But, this incident has generated too much violence already. We would like to end it without the necessity of more. We would be willing to trade you your life for the safe return of our property."

I was afraid to admit that I had no idea what he was talking about.

"And what is that?"

"Don't be a fool, Mr. Rutherford. Either you know or you don't know. If the latter case is true, we can terminate this conversation now and you and Miss Li can finish your wine. You'll not make it home alive."

"Okay. I'll cooperate, but it's not that simple. I'm not sure that I know enough..."

"I'm sure that you'll be able to garner whatever pieces of the puzzle you are missing. Go back to Walkerville. We're no threat to you at the moment. Keep the phone close to you. There's a charger in the bottom of the box." The speaker paused for an instant and then said, "One bit of advice. I'm sure that I don't need to tell you that you must not inform your hosts that we've made contact. If we find evidence that you've betrayed this confidence, we'll simply kill you both without further warning. We're quite serious. Please remember that." There was another brief pause, then, "We'll be in touch." The line went dead.

"What did he say?" Lisa asked.

"I'll tell you later," I replied, grabbing the box and standing up. "Let's go."

The waiter saw us rise from the table and rushed over. "I hope you're not leaving. I trust the wine is good?"

"We need to leave," I said.

"But that's a four hundred dollar vintage bordeaux," he stammered. "I really would hate to see it go to waste."

"Then drink it yourself," I said and headed for the exit.

Halfway there I stopped and turned around. The waiter was still staring, uncertain what to say. "One question," I asked.

"Yes?"

"The man who paid for the wine and left the gift. What did he look like? Did he give his name?"

The waiter looked relieved that I was not complaining about the quality of the wine. "I didn't see him. He called and arranged it all over the phone. Said it was a birthday surprise for you. He left the gift and an envelope of cash at the front desk where I picked it up."

"His name? Did he give a name?"

"Yes. He said that he was an old friend of yours. Stewart Jarrard."

27

I GRABBED LISA'S HAND, nearly pulling her out of the wine bar. "What did he say?" she asked again, more insistent this time. I didn't answer. I studied the crowd on the street. Throngs of summertime visitors filled the sidewalks, window shopping, talking—or watching us?

A man across the street sat on a bench, looking intently in our direction. As we reached the sidewalk he leaped up suddenly, wading through the traffic in our direction. He was carrying an oversized shopping bag.

Holding on to her hand, I nearly jerked Lisa off her feet as I tried to weave my way though the crowd toward the car. A gaggle of senior citizens, apparently on a summertime bus tour, blocked our path as they slowly inched their way down the sidewalk. I stepped out toward the street to get around them. The man with the shopping bag was getting closer. I saw him reach inside and yell, "Hey!"

He withdrew a small dark object from his sack. I looked around, terrified, just in time to see him hug an obese woman in a yellow pants suit and say, "Where have you been? I've been looking for you for an hour. I got the damned carved bear you wanted—cost me fifty bucks. What a rip-off." He held out a wood carving for her inspection. I breathed a sigh of relief.

"Matt!" Lisa said. "Slow down. What's going on?"

"Let's go for a ride. Someplace where we can talk."

We drove west this time, toward Franklin. The road narrowed, twisting and turning down the mountain as it hugged the edge of a rocky stream. We found a deserted overlook with a view of the creek below and parked. "So what did he say?" Lisa asked.

"Nothing really. Just that he—or whoever he represents—wants our cooperation. He said that we're safe and that he'd call. I'm supposed to keep the phone with me."

"That's it? Nothing more?"

I gave her a detailed account of the conversation, as well as I could remember it. Lisa stared off at the creek as I spoke, then picked up a rock and threw it over the railing. She watched as it clattered on the stones far below before bouncing into the stream. "So what do we do?"

I picked up another stone and threw it after hers. It hit a tree and bounced back onto the hillside. "Looks like we have our choice of two unpleasant options. We can stay here—our every move watched—or we can leave."

"And go where?"

I threw another stone. This time it landed on the edge of the creek. I turned things over in my mind and said, "Home. Walkerville."

"Why?"

"Why not? Staying here has no advantage any more. Our cover's been blown. And like the man said, we're fish in a glass bowl. We can't risk telling the FBI—they don't trust us anyway. Maybe the guy that called has an inside track—a source on the inside. How else could he have found us?"

"You don't suppose it might just be more government games? If they think you know something, another way to flush you out?"

"Possible, but I just don't think so."

I picked up another stone and tossed it. It landed squarely in the creek this time. The impact startled a foot-long rainbow trout that leaped out of the water, its scales shimmering in the sunlight.

Lisa propped against the hood of the BMW, turning the options over in her mind. "All it does is buy us time. You—we—have no idea what secret Jarrard was hiding. Where do we even start? As long as anyone believes that we hold that information, we're not safe."

"Any other suggestions?" I asked.

Lisa tossed another stone, then paused and took a deep breath. "No. Not really." She then smiled and said, "But if we're leaving, I need to take care of a few things. Mind if we stop at the hardware store on our way back through town?"

□□□

THE SUN WAS APPROACHING THE TOP of the mountain range to our east as we pulled in through the iron gates. We parked under the portico and spent the next half-hour packing up the few belongings that we'd brought.

Once we had everything stowed in the car, Lisa whispered, "How about going down to the basement and cut the main power switch? It will take ten or fifteen seconds for the generator to power up. Keep the power off for about thirty more seconds after the lights come on, then cut the main power back on. The generator should shut off automatically then. I've got a little work to do in the kitchen."

I did as I was told. I pulled the main power switch at the basement electrical panel. There was sudden darkness. With a whirring, then a low muffled roar, the diesel generator caught and fired up. The lights came back on, a low glowing yellow at first, then at their full luminescence as the power returned to normal. I looked at my watch, waited thirty seconds, then cut the switch back on. The lights blinked briefly, then came back on as the sound of the engine died.

I sprinted back up the stairs to find Lisa seated at the kitchen table, working on a piece of lamp cord that she'd bought at the hardware store. A roll of electrical tape lay next to her.

I whispered, "Are you worried about…"

She shook her head as she worked, pointing silently at the clock on the wall that concealed the camera. A black strip of electrical tape was stuck over the small hole that concealed the lens.

"Nope. Think we're just fine here."

Fishing two alligator clips from the white Ace Hardware bag, she stripped one end of the electrical cord and screwed the clips on each of the two wires. On the other end, she affixed a clip on the electrical plug.

She stood up and leaned next to my ear to whisper, "The

upstairs circuit breaker box is in the utility room. Open it up and wait. As soon as one of the breakers trip, the lights may go out here in the kitchen. Just reset it and they'll come back on."

"What are you going to do?" I whispered.

"Watch."

Lisa lifted the clock-camera off the wall and let it dangle at the end of the blue Cat-5 cable. Using a small screwdriver, she loosened the rear panel of the clock and slid it to one side. At the point where the wires were connected to the small circuit board supporting the camera, she attached an alligator clip to each side. "Now get ready," she said.

I stood waiting in the doorway of the pantry. Lisa took the other end of the lamp cord and plugged it into an electrical outlet. There was a blue flash accompanied by a loud pop. The lights under the kitchen counter blinked, then shut off. Lisa smiled, unplugged the cord from the socket, removed the clips from the clock and said, "You can flip the breaker on now." I did and the counter lights came back on.

"Now," she said, no longer whispering, "Let's do the same thing for the network connections to the computer. That should pretty well wipe out most of their surveillance equipment."

"Did you do what I think you just did?" I asked.

"Yep. All this stuff—cameras, microphones, computer wiring—is low voltage, twelve volts max, but usually less. It's got all kinds of protection from lightning and electrical surges from the outside, but none from the inside. I just ran enough juice into the system to fry every component in that closet downstairs. We'll do the computer just to make sure. I'm not going to let those assholes turn me into a porn star."

Twenty minutes later we pulled onto the highway back to Highlands and home. We found the gate stuck open, its control system apparently burned out by Lisa's lamp cord. I drove this time. It felt strange to be behind a steering wheel again.

As we drove through town, Lisa asked, "Mind if we stop at a convenience store and pick up a Coke and some crackers? We haven't had much to eat today."

I was topping the tank off at the gas pump as she emerged, clutching a bag in her right hand and holding a newspaper in her left. She had a worried look on her face.

"Everything all right?" I asked.

"Just dandy," she said. "We were wondering how whoever's been watching us found out about the cameras."

"And..."

"I have an idea," she said, handing me the newspaper. It was a copy of "The Highlander," the local twice-weekly newspaper. Emblazoned in bold print under the masthead, the headline read, "*LOCAL MAN FOUND DEAD AFTER APPARENT HIT-AND-RUN.*" The article below began, "Horace A. Nesselrode, aged 64, of Turtle Pond Road in Highlands, was found dead yesterday afternoon near his home. The body was discovered in a ditch by a jogger who reported it to local police. Official sources stated that his death appears to be due to a hit-and-run accident, based on the amount of trauma suffered by the victim. Nesselrode, a former FBI agent, was divorced and lived alone..."

"Damn," I said.

"Yeah," Lisa said.

I read fear in her eyes.

28

IT WAS AFTER DARK when we arrived in Walkerville. Even though I'd been gone for nearly two months, little had changed. The stucco and brick sign marking the city limits still read "Welcome to Historic Walkerville, 1793" next to a small forest of notices advising the wayward traveler that this town held its full measure of Lions, Rotarians, Kiwanians, and Optimists. High school students, bored during the long summer, still congregated on the City Square, scoping each other out with an intensity made possible only by teenage hormones. The pleasant warmth of June had given way to the mugginess of August. Broad fields of yellow grain were replaced by row upon row of green soybeans maturing for the fall harvest. Life had continued, apparently none the worse from my absence.

We debated about calling to let someone know we were returning. In the end, we just decided that we'd show up. To alert Uncle Jack or my mother meant that there'd surely be a welcoming party complete with covered dishes of fried chicken and a parade of well-meaning—or curious—neighbors showing up to have a look at the survivor of Walkerville's only known car bombing. I had no real plans about what we'd do once we reached home. I simply wanted to sleep in my own bed.

Rutherford Hall loomed as a dark, bulky shadow as we pulled in the driveway. Under the glare of the headlights, the stable appeared to have acquired a fresh new coat of white paint. The hundred-year old camellia that had been only a few yards from my truck was simply missing. I could make out gashes in the bark of the elm trees in the yard, but the house itself was unchanged.

We parked the car in the stables, hidden from street view. I fumbled around in the dark until I found the spare key to the back door that I kept hung on a nail in one of the stalls. Loading up with our bags, we climbed the steep back stairs to the stoop, the exact spot where I'd last been standing when my memories of June 14 abruptly ceased.

"I hope no one's changed the locks or the alarm code," I said, finding the hole and slipping the key in. It turned easily. The rear door swung open into the entryway, greeted by the sharp beeping from the security alarm key pad. I punched in my old code and the beeping stopped.

I opened the second door to the wide central hall. The house smelled at once musty and old, but it was home. A gentle glow from a streetlamp beamed through the front door side panels at the far end of the hall. For an instant, I thought I saw a shadow play against the wall, but wasn't sure.

Rather than turn on the light, I grabbed Lisa's hand and whispered, "Hold still for a minute. I thought I saw something move."

"Where?" she whispered back. An audible creak echoed from somewhere in the front of the house. Lisa pressed herself against the wall in the shadows. I picked up a heavy cloisonné vase from a side table and advanced slowly down the hall. The shadow on the wall moved again. This time I was sure. I kept still. The floor creaked once more, nearer this time. I began to pick up the sound of someone's rapid breathing.

I slipped quickly into the shadow of the stairs. My eyes were becoming accustomed to the dark as a figure moved slowly toward the spot where Lisa stood motionless. He stopped, listened, and then began to inch in the direction of the front parlor. I reasoned that if I crouched and took a flying leap I could tackle him, or at least slam him into the wall. Grasping the vase firmly with my right hand, I braced my legs to wait for the right moment.

I saw the figure make a sudden move toward a table against the opposite wall. Tensing my muscles, I prepared to leap. The click of a switch flooded the hall with bright light. Eula Mae stood wide-eyed in a long pink nightgown, her head wrapped in a plastic shower cap and her hands nervously pointing my father's double-barreled shotgun right at my chest. She screamed at the sight of me.

"Good God, Mr. Matt! What you trying to do? Get yo'self kilt? Come sneaking in here in the middle of the night like you some kind of burglar man? You oughta be ashamed of yo'self. And what's more..."

She saw Lisa and stopped abruptly. She laid the gun on the table and ran toward her.

"Praise the Lord, is that Miss Lisa? Now I *knows* things is gonna be okay." She hugged her, crying, then turned and hugged me. "Mr. Matt, we been so worried about you. We thought you was gonna die. Been off in some hospital in Florida, they says, bad hurt. You are a sight for sore eyes. If I'da known that..."

I hugged her back, then said, "Eula Mae, just what are you doing here in the middle of the night?"

Out of the corner of my eye, I saw Lisa dab a tear from her cheek.

"Well, you got this big old house full o' them antiques. You don't speck me to just stay home and wait for somebody to rob 'em, do you? No, we can't have that. Your Uncle Jack, he say it be okay if I jus' stayed here to look after things 'til you gets back. So I been staying here—ever since you got hurt. The house is clean and I been keeping your favorite food in the 'frigerator jus' in case you shows up like you jus' done." She paused, standing back to look at me. "Lord, you looks a world better than you did in that hospital over there in Augusta. Come on in the kitchen. Let me get you some food. The boss is home and things are gonna be jus' fine!"

□□□

AS I PREDICTED, the next day brought a steady stream of visitors to the back door, beginning at 7:30 with my uncle who showed up to "check on things" and was shocked to find that we'd returned. Around 10:00, my mother and three of her bridge club friends arrived with a large tin of cheese straws and grocery sack of late summer squash and Vidalia onions. I told Eula Mae to screen the phone calls—telling everyone that I was still recovering, or something like that, and that I'd try to call them back when I was more rested.

"You looks in good shape to me," she'd replied, somewhat indignant at my instructions.

My mother and her friends were just leaving when Eula Mae stuck her head in to say, "Mr. Matt, there's a man on the phone says he's with the FBI. Agent Davis. You wants me to tell him to call back?"

I looked at Lisa and shrugged. "Tell him I'll be right there."

"Let me get it," Lisa said and headed toward the kitchen without waiting for my reply. I followed her, curious. I could hear her side of the conversation.

"This is Lisa Li. How are you, Mr. Davis?"

She listened for a moment and said, "Late yesterday afternoon. Matt has been doing so much better and he just decided that he needed to be at home."

Another pause, then, "Oh, really, I'm so very sorry. Well, there was that big thunderstorm you know. Knocked out the phones. We would have called but they just weren't working." A pause. "I don't know what the weather report said, Mr. Davis. All I know is that we had a terrible electrical storm up there on that mountain. Lightning striking all around. I know it hit the phones—probably got the computer, too."

Lisa held her hand over the mouthpiece and giggled. She listened for another full minute, occasionally saying, "Uh, huh," or "Is that so?" Apparently cutting him off, she ended with, "Well, I hope you get it all fixed. We'll look forward to seeing you in a few days. I'll tell Matt that you called." She hung the phone up without waiting for a reply and burst out laughing.

"Seems like the lightning knocked out their satellite dish system. I think he was more worried about that than he was about our leaving without saying good-bye. He said that he'd call or come by next week."

By two, the crowd had drifted away. Eula Mae, now satisfied that I was alive and well, decreed that she was taking a few days off and would be back as usual Wednesday morning. I didn't argue. She called a friend to pick her up and was waiting on the back steps when Sheriff Arnett pulled in the yard. He spoke politely to Eula Mae, then trudged slowly up the steps, hat in hand. I greeted him at the door.

"Matt, I don't know what to say. I'm just so sorry. I feel like in some way I am responsible for getting you into all of this. If I'd had any idea that…"

"You don't have to apologize. It wasn't your fault."

"But what are you doing here? The last time I spoke to Agent Kight, you two were somewhere up in North Carolina—some secure facility the feds have got up there. Then I get a call this morning from Agent Davis saying you'd disappeared. I told him the word was you got back in town last night. He said he was going to call you."

"He did," Lisa said, having appeared behind me in the doorway.

"How are you, Miss Li?" the sheriff nodded politely.

"I'm fine, thanks." She put her arm around my waist. "And Matt is, too. He just needed to come home."

"Mind if I come in? Davis was all upset and worried—and then Kight called, too. They think you may still be in danger. Worried about you being back down here without protection. They wanted me to come over and talk with you. See why you left without so much as giving them the time o' day."

"I'm better. I just wanted to get home. Come on in. We'll talk."

We sat around the kitchen table drinking coffee. I talked. Lisa talked. Arnett listened. On our drive back, we'd decided not to say anything about our discovery of the fact that our every move in our so-called "secure" refuge had been watched, or about Horace Nesselrode, or the note and photographs, or our contact with the person who appeared to have ordered Jarrard's death.

Instead, we ended up telling Arnett everything. It wasn't that Lisa or I had anything to confess; it was more a sense of hopelessness, a feeling that we were overwhelmed by events beyond our control. We needed an ally. Someone with a different perspective on the situation. Someone we could trust. For the most part, Arnett sat silently, sipping his coffee and listening. In the end he said, "I think you're in a hell of a mess, and I don't have any idea what to do."

29

IT'S THE SORT OF THING that you turn over and over in the back of your mind. Whether you're awake or asleep or eating or taking a shower, it's just there, a persistent shadow that stalks every moment of your existence. Lisa tried to put up a good front, as did I. We said, both by our words and actions, that things were going to work out. In truth, neither of us believed it. I had acquired a mortal enemy who had promised that should I not be able to return to him whatever it was that had been stolen, I would die, and, most likely, Lisa would die with me. The problem was that we had neither any idea what we should be searching for, nor any way of defending ourselves from our equally unknown adversary.

Arnett continued, "I don't know what I can do to help you. Of course, we need to let the FBI know what's going on."

"No!" I said.

He seemed surprised. "Why not?"

"Because we have no idea who we're up against. This person who called me—he kept referring to 'we.' I don't know how he—or they—managed to track us down in North Carolina. Unless they got the information from Horace Nesselrode, how did they know about the camera and microphones in the house? It's possible that they have a source on the inside. We're supposed to recover something that has been stolen. We don't know what we're looking for and we have no idea where to start. If we fail, we die. We need more information, but the last I heard from Davis, no one's made much progress in the investigation. You don't have

138

any fresh news, do you?"

Arnett shifted uncomfortably, "Not really." He took a sip of coffee and said, "How much detail did you get from Davis the last time you talked?"

"Not a lot. Just the big picture, really. He said that they'd followed up on a lot of leads, done a bunch of interviews, that sort of thing."

"Maybe I can help. Up until someone tried to kill you, this was pretty much a joint investigation. Chief Mathis and I had each assigned a couple of our men to work on the case full time. We were handling the local end while the feds were following up on leads outside the area, like old cases Jarrard had worked on, any problems that he might have had in New York and the like. We shared files and reports, including all the stuff the FBI collected. Now, all that is confidential of course..." His voice trailed off.

"Are you going to repeat any of what we told you to the FBI?"

"I should. I have to, really. They could charge me with impeding the investigation. If something happened to you, Matt…" He stopped a second time without finishing his sentence.

"If you do, it could get us killed," Lisa said.

Arnett rubbed his chin nervously. "Mind if I have a little chew?" he said, reaching in his shirt pocket for a bag of Red Man and plopping a large pinch in his mouth. He thought for a minute and looked at his watch. "Okay. We haven't had this conversation. I need to run over to my office for a few minutes. You're not planning on going anywhere, are you?"

We said that we weren't.

"I'll be back in half an hour or less."

Twenty minutes later, Arnett appeared at the back door with a bulky expandable file folder under his arm. He came in and sat down once again at the kitchen table, looking at his watch. "Here is the entire investigation folder on the Jarrard murder. It's not supposed to leave the office. I'm willing to summarize it for you, but officially you can't see what is in these files." He glanced at his watch again, just as his cell phone rang. He unclipped it from his belt.

"Arnett here."

There was a pause, then "Okay." He hung up. "Looks like

I've got a call. I'm going to be gone for three hours, and then I'll drop back by and we can talk." He got up and walked out without another word. The thick folder lay on the table.

I looked at Lisa. She said, "Does your photocopier still work?"

"It's even got a document feeder."

"You know, he's a nice guy," she said.

"I think he feels guilty," I replied.

□□□

ARNETT RETURNED PROMPTLY three hours later. The file folder lay on the kitchen table where he'd left it. "Oh, gosh," he said. "I forgot and left the Jarrard files here. Again, they're confidential. I hope you didn't disturb them."

"No," I said. "There're exactly as you left them."

"Good," he said. "Gotta go. We'll talk in a day or two. I'll help you in whatever way I can." He scooped up the folder and walked toward the door. He stopped, turned around and said, "It's good to have you back in town, Matt. Really." He flashed a terse smile and left.

□□□

WE MOVED THE EPERGNE from the center of the dining room table and began to sort the copies from the Jarrard murder investigation file. We'd used more than three reams of paper in copying them, some seventeen hundred pages in all. Two hours later, we'd divided them into three big piles. The largest was information related to the first attempt on Jarrard's life, plus everything directly having to do with the local investigation of his murder.

The second pile was a series of reports of various origins on Jarrard's background. There were lists of essentially every legal case in which he'd played a substantive role for the past twenty years. There was a copy of his divorce decree with an attached schedule of the property settlement. Ten-odd pages represented a detailed analysis of his financial status. A summary report from the FBI crime lab in Washington contained an annotated list of the contents of the hard drives of his laptop and the computers at his office.

The third pile was made up of interview reports, some sixty-three in all. A few of these were local, but most were of friends, former business associates, and family, including his ex-wife and ex-father-in-law.

"You know," Lisa observed, "there's something vaguely obscene about all this. A man's whole life, laid out in stacks of reports, every little detail picked apart. And his death, not so much mourned as clinically dissected under the spotlight of the police and FBI. Do you think it's going to be that way with us, Matt? What if things don't work out? Is all that remains of us going to be a thick file folder gathering dust on the shelf of some backwoods Georgia police station?"

"I can't say, but not if I have a choice. Which pile do you want?"

"I don't know much about Jarrard…" she began.

"Neither do I."

"But at least he was more to you than a stack of reports. I'll start with Jarrard's background.

"Good. I'll work on the interviews."

An hour later, we took a brief break to eat some vegetable soup that Eula Mae left for us in the refrigerator. Three hours later, we were both exhausted and decided to call it quits for the night. We were none the closer to a solution.

□□□

THE SOFT RING OF THE CELL PHONE awoke me at 7:30 the next morning. "Good morning, Mr. Rutherford," the same mechanical voice said. "I trust you made it home safely?"

"Yes."

"That's good. I hope that you and Miss Li are rested."

"I appreciate your concern. What do you want?"

"First, I want to reiterate my request that you do not communicate to the authorities the fact that we have been in contact."

"I haven't," I lied.

"Second, I want you to help us discover the whereabouts of what Mr. Jarrard took from us. We have reason to believe that he gave you certain information before he died."

"Where do I start, then?"

"I was hoping you wouldn't have to ask that. I have every reason to believe that the information is right in front of you somewhere. And knowing Stewart as I did, it may be hidden in the most obvious place. He always was fond of his little games, his puns, the little mysteries that he used to demonstrate his cleverness. If you haven't figured it out, I'm sure that you will." The caller paused.

"Remember this: We have discussed the matter at length. Our position has boiled down to two alternatives. In an ideal world, we would be able to recover that which has been lost. If we do so, and it is done quietly without anyone's knowledge, you and Miss Li have our assurance that you will be left alone. On the other hand, we could remove our uncertainty about what you know by eliminating you. If we do that, though, it is likely that we will never recover what we seek. We are willing to delay the second alternative in hope that you can accomplish the first. If, after a reasonable period of time, you do not, we will have little choice but to permanently silence you. Is that very clear?"

A cold chill ran through my body as he spoke. "Very clear. Where should I start looking?"

"That's up to you. I'll call again in a week and expect to hear that you're making progress." With a click he was gone.

Lisa had been lying quietly beside me, listening to the exchange. "Victor again?"

"Yes."

"What did he say?"

"Briefly, that we find what Stewart Jarrard took, or we'll be killed."

30

WE ATE BREAKFAST. Lisa took her coffee and a stack of papers to the dogtrot. I sat at the dining room table, reading. I finished the summaries of the interviews and attacked the pile having to do with the local investigation of Jarrard's murder. In large part, it was a rehash of what we already knew. By 10:30 I was just finishing up.

Lisa stood in the dining room door, yellow legal pad in hand. "Want to go over things?"

"Sure. Did you learn anything?"

"I feel like I grew up with Stewart Jarrard. I have to say the investigators did a good job. I can't see where they've missed anything in his background. He sounds like a nice-enough guy. Born in Connecticut, did well in college—he was Phi Beta Kappa, by the way. Graduated fourth in his class from Yale Law. Apparently had some excellent offers in New York, but he wanted to 'practice real law,' according to one report, and took a job as a federal prosecutor in Atlanta. He did that for about eight years, working his way up to the top of the stack. Did quite a few high profile cases.

"When he was in his mid-thirties, he was recruited by the firm in New York, what is it…" She looked at her notes. "Dewey, Naughton, Pierce, et cetera. Made partner after a year and did extremely well, according to the financials filed with his divorce. He was pulling down a mid-six-figure salary toward the end there. Apparently, most of what he handled was civil litigation, plus an occasional white-collar criminal defense case. Met his future wife in Atlanta when they were both in their late-twenties. Got married at thirty, two kids, the usual. Oh, by the way, the wife's maiden name was Habersham. She's the only daughter of Pendleton Brewster Habersham, apparently some bigwig in the New York art and antiques scene."

"Yeah, there were interviews with both the ex-wife and ex-father-in-law in my stack. I think Habersham runs an art auction house."

"Anyway," Lisa continued, "he sounds like an pretty good guy. The only real blot on an otherwise stellar career was the divorce. You have to do a little reading between the lines, but the implication is that he was caught *en flagrante delicto* with a female associate. Jarrard was doing her on a desk late one night when the janitor walked in on them. I guess the guy'd spent too much time working around lawyers. He turned around and sued the firm for creating a hostile work environment.

"Of course, once news of the suit became public, it was matter of damage control. It looks like that's what got him fired from the firm. It seems that his father-in-law was a big client and that Jarrard had been handling all his cases to the tune of a million-plus dollars a year in fees. With the divorce, Habersham pulled his business, and the firm retaliated by firing Jarrard, hoping to get it back."

"Did they?"

"Don't know. What did you learn from the interviews?"

"Not a lot. Like you said, everybody seemed to think he was a nice guy. They talked to a lot of his colleagues dating back to his days in Atlanta, his friends and associates in New York, and of course the ex-wife and ex-father-in-law. There was a codicil that Jarrard attached to his will just days before he was killed. A list of people that he wanted notified in case anything happened to him. They talked to everyone on it—all twenty-nine of them."

"And…"

"Nothing. The conclusion seems to be that he didn't have anyone that he was close to here in Georgia, and just in case someone did him in, he wanted the world to know."

"Oh," Lisa said, thinking. "So, the only hint that Jarrard ever gave to anyone that he might be hiding something from his past was what he said to you just before he was shot?"

"Right."

"Another dead end?"

"Maybe."

"What about his friends?" Lisa asked. "How about those two guys—I remember you said that one of them was a proctologist—who came down for his memorial service?"

"Bonifay and Cordy? Apparently no connection. The only thing they shared in common was their hobby of crossword puzzles. All three of them have contributed puzzles at one time or another to the *New York Times*. The local cops and feds talked to them when I took them over to the sheriff's office on the day of the service.

"But speaking of that," I continued, "several people that were interviewed mentioned Jarrard's obsession with puzzles and little mind-twisters. A couple of people said he had a way of making you feel stupid without really meaning to do so. He was bright, for sure."

"Didn't help him. He's dead now."

□□□

THE COURTHOUSE CLOCK WAS CHIMING noon when Eula Mae slipped in the back door.

"What are you doing here?" I asked. "I thought you were taking a few days off."

"I said that, I know," she said. "But I'm jus' glad to have you back. You 'bout my only family these days and I jus' hated for you and Miss Lisa to be over here without nobody to cook for you." She headed off to begin rattling dishes and filling the sink.

Lisa and I continued to talk in the dining room. Eula Mae sang softly to herself in the kitchen. Fifteen minutes passed. She stuck her head in the door and said, "You got any laundry? Might as well run a load..." She stopped and stared at the dining room table. "Good Lord. What is all them papers you got strewn all over the place? You ain't expectin' me to straighten 'em up, is ya? 'Cause if you is, I..."

"No, thanks. We'll take care of them. They're just some legal papers."

"They's about that Jarrard fellow. I knew it. I ain't one to rub no salt in your wound 'cause you nearly got yerself kilt, but I told you so. I hope you ain't gonna never do nothing stupid like that agin. It liked to kilt me, too, ya know? First the police running all over the house, poking into things, and then you nearly getting exploded, and…"

I had an idea. "Eula Mae. After Jarrard's murder, you cleaned up his room, right?"

"'Course. But the police done hauled off everything there was of his'n. Weren't much to clean up. Jus' sweep and dust and change the sheets and scrub the tub and clean the bathroom."

"You didn't find anything unusual or different?"

She gave me an odd look. "What you mean? No. There weren't nothing different so far as I seen. And then I done spent nigh on two months here in this house day and night cleaning and dusting and polishing every square inch o' this place. There ain't nothing here what ain't here before."

Lisa wrinkled her forehead. It took a moment for the translation to sink in. "You checked all the rooms, then?"

"Well, I weren't looking for nothing, but if it was there I dusted it or polished it. It got mighty lonely waiting for you to come home. I even straightened up in Miss Lillie's old office where you keep yo' computer. I know you don't like me doing that, but I did it anyway, and I have to say I'm sorry."

"Why are you sorry?"

"About the vase. I broke that little vase you keep on the desk there next to the lamp. Knocked it right off while I was dusting."

"To be honest, I hadn't noticed, but for God's Sake don't worry about something as minor as that."

"I thought it might be worth somethin'. One of them antiques. Yo' aunt said it was eye-mary. She got it in Japan."

"Imari?"

"That's what it was. But I saved the pieces for you in a box in case you want to get somebody to glue it back together, and I put that little computer thing in the desk drawer so you could find it."

"What computer thing?"

"I don't know what you call that thing. You got some of 'em sitting there next to the screen part. Let me get it for you." She headed toward the study.

"What's that all about?" Lisa asked.

"I have no idea."

Eula Mae returned gripping a small object in her fist. She held it out for me to see. "Ain't this a computer thing? You got some others look like it in there."

A small flash drive lay on her open palm. The last time I'd seen a similar one, Stewart Jarrard was holding it and asking if he could borrow my computer to send an e-mail.

31

THE FLASH DRIVE held an odd assortment of files. I watched over Lisa's shoulder as she pulled them up on the computer screen. There were two main folders, one labeled "Notes" and another labeled "Puzzles."

"I'm surprised it's not password protected," she said, tapping away at the keyboard. The screen filled with page after page of text. "It looks like—and I'm guessing here—he composed and filed his e-mails in the 'Notes' folder. And this other one," she paused, striking a few more keys, "looks like it's full of crossword puzzles, seven in all, just labeled 'Puzzle #1,' 'Puzzle #2,' and so on. Let me print out the contents of the 'Notes' folder first." She highlighted several files and clicked "Print." With a whirr, the laser printer sprang to life.

We cleared a spot on the dining room table and spread out the sheets. There were five messages in all. "I'd assume that rather than writing his e-mails at the computer like most people do," Lisa observed, "he composed them elsewhere, then copied and pasted the text into a web-based e-mail program. You said the cops couldn't find any trace of the e-mails he sent from your computer the night before he was killed, right?"

"Right."

"That would support that hypothesis. Okay, I'll read and you listen. Tell me what you think."

The first file was titled "B&C." Lisa read:

Hi, guys. I'm sending a puzzle for you two

to review. I know this one's a little different, but I have plans. Look it over. I've got another for you that I'm working on which I'll send just as soon as I finish it. I'll try to give you a call in a few days, maybe this weekend, with some more info, but right now I'm in a real rush. After I send the second one hang, on to them. We'll talk later.

Thanks, Stewart

The next file was titled "Doug1."

Doug,

I know that we've had our differences recently, but we go back a long way. Life has been pretty bad for me lately, as you know, but I've been trying to make a fresh start down here in Georgia, and things seem to be coming together. Something's come up, though, and I need help. I'm not one to beg, but if you would agree to at least consider doing me a personal favor, I'd appreciate it. It doesn't involve the firm or anything professional, so there'll be no implications for DNPWYE.

Thanks. Let me hear from you as soon as possible.

Stewart

The file titled "Doug2" read:

Doug,

Thanks for agreeing to help me out. I know this sounds mysterious, but if anything happens to me, I want to be sure that certain people get copies of the attached files. You know of my obsession with puzzles and games, and I thought these might make a fitting obituary. I'm not being morbid, but I am getting older and don't have many close friends down here (yet!). The e-mail addresses of where you should send them can be found listed next to the puzzle clues.

Thanks again—for old time's sake.

Stewart

A file titled simply "YHA" read:

I know you're behind this, but it looks like I dodged the bullet this time. I thought we had an agreement. I'm here, you're there, and no one is the wiser. It'll stay that way so long as I'm left alone. I thought my knowledge alone was sufficient insurance. Never did it occur to me that you'd consider putting out a contract. But this is a game two can play. I have taken out additional insurance with additional beneficiaries. All anyone will have to do is scratch the surface and the truth will be known. I have mixed feelings about this, because if anything happens to me it will inevitably lead to your downfall and hurt the ones I love. I had gotten in too deep anyway. This had to stop somewhere. The truth will make you free (as they say) in my case, but in yours, it will be life plus twenty, if you can avoid the hangman. Leave me alone.

SJ

A fifth file titled "B&C2" read:

Guys,

I know we've been friends for years through our mutual interest in puzzles. Even though I feel like we know one another well, our association has mainly been limited to our common recreational pursuit. I know that you have your families, and at one time I had mine. With all the changes that have taken place in my life, I've lost many of the relationships that meant so much to me over the years. These days, you guys are about as close as I come to having family, and XXX—got to work on this!!

What I want to ask of you is a deeply personal favor. If anything happens

Lisa finished reading and handed me the printout. The message appeared to be unfinished.

"Can you make any sense of them?" Lisa asked.

"I'm not sure. B&C may refer to Bonifay and Cordy, but I have no idea who 'Doug' or 'YHA' are. What about the puzzles?"

Again I stood in front of the computer looking over Lisa's shoulder. She typed a few strokes and a completed crossword puzzle grid popped on the screen. "What are we supposed to make of that?" I asked.

"I don't know, but here's another one. And another."

A series of grids filled with letters flashed on and off the screen.

"Which one of these did he send to Cordy and Bonifay?

"How should I know?" she said with some annoyance. "I have an idea that we may be looking at whatever secret Jarrard was hiding, but it's coded somewhere inside of all of that." She stabbed at the screen with a pencil. "I wouldn't even know where to start. And look at this one," she continued, bringing up another puzzle grid. "See, it's half done—look at all the empty spaces. It looks like he was working on it but didn't finish it before he was killed."

"Why don't we work on the e-mails first, then? See if they'll give us some direction. I know that the feds didn't follow-up again with Cordy and Bonifay. They dismissed them as being unimportant after the first interview. At least we'll be working on unplowed ground."

"Matt," Lisa said, swiveling her chair around to face me. "Are you sure that we don't need to let the FBI in on this? If we can't figure this out—or if we screw up somehow—Victor's promised to kill us. And what if we do find whatever it is that they're looking for—who's to say that he won't have us killed anyway?"

I wasn't sure how to answer her. I pulled the curtains back and looked out on the side yard. It was a perfectly normal August day.

A couple of kids, maybe ten or twelve, rode their bicycles down the sidewalk along Main Street. Off in the distance, I could hear a lawnmower. At that one moment, in time it seemed impossible to believe that anyone would want us dead. We had no choice. We had to make a decision on which our entire futures hinged.

"You may be right," I said, "but we have two things going for us. First, Jarrard was confident that the mere knowledge of whatever he was hiding was sufficient to protect him from his killers. I'm guessing that they didn't know he had 'insurance'—to use his word. They thought if they silenced him the problem would go away. I think we can use his ploy to our advantage. Make them believe that we've got the information and threaten to go to the feds. It'll buy us some negotiating time."

"And the second thing…" Lisa asked.

"You. You've done it before. You can do it again."

"And if I fail?"

"You won't."

32

WE DECIDED TO WORK on the e-mails first. "B&C" were likely Bonifay and Cordy, but "Doug" and "YHA" were unknowns. The only clues in the e-mails to "Doug" were the references indicating they had known each other for some time, and that he probably lived in New York as Jarrard had written, "down here in Georgia." "DNPWYE" had to mean Dewey, Naughton, Pierce, Williams, Young, and Eaton, since Jarrard had promised that the favor he was requesting "doesn't involve the firm." But who was "Doug?"

I checked the list of persons that Jarrard wanted notified in case of his death. Near the bottom was Douglas Q. Eaton, III, of Dewey, Naughton, et al. It didn't take long to find his photo on their Web site. He was listed as "Managing Partner," with a special interest in estates and trusts. I scribbled down his phone number and moved on to check out Bonifay and Cordy.

Their names and addresses were also on the list. It took one call to directory assistance to get Cordy's office number in Nashville and Bonifay's home number in Greensboro, North Carolina.

As for YHA, both Lisa and I hit a dead end. We couldn't connect the initials to any person, place, or thing that we'd seen in the Jarrard murder file. We logged on to the internet and tried looking up law firms whose names started with the letters "Y," "H," and "A." No luck. We brainstormed about possible abbreviations ("yellow-headed aunts" or "young hot Armenians"). Nothing. We finally gave up and put YHA on the back burner with the crossword puzzles.

I looked at my watch. It was 4:10 in Greensboro and 3:10 in Nashville. I reasoned that I could catch Cordy at his office, and Bonifay later at home. I dialed the Nashville number. Lisa picked up to listen on the extension. The receptionist answered on the eighth ring. "Proctology Associates. How may I help you?"

"My name is Matt Rutherford. I'd like to speak to Dr. Lawrence Cordy, please."

"Are you a patient?"

"No."

"A physician?"

"No."

"I'm sorry, Dr. Cordy doesn't accept phone calls from just anyone. What is the purpose of your call?"

"I'm a friend of the late Stewart Jarrard. I was calling Dr. Cordy about a mutual matter of interest."

There was a pause. "So you're a dead man's friend and you're calling a proctologist about a matter of mutual interest?" She sniffed audibly. "Whose interest, may I ask? Yours and the dead man's, or yours and Dr. Cordy's, or Dr. Cordy's and the dead man's, or something between the three of you?" I could see Lisa convulse in laughter, her hand held over the mouthpiece.

"I think I'd have to answer the three of us."

There was another pause. "You're not a lawyer, are you?"

"No," I said, thinking quickly, "I'm a cruciverbalist."

The receptionist's voice immediately warmed. "Oh, of course! Why didn't you say so? Let me check with him." She came back a moment later to say, "Dr. Cordy is right in the middle of a procedure at the moment. If I can have your contact information he'll call you back just as soon as he's finished." I repeated my name and that of Stewart Jarrard and gave her my number before hanging up.

Lisa was still laughing. "You just get no respect, Matt. Calling a proctologist and saying you're a friend of a dead man. No respect," she giggled and headed toward the kitchen.

Dr. Lawrence Cordy called back twenty minutes later. "Mr. Rutherford, I apologize for not being able to take your call. I was doing an anoscopy and couldn't exactly get away. It's one of those procedures where you're gloved and gowned and have the patient up in the knee-chest position. You…"

"There's no need to apologize, Dr. Cordy." In truth, I didn't want to hear the details. "I know that you talked with the police when you were down for Stewart Jarrard's memorial service. No one's contacted you since then, have they?"

"No. No reason to, really. We—Phillip and I—couldn't be of much help to the authorities. Told them what we knew."

"I recall that you said Jarrard e-mailed you a crossword puzzle just before he was killed, is that right?"

"Yes. Sent exactly the same e-mail to both Phillip and me."

"Do you still have it?"

"I don't see why I shouldn't. They're probably somewhere on my computer. Why do you ask?"

"I'd like to look at the puzzle. Would you have any objection?"

He hesitated. "No, I suppose not. You're not going to involve us—rather, me—in any police investigation, are you?"

"No, no chance of that. Stewart had gotten me interested in crossword puzzles and I was just curious. You said it wasn't of top quality."

"Sure, then. I can just find and forward his e-mail to you tonight. That be okay?"

I thanked him and gave him my e-mail address.

□□□

NEXT, I TRIED DOUGLAS EATON, again with Lisa listening on the other phone. The Dewey Naughton Web site listed a direct number. An efficient-sounding female voice answered on the second ring. "Mr. Eaton's office."

I identified myself and told her that I was calling Mr. Eaton about a business problem. After a brief delay, he answered with a simple hello.

"Mr. Eaton," I said, "my name is Matt Rutherford. I was calling about Stewart Jarrard. I…"

He cut me off. "Mr. Jarrard is no longer with this firm. In fact, he's no longer living. We've closed all of his case files. Were you aware of that?"

"Yes."

"Then what can I do for you?"

"I want to discuss a matter of business that involved Mr. Jarrard."

"Where are you located, Mr. Rutherford. I seem to detect a southern accent."

"In Walkerville, Georgia. Where Stewart was living."

"Fine. I don't give advice or discuss legal matters over the phone, especially with someone I've never met. If you'd like to meet with me in person, you're most welcome to call my assistant back and make an appointment." The line clicked, followed by a dial tone.

"That guy needs a proctologist to help him relieve the load on his ego," she said. "What are you going to do?"

"Go to New York," I said as I redialed the number for Eaton's assistant.

33

THE 12:40 DELTA FLIGHT from Savannah arrives at La Guardia at 2:45. Without too much difficulty, I talked Eaton's assistant into "working me in" at 4:30 the next afternoon. It would be tight, but I thought we could make it. It was 4:22 when our taxi dropped us in front of a steel and concrete edifice on the Avenue of the Americas a couple of blocks from Times Square and Bryant Park. The Law Offices of Dewey, Naughton, Pierce, Williams, Young and Eaton, LLC, sprawled comfortably across the fortieth floor, midway between the old money of the upper east side and the waxing and waning fortunes of the lower Manhattan financial district. We passed through two metal detectors before giving our names to the guard at the desk who called to confirm that we were expected and handed us color-coded visitors' passes.

The walnut-paneled elevator opened directly into a small lobby, elegantly wainscoted in muted shades of cherry and softly illuminated by light from polished brass sconces. The receptionist, a woman in her late twenties with the demeanor of a Vassar graduate of 1950, smiled primly and asked if she could be of assistance. I told her that we had an appointment with Mr. Eaton. She told us to have a seat while we waited. I got the impression that waiting was part of the game. It would be unseemly to admit that five-hundred buck-an-hour attorneys might actually be operating on time.

Lisa, dressed for the part in a conservative Talbot's linen suit, settled down on one of the silk-covered settees and started thumbing through a copy of *Town and Country*. I stared at the

Dewey, Naughton, etc., name in buffed brass above Miss Vassar's desk and played mental games trying to make new words out of the partners' names. I'd come up with "you anti-impotence drug swallowing hyena"—with two letters left over—by the time Eaton's assistant appeared at the door and told us he would see us now. It was 4:58.

I wasn't really sure what I was going to say to Eaton. Our brief conversation the day before had left a bad taste in my mouth, but I didn't want to pre-judge him. Maybe he'd just been having a bad day. From his Web site photo, I'd have thought him to be in his late forties, athletic, and with a patrician demeanor befitting someone who swam in the lofty world of estates and trusts. The man who rose from behind the antique English partners' desk to greet us was fifteen years older, twenty pounds heavier, and possessed considerably less hair than his namesake on the Web. I forgave him; the law, like many of the learned professions, requires one to keep up appearances.

On the drive to Savannah, Lisa and I had talked strategy. We decided that to get the most out of Eaton, a little deception would be in order. Despite any protestations to the contrary, the legal profession is more interested in money than in justice. We'd have to ad lib the exact script, but we knew the general plan.

"Mr. Rutherford," he said, pumping my hand. "So glad that you were able to come up. I much prefer face-to-face meetings. Gives us both a chance to get to know each other personally. That's so important in my line of work. You see, we here at Dewey Naughton specialize in unique solutions for unique…"

I interrupted him. "Allow me to introduce my associate, Ms. Lisa Li." Lisa nodded demurely and extended her hand.

"I'm honored to make your acquaintance, Ms. Li. Please sit down," he said, gesturing toward a comfortable couch and a pair of matching wingback chairs. My eyes swept around his office. It, like the reception area, sported cherry wainscoting and brass lamps. I noted that his desk was essentially bare, with only a lamp, telephone, and two near empty boxes labeled "In" and "Out." Heavy damask curtains lined a window looking out on Bryant Park and the Empire State Building in the distance.

"Can I offer you something to drink?" Eaton said. "Coffee, perhaps, or…" he looked at his watch, "it's nearly five, something stronger?" I perceived a faint redness of his cheeks. Probably a heavy drinker.

"Thank you, but no. It is late, and we don't want to take up too much of your time."

"I'm here as long as I need to be, Mr. Rutherford. So often our younger associates forget that we're in a service business. With our type of clients, of course, you never know when you'll be needed." He paused, "So, tell me, what line of work are you in?"

"I inherited well." I heard Lisa take a sharp breath.

"Ah. Not a bad problem to have." I could see him mentally licking his chops. "I take it that since you mentioned Stewart, he'd been doing some estate work for you down there in Georgia. He was one of our finest. So sad about what happened."

"Yes, a real tragedy. It's strange how things seem to work out. Stewart moved to Walkerville just a few months after I came into a rather substantial inheritance. Family money—a good bit of cash, securities, timberland, and the like. I hate to admit it, but it has been nearly overwhelming to me. I didn't realize the time commitments necessary to manage it all. I met Stewart at the Rotary Club, we got to talking, and he said that he thought he could help. He mentioned that he'd been with your firm here in New York and that you specialized in estates and trusts."

"Yes, we do. For more than fifty years we've helped families like yours who possess significant private wealth. We focus on asset management, wealth preservation, and trans-generational issues through what we think are a series of creative and innovative strategies designed to maximize your returns and minimize your tax obligations while shielding your hard-earned assets from outside challenge."

All this rolled off Eaton's tongue with such ease that I couldn't help but think he'd given this same spiel hundreds of times before.

"That's exactly what Stewart said," I replied with a straight face. "He made a proposal for a series of trusts and managed investments that would accomplish just that. In fact, he gave Ms. Li and me a preliminary presentation just a few days before his death. He wanted me to think it over, and if his suggestions seemed appropriate, he was going to contact you here in New York to get some assistance."

Eaton seemed puzzled. "How so? Stewart was an excellent attorney. I'm not sure how we…"

"I think it was something about the size of the estate."

"Oh, I see." The wheels in Eaton's head were churning. "And what asset range are we talking about?"

"I'm not really sure. My grandfather bought a bunch of Microsoft stock back in the 1980s, and then there was the family farm up near Atlanta that they sold for an office park. Somewhere in the range of a hundred million, I think."

Eaton's eyes glowed. "Certainly. For an estate of that size, he'd…"

"You see," I continued. "The plan was that I'd just turn it over to Stewart to manage. He'd take care of the details and make certain that I had a good income."

I didn't need to mention that such an arrangement would generate seven-figure management fees.

"Oh," Eaton said. "Are you certain that I can't get you something to drink?"

"No, thanks," Lisa said. "Mr. Rutherford doesn't drink." I wanted to kick her.

"Anyway, after Stewart's death, I just put everything on hold," I said "I've hired Ms. Li to help me manage, but she agrees that we need some outside assistance. That's why we're here."

"Well, you've certainly come to the right firm, Mr. Rutherford," Eaton said. "But I'm a little curious. Why New York? We do have an office in Atlanta. Stewart worked there at one time. I would have thought…"

"I don't think it was the firm, Mr. Eaton. It was you. He mentioned you several times as being one of the best. That's why he wanted your advice. In fact, just before his death, he'd mentioned that he e-mailed you to seek some advice about how to proceed. I guess he didn't hear from you before he died."

Eaton's ruddy face took on a deeper shade of red. He sighed. "I shouldn't admit this, but I did get an e-mail from him just a few days before his death. I, er, I didn't read it. I deleted it."

"What? Why?" I tried to look a little shocked.

Eaton took a deep breath. "I have to be honest. Did Stewart ever tell why he left this firm?

"No. I know there was a divorce. He said that he wanted to

make a fresh start. I recall that he said he resigned. Was there more?"

"Yes, there was. I'm tempted to gloss it over, but the whole story is fairly well known. If you asked around enough you'd probably find out. I've got to be honest. Stewart was asked to resign because he was having an affair with one of our younger female associates. He…"

"Ms. MacFarlane?" Lisa asked.

Eaton looked shocked. "Er, no. Not Ms. MacFarlane. It was Ms. Southerland. Chrissy Southerland. She's no longer with the firm. Did he mention Ms. MacFarlane?

"No," Lisa said. "I never met Mr. Jarrard."

"But…" Eaton began, and then reconsidered, but then continued. "Anyway, the affair came to light in a most embarrassing manner. And it got worse. There was a lawsuit and a very messy divorce. The Partners' Committee met and discussed it. We terminated Ms. Southerland and asked Stewart to resign."

"But he always spoke so highly of you," I said. "I'd have never thought he left under a cloud."

"He did. It cost the firm quite a large sum in terms of lost clients, settlement of various lawsuits and, of course, Stewart's buy-out. But we've moved on." Eaton evidently wanted to change the subject. "So let's talk more about…"

"You said you deleted Stewart's e-mail?"

"Yes." Eaton appeared uncomfortable. "I glanced at it. As I recall, he said he wanted a favor. I thought a clean break would be best, so I ignored it. Deleted it."

"You got just one e-mail then?"

"Yes? Why?" He was becoming suspicious.

"I just thought he would have tried harder. But who knows?" I glanced at my watch. Turning to Lisa, I said, "It's late. We need to check into the hotel." Then back to Eaton: "Let me do this, Mr. Eaton. I'll have my accountant send you a synopsis of the estate and perhaps you can work up a plan for me. I'd rather deal with the home office than those hicks down in Atlanta." I stood up to leave.

"That'll be great." He handed cards to both Lisa and me. "I'll look forward to hearing from you." He walked to the door to show us out, then paused and turned toward Lisa.

"Ms. Li. Did I hear you say that you'd never met Mr. Jarrard? How did Ms. MacFarlane's name come up?"

"I don't recall, exactly. Perhaps I saw it on your Web site. I guess I was just confused."

I couldn't exactly read Eaton. He wore a look between uncertainty and confusion. We shook hands and left.

In the lobby, I asked Lisa, "Who the hell is Ms. MacFarlane?"

She smiled, coyly. "His lover. I wanted to rattle the sleazy bastard's cage."

34

"**HOW DID YOU** come up with that?"

"You're a man. You'd never understand," Lisa said as she pushed her way toward the curve and flagged down a taxi.

"Try me."

I gave the driver the name of our hotel. We settled in the back for the ride uptown.

"We went to see Eaton with the goal of finding out about the e-mails," Lisa said. "He made it clear that he only got one, and that he didn't pay much attention to that. It occurred to me as we were sitting there that we may be looking under the wrong rock. Eaton's not going to volunteer any information that he doesn't have to. He's after those fees and commissions on your fictitious hundred million dollar-estate. But who might want to talk? Jarrard's ex-lover. We know she's an attorney. We know her name. Now all we've got to do is track her down."

"But where does this MacFarlane woman come in?"

"She's his assistant, silly. You didn't see her name on her desk as we walked past it to Eaton's office?"

"No, but you seemed to hit a nerve when you mentioned it. What…"

"Good guess. Eaton's the classic nasty old man. I could feel his eyes undressing me as we sat and talked. God, I feel like I need to take a shower. As she showed us in, I watched her watching him watch me. You could read the jealously on her face. It was a stab. A lucky one. I bet if we track down Chrissy Southerland we'll get an ear full."

□□□

WE CHECKED INTO THE WALDORF on Park Avenue. I stayed there frequently during my high-tech days, but I didn't expect them to remember me. Just another fallen has-been from the dot-com era. Our room on the twenty-seventh floor Concierge Level was quiet, luxurious, and had high-speed internet access. I ordered from room service while Lisa fired up her laptop.

Ten minutes later, she said, "There's nothing helpful on Dewey Naughton's Web site. I guess they purged it of all references to Jarrard or Southerland. We don't even know how 'Chrissy' is spelled—either with a 'K' or a 'C'—and whether or not that's her name or a nickname. *But,* if you narrow the search down to people whose last name is Southerland, whose first name begins with a 'K' or 'C,' and who are either identified as lawyers or appear on lawyer-related Web sites, you come up with four names. Two of them are Carl and Clayton, and the other two are Catherine and Christine. I'd put my money on Christine. Looks like," Lisa said, poring over a list on the screen, "she's a legal services attorney with the City Bar Justice Center. It appears she's a staffer on the branch of the New York City Bar Association that handles *pro bono* work. We can probably track her down with a couple of phone calls in the morning."

Promptly at nine the next day, I was on the phone to the offices of the New York City Bar Association. After several transfers, I was connected to a voice that said, "City Bar Justice Center." I identified myself as Douglas Eaton of Dewey, Naughton, et al., and asked if I could get in touch with Christine Southerland.

"Ms. Southerland's in court today," the voice said, the harsh Brooklyn accent scratching across my ear drums like fingernails across a blackboard.

"I have some pleadings that I need to get to her right away. If you could tell me where she is, I'll send them over by messenger."

"Hold on," the voice scratched, "She's in Housing Court, down on Centre Street. You know it?"

"Yeah," I said, trying to sound New Yorkerish. "Thanks. I'll find her."

It took us twenty-five minutes through mid-morning traffic to reach the Housing Court building. Once again passing through a metal detector and the scrutiny of multiple security guards, we were directed to an information desk where a fat black woman with a Jamaican accent fended off a long line of direction-seeking plaintiffs and defendants. It took us fifteen minutes to reach the head of the line, to which she said, dreadlocks bobbing with each chew of her gum, "Yeah?"

"I'm looking for Christine Southerland. She's an attorney."

"Plaintiff or defendant?"

"Neither. I think she's pleading a case."

The woman buried her head in a thick print-out, rapidly flipping pages, then stabbing one with a long-nailed finger. "Third floor, Courtroom D. The lift is there." She pointed to her left at a bank of elevators.

The third floor hall was a human zoo. Long wooden benches were filled to overflowing with a cross-section of New York society. I caught conversations in French, Spanish, Russian, and half a dozen other tongues whose origin I could only guess. We found Courtroom D, a smallish room equipped with an elevated bench, a small jury box, and eight or ten rows of wooden benches that served as a gallery. Lawyers, whom I recognized by their suits and worn briefcases, wandered in and out, holding informal conferences with their clients in the hall or in whispered tones on the back benches of the public seating area. A guard at the door said that Ms. Southerland's case had just been called, a landlord-tenant dispute. Lisa and I took a seat on a middle row to watch the proceedings.

Unlike Eaton, I didn't know how I expected Chrissy Southerland to look. Perhaps I'd been influenced by the tony décor at Dewey Naughton. I'd imagined someone upscale—a graduate of some Ivy League school—demure, but forceful, dressed in a custom-made silk and wool suit while struggling to bring justice to the underclass. I was wrong. The person addressed by the judge as "Ms. Southerland" was short, a little hefty, and dressed in a plain blue skirt with a wrinkled white blouse. Her hair was pulled back in what had probably started the day as a French braid, but was now the cross between a ponytail and bun.

The proceeding—neither Lisa nor I were sure what was

going on—lasted approximately five minutes. Southerland and the lawyer for the opposing side huddled in front of the bench for most of this time, whispering back and forth with the judge. Southerland turned away with a scowl as the judge banged her gavel and called for the next case.

I caught the former Dewey Naughton associate as she stormed down the aisle toward the exit.

"Ms. Southerland?"

"Yeah? Whatcha need?" Definitely not a graduate of the Seven Sisters.

"I'm Matt Rutherford. Could I talk with you a moment?"

"Why?" She looked at the clock mounted over the rear door.

"About a personal matter."

"I don't do that kind of work. Get yourself a private lawyer." She started to walk away.

I touched her sleeve. "I was a friend of Stewart Jarrard."

Southerland whirled around, blanched, and then turned red. "Did I hear you right? Stewart?" Her face softened slightly. "What do you want?"

"Just to talk. Information only. Nothing that will involve you."

Southerland looked at the clock again. "Meet me at 5:30. Moe's on Waverly Place near Washington Square Park. It's a bar. It'll be crowded. I'll be upstairs in the back." She rushed out the doors, bulging briefcase in hand.

□□□

MOE'S WAS INDEED CROWDED. The patrons were an eclectic mix of Soho artists, office workers from the financial district, and students from nearby NYU. We wormed our way through to the stairs, then up to a mezzanine level where Chrissy Southerland sat alone at a table in the back. There were three empty highball glasses in front of her. She stood up unsteadily as she saw us approaching. "You made it. I didn't think you'd come."

"Why not?"

She took a deep breath. "I spent the entire day trying to believe that I'd misunderstood you. Trying to convince myself that you didn't say 'Stewart Jarrard.' I was wrong, right?"

"That's what I said."

"I thought so." She finished her drink with a long draw and signaled for another. "I guess you can see that I got here early. I... I normally don't drink like this. It's just that, well..." She didn't finish.

"I understand that you and Jarrard were close at one time," Lisa said.

"Yeah." Her drink arrived. She twirled the swizzle stick and said, "Look what it got me. A nasty little job representing Puerto Ricans suing slumlords. Not something you want to call home about. 'Hey, Mom, Dad! Look at me. Honors graduate of Columbia and a miserable failure before thirty.' Yeah, right." She took a gulping drink.

"We don't mean to open old wounds," Lisa continued. "We just need some information." I figured it was better to let her do the talking.

"I don't even know who you are. You just mention the name of the one man I ever loved and just like that I agree to meet you here in a bar, but have to get soused to do it. I'm really a mess, you know. Why are you here? Why do you want to talk to me about Stewart?"

"I got to know him after he moved to Georgia," I said. "We had some business dealings. There were some issues about things that had happened when he lived here in New York. We're trying to resolve them."

It was a totally inane answer that made absolutely no sense, but Southerland didn't seem to notice. She was already drunk.

"Why don't you tell us what happened?" Lisa said.

Southerland pursed her lips and stared out across the room. "Why not? He's dead, and anyway, my shrink has heard the story so many times that I've got it memorized." She took a short sip and pushed the drink away. "I'll start at the beginning..."

35

CHRISSY SOUTHERLAND WAS a totally decent person whose life was a complete train wreck. Her parents were hard-working dairy farmers of German stock from upstate New York. She attended Syracuse University, was Phi Beta Kappa, and finished near the top of her class. She'd moved on to Columbia Law School, graduating with honors and snagging a prestigious two-year clerkship with one of the justices of the New York Court of Appeals. She had a real interest in—and knack for, she said—tax law. After receiving several good offers from Manhattan law firms, she signed with Dewey, Naughton, Pierce, Williams, Young and Eaton, based mainly on their reputation as one of the city's leading wealth management firms.

In law firms, Chrissy explained, most new hires start out as associates. The hours are terrible and the pay not much better, but if you can take the stress and turn out the billable hours, you stand a fair chance of making partner. The hardest part is the first three or so years. Hundred hour weeks are common. Burnout and suicide among associates is not unheard of.

"I'd been there about two years when Douglas Eaton took an interest in me. I wasn't surprised; I'd done some great work on a couple of his cases and he had reason to notice me. I was really flattered at his attention. If you're really serious about making partner—as I was—you need a mentor. Someone who'll show you the ropes, introduce you to the right people, broadcast your triumphs, and show you how to gloss over your errors. He arranged for me to work directly under him."

Things went well for several months. Then, when they were both in Chicago on some of the firm's business, "we got involved," Chrissy said. "It wasn't that I found him especially attractive, and I knew he was married, but it just happened. We'd just landed a huge trust account and we went out to celebrate. We had drinks, then dinner with a couple of bottles of wine. One thing led to another. I woke up the next morning in his bed and said to myself, 'Just what have you gotten yourself into?'

"It wasn't bad at first. I wanted to write it off as a one-time thing—a little slip. I figured that we'd just pretend it never happened. And for a while we did. But a month or so later, Eaton had to be in Miami for a week. He asked me to go with him, said he was going to need some help. I didn't think anything about it until we arrived at the hotel and found out that he'd booked just one room."

Chrissy reached for her drink. Lisa gently put her hand over it and said, "Maybe you should slow up."

"It got worse after that," she continued. "He kept asking me to stay late, and help him with some project or another. Sometimes he had work for me to do. Most of the time he just wanted to sit around, have a few drinks and screw me on that damned couch in his office." A tear trickled down her cheek. "What could I do? He was subtle about it, sure, but he made it very obvious that if I didn't play the part of his little in-house whore, I could forget the idea of ever making partner. So I went along with it. I pretended to enjoy it. I got depressed. Started drinking too much. Tried seeing a shrink, who said I was under too much stress—put me on Xanax and Prozac. Of course, I never told him about Eaton. One Friday night, Eaton wanted me to stay late. We had sex. He kept talking about how he'd like me to do a threesome with a hooker. I couldn't take it anymore. I went home, half drunk, and swallowed every pill I had in the apartment. I woke up two days later in a Lenox Hill Hospital psych ward. The super had seen me come in and for some reason decided to check on me. If he hadn't, I guess I wouldn't be here.

"I was out of work for two weeks. Eaton called, sent flowers, the usual. I went back and for a week nothing happened. Then, one Friday afternoon, he asked me to work late with him again.

It was amazing. He thought we could just start back where we left off. I slapped him. Threatened a sexual harassment suit—the whole nine yards. So he backed off. Promised to support me when I came up for partner. I transferred to the section that dealt mainly with civil litigation. That's where I met Stewart Jarrard."

Chrissy was obviously drunk. I felt sorry for her. But she was talking and was probably the one person available to us who knew what Jarrard was up to when he left New York. She continued, "It wasn't love at first sight or anything like that. My God, Stewart was twenty-something years older than me, and a little overweight and all, but he was a *nice guy*. He helped me, he encouraged me. I knew that he was having problems with his marriage, his wife— ex-wife, now—is a real bitch, by the way, but he never talked about it. I just woke up one Saturday morning and realized that I missed seeing him. It was me, not him, who was the moving party. I seduced him. I was lonely, sure, but I'd come to care about Stewart. I wanted to be close to him. So we became lovers.

"Normally, we would avoid any semblance of involvement at work. We'd meet in hotels or sometimes at my place. He was very devoted to his kids, and wanted to keep his marriage together because of them. We shouldn't have gotten caught. It was stupid. I was working late one night. Stewart came back to the office because he'd forgotten to put a proposal in his briefcase and needed to study it for a meeting the next day. He was as surprised to see me as I was to see him. We talked for a few minutes, and, well... The goddamned janitor walks in on us. Just opened the door, stared for about five seconds then says, 'Sorry,' and leaves. He resigns the next day and a week later the firm gets slapped with a suit from a plaintiff's attorney who specializes in workplace issues. The worst part is that the bastard holds a news conference to announce that he's suing one of the city's leading estate and trust firms—trying to drum up more business no doubt. Of course, Stewart's wife got the news, kicked him out and hired the same plaintiff's firm to do the divorce. It was a real cluster-fuck."

"But what were the grounds for firing you, and forcing Jarrard to resign?" Lisa asked.

Chrissy took a long pull on her drink. She laughed, "You really want to know? The truth? It was Eaton. He was livid that someone else in the firm was dipping into his little honey pot.

Called me in and accused me of seeing Jarrard all along. Said the 'so-called suicide attempt' had just been a ploy to break it off with him. Promised me that he'd make sure that I'd never get a decent job with any firm in New York state if he had anything to do with it. The only way I got hired with the City Bar was that my dad leaned on his assemblyman and called in a favor he'd done him one time. As for Stewart, he was a partner, and there didn't appear to be much they could do until his father-in-law got in on the act."

"How so?"

"You knew Stewart's ex-wife, Emily, is the daughter of Pendleton Brewster Habersham—the guy that owns Habersham's, the auction house?"

We nodded.

"Well, toward the end there, about all that Stewart and I were doing was defending a series of lawsuits from plaintiffs who'd bought art at auction from Habersham's. There were a total of four of them—all brought by the same attorney—alleging that the pieces that his clients had been sold had somehow been misrepresented by the Habersham firm. He claimed they were fakes or something like that—we never really got into deposing his alleged experts. Anyway, after his daughter filed for divorce, old man Habersham pulls all the firm's business from Dewey Naughton. I'm not sure what happened after that, but I do know that it cost the partners a bundle in lost fees."

"Was that why they demanded Jarrard's resignation?" I asked.

"I think so. It may be that they found out that he was doing a lot on the side for Habersham's. Stuff outside of work that he wasn't billing for, but hell, the guy was his father-in-law. You'd expect him to do that. I really don't know the details."

"So Jarrard was just working on that one client account toward the end?"

"Right."

"Was there anything unusual about the lawsuits?"

"No. Like I said, one plaintiffs' attorney was handling all of them. He may have been soliciting clients—Habersham has deep pockets. He may have seen a chance to get into them, I don't know. I was fired right in the middle of it."

"You don't still have a list of the cases, by any chance, do you?" Lisa asked.

Chrissy finished her drink and said, "Sure. I've still got my copies of the case files at my apartment. They made me clean out my desk and leave once they fired me. Told me I was banned from the premises. I wasn't about to take 'em back. You want to see 'em?" She was beginning to slur her words badly.

"I think we need to make sure you get home safely. We'll ride with you in the cab," Lisa said.

I waved to the waitress and threw a fifty on the table. Lisa took Chrissy to the ladies room. I waited outside on the sidewalk watching the early evening Greenwich Village foot traffic. Fifteen minutes later they emerged, Chrissy looking tired and pale and Lisa a bit frustrated.

"Sorry," Chrissy said. "I had to puke."

I looked at Lisa and she raised her eyebrows in a somebody's-gotta-do-the-job expression.

I hailed a cab and gave the driver the address of Chrissy's apartment on lower Greene Street in SoHo. She sat between us in the back, her hair and make-up a mess, her wrinkled white blouse now stained with little yellow flecks on the front.

"You want to hear something funny? When I first went to work at Dewey Naughton, a girl that had been there as an associate for nearly five years warned me about Eaton. Said he was a real predator. Always had a mistress nearby. Told me to be careful. But this is the funny part—she said, 'Do you know what Dewey, Naughton, Pierce, Williams Young, and Eaton stands for?' I told her I didn't. She said it's all in the initials, DNPWYE. They stand for 'Do Not Piss Where You Eat.' I guess I shoulda listened to her."

She was silent for a moment and then laid her head on Lisa's shoulder and began to snore softly.

36

CHRISSY LIVED IN A TWO-ROOM WALK-UP on the third floor above an art gallery. The building must have at one time housed a manufacturing facility of some sort, but now was divided up into the tiny sorts of spaces that they call apartments in Manhattan. We half-carried her up the two flights of stairs, helped her with the triple lock on her door, and sat her down gently on a piece of furniture that served as a couch during the day and a futon bed at night.

The place was a mess. Clothes were hung haphazardly on a rack in one corner. The narrow sliver of space that passed as a kitchen was adorned with unwashed dishes and empty Chinese take-out cartons. An ancient refrigerator contained only wilted celery, two bottles of orange juice and half a dozen containers of fruit-flavored yogurt. A single dingy window faced out toward a fire escape and a brick wall across the narrow alley. Chrissy sat for a moment, said, "Sorry about the mess—I wasn't expecting guests," then lurched toward the closet-sized bathroom and made retching noises from behind the closed door. We stood quietly and waited while she threw up.

She emerged, still looking pale and clearly embarrassed. She seemed a bit more sober. "I am so sorry. I guess when I heard Stewart's name today I just lost it. Things have been pretty rough for me—but you can see that, though."

"Yeah," I said. "Can we do anything to help?"

"No, thanks. I just need to get a good night's sleep and spend a few extra hours with my therapist." She paused, looking around the room. "You said you wanted to see the files on the cases Stewart and I were working on, right? They're here somewhere…" She focused on what appeared to be a pile of laundry in one corner and began to dig in it, unearthing a storage box-file labeled "Habersham" in black marker on one end.

"Here they are," she said. "I don't really remember what's in there. I haven't touched it since I got fired. Why don't you take the box with you? There might be some confidential stuff, but I don't care. What are they going to do to me? Fire me again? I think the cases have been settled, anyway." She hefted up the heavy box and handed it to me. "Be careful going down the stairs. They're steep."

"Are you sure we can't do anything for you?" Lisa asked.

"I'm sure. I'll survive. I always have. Things will get better one day." She smiled for the first time, still looking a bit drunk.

□□□

THE BOX OF LEGAL FILES contained four thick expandable folders, each labeled with the name of a case. There was "Vermentino v. Habersham" and "Crouse v. Habersham," among others; nothing to give any hint of what lay inside. I put two on the hotel room desk and the other two on the bed. "Your choice of piles," I said.

Lisa flung herself on the bed and said, "I'll start here. That way if I get bored, I can summon you over for a momentary distraction." Two hours later, nothing was any clearer.

The cases all had a common thread. The plaintiffs alleged that they had purchased valuable works of art from Habersham's, LLC (referred to as "the Defendant"), and that the auction house had given explicit or implicit assurance that the works were genuine. At some point after the sale, usually when they tried to insure or resell their purchases, they were told that the work was either a fraud, or was of uncertain provenance. The tort alleged was that their "investment" was worth, at best, a small fraction of the price that they had paid. All were seeking both restitution and punitive damages in unnamed amounts. Judging from the dates, it looked like the suits had been filed over a sixty-day period about three months before Jarrard resigned from Dewey Naughton.

"What do you make of it?" I asked Lisa after we'd compared notes.

"Nothing. We are probably totally off-base. There was a report in Jarrard's murder investigation file that mentioned he'd been working on a series of civil cases involving alleged fraud, but no one seemed to think it was important."

"What about Chrissy's mention that he'd been doing legal work for his father-in-law on the side?"

"So? This is New York," Lisa said. "Everybody's got a friend in the business. I don't see how that's so strange."

"True, but why don't we check the guy out while we're here? Chrissy's a pitiful soul and Eaton's a philandering jerk, but we still don't have a hint about what we're looking for. The Habersham connection is probably a dead end, but we haven't come up with much else."

□□□

WE WERE JUST FINISHING our room-service breakfast when the cell phone rang at 7:30 the next morning.

"Good morning, Mr. Rutherford." It was the same mechanical voice—Victor. "Rumor has it that you're in New York. That's good. I take it that you're following up on the information Mr. Jarrard left you?"

"That's right. How did you know where we were?"

"The same way I know a lot of things. My sources are varied, but accurate. I trust that you will be able to deliver the missing goods to me at some point in the near future?"

"Yes. It would appear that way."

"Good. The cell phone that you have is capable of receiving photographs. Once I ring off, you'll be getting one. Don't bother trying to trace it. It's being forwarded from an anonymous e-mail address. Just a reminder." The line went dead. Thirty seconds later, the phone beeped, notifying me that I had received a message. I pressed the retrieve button. A photo of my mother, uncle, and aunt leaving church appeared on the screen with the text message below: "WE CAN DO THREE AS EASILY AS ONE."

□□□

I DON'T THINK EITHER OF US wanted to say it, but privately, both Lisa and I thought we were wasting our time chasing down this possible lead. We tossed suggestions back and forth as to how to approach him, finally agreeing on one thing that seemed to work in New York—money. The hint of it had gotten us an appointment with Douglas Eaton. Lisa suggested that the same thing would probably work with Habersham.

There are, as I later learned, four leading art auction firms in the world. Sotheby's lays claim to being the oldest, having held its first auction in London in 1744. Christie's and Bonham's followed suit before the end of the eighteenth century. Despite—or perhaps because of—wars and revolutions, they all three have managed to survive, prosper, and grow by providing a discreet and socially acceptable way for the wealthy to dispose of their baubles when times are a little hard. Habersham's, on the other hand, was a relative newcomer, a brash upstart that had fought its way to the top next to the hoary old veterans in this international game of wealth redistribution.

Pendleton Brewster Habersham, according to the glossy brochure on the table of Habersham's Fifth Avenue salesrooms, emigrated from England to the United States as a teenager in 1946. His parents had been killed during the German bombings of London in 1940. With the war over and Europe in ruins, he saw America as the land of opportunity.

"Having grown up with antiques and the finer things, I realized that there was an unmet demand in this country. I was determined to fill it," he was quoted.

"My first real break came when a certain member of European Royalty wished to anonymously dispose of a jeweled necklace that had been handed down in his family for more than six generations. By using my contacts with discerning buyers in New York, I was able to obtain for His Excellency a sum that vastly exceeded his highest expectations. In gratitude, he told others among his peers of my success, and soon I was able to offer a wide selection of unique and important European paintings, furniture, jewelry, and other *objects d'art*."

The brochure went on to say that today, Habersham's has salesrooms in New York, Los Angeles, London, Tokyo, and Dubai, and representatives in most major world capitals.

Habersham's had a certain snootiness about it, a sense that

being allowed to visit was an honor not bestowed on all men. Despite this, obtaining an appointment with Pendleton Brewster Habersham himself on short notice had been surprisingly easy. I called the main number and asked to speak to his secretary. I explained that I'd just inherited a large estate with lots of antiques, the sorts of things that didn't fit my lifestyle. I said that I was in town on business, and wanted to discuss the possibility of selling them through Habersham's. She put me on hold for a moment, then returned to say Mr. Habersham could see me today at 2:30 if that was convenient. I told her I'd be there.

Unlike Douglas Eaton, Pendleton Habersham looked exactly like his photos in the brochure. Tall, thin, and aristocratic with flowing white hair above olive-complected skin, he was dressed in a blue linen double-breasted blazer with a heraldic crest embroidered on the pocket. A finely striped Turnbull & Asser cotton shirt and a red silk tie gave him the prefect look of an English gentleman.

He extended a boney hand with a firm grip saying, "So good to meet you, Mr. Rutherford." Sussex accent, Etonian overtones.

I introduced Lisa and said, "So good of you to meet with us on short notice, Mr. Habersham."

"My pleasure, and also my policy. Despite our success, I remain very much involved in the day-to-day operations of the business. Also, many of our clients are individuals who are not accustomed to dealing with underlings. The decision to part with a family inheritance is a significant one, and I want you to know that our commitment to obtaining the best return comes from the highest level."

"We appreciate that," I said, slightly exaggerating my southern accent.

This guy was smooth. I decided that I'd have to play a bit of a naïf in the big city to get the most out of him.

"My secretary said that you'd inherited an estate that includes some significant works of art and nineteenth century American furniture. I understand that you're interested in having us help you market it, is that correct?"

"Yes, it is. You see, I've been living on the West Coast for the past few years and just now returned home to Georgia after my aunt's death. I inherited her place, you see, and I've been living there now for about a year. It's a big old house with lots of what I'm told is valuable furniture, some of it made here in New York before the War. I…"

"Which war?" Habersham said, his brow wrinkling slightly.

"The War Between the States," I said.

"Of course. Please continue." He smiled graciously.

"I'm told there are some valuable pieces, but quite honestly, I'm thinking about moving back to California and they just don't fit my lifestyle. To give you an example, there's a matching pair of hall tables made by a fellow from up here named File, or Fight, or something like…"

"Phyfe," Lisa corrected me. "Duncan Phyfe. The local museum wanted them because they'd been written up in a magazine years ago."

"Thanks," I said. "Never could remember that name." Habersham nodded, his eyes gleaming. "Anyway," I continued, "I thought I'd just put everything on the market. I was told that you were one of the best, Mr. Habersham, and that's why we're here."

"I'm flattered," he said. "We try to do our utmost. I'm sure that we can work with you." He paused, picking up a small notepad. He scribbled my name across the top and said, "You seem to be a long way from home. Tell me, who referred you to Habersham's?"

"It was my attorney, actually. Unfortunately, he's deceased. His name was Stewart Jarrard."

A brief shadow flicked across Habersham's face.

37

"ALAS, POOR STEWART. I knew him well. We were all so saddened to hear of his death." Habersham's voice had a certain perfunctory tone about it. "And how was it that you made his acquaintance?"

"Well, he moved down to Georgia earlier this year, not too many months after I moved back from California. I got to know him through the Rotary Club, and he seemed like a nice fellow."

I wondered if I was getting a bit thick with the southern drawl.

"One of the problems I've had is figuring out what to do with my inheritance. It's family money, of course, but I'm just not into hands-on management. I'm more of a big picture sort of guy. My idea was that I could sell the house and property and combine the proceeds in with the other investments in an account that would provide me with a good income. I approached several of the local attorneys that I'd known growing up there in Walkerville, but I think the main thing they do is real estate work and DUI defense. They suggested that I hire someone out of town, maybe in Atlanta. About that time, I met Stewart. He said he'd worked with estates and trusts up here in New York before he came south. Sounded like he knew what he was doing.

"To make a long story short, he came up with a proposal for a series of income-producing trusts to manage my affairs. Not long before he died, I asked him about helping me sell the house and its contents. He said that I'd get a far better price if I worked with one of the big international auction houses, and told me he thought you were the best of the best. So, while Lisa and I were up here, I thought I'd come by and meet you. See if you could help me."

Habersham smiled. "I do appreciate Stewart's recommendation. We were close for many years. I don't suppose you knew he was my ex-son-in-law?"

"Oh, my God, no." I tried to sound shocked. "I didn't realize… I apologize…"

"No need to apologize, Mr. Rutherford. It's one of those sad facts of modern life. Divorces happen. He was married to my daughter, my only child. I will admit that she can at times be difficult, but it was hardest on their children. And of course his death has compounded the tragedy." He paused briefly, and then continued. "Did you know if they've made any progress in tracking down his murderer?"

"Not from what I hear, but I'm not privy to a lot that goes on with the local police." I watched closely for Habersham's response. I was having trouble reading him. He was too polished, too urbane to allow his true emotions to show.

He said, "We can only hope they do their job. Yes, I do miss Stewart's advice and expertise. As I'm sure you well know, one of the greatest problems facing the world's more affluent families is the constant necessity of structuring wealth and income in such a way as to shield it from the greedy hands of government. For many of our clients, their single-largest expense is the amount they pay in taxes. For someone like me who has business interests around the globe, it is a daunting challenge. Stewart's forte was wealth preservation. I'd given him a lot of responsibility with my own personal assets. He…" Habersham paused again, then said, "I digress. Tell me more about your inheritance."

We spent the next twenty minutes in a general discussion of Habersham's policy on consignment sales, the necessity of expert appraisals, and the like. He suggested that I send him a list and photographs of items that I wanted to offer for sale. Based on his experts' preliminary assessment of what I had to offer, they would likely send one or more appraisers to Walkerville to view the pieces first-hand. Depending on the number and quality of items available, they could offer to purchase some or all of the entire estate outright, or alternatively offer it at auction on consignment.

"I'll be perfectly honest with you, Mr. Rutherford," Habersham said. "To a degree, most international art auction houses act very much like pawnbrokers. The world's wealthy, just like their poorer brethren, run short of cash. They must keep up appearances, however, and often turn to me and others in this field when they need to quietly convert their baubles into spendable assets. Selling works on consignment takes in excess of a year, and there is no real guarantee as to what they'll bring at auction. Oftentimes we will buy individual pieces for cash at somewhat discounted prices, hoping to make our profit by reselling them later. This can be done quite anonymously, so the world need never realize that Count So-and-So had to sell his mother's diamonds to pay the rates on his villa at Cap Ferrat."

"Well, I don't think I'm exactly in that situation, Mr. Habersham," I said, "but we'll be in touch with you in a few weeks." I rose and reached out to shake his hand. "It's been a pleasure."

"Mine, I assure you," Habersham said. He walked us to the lobby and smiled genuinely as we left.

On the way down in the elevator Lisa said, "It was all I could do to keep from gagging with that Southern accent you put on back there."

I grinned and drawled, "Jus' showin' my roots, honey." Then, in my normal voice, "But I'm not sure that I'm the only one that's faking it. There's something strange about Habersham. I can't quite put my finger on it, but something's just not right."

"How so?"

"I'm not sure, but if I had to guess, I'd say that I'm not the only one exaggerating an accent." We walked back to the hotel in silence. Habersham bothered me. There was not one particular thing that made me uneasy about him. He just seemed too perfect, too much the stereotypical English gentlemen.

In the hotel bar over coffee, I asked Lisa, "What was your general impression of Habersham?"

"British. Upper class. Refined. Discreet. Just the sort of fellow who you'd feel comfortable dealing with if you were very rich and had fallen on hard times. I didn't get any negative vibes. What do you think? Any connection to Jarrard besides the obvious?"

"No, but after today I want to take a closer look at those lawsuits against him that Jarrard was defending. That's one thing Habersham didn't mention."

□□□

WE TOOK THE EVENING FLIGHT back to Savannah and were back in Walkerville by midnight. I bought a cheap suitcase in the hotel gift shop and stuffed it full of the case files we'd gotten from Chrissy, checking it through with our other luggage. I checked my e-mail before going to bed. Dr. Cordy had found and forwarded Jarrard's e-mail back to me, together with an attachment that contained the crossword puzzle and its clue list. I found a note on the kitchen table from Eula Mae saying that Sheriff Arnett came by to visit. She told him that we were out of town and he said that he'd check back later. Otherwise, nothing happened in our absence.

There were two things we needed to work on: the crosswords on Jarrard's flash drive and the legal files from New York. After breakfast the next morning, I lay claim to the dining room table while Lisa gathered up the various crosswords and e-mails and headed toward the study with her laptop. Grabbing a huge mug of coffee, she said, "See you at lunch," and shut the door.

I spread the case folders out in front of me and began work. I wasn't sure what I was looking for, so I ended up making notes as I read. As we'd figured out in New York, the cases were all filed during a relatively short period of time, and all involved alleged fraud on the part of Habersham's. Based on the depositions, the plaintiffs represented a selection of wealthy individuals from New York, Connecticut, and New Jersey. Two described themselves as investment bankers, one was a plastic surgeon, and another reported his occupation as "retired." The prices paid ranged from $185,000 for a landscape by Paul Nash to $660,000 for a 1770 portrait of Lady Sarah Whitfield by Sir Joshua Reynolds. They had been purchased over a period of three and a half years, the last one having been bought about eighteen months prior to the filing of the lawsuits. The one thing that the works had in common was the statement that all had originally been purchased by Habersham's from "private European" collectors or collections, and were offered for resale at auction.

I had filled four pages of a yellow legal pad with notes by the time Lisa emerged from the study, coffee mug in hand, heading toward the kitchen. "How's it going?" I asked.

"I hate crosswords," she said on the way back, once more shutting the door and leaving me to ponder the depositions.

I sifted the data back and forth on paper, making lists, drawing arrows, trying to establish some hidden pattern or connection. I finally realized that was no real pattern, just a group of four individuals suing a major art auction house. Chrissy said that she thought all of the cases had been settled. If that were so, it would be doubtful if any information would be available in the public record. I flipped through the "Crouse v. Habersham" file until I found the service page giving the plaintiff's attorney's contact information. His name was Granger Shenck, of Aaron, Levin, and Shenck, LLC. A New Jersey phone number was listed.

A nasal Bronx accent answered the phone. "Aaron, Levin, and Shenck. How may I direct your call?"

I identified myself and asked to be connected to Mr. Granger Shenck's office. There was a slight pause, then, "Mr. Shenck is no longer with the firm, but I can connect you to Mr. Aaron, who took over some of his cases." I said that was fine.

After going through one more secretary, I was connected to a voice that announced, "Lawrence Aaron."

"Mr. Aaron, my name is Matt Rutherford. We've never met, but I called your firm to see if you could help me with a little problem I've discovered. About four years ago, I purchased a rather expensive painting at auction from Habersham's in New York. A few months ago, I decided to sell it to a collector, but before he bought it, he wanted it independently appraised by an expert. I can give you the details, but the bottom line is that the fellow says it's a fake. A good one, mind you, but not perfect. Of course I was upset. I called Habersham's but didn't get very far with them. They deny any liability. I got to checking around and found out that Mr. Granger Shenck, who was with your firm, handled some similar cases a year or so ago. I was told that they were settled. I wanted to get in touch with Mr. Shenck and see if he could give me some advice—maybe take the case if he thinks it's worth it."

"Of course. I understand your concern. We've handled a

number of art fraud cases over the years. I wish that I could refer you to Granger, but unfortunately, he's no longer with us."

"I'd really like to talk with him, if possible. If you could tell me how to get in touch with…"

Aaron cut me off. "When I said he's no longer with us, I meant it. He's dead, Mr. Rutherford."

38

"DEAD?"

"Yes, I'm sorry to say. Hit-and-run last year. They never caught the driver. We miss Granger—he was a fine man and a real asset to the firm."

"What about his cases?"

"We split the active ones up among the other attorneys. The Habersham suits had the potential to be quite lucrative, but it also turned out that the attorney who was defending them quit the firm he was with and moved somewhere down south."

"Would that be Steward Jarrard?"

"I believe that was his name, yes. Do you know him?"

"No," I lied. "His name came up along with Mr. Shenck's when I was researching how to proceed with my problem."

Aaron took a deep breath. "Mr. Rutherford, I'd like to discuss these cases with you, but they were settled shortly after Granger's death. With both the plaintiffs' and defendant's attorneys out of the picture, I think all parties thought it would be best to handle it that way rather than start over. The extra legal fees alone would have been horrendous. What I need to tell you, though, is that this firm and our clients are bound by the terms of the agreement not to divulge any details of the settlement. I *can* tell you that our side was quite pleased with the outcome, but that's all I can say. The court sealed the records."

"So I take it that you wouldn't be able to consider taking another similar case?"

"As much as I'd like to, the answer would have to be no. We'd be happy to refer you to another firm."

"Thanks. I'll just keep looking," I said, and hung up. I wondered if I had already found something.

I got my notes out and started going over them for the nth time. I could see how Habersham would be eager to settle. The loss of a civil suit involving art fraud could destroy his business. Shenck must have felt confident to bring four separate cases. Aaron said his clients were "quite pleased." Perhaps he was right, maybe Habersham saw a settlement—even an expensive one—as the lesser of several evils. But when juxtaposed with Jarrard's death, it begged the question: Was the hit-and-run an accident or something more?

The door to the study flew open. Lisa collapsed against the door frame. She was holding several sheets of printer paper in her hand.

"I've had it. That's it. I will never—and I repeat, *never*—look at a crossword again. I'm up to my ears in so-called 'clues.' You want a list of four-letter names for antelopes of the Serengeti? How about topi, oryx, kudu, puku, and suni? Or three- and four-letter flightless birds? Try emu, rhea, kiwi, or—if they're extinct—moa or dodo or auk. These people are fiendish.

"And I tell you," she continued, sinking into an armchair at the head of the table, "the clues are even worse. It reminds me of what one of my professors said when I was taking a course in cryptography as part of the core stuff for my Ph. D. We were sitting in his office one afternoon talking about what I thought was an insoluble problem. He reached behind his desk and picked a thick, dog-eared old book off the shelf. It was so worn in fact that you couldn't even see the name on the spine. He held it up and said, 'Miss Li, do you see this book I'm holding in my hand? You've been looking for a solution to what you say is a problem that can't be solved. This book contains all the answers to every question that man has ever asked, or ever will ask. They're all in there, every single one of them.' He laid the book in front of me on his desk. It was a dictionary. He said, 'All you've got to do is put the words in the right order. Remember this: Every problem designed to have a solution has a solution. It's just up to you to find it.' Where is that magic dictionary when I need it?"

I told her what I'd learned about the fraud suits against Habersham.

"Suspicious, I grant you, but nothing definite," Lisa said. "But I think I've found something that might be important. In the depositions, the plaintiffs said they'd gotten fake art, or something like that, right?"

"Yes."

"Do you have a list of the four artists whose works are in question?"

"Sure, it's right here." I scanned my notes and read out the names. "Okay, one of the investment bankers said that he'd bought a small abstract bronze casting done in 1956 by Giocomo Manzù. The plastic surgeon got a landscape dated 1938 by a British painter named Paul Nash. The other investment banker paid big bucks for a 1780 portrait of a man by an American painter named Ralph Earl. The retired fellow bought the Reynolds for nearly seven hundred thousand."

"Good," Lisa said, her eyes gleaming. "And how much did those four works bring all together?"

I looked at my notes and added the numbers quickly in my head. "A little more than a million and a half, plus 10 percent more to Habersham for the buyer's commission."

"Did you see any mention of works by artists named Claus Oldenburg or R. B. Kitaj?"

"No. Who are they?"

"I'll get to that in a minute. I didn't know either but I Googled them. They're both considered American artists, but Oldenburg was born in Sweden and Kitaj did a lot of his work in England. Look at this." She extracted a sheet of paper from her pile and slid it across the table to me. Printed in the middle of it was a completed crossword puzzle grid.

¹A	²C	³M	⁴E	■	⁵A	⁶D	⁷A	⁸M	⁹S	■	¹⁰A	¹¹R	¹²K	¹³S
¹⁴B	R	A	E	■	¹⁵M	A	R	I	E	■	¹⁶C	A	N	E
¹⁷R	E	N	C	¹⁸O	U	N	T	E	R	■	¹⁹C	L	E	W
²⁰A	D	Z	■	²¹A	L	K	Y	N	E	■	²²O	P	E	N
²³M	O	U	²⁴S	S	E	■	²⁵N	²⁶A	S	H				
■	²⁷K	I	T	²⁸A	²⁹J	■	³⁰I	N	T	E	³¹N	³²D		
³³B	³⁴U	³⁵O	Y	S	■	³⁶F	U	³⁷S	T	Y	■	³⁸A	I	R
³⁹I	S	L	E	■	⁴⁰R	A	L	L	Y	■	⁴¹A	R	C	O
⁴²R	E	D	■	⁴³E	E	R	I	E	■	⁴⁴S	H	L	E	P
⁴⁵D	R	E	⁴⁶G	G	Y	■	⁴⁷E	D	⁴⁸U	C	E	■		
■	⁴⁹N	E	O	N	■	⁵⁰N	O	M	A	⁵¹D	⁵²S	⁵³S		
⁵⁴B	⁵⁵A	B	Y	■	⁵⁶O	⁵⁷M	⁵⁸E	⁵⁹L	E	T	■	⁶⁰B	O	A
⁶¹O	N	U	S	■	⁶²L	E	V	I	A	T	⁶³H	A	N	S
⁶⁴L	O	R	E	■	⁶⁵D	E	E	M	S	■	⁶⁶U	S	E	S
⁶⁷E	N	G	R	■	⁶⁸S	T	R	A	Y	■	⁶⁹T	H	E	Y

"Look at 3-down, 11-down, 25-across, and 40-down. There are your four artists."

I studied the puzzle. "Damn," I said. "You're right. Which puzzle was this?"

"It was the one on the flash drive that Jarrard e-mailed to Cordy and Bonifay." Lisa leaned back and gave me a smug look.

"What about those other two artists you mentioned? They're on here, too. Oldenburg is 35-down, and the other one—how do you pronounce his name..."

"Kitaj"

"Right—he's 27-across. How do they fit into the picture? And how about other names like Adams and Abram and Bole, couldn't they also be the names of artists?"

"I don't know—they may all be important. That's just the problem. I have a funny feeling that this crossword puzzle and the others on that flash drive are like that dictionary. We've got all the words to answer all the questions, we've just got to put them in the right order. The one thing we've got now that we didn't have before is direction. Our job is to connect the dots. Jarrard wrote the crosswords hoping to save his life. Jarrard was also doing legal work for Habersham's. Hidden in the crosswords are names of art works sold by Habersham's. Draw the lines: Crosswords to Jarrard, Jarrard to Habersham's, Habersham's to crosswords. *Voilà*, it starts to come together."

I looked at the crossword and then back at Lisa. She continued, "Obviously, Jarrard had some kind of game plan, something that he thought could keep him alive. We need to understand it. Whatever the answer is has to be important to our friend on the other end of the telephone, otherwise we'd be dead. After we put the pieces into place...." She stopped, thinking.

"And if we don't?"

"We will. There are no other options."

39

"SO, WHERE DO YOU think all of this is leading?" I asked.

Lisa stood up and started pacing back and forth on the other side of the dining room table. "Okay," she said, "Let's look at what we've got. First, there's a dead lawyer who was killed either because he knew something or had stolen something, probably both. He thought whatever knowledge he had could protect him, and was determined to use the threat of its being made public as a shield. You said in those few days that he stayed here before he was killed he would come in at night and go up to his room—sort of strange behavior for a man who is essentially a house guest, don't you think? And then the night before he was shot he wants to borrow your computer to send some e-mails. Think about it, Matt. He had internet access at his office. He could have waited until the next morning, but he wanted to get the information out *right then*. To him it was vital information, something that couldn't wait.

"Now, think about the e-mails. We can divide them into three groups." She selected five sheets of paper from her bundle and laid them in three piles on the table. "We can assume that two of these were for Cordy and Bonifay, two were for Douglas Eaton, and one was for whoever 'YHA' is. If Cordy and Bonifay are telling the truth, they each got the same e-mail, this one." She held up the printout of the file named "B&C." "In the message, Jarrard says he's 'sending a puzzle for you to review' and that 'We'll talk later.' Cordy forwarded his copy to you so we know which one of the seven puzzles was attached to it. The second e-mail, the one named 'B&C2,' was a partial rough draft. Jarrard probably intended to give them some instructions about the contents of the crossword puzzle he sent with the first one.

"As for Eaton, Jarrard's first e-mail was to ask for a favor. He must have felt confident that his request would be granted, because he'd already written a follow-up note that he intended to fire back just as soon as he got Eaton's reply. Again, assuming that Eaton is telling the truth and deleted the message after just glancing at it, the second e-mail to him never got sent either. But listen to what Jarrard was saying."

She picked up the sheet and read, "'if anything happens to me, I want to be sure that certain people get copies of the attached files.' Apparently the 'attached files' were other puzzles, but we don't have any idea which ones of the *other* six on the flash drive. He goes on to say that the e-mail addresses where Eaton was supposed to forward them are written next to the clues, but I couldn't find anything like that anywhere."

Lisa sat down and propped her chin on her hands. "I've been going back and forth trying to figure it all out, and I've reached this conclusion: I think that whatever we're looking for is hidden in the puzzle e-mailed to Cordy and Bonifay, and the key to finding it is in one of the other puzzles that he intended to send to Eaton."

"The second e-mail for Eaton just says that he should send the puzzles to 'certain people.' Why does that have to mean Cordy and Bonifay?"

"I don't know. It's a total guess, but it's logical. Look at it from Jarrard's viewpoint. He was hiding some great secret, something that would hurt and embarrass his family if the knowledge became public. He wanted to keep the information hidden, but in a worst case scenario, he knew the truth would have to come out. So what does he do? He slices and dices the clues to whatever he's hiding and mixes them in with the word salad of a crossword puzzle. He then does the same with the key to unlock the code. He then plans to put each half in the hands of individuals who never in a thousand years would randomly meet each other and leaves instructions that contact be made only in the event of his death. Pretty clever, I'd say."

I walked around the table and looked at the e-mail messages, then picked up the puzzle printouts and sifted through them. "We know which one was sent to Cordy and Bonifay. Which of the others contains the key?"

"I don't know," Lisa said.

"And," I said, tapping my finger on the lone e-mail to "YHA," "who is this, and how does he figure into the picture?"

"I don't know that either, but I suspect you've been talking with him." She motioned with her head toward the kitchen. "Didn't I see a bottle of chardonnay in the fridge? I think I need a drink."

We sat on the dogtrot sipping wine and talking. "How did you figure out that there were names of artists hidden in the puzzles?" I asked.

"Luck, mainly," Lisa said. "I've never really been a fan of crosswords, so I didn't know where to start. I looked at the clues, at the answers, at the patterns of the grid, and basically came up with nothing. I then backed off and asked the question, if this were a code or cipher of a sort I'd never seen before, how would I handle it? I'd start looking for patterns. One of the things I tried was sorting all the answers by category. That's where I came up with the animals of the Serengeti and the flightless bird lists. In one puzzle, though—the one we looked at—I noticed that a number of the answers were the names of artists. I remembered seeing the name Manzù mentioned in one of the depositions from Dewey Naughton. After that, things fell into place."

"All right, assuming that you're correct and the 'important' words are sprinkled in with the rest of the puzzle answers, how do you account for the other names that appear to be artists, like Oldenburg, and that other guy with the unpronounceable name that starts with a 'k'?"

"Kitaj."

"Right."

"That's what worries me, the possibility we'll think something's unimportant because we can't make it fit into our theories. See this scar right here?" She lifted up her hair to reveal a small scar just at the top of her forehead. "When I was eight years old, my dad bought me a new bike. I wanted to see how the gears worked, so one afternoon after school, I sneaked it out to the workshop behind the house where nobody could see me, got his wrenches and took it all apart. And then I got scared that I'd get caught, so I quickly put it all back together. Problem was, I had these little flat things left over. They didn't seem to fit anywhere and the bike worked okay, so I assumed that they weren't important. Turns out they were lock-washers that kept the wheels from falling off. I was riding down a hill two days later when the front end just collapsed—threw me onto the concrete sidewalk. I got ten stitches in my head and was grounded for three weeks. I swore that would never happen to me again." She gulped down her remaining wine and poured herself another glass.

I guess sometimes you can become too close to a person. Lisa was part of my life. She was at my side when I woke up in the hospital and had never left. She knew my life was in danger, and, by staying with me, hers equally so. But she never considered the option of leaving. The thought of Lisa as a child, riding on her bicycle down a California hill, jolted me back to reality. I looked at her now, her long black hair streaming over her finely sculpted face, looking back at me. "What are you thinking so hard about?" she asked.

"Nothing, really," I replied. "Just being amazed by you."

"You can be amazed all you want, but what we need is some way to test our theory. For all I know, Jarrard could have been making a 'theme' puzzle—one that featured names of artists. He could have just chosen those because he was familiar with them."

I thought silently for a minute. Lisa waited, twirling her wine glass and watching the rivulets run down the side. "Okay," I said, "I have an idea that might work. We're sure both Oldenburg and Kitaj are artists, and there's nothing we've found to connect them to Habersham, right?"

"Correct."

"Is there any way we can find out if a work by Oldenburg or Kitaj has been sold at auction by Habersham's?"

Lisa pursed her lips, thinking. "I believe so. I think there are Web sites listing the prices for art sold at auction. Buyers and sellers use them to gauge the market. I doubt if the individual buyers would be listed, though. It's not that the information is secret, but if I were a buyer and had just paid a million bucks for a painting to hang in my beach house, I wouldn't want the world to know—it'd be an invitation for thieves."

"A lot of the stuff Habersham sells is pretty high dollar.

Wouldn't the sale of a work by a well-known artist get some press coverage?"

"Who knows? All we can do is look. Where are you going with all this?"

"The goal is to find out if the presence of Oldenburg's or Kitaj's names as a puzzle answer is important. First, we have to establish that Habersham sold one of their works. If we do that, and can track down who bought it, we might be able to contact them to see if anything strange has gone on."

"It won't hurt to try," Lisa said. We settled in front of the computer in the study. After some searching, she settled on artprice.com, a site that purported to list more than four million auction records going back to 1987. I gave her my credit card number and she purchased a one-day pass.

"Let's try Oldenburg first," she said and with a few clicks brought up a screen listing the results of more than eight hundred auction sales going back to 1986. "Let's try sales during the years 1999 and 2000. That would be roughly in the right time frame and it would catch the sales before the high-tech stock crash." She studied the screen for a moment and said, "I count twenty-eight sales records total from major auction houses worldwide. Now I've got to go through them to see if any were sold at Habersham's. This is going to take a while, Matt. I'll let you know if I come up with something." Lisa clearly didn't want me standing over her while she worked.

I wandered back out to the dogtrot and splashed more wine in my glass. Fifteen minutes passed. I walked out to the boxwood maze and wondered what Jarrard's killer must have been thinking as he lay in wait with his rifle. I looked at my watch. Thirty minutes. Lisa appeared at the window, tapping to get my attention and motioning for me to come in.

"Find anything?" I asked.

"Yeah," she said, a bit grimly. "Among the Oldenburgs, two were sold by Habersham's, both in March 2000. There were a total of six sales of works by Kitaj, and only one of those from Habersham's in October 1999. I did manage to get copies of the catalogues, and all three works sold at Habersham's were listed as having been purchased from 'private European collections,' with the auction house being the owner of record at the time of the sale.

So far, so good.

"The next thing was to try to come up with who bought them. I struck out on the two Oldenburgs, but on the Kitaj, I came up with this." She handed me a new item printed from the archives of the *New York Times*:

Princeton Alumnus Makes Gift to University

Princeton, NJ—Morton H. Steinberg, banker and well-known figure in the art world, was revealed today as Princeton University's benefactor through his donation of a major work by American artist Ronald B. Kitaj. The painting, a 1962 oil-on-canvas surrealist landscape executed by Kitaj during his London years, was sold to an anonymous buyer at Habersham's this past October, setting a new record sale price for a work by this artist. In an announcement of the gift, Princeton University officials...

"That's great. It's a start," I said. "If the work is owned by the University, we should be able to..."

"Not so fast, Matt. There's more. When I starting researching Steinberg, this is what I came up with."

She handed me another item from the *Times* obituary section:

Prominent Banker Murdered in Home Invasion

Morton H. Steinberg, prominent New York banker and patron of the arts, was found murdered today at his vacation home in the East Hamptons. The motive appeared to be robbery, but police are unsure at this point...

The article was dated shortly after the filing of the lawsuits against Habersham's.

40

"THAT'S IT," I SAID. "We've got to get the FBI in on this."

"Do you trust them?" Lisa asked. "Especially after what they did to us in North Carolina? And how do we know that Victor doesn't have a source on the inside? How else could he have tracked us down in Highlands?"

"Any other suggestions?"

Lisa hesitated before answering. "You're probably right. We're eventually going to have to talk with them, but I think we should wait."

"Why?"

"Several good reasons. Even if we did trust them, as far as we know, they still think Jarrard told you something before he died. We go to them now with his secret, that'd only confirm their suspicions that we knew it all along and were holding back. They'd charge us with hindering a murder investigation. Second, I think we've just scratched the surface. We still have no idea what we're looking for. If we don't find it, we're dead. If we do, we've got a bargaining chip. If we find what it is, we'll find who wants it. If we find who wants it, we find who killed Jarrard and tried to kill you. At this point, there are too many loose ends. I'm making progress—give me a couple more days."

I started to object, but I didn't want to argue. Instead I said, "Okay. What are you going to work on?"

"One of the five e-mails is unfinished. Same thing for the puzzles. It looks like Jarrard was still working on one of the seven

196

when he was shot. I've been studying his style. It's pretty clear that he started with a list of words he wanted to include in the puzzle. He'd put those in first, then filled in the rest of the grid with words that fit the spaces left over. I think he only sent one puzzle to Bonifay and Cordy because he was still working on the second one—that's why his other e-mail to them is still in draft form. And it's obvious, too, that he filled in the puzzle grid before he wrote the clues. Here, take a close look at the unfinished puzzle, the one he called 'Puzzle 2.'" She handed me a printout.

```
 1R  2A  3S  4P  ██  5K  6W  7A  8I  ██  9D 10R 11I 12F 13T
14T   B   A   R  ██ 15N   E  ██ 16E   A   R   T   H
17D   O   V   E 18C   O   T   E   S  ██ 19S   E   R   G   E
20    V   I   E  ██   B   C  ██ 21    P  ██      E  ██
22J   E   N   N   Y  ██ 23H 24A 25T   E   F   U   L   L 26L 27Y
28E   N   G  ██ 29A 30N   O   T   H   E   R  ██ 31I   I   U
32T   O   S 33  ██  ██ 34     P  ██ 35      G   P   A
36T   R   A   N   S   P 37L   A   N   T   A 38T   I   O   N
39I   M   C  ██ 40  ██ 41O  ██  ██   O   P   L
42E   A   C  ██ 43P   U   Z   Z 44L   E   R  ██ 45U   R   I
46S   L   O 47F  ██  ██ 48  49   B   S   O   N
    ██ 50U   I  ██ 51A 52B   S   E   N   T  ██
53B 54A   N   F   F  ██ 55S 56E   V   E   N   T   E   E 57N
58     T   T  ██ 59A   V   E   S  ██ 60A   S   I   A
61     S   Y  ██ 62N   E   S   T  ██ 63S   S   N   S
```

"This is a work in progress," she said, "and he'd run into problems making it work. You can see why he wasn't finished. Look at 20-Across, or 46-Across, for example. When I was working with this yesterday, I couldn't find any word or phase in English or any other language that he could put in those slots. I think he'd gotten hung up."

Lisa handed me another sheet. "The other thing is this clue list—it's unfinished. He's written some clues, but not all of them. Look at 5-Across. It reads, 'Alec Guinness's character built the span over it in the movie.' The answer is 'Kwai,' from *The Bridge Over the River Kwai*. But for some answers, like 1-Across, or 19-Across, he's not written clues. It's always hard to guess what someone was thinking, but I'm betting that the important stuff is included in the words and clues he's written, and the rest of the puzzle is fluff—just camouflage to fill up the spaces. He's trying to work unimportant stuff around the important stuff, and that's why it must have been so difficult. I want to focus on the words and clues he *did* finish to see what I come up with."

I looked at my watch. "It's late. You've really been going hard at this. Why don't we take a break and go out for dinner? I need some Lisa time without any computers to distract us."

Lisa smiled, half surprised. "Am I hearing this? From Matt Rutherford? That head injury must have rattled some things up there. Sure, I'd love to. Some good wine and great food sounds wonderful. Just let me close down these files and change into something sexy and we're outta here."

"Uh, Lisa," I said as she typed quickly at the keyboard.

"Uh-huh?" she replied, not looking up.

"We're in Walkerville."

She stopped and looked up. "So?"

"I think the closest we'll come is fried fish and beer."

She resumed her typing. "With you, silly, it's caviar and champagne."

□□□

WE ENDED UP GOING to McLester's Pond. In Georgia, it's what they informally call a fish camp restaurant. To qualify, the place has to be next to a body of water, usually a river, and in the middle of nowhere. It has to have a bar—neon signs are a plus—and be located in a county where the local cops are less interested in sticking you with a DUI citation than making sure that you make it home safely. The décor is cozy—rustic even—and the music loud. The parking lot is a mélange of vehicles ranging from pickups to Cadillacs, but inside you can't tell the bankers from the construction workers sidling up to the bar. It's the sort of place where a nineteen-year-old kid with a three-day stubble can get a beer. I'd spent a lot of good nights at McLester's during my high school and college days.

The place was located at the end of a dirt road, which branched off a thinly paved county road, which itself turned off of Highway 15 south of town. The name McLester's Pond came from the fact that the main building, a ramshackle construction of wood and tin, sat on the edge of a long ox-bow lake connecting to the Opahatchee River. It was owned by "Red" McNair, reputedly a distant relative of the McLesters, but, more importantly, Sheriff Arnett's wife's brother-in-law.

Lisa eased the BMW in between a pickup and what appeared to be the detached cab of a logging truck. "Are you sure this is the right place?" she asked, trying not to sound disappointed.

"I promise. The food's great—you'll see."

Red himself greeted us at the door, his belly jiggling over his belt. I hadn't seen him in at least five years, but he remembered me instantly.

"Matt Rutherford! How ya been? Haven't seen you down here in a month o' Sundays. And who's the young lady?" He eyed Lisa lasciviously.

"This is my friend Lisa," I replied.

Lisa smiled and nodded, eying the patrons in the crowded bar suspiciously. Red found us a quiet table in the corner of one of the patchwork of dining rooms and volunteered, "I'll send over a pitcher of beer. Compliments of the house for old times' sake."

Lisa whispered, "Remember that bar scene from the first *Star Wars* movie, the one where Luke Skywalker meets…What's his name? The character played by Harrison Ford?"

"Han Solo?"

"That's it. I think we just walked into the local branch of that franchise."

The waitress appeared with a pitcher of beer and two frosty mugs. She suggested the "Fisherman's Platter for Two," which was especially appealing, she emphasized, since it came with "free trips to the salad bar." I said it sounded good. Lisa nodded somewhat numbly while quaffing a swallow of beer.

Forty-five minutes later, Lisa said, "This is one of the best meals that I've had in months." We were into the second pitcher of beer and a third order of freshly caught fish. "Who'd have thought…"

"Matt." A voice called from across the room. "What are you doing down here?" It was Sheriff Arnett, dressed as a civilian in faded jeans and a plaid shirt, wife in tow. They waded across the room as I stood to greet them. He introduced his wife, an oversized, dowdy woman with big hair and too much makeup. I introduced Lisa to her.

"We were just leaving and saw you two in here," Arnett said.

"I came by your house to see you the other day. Eula Mae said you'd gone out of town." He looked around to be sure that no one was paying attention, then said, "Making any progress?"

I nodded at Lisa, who was picking at a bit of fried bream. She looked up, and said "I think so. A day, maybe two at the most, and I should know something."

Arnett scanned the room again. His wife stood stoically, inured to her husband being the center of attention. "No calls from your friend?" he said in a low voice.

"Yesterday morning. Nothing new, just more threats."

"Hmm. We need to talk. How about I drop by tomorrow?"

I said that would be fine. With the usual nodding of heads and handshakes, Arnett and wife moved on to another table occupied by voting citizens of Adams County.

"Don't you think he's a little too friendly?" Lisa asked once they were out of earshot.

"The Sheriff is an elective office. He's a typical politician in an election year."

"I think he's too friendly," Lisa said, and continued picking at her fish.

41

I AWOKE THE NEXT MORNING to find the bed empty. I'd been in the middle of a dream. I was back in the ICU. I could hear a male voice saying, "We're not sure if he's going to wake up," and then Lisa's voice, "He's got to. He has to know I'm here." I tried to speak, but couldn't. My eyes wouldn't open; my hands wouldn't move. I tried to say, "I hear you," but the words hung in my throat. I couldn't see her, but I knew where she was. I willed my hand to move. Nothing. Then, a slight twitch. If I could only reach out and touch her...The hand moved, and grasped toward the sound of her voice. She wasn't there. I was suddenly awake.

The faint light of morning seeped through the curtains. From somewhere, the smell of coffee drifted into my consciousness.

"You're awake," Lisa said. She was sitting in the overstuffed bedroom chair, her legs folded under her and a steaming mug cupped in her hands.

"What time is it?" I asked.

"A little after six. I woke up at 4:30 and couldn't go back to sleep. I've been sitting here sipping coffee and watching you breathe."

"Are you all right?"

"Sure. Just thinking. Trying to pretend that I'm Stewart Jarrard. Trying to think like he would have thought." She stood up and smiled, her short nightgown barely covering her thighs.

"Want to come back to bed for a while?" I asked, reaching out toward her.

"I do. I really do, but I've got an idea and I have to try it out. I'll be in the study on the computer. There's fresh coffee in the kitchen." She grabbed a robe and disappeared through the door.

Half an hour later, I had finished my shower and was combing my hair when I heard her bounding back up the stairs. The bedroom door flew open. Lisa said, "I've got it. I know what Jarrard was hiding. It's money—or at least I think it is—in a bank in New Jersey."

"Are you kidding?"

"Of course not. I haven't got all the details worked out, but I've solved enough of it to get the name of the bank and what is probably an account number."

"But how…"

"Come downstairs. I'll show you."

She cleared a spot on the dining room table and laid out two puzzles. "This," she said, pointing at the partially filled puzzle grid, "is 'Puzzle 2,' the one that we talked about yesterday. The one that he hadn't finished."

"Now, here's another one, the one Jarrard called 'Puzzle 3.'" She placed an irregularly shaped puzzle next to the first.

202

"Look at it. What do you see?"

I studied the numbered grid for a moment. "Well, it's different."

"Of course. It's the only one of the seven that is not symmetrical, and the only one that's not filled in with answers. But—and here's the good thing—the clue list is different, too." She placed another sheet next to the irregular puzzle grid.

Puzzle 3 Clues
1-26. Crazy bankers
27-41. Where it's at, baby.
42-52. = 53-58
59-70. 13D, 43A, 52D

93, 21, 152, 40, 70, 12, 136, 150, 91, 76, 88, 40, 1, 87

I tried to make sense of the letters and numbers. I couldn't find a pattern. "Okay, I give up. What am I supposed to see?"

"It's what you don't see, Matt. Puzzle writers have to be meticulous, compulsive people. There can't be loose ends. Everything has to fit. First of all, this clue list has mostly numbers instead of definitions. The clue lists for the other puzzles are word hints. Second, the numbering system is totally different. In the other symmetrical grids, not every square is numbered, only the ones that represent the start of a word either across or down.

"Anyway," she continued, "what pushed me to connect this

irregular grid with the unfinished Puzzle 2 was the word length. Look at the lines in this one—Puzzle 3— that start with 12 and 27. They are fifteen-letters long. It was like a light bulb lit up in my head. All the symmetrical puzzle grids measure fifteen-by-fifteen block squares, but only Puzzle 2 has fifteen-letter words as answers." She pointed at 3-down, 11-down and 36-across.

"There are three of them: savings accounts, irreligiousness, and transplantation. See the second clue for Puzzle 3 that says, 'Where it's at baby'? Sounds Austin Powers-ish, but if you had to choose one of those three fifteen-letter answers, the obvious one would be *savings accounts*. That fills the line that starts with twenty-seven.

"So that made me think that the first three lines, numbers one through twenty-six, are to be filled with individual words. The first word has to be seven letters, the second four letters, and the third fifteen. We know that the third word is either *irreligiousness* or *transplantation*. Remember Puzzle 2 is not finished, so that narrows the potential answers even further. There are only four seven-letter answers and nine four-letter answers. If you do the math, that gives you only seventy-two combinations, which to a code breaker is child's play—stuff that you can almost do in your head."

"Hold on—you've lost me. You said…"

"Just bear with me a sec. Your degree is in linguistics. My Ph.D. is in math, remember? Pretend you understand if you don't."

I nodded.

Lisa continued, "Now, the word clue is for number one through twenty-six is 'Crazy bankers.' You have to think about it. What does 'Crazy' mean? Demented, loony, sick, or perhaps mixed-up. That last definition—mixed-up—could also mean that the words or letters in the true answer are jumbled. And then it hit me. The three lines that make up one through twenty-six represent an anagram of a bank name. If you pick the right words and unscramble them you should come up with it."

"So how did you…"

"Let me finish." She was on a roll. "I just whipped up a little program to look at all seventy-two possible combinations of words, take the letters, and rearrange them into standard English words, and..." she paused for effect, "I found only one solution that worked. Using the word another in the first slot, knob in the second and transplantation in the third, I come up with 'North Patterson National Bank,' which just happens to be the name of a small chain of community banks in northern New Jersey just outside of New York City." She leaned back, crossed her arms across her chest, and gave a huge smile.

I felt like a huge weight had been lifted off my chest. "So you've figured it all out?"

The smiled faded. "Well..." she hesitated, "not completely. There is a loose end or two. I got online and went to the North Patterson National Bank's Web site. They're like everybody else—they have internet banking. You need a user name—which I think is an account number—and a password to sign on."

"So we're close?"

"Close, but not there. Give me another hour. Why don't you go to McDonald's or somewhere and get us some breakfast? I need to work." Lisa obviously wanted me out of her way for a while.

"Eggs McMuffin with hash browns?"

"Yeah, whatever," she said, tossing me the keys to the BMW with a smile. She headed back to the study and shut the door.

I slipped into jeans and a T-shirt and headed toward the stable. The morning sun was painting the late summer tree tops a shade of reddish green. I thought about the light at the end of the tunnel.

42

LISA WASN'T REALLY HUNGRY. She's the type of person who compartmentalizes things. When she perceives that she needs to work, she turns off the Lisa that I know and love and care about and transforms herself into the brilliant mathematician that lives inside that lovely body. I respect that part of her, and have learned to keep my distance when necessary.

I took my time at McDonald's. I picked up the Atlanta paper at a convenience store, ordered a big cup of coffee, and hid in a corner booth for an hour, reading. I realized that I'd been unconsciously avoiding people since we arrived back in town from North Carolina. A steady stream of well-wishers, seeing me sitting alone reading the paper, paraded by to say that they were glad to see me out and about after "all that happened." I suppose they wanted me to fill them in on the details of my ordeal, but I just smiled politely and thanked them, refusing to engage in the usual small town small talk.

I'd read all the letters to the editor and was to the point of scanning the want ads before I decided that I'd been gone long enough. I ordered an assortment of breakfast foods from the sloe-eyed teenager behind the counter and was back home ten minutes later. I found Lisa sitting at the kitchen table flipping through the day's Macon *Telegraph,* which she'd retrieved from the front porch. She looked up and smiled.

"Hungry?"

"I am now, for real." She dug in to the sack, extracting a

Sausage McGriddle, laying it on the table before her and carefully unfolding the paper. She took a big bite.

"Any luck?"

Her reply sounded like "Ymmm" as she chewed. I waited for her to swallow. Pausing for a moment, she said, "Of course. I'm good."

"I know that, but did you make progress on the rest of the puzzle?"

"Yeah." She took another bite and chewed slowly, then, "I've got most of it. The account number at least."

"That's great!" I said. "We're there. What's..."

"Well, not quite. There's one little thing I still need. Let me finish my breakfast and I'll show you." She popped the last bit in her mouth and peered back into the sack, looking up to say, "Did you pick up any Eggs McMuffin?"

Ten minutes later, we were back at the dining room table with Puzzles 2 and 3 laid out in front of us.

"Okay," Lisa said, "This is what I've done. The letters in the first three lines, when rearranged, spell 'North Patterson National Bank.' The fourth line presumably tells us what we're looking for—one or more savings accounts. The bank's Web site asks you to enter a seven-digit account number and a password to gain entry to the system, so you can assume we need to come up with some sort of number.

"Now, let's look at the clue list again." She placed the sheet on the table.

Puzzle 3 Clues

1-26. Crazy bankers
27-41. Where it's at, baby.
42-52. = 53-59
59-70. 13D, 43A, 52D

93, 21, 152, 40, 70, 12, 136, 150, 91, 76, 88, 40, 1, 87

"The clue for spaces forty-two through fifty-two—that's three lines on the grid—is '=53-59,' which are the numbers for a complete new line. That is a mathematic expression, so it follows that all four lines must be numbers. The last of that group, the line with numbers fifty-three through fifty-nine, is probably the sum of the three lines above it. There are two problems, though. First, there are no numbers—only words—in Puzzle 2. Next, the second and third lines only have two spaces. There are no two-letter words in the puzzle. That got me for a minute. Then I saw something."

She handed me the clue list for Puzzle 2.

"See here, number 47-down. The clue is 'Ways to leave your lover.' The answer has to be fifty, from the Paul Simon song. Same thing with 55-across. The clue is 'A bad year for Janis Ian.' If..."

"Who is Janis Ian?"

Lisa gave me an annoyed look. "Philistine. She was a singer—still is as far as I know, but she's got to be old now. She had a big hit back before I was born, 'At Seventeen.' Jarrard would have been in his twenties at the time and would have remembered it. So that gave me a couple of word answers that were also two-digit numbers, fifty and seventeen. And, since two out of three were numbers derived from song titles, it didn't take much to figure out the other one. Look at the clue for 22-across: 'Who Tommy Tutone called.'" She pointed at the puzzle and waited for my reply. I stared at it blankly, feeling really dumb.

"Don't you remember?" She gave me a bemused look and then sang,

> "Jenny, I got your number,
> I need to make you mine.
> Jenny, don't change your number,
> 867-5309..."It's a song, dummy, '867-5309/Jenny.'"

I wanted to hug her.

"There're two possible answers, depending on whether you put the fifty or the seventeen on the first two-digit line." She quickly penciled in the numbers and added them up. "Here's one way:"

A	N	O	T	H	E	R

(8) K (9) N (10) O (11) B

T R A N S P L A N T A T I O N

S A V I N G S A C C O U N T S

8 6 7 5 3 0 9

1 7

5 0

8 6 9 7 3 0 9

Erasing them, she penciled the numbers in the reverse order, saying, "And here's the other:"

A	N	O	T	H	E	R

(8) K (9) N (10) O (11) B

T R A N S P L A N T A T I O N

S A V I N G S A C C O U N T S

8 6 7 5 3 0 9

5 0

1 7

8 7 2 7 0 0 9

"I'm betting the account number is either 8697309 or 8727009."

"Then let's see what Jarrard was hiding," I said.

Lisa pursed her lips. "Remember I said that I still need just one little thing?"

"Yeah?"

"We can't get into the system without the password, and I

can't figure it out. I'm a little stumped."

"What's the problem? You've been cutting through Jarrard's puzzles like a hot knife through butter."

"The last line in the puzzle has to be the password. It's twelve letters, see?" She pointed at the puzzle grid. "The clue seems easy enough. For sixty through seventy-one, it's '13D, 43A, 52D.' Those three words in Puzzle 2 read—if you rearrange the order—The Best Puzzler. There are fourteen letters. I tried running them in my anagram program and came up with about eighty-five different combinations of English words that you can make using all the letters, but nothing seems obvious. I guess I'll just have to…"

"What about those numbers at the bottom of the list?" I asked, running my finger across the line that read "**93, 21, 152, 40, 70, 12, 136, 150, 91, 76, 88, 40, 1, 87.**"

"I don't know what they are. They just don't seem to fit anywhere. Maybe Jarrard was making a note to himself. I tried fitting them in to all the other puzzles, but I came up with zip."

I stared at the grid for moment. "Wait a minute," I said. "We think this puzzle was going to go to Cordy and Bonifay, right?"

"Right," Lisa said, sounding uncertain.

"And these guys have egos, right?"

"Big ones, I'd imagine."

"So if you had a big ego, wrote a crossword puzzle, and sent it to other crossword puzzle writers, and referred to 'The Best Puzzler,' who would you be talking about?"

"Yourself, of course." Lisa gave me a disappointed look. "I thought of that first thing. 'Stewart Jarrard' has thirteen letters. Close, but no cigar."

"No, it's not that. The first day he came to my house, he mentioned that he wrote crossword puzzles and a bunch of them had been published in places like the *New York Times*. He said that he sometimes wrote under a pseudonym. I can't exactly remember the name." I was still discovering patches of memory that seemed to have disappeared with the bomb blast.

"Think about it. Was there something special about the name? Do you associate it with anything?"

I racked my brain and drew a complete blank. "No, but I know who'd have the answer." I nearly sprinted to the dining room and began to sift through the stacks of paper that we'd accumulated in trying to chase down Jarrard's secret. I found what I was looking for and dialed a phone number.

"Greensboro Warehouse and Storage," a male voice answered.

"Phillip Bonifay, please."

"You got him."

"Mr. Bonifay, this is Matt Rutherford in Walkerville, Georgia. We met a few months ago when you and Dr. Cordy came down for Stewart Jarrard's funeral."

"Yeah, how you doing, Mr. Rutherford? I heard you were injured in an accident somehow or other. You okay now?"

"I'm fine, thanks." I didn't want to get into the details. "Listen, I'm calling to ask if you could help me out. Stewart mentioned to me one time that he sometimes wrote crossword puzzles under another name. Do you have any idea what I'm talking about?"

"Sure. A lot of the great puzzle writers used to do it. Back in the 1930s and 1940s, before my time. These days most folks just use their given name."

"But do you remember what name he used?"

"Of course, but I'm not going to tell you just like that. It'd be too easy. Why don't you guess it? Here's the clue: 'Roman general who was governor of Jerusalem in the first Century A.D.'"

I was not in a mood to play games, but it looked like I didn't have a choice. "It has twelve letters, correct?"

"Hey, you're hot. But I need a name. Anyone can count squares."

"I give up," I said. "I majored in Linguistic Anthropology and then worked in high-tech. Not many of my friends were into Roman generals."

"Come on. Try. I'll give you a hint: Masada."

I thought I knew the word. "That's something you get in an Indian restaurant, isn't it?"

Bonifay took a deep breath and exhaled before saying, "No. You're thinking of *garam masala*, which is a spice used in northern Indian cooking. I said 'Masada,' spelled with a *d*."

"Mr. Bonifay, I really don't have time…"

"Oh, come on. It's a game."

In that very moment, I realized that I hated cruciverbalists. Trying to control my anger, I said, "How about talking with my associate, Ms. Li?" I stuck the phone in her face.

Lisa took the handset and gave a tentative hello. She listened quietly for a moment then said, "You're talking about the commander of the famous Tenth Roman Legion, the governor of Judea at the time, right?"

I couldn't hear the response on the other end, but Lisa replied, "I know it. Now you do, too." She hung the phone up.

"What did he say?" I asked.

"That I must be brilliant, because nobody ever gets that answer right." She grinned. "Let's try logging into the North Patterson National Bank."

43

"**ARE YOU GOING** to tell me what Bonifay said?"

"He didn't say anything. He gave me the same hints that he gave you, and I gave him a hint back. Neither one of us gave the other the answer."

"Lisa, are you crazy? What are you trying to do? If we've made it this far, we've *got to* know the password."

"Bonifay is a gamester, Matt. And a very bright one at that. I was just trumping him at his own game. He's an obnoxious pedant, and proud of what he knows. What better put-down than finding someone who may know more than he does?"

"Do you?"

"If I hadn't been reading an article in a magazine on the plane when I flew in from San Francisco, I'd have had no idea whatsoever what he was talking about."

"Like I said, do you?"

"We'll see."

Lisa logged on to the North Patterson National Bank Web site. She clicked the icon for "Internet Banking" and was presented with a page that asked for a User ID and Password. Consulting the sheet of paper where she'd scribbled down the two possible account numbers, she entered the first one into the User ID box. She tabbed to the Password box, quickly typing in twelve letters which appeared on the screen as "************." She hesitated, then pressed "Enter." A message in red letters flashed on the screen: "Invalid User ID and/or Password. Please re-enter or

213

contact Customer Service."

"One down, one to go," she said.

"Are you going to tell me the password?"

"If we get in, yes. If not, then I've made a fool of myself with Bonifay and I'm going to call him groveling and beg him for the answer." She looked up at me with a slight grin. "Even us technical types have egos, you know."

Glancing at the paper a second time, she typed in the alternate User ID, then tabbed and typed the password, saying, "Flavius Silva."

The screen went blank, then flashed: "Welcome to The North Patterson National Bank's Internet Banking Center, Mr. Jarrard. What would you like to do?" Below it was a list of options.

"We did it," Lisa said quietly, smiling.

"How did you know the password—what was it? Flavius Silva?"

"Just an article in an airline magazine. I remembered the name because he was a bad guy. He was one of the commanders of the Roman army that conquered Jerusalem. He was made governor and started what today we'd call a reign of terror. The piece focused on the fortress at Masada, where Flavius led an entire Roman legion against less than a thousand men, women, and children who'd taken refuge there. A pretty ugly bit of history, really. For some reason, the name stuck with me."

"I wonder why…" I started.

"Who cares? We're in." Moving the cursor over the menu, she said, "What's your pleasure? *Make A Deposit*? *Transfer Funds*? How about *View All Accounts*?" She clicked on the Accounts icon. The screen again went blank, then reappeared with a list of eight account numbers, with instructions to *Check The Account You Wish To View*. She clicked a first, then a second, and a third as we watched numbers fill the screen.

"Holy shit," I said. "The first three accounts alone contain more than five million dollars."

"And that's how we're going to buy our freedom."

We spent the next hour sifting through Jarrard's hidden treasure. The eight accounts contained just over nineteen million dollars, all of them listed in the name of Shortz International Trading Company, LLC, with an address in Trenton, N.J.

"You know who Will Shortz is, don't you?" Lisa asked. I said that I didn't. "He's the Puzzle Editor of the *New York Times*. Jarrard was really getting cute here."

It didn't take much searching to find out that the Trenton address was the same as that of a commercial mailbox firm whose Web site advertised "Discreet forwarding services with mail sent to the address of your choice in unmarked packages." Images flashed through my head of fat, sweaty men stuffing kiddyporn and cocaine into plain brown wrappers.

Other than monthly interest deposits, it appeared that the accounts had been dormant for more than a year. "It's hard to believe that kind of money would just sit idle in a bank account for a year," I said.

"Why not? They are loaning it out for more than they're paying to sit on it. The bank has no reason to want things to change. I'd wager that they don't even know Jarrard is dead. Why don't we ask?" Lisa moved the pointer to the top of the page and clicked on a box that read "Contact Us." A new screen appeared that invited the viewer to "Contact your Personal Banker," followed by a space for an e-mail message, plus a telephone number for Russell Denton, Senior Vice President at the Whittington Street Branch. She handed me the phone and said, "Suppose you can make Mr. Denton believe that you're Steward Jarrard?" she asked.

"I'll try," I said and dialed the number. The bank's operator transferred me to a female voice that answered, "Mr. Denton's office."

I said, "This is Stewart Jarrard. I'd like to speak with Mr. Denton," using my best New York accent.

"Of course, Mr. Jarrard. This is Sally, his secretary. We haven't heard from you in ages. Are you still down there in—where was it?—Georgia?"

"Right. I've settled in now." I seemed to have leaped the first hurdle.

Russell Denton came on the line, "Mr. Jarrard, How are you? I know you said that we'd probably not be hearing from you for a while and that the accounts would be inactive, but I'd really hoped that you'd keep in touch. How are things down South?"

"Things are going well, thanks," I replied. "Since it's been so long I thought I should check in."

"Well, we're following your instructions to the letter. You're one of our larger customers and we want to be sure that you're well taken care of." He paused briefly. "You haven't had any problems with your European suppliers, have you?"

I had no idea what he was talking about. "How do you mean?"

"I recall you said that you were a little concerned about the EU regulators, and how that might affect your overseas sales."

I was even more bewildered. I gave him a neutral answer. "No, all's well there. We will probably want to transfer some funds out of the bank in the next few weeks."

"We certainly hate to lose any business, but you've been a great customer so anything that I can do to help..."

"Thanks, Russell," I said. "Got a call on the other line that I need to take." I hung up without giving him a chance to say goodbye.

Lisa and I stared at one another. She said, "We haven't figured it all out, but do we need to? We know what Jarrard was hiding, and we know where it is. Now we've got to decide what to do. If we tell Victor, we've become part of the conspiracy. If we tell the FBI, Victor's promised to kill us. Not a good set of choices."

"We need to come up with some way to satisfy both of them. Problem is, I don't know where to start."

"Neither do..." Lisa started, her sentence interrupted by the sound of the door bell.

44

SHERIFF ARNETT STOOD on the back stoop, in full uniform this time, his wide-brimmed campaign hat in his hand. "Hi, Matt. Ms. Li," he said, nodding. "I told you I'd drop by to check on things today. Y'all doing all right?"

"We're fine, thanks." I wasn't really sure that I had time for this.

"You mind if I come in? With all that's gone on, I still feel responsible. And I want to get an update. We haven't talked since before you two went up to New York. Have you made any progress at all in finding out what Attorney Jarrard was hiding? And how about that Victor fellow? You heard any more from him?"

I opened the door and invited him in. I didn't have much choice. Other than Lisa and I, he was the only one that knew the whole story. And, or so I reasoned at the time, we could use him as a sounding board as we tried to decide the next step—about how or whether to talk with the FBI, and how to handle Victor.

We walked to the front parlor. As we passed the dining room, Arnett peered in at the stacks of papers strewn about the table and in piles on the floor, saying, "Looks like you're working on something." I didn't reply. He lowered himself on the settee, half leaning back and propping one leg up slightly on the cushioned silk. I noticed that he wore ostrich-skin cowboy boots under his sharply creased trousers.

Lisa and I sat opposite in two wing chairs. I spoke first, "Sheriff, we've discovered some things. I think it's safe to say that we know what Jarrard was hiding, and we know where it is and how to get it." Arnett sat up sharply, listening intently.

"There are *a lot* of loose ends and things that don't exactly fit into place," I continued, "but I'm pretty sure that we've stumbled onto what Victor wants. We still don't know who he is, or..."

"What is it?" Arnett interrupted. "He'd stolen something, right?"

I looked at Lisa. She shrugged with a certain look of resignation as if the information would have to come out sooner or later. "Money," I said. "Lots of it. More than nineteen million dollars in several bank accounts."

Arnett whistled. "Hell, that's more than the entire yearly budget of Adams County. How'd he..."

I cut him off. "That's all we know. Just where it is and the amount. We don't know how it got there, who the money belongs to, what Jarrard intended to do with it, nothing. We don't have any idea who Victor is, or who he's working for. We suspect that the money's got some connection to Habersham's, the auction house, but we don't have anything to prove that. We...."

"You met with Habersham himself when you were in New York?"

"Yes, but there was nothing unusual about the conversation. He was polite, acknowledged that Jarrard was his ex-son-in-law, and spoke highly of him."

"So why do you think..."

"That's really all we know, Sheriff," Lisa spoke up. There was something I didn't like about the tone of her voice. I looked at her but couldn't read anything on her face.

I continued, "We're faced with a dilemma. We need to let the FBI know what's going on, and we need to deal with Victor. If we call up Agent Davis or Agent Kight and say, 'Hey, we know where the money is,' that'll just confirm to them that we knew all along. And if we don't identify and permanently neutralize the threat from Victor, we're sitting ducks. What's your advice? How should we proceed?"

Arnett reached in his pocket and pulled out a pouch of Red Man, taking a small pinch of the dark tobacco and sticking it in his mouth. He chewed for a moment and said, "You do have yourselves in a pickle." He chewed quietly, apparently thinking.

The ticking of the grandfather clock in the hall echoed softly off the walls. He shifted his chaw to one side and observed, "It's Chief Mathis, you know?"

"How so?"

"He's the one that convinced the Feds that you couldn't be trusted. He's still smarting over your cousin's murder last year. Thinks you had something to do with it. He doesn't like you, you know."

"So I've been told," I said.

"If it weren't for him poisoning the water with the FBI, they'd see you as a victim rather than a possible suspect. As it stands, though, you've got some explaining to do if you've come up with where the money is. How'd you find it anyway?"

"I found it," Lisa said. There was still something in her voice that I didn't like.

"Could you turn it over to the FBI right now if you had to?"

"I suppose so," I answered. "We've apparently got full access to the accounts."

"And you haven't told Victor that you found it?"

"He hasn't called, and I don't know how to call him."

Arnett chewed for a moment more and said, "Let me study about this for a while. You two going anywhere? Can I give you a call later on?"

"Sure. We'll be here."

Arnett rose to leave. "I need to think about this and do some quiet checking around. Let me see if I can get a hold of one of the FBI agents. Sort of ask for an update on the investigation and so forth. I'll feel 'em out as best I can and get back to you with what I think you oughta do. Sound okay?"

I showed him to the door and watched his patrol car drive out of the yard. Lisa stayed back in the parlor. She was still sitting there when I returned. "Are you all right?" I asked. "What was going on just then?"

"You didn't catch it, Matt?"

"Catch what?"

"Arnett. He asked if we met with Habersham in New York. We haven't told anyone that. He had no way of knowing."

"I didn't hear it that way. I think he was just inquiring if we met with the old guy. It's not like he was asking, 'Didn't you meet with Habersham when you were in New York?'"

"I think that's almost exactly what he *did* say," Lisa replied, a worried look on her face. "I don't trust him."

45

WE TOOK THE REST OF THE DAY OFF. It was one of those rare August days when the jet stream had moved south, bringing with it blue skies and a break from the stifling summer heat. One of the things I'd inherited from my father was a tract of timberland that bordered the Opahatchee River. Deep in the forest, down a small logging road, a high bluff crowned with old-growth longleaf pines hugged a lazy ribbon of water fifty feet below. It had been my own private refuge during my high school years in Walkerville. I rarely went there now, and never with anyone else. It was a private place. Somewhere to think, undisturbed.

We stopped by the grocery store to pick up cheap wine, plastic glasses, and snacks, then put the top down on the BMW and drove to the river. We locked the gate behind us, parked the car out of sight, and walked the quarter mile through the woods to the bluff, carrying our blanket and picnic sack.

"It's beautiful," Lisa said. "So quiet here, with just the sound of the wind in the pine needles."

"You know, I haven't taken anyone here in years. It's where I used to come to think."

"I guess we've got a lot to think about," she said, sipping wine and staring down at the river.

"We've been through a lot together in the last year. When you left and didn't call, I thought I'd never see you again."

She turned and looked at me with a soft smile. "I love you, you know?"

"I know. Just promise me one thing."

"What's that?"

"That you won't leave again."

"I promise," she said, and reached out to hug me.

□□□

IT WAS NEARLY DARK by the time we arrived back at Rutherford Hall. The lights on the City Square were beginning to blink on, and traffic on Main Street had fallen to a trickle. We'd almost finished bringing things in from the car when I saw the lights of a vehicle pulling into the back yard. I caught a reflection of light off the bar on the roof and realized that it was Sheriff Arnett, apparently returning to talk with us. I waited for him at the back door while he bounded up the steps.

"You must have just gotten home," he said. "I've been trying to call but didn't get an answer. I apologize for showing up unannounced, but I wanted to get back to you about the situation. You and Ms. Li got a few minutes to talk with me?"

I invited him in. We sat at the kitchen table. "You sure you're not expecting company?" Arnett asked. "I don't want to disturb any plans."

"No, we're still trying to decide what to do," I said.

Lisa was silent, still suspicious, I thought.

"I've been going back and forth all afternoon trying to come up with what's best for everyone involved. The way I see it is this: I think it's fair to say that whatever money's in those accounts wasn't gotten exactly legally, and so far as the government knows, it probably doesn't exist. That makes for a mighty attractive prize. That's one thing. The other thing is that there are a lot of people who've got dogs in this fight. You've got the rightful owner of the money, and I'm assuming that's your friend Victor. You've got the FBI who is interested in catching Jarrard's killer. I suspect they don't even know about the money. And you've got you two who're caught in the middle. You're sorta damned if you do and damned if you don't.

"The problem with your position is that you—and I guess now me—are the only ones who stand with one foot on each side of that line. Nineteen million dollars is a lot of money, at least to me it is. I've got to be honest with you two. Victor's been talking to me, too. Sent me a photo of my wife and told me what was going to happen to her if I didn't work with him. And like you, he offered me a carrot along with the stick. See, he didn't even tell you what you were looking for—just in case you decided to talk to the feds. He was a little more forthcoming with me, though. Told me it was money that Jarrard took from him and that he wanted it back. As for you, if you found the money and let him have it and didn't tell the Feds, he said you could walk away with your life. In my case, I got the same offer, plus 10 percent of what I helped him recover."

I felt a draft from the direction of the hall and turned to see a man dressed in black standing in the door. Arnett followed my gaze and said, "You remember Mr. Conan McKenna. You met him at Jarrard's funeral. He works for Mr. Habersham and has come to collect what's been stolen."

"Pleased to see you again, Mr. Rutherford. And to make your acquaintance, also, Miss Li." Hard consonants, soft vowels. Irish accent. He was holding a gun pointed at us. "If you fine people don't mind, we'll keep this simple and easy. All I need to know is where our money is located, and how to get it out. That's it, and I'll be gone."

I looked at Lisa. She spoke. "It's in a bank in New Jersey. We have the account numbers and access codes. That's all you need."

"It'll be a start," McKenna said. "You have it written down?"

"I can in a minute." Lisa arose from the table. I followed.

McKenna waved the gun at me. "You, Mr. Rutherford, stay here. Keep an eye on him if you will, Sheriff, while the young lady and I conduct our business."

Arnett drew his Glock .40 caliber and held it loosely pointed at me. Lisa gave me a helpless look and headed toward the study, McKenna following close behind. "Matt, I'm really sorry things had to work out this way. Don't worry. I don't mean you any harm. This is going to be a little secret that you and I and Lisa will share for the rest of our lives. 'Course, I'll be nearly two million richer and you'll have to keep your mouth shut. That's the deal. Habersham gets his money, I get my commission. You get to live. Everybody wins."

I wanted to heave the table in his face and ram the gun down his throat, but I said calmly, "It'll fall apart. The wheels will come off. Something always happens."

"Better for your sake that it doesn't. You're like Jarrard now. You know too much. You've got the sword of the Democrats hanging over your head."

"Damocles," I corrected him.

"Whatever."

McKenna and Lisa reappeared at the door. McKenna was gripping a folded sheath of papers tightly in his left hand, his gun still in his right. "You have a very efficient girlfriend, Mr. Rutherford. I think we've got all we need." Turning to Arnett, he said, "Sheriff, are you ready to take our friends for a ride?"

Arnett looked surprised. "Why?"

"Surely, we can't leave them here. Neither you nor I want to spend the next twenty years or so in prison."

"You got what you wanted, McKenna," I said. "We haven't talked to the FBI. We can keep our mouths shut. Just leave us alone."

"If things could be so easy, my friend. It was a race to see who'd bring us the goods first and it looks like you lost. You may not have talked with the FBI, but you *did* talk with the good Sheriff. I think you've given sufficient evidence that you can't be trusted." He waved his gun. "Let's go."

"You're making a mistake, McKenna," Arnett said. "There's been too much killing already. You…"

"I can kill three just as easily as two." He raised his pistol and aimed squarely at Arnett. "Take your choice, Sheriff."

Arnett hesitated, then said, "You don't leave me but one." Then to me, "Get up, Matt. Time to go."

McKenna scooped Lisa's car keys off the table. "You put them in your car, Sheriff. I'll drive the girl's BMW. A fatal accident outside the city limits would be investigated by your men, I presume."

Arnett nodded, a look of hopelessness in his eyes. He prodded me in the ribs with his pistol.

McKenna exited the back door first. He stood on the stoop, pointing his gun at us while Arnett locked the door. I noticed that the yard was unusually dark, and realized almost immediately that all the street lights on Main Street had gone out. We started to inch down the stairs, Lisa first followed by McKenna, then me with Arnett in the rear. We were suddenly stabbed by the beams of a dozen high intensity flashlights from all around us, accompanied by a voice through a bullhorn commanding, "This is the police. You are surrounded. Lay down your weapons and raise your hands high over your heads."

Arnett was behind and just above me on the steps. I couldn't see what he was doing, but I felt the barrel of his Glock ram into my back. In front of me, McKenna wrapped his left arm tightly around Lisa's neck and placed the muzzle of his gun at her right temple. He yelled out, "You want a dead girl? You bastards move back or you'll have to gather up her brains with a shovel."

The voice with the bullhorn boomed. "Drop the gun, McKenna. You're not going anywhere."

"So *you* think," McKenna yelled back and took a step forward.

I felt the gun poke in my back again and heard Arnett saying, "Move."

I'll probably never know precisely what happened next. I think Arnett missed the step. It was dark and we were blinded by the flashlights. I stepped forward and the next thing I knew he was falling into me, his gun hand flying up reflexly to balance himself. I felt, more than heard, a blast just above my head, then another just in front of me. I threw myself down. I caught a glimpse of McKenna silhouetted against the lights, his right arm raised and firing toward the flashlights, which seemed to bob and sway in slow motion as muzzle flashes erupted from around them. I saw Lisa pitch forward, falling off the steps toward the earth, and felt Arnett firing his gun wildly behind me before he screamed and crumpled in a ball that rolled down the long stairs. From my supine position, I looked up to see McKenna jerk as the bullets slammed into him, then lurch backwards as his forehead exploded in a mass of red. A small cloud of aerosolized blood droplets floated in the bright lights where he'd stood.

As suddenly as it started, it was quiet. I heard someone yell, "Clear." I tired to sit up as a flashlight beam blinded my vision. The lights that surrounded us began to approach cautiously. I looked for Lisa. I'd seen her fall over the side of the steps. Ignoring the bullhorn command that I not move, I leaped down to find her sprawled on the earth, lying on her back. An ugly river of blood flowed from her hairline, covering her lovely face.

"Lisa!" I screamed. "Lisa!" She didn't move. I touched her neck, feeling for a pulse. Two sets of strong arms pulled me away.

46

I'D BEEN SHOT and didn't know it. My back yard was almost instantly transformed into a carnival of flashing blue lights from police cars, red and yellow lights from two ambulances, and blinding white headlights that illuminated our shadows like huge finger-puppets displayed on the side of Rutherford Hall. Someone—I think it was one of the City patrolmen—said, "You're losing a lot of blood." I reached over my right shoulder and felt pain as my finger touched a sticky furrow plowed by a bullet across my upper back.

They forced me onto a stretcher while one of the cops and an EMT applied pressure to stop the bleeding. I could see them hovering over Lisa where she lay on the earth, my view half-blocked by the steps, but their shadows projected on the wall behind them. I tried to get up, insisting that I'd be all right, but they wouldn't let me. Two techs manhandled the stretcher into the ambulance and we went flying, sirens wailing, up Main Street toward the hospital.

The ER was expecting us. I was wheeled in and immediately descended upon by a hoard of green-clad nurses who rudely cut off my clothes with scissors and jammed an IV into my vein while a doctor whom I'd never met rolled me back and forth to examine my wound. He asked me if I hurt anywhere else, was short of breath or was allergic to anything. Getting a negative answer to all three, he told one of the nurses to "put him in Room 3 and get a portable chest. We need to keep Room 2 open for the female with the gunshot wound to the head."

I tried to sit up. They pushed me back down. "That's Lisa. I've got to see her."

The ER doc said, "We don't know how badly she's hurt. You'd only be in the way. Let us do our job, okay?"

They rolled me in a room where an RN and an aide hovered over me, checking my vital signs, connecting me to a monitor, and making sure that the bloody bandages on my back were controlling the bleeding. From the hall outside, I heard the automatic doors swish open and someone yell "Coming through," while another voice said, "Put her in Trauma 2." A portable x-ray machine was wheeled in and a hard cassette placed behind my chest. Everyone except the lead-aproned tech left the room while the machine beeped and zapped me with radiation. Ten minutes later, the surgeon appeared briefly at the door and asked, "Everything stable?"

The nurses nodded. "Chest x-ray's okay. No pneumothorax. We're still working on the other victim. Go ahead and clean the wound and I'll come and repair it when I get a break." The only thing I'd heard was the word "victim." He didn't say "Lisa," he said "victim."

Half an hour passed. I asked the RN to check on Lisa. She left and returned to say that they couldn't really tell at this point how severe her injuries were, that they had just finished a CT scan of her head, and that the helicopter should be arriving within the next ten minutes. Was she conscious? No, I was told. Helicopter, I asked? She's going to Shock-Trauma at the Medical College in Augusta. What did that mean? That she's badly hurt, was the reply. I tried to get up again and they pushed me back down. Fifteen minutes later, I heard the doors swish open and they rolled her out toward the helipad. The ER suddenly became very quiet.

Chief Roger Mathis appeared at the door of my room. "How you doing, Matt?"

"I'll be fine. How's Lisa?"

"She's been shot in the head. I don't know the details. I'm not sure they're good." He paused. "You want to know what happened?"

"I guess so."

"You want to hear it from me or from the FBI?"

"It doesn't matter," I said. I was numb. I didn't care.

"We've been on to Arnett and McKenna for a while. To be honest, we didn't think things would come to a head so quickly. We knew you and Lisa were on your way to figuring out where Jarrard hid the money, but the FBI thought they'd let you make contact with Habersham and arrest him when he tried to transfer it."

"Oh," I said, still thinking about Lisa.

"Maybe we need to fill you in later. You've been through a lot tonight. Let me just say that things are gonna be fine. We got the bad guys."

He put his hands in his pockets, hesitated a moment, and then said, "I guess I shouldn't say things are fine. I'm real sorry about Lisa." Changing the subject, he continued, "Your folks are out in the waiting room. Want me to see if I can get the docs to let 'em come back and see you? They're worried to death about you."

Uncle Jack and Aunt Margie hovered over me, squeezing my hand and rubbing my forehead, as if touching me would confirm that I was alive and well. My mother, I was told, was not feeling well (which meant that she had been drinking) and planned to see me in the morning. I asked about Lisa again, and Jack went to see what he could find out. He returned to say, "The only thing they'd tell me is that she's been shot in the head. The helicopter got to Augusta without problems and they're evaluating her now."

The surgeon stuck his head in to say that he'd be repairing my wounds and that the family would have to leave. The nurses turned me over on my belly and proceeded to torture me with some sort of warm liquid while they were "cleaning" my wound. Ten minutes later, the surgeon returned, placed a drape over my back and began injecting me with lidocaine. "This will sting a little bit," he said, "but you were lucky. A few centimeters in the other direction and the bullet would have severed your spine."

"How is Lisa?" I asked.

"The oriental girl with the head wound?" The bastard hadn't bothered to learn her name.

"Yeah."

"Don't know. She was shot at close range with a 9 mm. She's unconscious. We should be getting a report from Augusta in a few hours." I flinched as he jabbed the needle into my back. "Say," he continued, "weren't you in here a few months back after you were injured in an explosion?"

"Yeah," I said again, trying to ignore the pain.

"We don't give out frequent flyer miles," he said.

I didn't respond. "How about the other two—Arnett and McKenna?"

"Dead, I hear. Must be because we initially got a report that four people had been shot, but only you two came in. That usually means the others are dead on the scene. They'll take them straight to the state crime lab for an autopsy, especially in this case, because they were killed in a shoot-out with the cops." He was quiet for a moment as I felt him continue injecting the anesthetic. The pain was beginning to ease off. "You've got a hell of a wound here, you know. I measured it at twenty-seven centimeters—that's more than ten inches. The bullet just dug a trench from your right side to your left over both scapulae. Barely missed your thoracic spinous process at about T-4. You'll have a fancy scar, I can promise that."

I wasn't paying attention. I was thinking about Lisa.

47

THE ER STAFF MADE NOISES about keeping me overnight for "observation," but I insisted on leaving. They made me sign a waiver before they'd agree. Against my better judgment, I allowed them to inject me with 75 mg of Demerol, which eased my now-painful back but made me groggy. They wheeled me out down the ambulance ramp with a huge bandage wrapped around my chest. Jack and Margie insisted that I stay at their house, at least for the night. I was asleep in the car before we drove out of the parking lot.

I awoke the next morning in a strange bed, my upper back in pain and my head still foggy from the medicine they'd given me in the ER. The bedside clock read 7:10 a.m. I stumbled downstairs to find Jack at the breakfast room table, reading his newspaper, and drinking coffee. "Good morning," he greeted me. "Are you sure that you should be up so soon?"

"I'm fine," I said, still a little unsteady.

"You had a bad day yesterday. By the way, Agent Kight from the FBI called last night. He wanted to come by and speak with you. I told him you were sedated. He said he'd be by to see you first thing this morning. You want some breakfast?"

I told him I wasn't hungry. "Have you heard from Lisa?" I asked.

"I knew you'd want to know, so I called when I first woke up at 6:00. She's still in the ICU, but that's all I could find out. They told me the doctors make rounds at 9:00, and I could call back then and speak to one of them."

I looked at my watch. I could make it there by 9:00. "Mind if I borrow your truck?" I asked.

Jack folded his paper and stood up. "I knew you were going to ask. You're in no condition to drive. I'm your chauffeur and ready when you are."

An hour and forty minutes later, I was standing outside the Trauma Unit at the Medical College Hospital pressing the call button for the nurse. The door opened to reveal a familiar face, one of the nurses who had cared for me there a few months earlier. I couldn't remember her name. Her badge read, "M. Santos, RN."

She seemed surprised. "Matt? Matt Rutherford? Is that you? What are you doing here?"

"You have Lisa back there?"

She seemed puzzled. "I don't think so, no." A chill ran through me.

"But she's here. She came in last night. A head wound…"

"Oh, *that* case." She reached in her pocket to consult a list. "But that's not her name—or is it? We have the patient in Room three listed as "'Mona L. Li.'" It occurred to me that I had never known that Lisa wasn't her first name. "She's here, but..," she turned around to look back into the intensive care unit, "the doctors are making rounds right at the moment. Could you wait a while?" A look came over her face, then, "That's not the Lisa who was here with you day and night, is it?"

"Yes. How is she?" I demanded.

"I didn't recognize her. I wouldn't have recognized her—the bandages, and her face is so swollen. I know your Lisa, but…" A middle-aged man in a scrub suit walked behind her. "Oh, there's Dr. Scott. Let me catch him for you."

Dr. Scott introduced himself. He was a neurosurgeon. He didn't waste time. "The patient's had a close call. A medium caliber wound from a pistol fired at extremely close range. She should be dead, really, but… I guess somebody had a guardian angel watching them last night. Do you…" he hesitated, "Do you want to see her?"

Tears welled up in my eyes. "Yes. Please. If I can."

"Well don't be shocked. There's swelling and…"

I walked past him toward Room three. Ms. Santos moved

to block my path, but Scott shook his head. The Trauma/ICU "rooms" were little more than glass-walled cubicles, each perhaps twelve feet deep and ten feet wide. The lights in Lisa's cubicle were dim. A monitor above her bed traced out a steady heartbeat while other readouts displayed pulse, temperature, respiration, and blood oxygen saturation. Her head was swaddled in a huge turban. Her right eye was swollen shut with an ugly bluish-black discoloration.

I pulled the sliding glass door back and stepped in. The only sound was the hum of the air-conditioning unit and the soft beeping of the monitor. I watched for a moment as Lisa's chest rose and fell slowly with each breath. I reached out and touched her hand. It was cold. She didn't respond. A wave of anger swept over me. I wanted to yell, to pound my fists, to demand retribution from... who? Arnett? McKenna? They were dead. The cops? They were trying to save us.

Slowly, I touched her swollen cheek. She took a deep breath and her left eye fluttered open. A slow smile formed on her lips and a tear trickled from her good eye. "Matt..." she said, hoarsely and barely audible.

"Yes? I'm here, Lisa."

"Matt..." she said again, trying to find her words. I was still holding her hand. She squeezed mine, then motioned with her finger for me to come closer. I moved my ear near to her lips.

"Matt..."

"Yes?"

"Those assholes cut my hair." And then she began to cry. And I cried. And Uncle Jack, who by that time was standing behind me, began to cry, which led to Nurse Santos's snuffling and quickly leaving the room.

"She's going to be fine," I heard the doctor saying behind me. "She's still sedated from the anesthesia, but it'll wear off soon. Probably have her out of here and home in three or four days, max."

I couldn't decide if I wanted to hug him or slug him.

"Like I said, she was lucky. The bullet grazed the frontal bone just anterior to the frontoparietal suture line. It cracked the outer table, but to everyone's amazement, she had no intracranial injury at all. In fact, if we'd known last night what we do this morning, she could have stayed over in Walkerville at Adams Memorial. Since she was here, though, we had our plastic guys do a good scalp repair. Once her hair grows out, you'll never see the scar."

It was all gobbledygook to me. I didn't care about frontoparietal sutures or outer tables or intracranial crap. All I cared about was Lisa.

48

THEY LET ME STAY FOR AN HOUR and then told me I had to leave. Lisa drifted in and out of consciousness. She tried to talk, to ask me what happened, but I shushed her. I held her hand. She held mine.

The ICU staff told us that it would be best if we came back the next day. Lisa would probably be moved to a regular room within twenty-four hours, they said, and she was too sedated to appreciate our presence anyway. I told them I'd be back tomorrow morning.

Agent Kight and another FBI agent named Eubanks were at my uncle's waiting for us when we returned. I was not in a good mood. Kight stuck out his hand. I said, "You son of a bitch," and ignored it. He said that they needed to talk with me, to explain things. I agreed, but more out of a combination of anger and curiosity than a sense of cooperation.

"Matt, I'm sorry for the way things turned out. If we'd had any idea that…"

Anger seeped from my voice. "Just tell me what's going on. Skip the details. Give me the big picture. Tell me why last night happened."

"It wasn't supposed to end this way," he started. I could hear a combination of embarrassment and guilt in his voice. "I'm sure when things all sort out you'll get a full report of the details. But let me try to give you the high points."

We went inside to the family room. They sat on the couch. I

sat in a chair opposite them, staring back. Aunt Margie disappeared upstairs. Uncle Jack hovered in the background. Kight said, "We've been suspicious of Habersham a long time, and we've been aware of Jarrard's family connection to him for years. Let me start at the beginning.

"The man you met in New York, Pendleton Brewster Habersham, was born in Palestine in the early 1930s. His real name is Yasir bin Hamid al-Aziz. His parents were middle-class Palestinian Arabs, the father a shopkeeper and the mother a teacher. His father was an ardent nationalist and an active participant in the Arab uprisings against British rule in the 1930s. His mother, on the other hand, was an anglophile, and realized that the future for her son lay not in any free Arab state, but rather in Europe or the U.S. She didn't want her son to turn out like her husband, so she sent him to British School in Jerusalem. That's where he acquired his perfect command of English and learned about the world outside of his village.

"During the mid-1940s, the war was winding down in Europe, and the Zionists were struggling against the British for the establishment of a Jewish state. By that time, al-Aziz's father had become a prominent pan-Arabist leader. In 1946, he, his wife, and their two oldest children were murdered by Jewish resistance fighters, leaving the young boy an orphan. His relatives decided that Palestine was not a safe place for the kid, so they shipped him off to live with some distant cousins who'd emigrated to the States years before. Getting him in was no problem. He was a teenager and an orphan, and he had relatives to vouch for and support him.

"We really don't have much information on him until the early 1950s. He lived for the first few years in the Atlantic Avenue area of Brooklyn where his cousins had a small furniture store. We know that he changed his name shortly after arriving in the U.S. to Pendleton Brewster Habersham. In doing some background checks, we had several acquaintances say that al-Aziz seemed ashamed of his heritage and was always trying to pass himself off as an upper-class Englishman displaced by the War. He started out selling used furniture, had a few lucky breaks, and by the mid-fifties had established Habersham's Auction house, together with a whole new identity for himself. And you have to give him credit, he did well. He became fairly wealthy, married a native New Yorker from a good family, and had a daughter, Catherine. By the 1970s and '80s, they were a well-known couple on Manhattan's social scene. Everyone seemed to have forgiven or forgotten Habersham's real name and background. Catherine met and married Stewart Jarrard, they had two kids. It was shaping up as the perfect American success story. But something happened.

"Sometime in the early 1990s—we're not really sure when—Habersham developed an interest in the Palestinian cause. We don't know the details, but we were able to trace fairly substantial donations from him to several European-based pro-Palestinian organizations. Around the time Arafat won the Nobel Peace Prize, word got out that he'd been a supporter and almost immediately he was shunned by New York's Jewish community. It began to hurt his business. And so the support stopped, or everyone thought it did. Are you with me thus far?" Kight asked.

"I am," I said. The wound in my back was aching.

"Have you ever heard of the MMB—the Muhaddith Martyr's Brigade?"

"No. Should I?"

"Probably not, unless you live in Israel or follow Middle Eastern events closely. They are among the most violent of the anti-Zionist movements, responsible for dozens of suicide bombings and hundreds of deaths in Israel. Very secretive group. Very opposed to the Oslo Peace Accords. Israeli intelligence tried to infiltrate them and ended up with half a dozen dead agents. They tried assassination, but they've only gotten middle- and lower-level leaders. They did have some success in tracking their funding sources to European banks.

"About two years ago, the Israelis came to us for help. They thought they'd tracked some MMB funds through a very complicated series of transactions back to Habersham. We tried to sort it out on our end, but got nowhere. The guy's got offices—and bank accounts—all over the world, some of them in places that are not friendly to either the U.S. or Israel. So, we'd been keeping an eye on him. Jarrard was never really in the picture.

"Last year, when things went south for Jarrard, it occurred to somebody at headquarters in Washington that the divorce might give us an opening. The breakup was a pretty ugly one, in part because Habersham stepped up to the plate to help his daughter. Bought her the best divorce lawyer in New York, that sort of thing. We knew that Jarrard had been doing some financial work for Habersham's, and he was the one person who might want to talk. We had absolutely nothing to indicate that any U.S. laws had been broken, and besides, we've been more focused on anti-terrorist activity. We were just doing the Israelis a favor, but it wasn't top priority.

"We approached Jarrard, tried to get him to talk, but he stone-walled. The agent that interviewed him knew that it was a shot in the dark, but came away thinking that Jarrard knew a lot more than he was willing to admit. In his report, he said that he believed that the man was concerned about his ex-wife and children. Didn't want their reputations sullied. So that was it. The Bureau stuck the case files in the cabinet and just sat on them.

"Then came the first attempt on Jarrard's life, and his murder a week later. That's where I came in. The case suddenly opened up. When Washington got the word, their first question was about his Habersham connection."

I heard the phone ringing in the kitchen. I glanced at the clock on the mantlepiece. Ten 'til noon.

Uncle Jack, his hand over the receiver, said, "Matt, it's your mother. Want me to tell her that you'll call her back?"

I wasn't eager to talk with her, but I had to get it over with eventually. I said, "No, I'll speak to her. She's probably worried that I haven't called." Jack handed me the phone.

I excused myself from the agents and walked out on the back patio. I said hello.

My mother, obviously on her cell phone, nearly screamed, "Matt, for heaven's sake, what is going on over here at your house? I heard there was some ruckus over here last night and I thought I'd come over and make sure that you were all right and now…" she seemed to be fuming "now, all this."

"What is all this?"

"Trucks. Televison trucks. And yellow tape that says 'Crime Scene.' Matt, there is a policeman here who won't even let me drive my car into my only son's yard. I told him that I am your *mother* and I *demand* my right to come see how my only son is…."

"Just hang on, mother. I'll be right there."
I hoped she was sober.

49

JACK DROVE ME HOME. I told Kight and Eubanks we could finish talking later. They insisted on coming with us. Jack and Margie's house is in one of the nicer subdivisions north of town. Rutherford Hall is on Main Street, a couple of hundred yards from the City Square. I could see the traffic jam from a quarter mile away as we approached. My mother had been right. Three vans from TV stations in Augusta, Atlanta, and Macon were double parked on the street in front of the house, slowing traffic to a crawl. A CNN van was parked in the driveway of the house next door, its satellite dish pointed toward the southern sky. Two police cars with their lights flashing were parked on either side of the TV vans. The entire yard and sidewalk were once again fenced by yellow crime scene tape. A City of Walkerville police officer stood in the driveway arguing with a woman in a large late-model Cadillac. "I see your mother has arrived," Jack observed.

We pulled in behind her. Jack said, "You stay in the car. I'll handle this." He knew I was angry. He said a few words to the officer, who nodded, touched the brim of his hat, and stood back for my mother to drive into the back yard. We followed. I could see the telephoto lenses focused on us as we both got out of the car.

My mother scurried over to hug me. I caught a faint whiff of vodka, her drink of choice before noon. "Oh, Matt. I am so embarrassed about all this. What have you gotten into now? I heard there was a shooting and that the sheriff and somebody else got killed, and that you got shot, and…"

Jack put his arm around her and began speaking in low tones, gently drawing her away. I looked at the house. It was a mess. The back door was splintered in a dozen places where it had been struck with bullets. Its glass was shattered, the lace curtain behind it hanging limply. A diffuse flock of crime scene techs huddled here and there, discussing, photographing, examining. I approached the back steps but was stopped by a patrolman. Streaks of deep red gleamed against the dull grey enamel paint on the stairs. Three dark red patches stained the earth where Arnett, McKenna, and Lisa had lain.

Kight and Eubanks pulled in the yard and parked behind us. Jack walked over and engaged them in a conversation. I saw the agents shaking their heads, and briefly heard Jack say, "It's the least you can do, dammit." He walked back over to me and said, "Agent Eubanks is going to drive your mother home. Kight will wait here with us until he gets back."

We were allowed inside via the front door. Again, telephoto lenses tracked our every move. The house was cool and quiet. We sat in the relative privacy of the front parlor. "You want to hear the rest of it?" Kight asked.

"Might as well."

"The first attempt on Jarrard's life frightened the hell out of him, as well it should have. We—the FBI—were originally called in because of the supposition that someone he'd prosecuted years ago had put out a contract on him. He apparently didn't have anyone he was close to, but before he was shot, he mentioned something to the Sheriff about 'a secret,' or something to that effect, and that he 'needed someone to confide in.' Jarrard said that it didn't have anything to do with what appeared to be an attempt to kill him, and that he thought he could trust you. That's it. Based on what Arnett said, we didn't know what Jarrard may have told you before he was killed. We had a number of meetings discussing the case, and every time Arnett would say, 'That boy knows a whole lot more than he's saying.'"

"Arnett told me that Chief Mathis was the one who kept trying to convince you that I was holding something back."

Kight half-laughed, "Just the opposite. Mathis is not one of your greatest admirers, but I will say that he defended you. Said something like, 'I know the boy's family. I don't think he's lying.' Anyway, it all just seemed to come together after they tried to kill you. And if you think about it, it sounds logical. Jarrard admitted that he was hiding something. He told Arnett that he was going to confide in you. You were not especially cooperative, and then—next thing you know—someone's trying to do you in. It made us take a second look at Arnett's theory.

"So, we thought we'd kill two birds with one stone. You needed a place to recover. You needed protection. The North Carolina house was perfect. We could quietly keep an eye on you while…"

I started up to lunge at him. Jack was quicker. He caught me before I reached Kight. The agent fell back on the settee, instinctively reaching for his gun. "Easy, Matt," Jack said, waving him off.

"You know the whole damned place was full of microphones and cameras," I said to Jack.

"I know," Jack said quietly. "I knew all along."

I looked at him in shock. "You, too?"

"I didn't believe it, but it was the only way to completely clear your name."

I sank back in the chair, my heart racing, the wound in my back throbbing.

"It saved your life, Matt," Kight said.

I looked at him, puzzled.

"What are you talking about?"

"Last night? Do you think all that was just chance, the street lights going out to darken your yard? Half the Walkerville police force showing up with guns drawn? Haven't you figured it out?"

I supposed I'd been in a daze. It suddenly became so obvious. "So that's it?" I looked at the agent and my uncle. They nodded.

"We bugged this house, too. Your phones, your computers. Microphones, no cameras this time. You should have realized it after you discovered the set-up in Highlands."

It had never occurred to me. I turned to Jack. "You let them do this?"

"I thought it was for the best, Matt. We care about you."

I stood up and walked over to the window, pulling the curtains back. The TV vans were still in place. The crime scene crew was just pulling out. I turned around and asked, "Is there anyone that I can trust?"

There was silence for a moment, then Jack said, "Lisa."

"Did she know, too?"

"Of course not."

"You almost killed her."

"That's where things went wrong, " Kight said. "By the time you left North Carolina, we were pretty sure that you had no idea what was going on—or if you had, you hadn't shared it with Lisa. But when you came back here, and we started listening to what you were doing, we realized that either you'd been in contact with this Victor fellow or he'd gotten in touch with you. We started to move in then, but Arnett argued against it. Told us to wait, to see what you'd come up with."

"Where did Arnett come into all this?" I asked. "Why were you suspicious of him?"

"I can't give you a straight answer on that, Matt," Kight answered. "Call it cop sense, or whatever. I didn't trust him. He was too nice. Too eager. Too obliging."

"They didn't tell him that they'd bugged your house," Jack said.

"So he didn't know…"

Jack answered, "No one here knew except me."

"We suspected Arnett was dirty," Kight said. "We put the microphones in right after they blew up your truck. We slipped a couple of our guys in with the ATF fellows who investigated the bombing. They put in the sensors under the cover of a Federal crime scene investigation. Just as soon as we pulled out, Arnett was in here nearly tearing the place apart looking for something. He must have suspected you'd hidden it. It didn't make sense otherwise. But last night was… well, a total surprise. We knew that McKenna and Arnett had talked, but we had no idea that they'd show up together. When they did, it caught us unprepared. Our guys were monitoring everything from Atlanta. We called Chief Mathis. We had to stop them before they took you away. It was all we could do…"

"Who shot Lisa?"

"I don't know," Kight said. "McKenna probably. All we know is that Arnett shot first. Mathis's men fired back."

"I think it was an accident," I said. "I think he tripped on the stairs and his gun went off."

Kight was silent for a second and then said, "Shit happens. He was a dirty cop."

50

THEY LET LISA OUT of the hospital five days later. I visited her every day, staying as long as she'd let me. I wanted to stay with her, to be there for her as she had for me, but she wouldn't allow it.

"You've got too much to do," she said. "And I have my pride. Here I sit, my head shaved, a black eye, no makeup, and wearing this thing that they call a gown. I don't want you to see me like this."

"It doesn't matter," I'd say, to which she'd reply, "To me, it does."

And she was right, I did have a lot to do. I spent hour upon hour with the local cops, FBI, the GBI, and a varied assortment of other law enforcement officials. It was the same thing over and over. "If you would, Mr. Rutherford, start at the beginning and tell us what happened." It got very old, very quickly.

I made my daily visit to Dr. Pike to have the dressing on my wound changed. He said that it was healing nicely and that the stitches could come out in about a week.

The Chairman of the County Commissioners dropped by to offer his apologies for Arnett, and to say that Adams County would be responsible for the repairs to Rutherford Hall and for Lisa's hospital bill. The repairmen arrived within hours, scooping up the bloody soil and caulking and patching the bullet holes.

I found out later from the County Attorney that the Commissioners were afraid that I'd sue. I wouldn't have, but I didn't tell him that.

Four days later, a team from the FBI arrived to remove the microphones from the house and wipe their spyware from the computers, all under the watchful eye of Agent Kight. I decided in the end that he wasn't such a bad guy. He was just doing his job. We sat at the kitchen table sharing a beer while he brought me up to date on the case. "Almost immediately after the shoot-out we got a warrant for Habersham's arrest and sent a team to his apartment in Manhattan to pick him up. The housekeeper said that he was at his weekend place in Connecticut, but when we got there we found he'd been gone about an hour. Looks like he found out what was going down and skipped. We'll get him, eventually. He's got money and friends, so it may take a while."

"Any idea where he is?"

"We're pretty sure he went to South America, possibly to Colombia."

"Colombia? That's not exactly Habersham's style. I can't picture the quintessential English gentleman on the hot streets of Bogotá."

Kight took a swig of his beer. "Me either, really, but we had a lead that someone resembling him chartered a private jet at Teterboro Airport in New Jersey. The pilots filed a flight plan for Miami, then amended it in-flight for Merida, in the Yucatan. They stopped there, refueled, and filed a flight plan back to Miami. Instead of heading for the States, they turned south. One of our planes in our drug interdiction force picked them up heading for the Colombian coast. It'll sort out. Money talks in that part of the world, but the Israelis really want this guy. I wouldn't be surprised if they find him and settle things right there. Who knows?"

"All I want to know is that it's over. I want Lisa home. I want to get on with our lives."

Kight finished his beer and said, "You can relax. Everything's under control. By the way, once we raided Habersham's office we figured out his game. He'd been selling very well-done forgeries of middle-tier artists, most of them painted by some real experts in China and Eastern Europe. He'd list them as having been purchased "privately" in Europe and once they were sold, transfer the proceeds out of the country to one of several offshore accounts. Jarrard's area of expertise was hiding the funds from the regulators, and he kept all the books. In fact, he was the only one who knew where the money actually went after it left New York. That way, if Habersham's were raided, he could plead ignorance, and his corporate records would back him up.

"Obviously, he trusted his son-in-law, but from what we've been able to reconstruct, Jarrard either didn't trust him, or they'd had a falling out over something. Jarrard hid the money where only he could find it. With the divorce, he saw a chance to make a clean break from Habersham, and used the threat of exposure as his 'insurance.'"

"So the fifth e-mail—the file labeled 'YHA'—was to Yasir bin Hamid al-Aziz, alias Pendleton Brewster Habersham?"

"You got it. And when this hits the press in a few weeks, you're going to have every museum and collector who's ever purchased anything from Habersham's beating down the walls for a refund. It's not going to be a pretty scene."

"How did McKenna fit in?"

"Interesting story. He's been in the U.S. for years, but since this whole thing came up, we found out from our friends at Scotland Yard that he's probably ex-IRA. Never directly implicated in any of the violence that took place back in the 1980s, but a suspect. The thinking was that he felt the heat and emigrated. He's been working for Habersham for years, and as far as any one knew, kept his nose clean."

"Amazing."

"Yeah, but it's all over now." He paused, then said, "You mind if I have another beer?"

□□□

BY THE TIME I picked up Lisa to take her home, the repairs to Rutherford Hall were finished. The newsworthiness of a couple of small town murders had faded and the herd of TV vans had migrated on to bloodier pastures. I packed a small bag for her homecoming—a soft silk blouse, some comfortable jeans and her underwear, plus her toothbrush and whatever she kept stuffed in her makeup kit. Her right eye looked better and her hair was beginning to grow out, but she put on dark glasses and a scarf, adamantly refusing to be pushed out in a wheelchair. She was pale and had lost weight. The doctors gave us no special instructions.

They told her that she was slightly anemic from blood loss and that she might have headaches for a few weeks, but that we didn't need to come back. "You'll be fine," they said, handing her prescriptions for iron and Vicodin. "See your local doctor in four or five days and let him take the stitches out."

Lisa was quiet on the way back to Walkerville. I started to fill her in on what Kight told me. She smiled and said she'd rather talk about it later. It was another beautiful day. The temperature was in the eighties. An occasional white, fluffy cloud drifted in front of the sun. I suggested putting down the BMW's top. She said that she'd rather not. She became increasingly anxious as we got closer to town, and almost shivered as we slowly pulled into the back yard.

"Are you okay?" I asked.

"I'm fine," she said unconvincingly. Then, peering through the windshield at the back steps, "It looks so... so normal."

"I had everything fixed."

"I see," she said and was quiet for a moment. "But that's not what I mean." She took off her glasses and turned to me, tears welling up in her eyes. "We almost died, Matt. Right there, on those steps. We almost died."

"I know, but everything's fine now. We're home, and we're going to take it easy for a while. We don't have to go anywhere. We don't have to see anyone. It'll just be me and you until you're feeling better. We can live on pizza and Chinese take-out."

She smiled and leaned over to hug me. "I love you, Matt."

She squeezed me so hard that my wound hurt, but I didn't care. She was home.

51

LISA DID NOT DO WELL. As long as I'd known her, she'd been bright, vivacious, active, and curious. Now she spent most of the day lying in bed, the curtains drawn. Her head hurt a bit, she said, but she refused pain medicine. I tried to get her to eat, but she stirred the food around on her plate, consuming only enough to make me think she was hungry.

She refused to leave the house to have her head wound checked, so Dr. Pike made a house call. He removed her stitches and pronounced her nearly healed. He told her that she could resume her normal activities if she'd like. She smiled wanly and said simply, "Thanks."

Eula Mae came and went, deciding after seeing Lisa that she needed to be there every day. She'd arrive promptly at eight and stay until six, trying her whole range of cooking skills in an effort to make Lisa eat. After a week she drew me aside and pronounced, "Miss Lisa's really down."

"I know," I said. "She's been through a lot. We both have."

"That may well be, but it ain't no excuse. You gotta get her out of this house, or she's gonna dry up and blow away. My thinking is, you gonna have to take her somewhere. Somewhere different where she don't know nobody, so as she won't be 'barrased 'bout her hair. You jus' don't know how womens is. Somebody's done shaved her head. It's like Sampson in the Bible. She's lost her power. She ain't herself."

"I know she's not herself, but things are fine now. The threat's gone. We just need some time…"

Eula Mae crossed her arms, "Mr. Matt, with all due respect, you don't know nuthin' 'bout women. That's probably why you ain't married. That girl laying in that bed up there loves you, but she's sick. Emotional sick. The minute she sets her foot out that door somebody's gonna say, 'There go that woman what been shot. Looka there. She done got her head shaved.' Now, if you was to take her somewheres where they don't know her, the people what see her jus' be thinkin' she got short hair."

"So you think it's all about her hair?"

"'Course not. There's more, but you got to start somewhere. You go up there and talk to her. Right now. Tell her you thinks y'all need to get away for a while. See what she says."

Eula Mae may have been right, but I doubted if the problem were that simple.

At the same time, I didn't think it'd hurt to try. I climbed the stairs and eased open the bedroom door. "How're you feeling?" I asked.

"Fine," Lisa said. "Still kinda tired. I'm going to get up in a while." It was 10:00 in the morning. She reached over and turned on the bedside lamp. Picking up a hand mirror, she studied her face, then ran her fingers through the thick dark stubble on her head. "Nearly an inch," she said. She felt the scar and held the mirror up to examine it before placing it back on the table.

"Uh, look, I've been thinking. Why don't we get away for a few days? Maybe go to a resort or hotel or somewhere that has good room service?"

Lisa looked up from the pillow. "Are you serious?"

"Of course. Some place where they don't know either one of us. We can just blend in with the crowds and…"

"You're not suggesting Highlands, are you?"

"Oh, no." I was shooting from the hip. I had no idea where I was talking about.

"We don't have to fly, do we? I don't want to have to deal with an airport and security and all that." She sat up and dangled her feet off the bed.

"How about the coast? It's a two or three hour drive. We could go to Hilton Head, or Savannah, or St. Simons or somewhere like that."

"I don't want to stay in a big resort with a lot of people. Not just now, anyway. Can you find something sort of private? With good food?" She smiled for the first time in days.

"I think so. Let me make a few phone calls."

Eula Mae was waiting at the bottom of the stairs. "Well?" she said.

"You're a genius," I replied.

"Ain't I been right all along?"

I didn't reply.

□□□

WE CHOSE THE CLOISTER at Sea Island. It was relatively small, upscale, and had a great restaurant. I booked an oceanfront suite in one of the Ocean Houses and was promised prompt room service. A change came over Lisa almost immediately. She still wasn't back to her old self, but for the first time she emerged from the bedroom wearing makeup and without a scarf covering her head. She seemed excited about the prospect of a change of scenery. She spent the afternoon picking through her wardrobe, laying out clothes on the bed, holding them in front of her as she stood before the mirror and—to use Eula Mae's term—"preening like a bird."

We left shortly before noon the next morning. I drove. This time, Lisa wanted the top down. She still wore a scarf and sunglasses, but now to protect her from the sun and wind rather than something to hide behind. She and Eula Mae had huddled upstairs in the bedroom for an hour with the door shut before she emerged with her short hair jelled in soft punky spikes. "Like it?" she asked.

"You're a new woman," I smiled.

"You work with what you've got," she replied, smiling back. "It was either punk or concentration camp gothic. I opted for punk."

"I trimmed it up around the ears and in the back," Eula Mae volunteered.

We took the back roads south through Soperton, Vidalia, Baxley, and Jesup, passing first through farmland and vast fields of cotton and soybeans, then down long straight roads lined with row upon rigid row of planted pines growing above palmetto fronds in the moist south Georgia soil. Lisa fiddled with the radio, finally settling on an FM station playing a song by the Counting Crows. I heard her singing quietly to herself.

> *How much longer will it take to cure*
> *this? Just to cure it cause I can't ignore*
> *it if it's love—love—Makes me wanna*
> *turn around and face....*

She stopped suddenly and smiled sheepishly when she saw me glance over at her. "I feel better," she said by way of explanation and turned to look out at the countryside.

We drove through the industrial and urban sprawl of the port of Brunswick, then across a long causeway through a vast marsh to St. Simons Island. Following the signs, we turned onto Sea Island Road and stopped when we reached the gatehouse at the end of another causeway. The massive hotel with its Moorish arches and tile roofs gleamed in the afternoon sunlight over the Black Banks River to our left. I gave the guard my name and was directed to the hotel for check-in. Lisa seemed excited.

Our room was perfect. The balcony overlooked sand dunes covered with waves of yellow sea oats. A broad beach was beyond, the smell of salt air pushed toward us by a gentle inshore breeze. The bellman arranged our bags while Lisa leaned over the railing, staring out at the ocean. I handed him a five, and he left. I joined her on the balcony. She turned to face me and put her arms around me. "I think..." she began, and stopped, choking a bit. "I think it's going to be all right." Then, without another word, gently guided me back into the room and onto the bed.

52

THE FIRST WEEK PASSED quickly. I'd told the hotel that we'd probably want the room for a couple of weeks, and that I'd give them several days notice when we decided to leave. Lisa's mood brightened daily. She started waking up at seven for a walk on the beach. Not her former early-morning five-mile jog, but in the right direction. Room service delivered our meals for a few days. Lisa fretted about the tiny amount of swelling and discoloration that remained about her right eye. She seemed more comfortable with how her hair was turning out.

On the morning of our fourth day, she said, "Why don't we go for a ride? Maybe see some of the island, eat lunch at the Beach Club? I hear the food's good."

We did, and it was. She went back for seconds. We rented bicycles and explored the residential area of Sea Island north of The Cloister, a long narrow strip of land served by a single oak-sheltered drive with short streets branching off to the ocean on the east and the marsh on the west.

The next morning, Lisa announced, "I called and scheduled an afternoon at the spa today. Hope that was all right?" I said that it was. "I think a facial and a massage would be good. They do hair, too, you know?" I didn't know and I didn't really care, so long as she was happy.

By the beginning of the second week, Lisa was approaching normal. She'd resumed slipping out of bed near daybreak, jogging north up the wide beach, then back down Sea Island Drive to our room. We'd have room service breakfast in our suite, eat a light lunch at one of the local restaurants, then have dinner with wine back at the hotel.

On our tenth day at The Cloister, I decided that Lisa had made a complete recovery. She'd headed for the spa while I spent a couple of hours with a shotgun trying to hit sporting clays at the Shooting School. I returned to the room to find her hunched over her laptop, deep in thought.

"What are you doing?" I asked.

"I'm a geek, remember?" she laughed. "I was having e-mail withdrawal."

"Any news?"

"Not really. Just a hundred or so messages from my friends on the West Coast saying that they haven't heard from me and wondering where I've been. It'll keep me busy for a while answering them all. They've got WiFi. I'll sit by the pool and write them back."

I saw her casually lay a magazine over a paper next to the computer.

"Are you sure that's all?"

"Yes. Why?" Then, "No, it's not Matt. I can't lie to you. There is something else."

A cold shiver ran through my body. She was going to leave.

Lisa walked over and put her arms around me, burying her head on my shoulder. "I think you know me pretty well by now, and…"

"Don't do it, Lisa."

"Why not? I have to. It's… it's just my nature."

I held her, trying to support myself against a sinking feeling. I said, "Please don't leave."

She dropped her arms, backed away a few inches, and said, "Who mentioned leaving? I was talking about the crosswords. Jarrard's crosswords. We never finished figuring them out. There were those last four…."

I kissed her. She kissed me back.

"I'm curious. I have to know," she said. "We figured out the first three and everything fell into place, but those others…"

"Why do you want to do that? They got the bad guys. We don't have to worry about any of that now."

"Oh, I know that, but it's the challenge. They're just there. I don't think he would have put the effort into writing them if they weren't important. Maybe they're just things he was working on—puzzles he planned to submit for publication. But they were on the same flash drive as the others, and I've got some time now, so…" She didn't finish.

"Sure," I said. "Go for it."

"Thanks."

□□□

BY OUR TWELFTH DAY at the hotel we had slipped into an easy routine. Lisa would rise early and go for a run. I'd get up, shower, and order breakfast. By the time she'd returned and finished her shower, breakfast would arrive. We'd eat on the balcony overlooking the dunes and the beach. That day, however, things changed.

We'd slept a little later than usual. I'd asked for breakfast to be delivered at 8:30. Shortly after eight, I heard the door open and shut. I was just drying off. "Lisa?" I said. There was no answer. "Lisa, is that you?" I called again as I wrapped the towel around my waist and opened the door. She was sitting in the overstuffed chair, her knees bent, and her arms wrapped around them. Her head was tucked down in what I could only describe as a sort of fetal position. "Are you all right?" I asked.

She looked up, fear in her eyes. "He's here, Matt. Here on Sea Island. I saw him. I know it was him. Sure, he's dyed his hair, but I saw that look in his eyes…"

"Lisa, calm down." I kneeled down beside her and put my arm around her.

"Who are you talking about? What are you talking about?"

"Habersham. I just saw him on the Drive. I looked right at him and he looked right at me. I can't forget that face. He didn't recognize me, I'm sure. I know I look totally different than I did when we met him in New York."

"Calm down," I said again. "It's not that I don't believe you, but I just can't imagine that he'd…"

"He's here, Matt. I *know* that was him." Lisa explained to me what happened. She'd started off her morning run as usual, jogging out to the beach, then north past the Beach Club down to Twenty-third Street where the sand narrowed. She then cut through to Sea Island Drive and ran up to Thirty-sixth Street. "That's halfway, about two and a half miles," she explained. "I've been jogging back down to the Beach Club, cutting through, and ending up back here. It's dangerous on the road, so I stick to the sidewalk along the Drive—it's on the inland side. You have to cross the little side streets that lead to the marsh, but this time of day there's not much traffic. Normally I just glance down the street and keep going. I'd just passed Twenty-first Street when I saw a car—it was a black Audi, one of the big models—pull up to the end of Twentieth Street ahead of me , waiting to turn onto the Drive. There were cars coming and the driver was looking both ways —he had to wait till they passed before he pulled out. As I got closer, I thought he looked familiar. He looked right in my direction, but he was focused on the traffic, not me. I slowed up a little bit and I realized that it was Habersham. His hair's a dark brown now, but it had to be him. He pulled out just as I reached him. The car had a Florida tag."

I didn't know what to say. Lisa was shivering. "The FBI thinks he's somewhere in South America—or they did the last time I spoke to Kight," I said softly. I didn't want to be harsh to her. "Why don't I see if I can get in touch with them, get an update."

"He's here, Matt. I saw him. I looked into his eyes. I know it was him."

Lisa took a shower. She emerged wearing a white terrycloth robe, looking somewhat calmer as she toweled down her hair. "I'm sorry. I shouldn't have gotten upset. I'm probably just imagining things." She wrapped the towel around her neck and leaned over to kiss me. "I guess it's been a little rough on both of us."

"Yeah. But I'll call Kight anyway. Just to be sure." A soft rap at the door announced that breakfast had arrived.

We finished eating. Lisa headed off for a 9:30 appointment at the spa. I sat on the balcony, turning the situation over in my mind. She'd been under a lot of stress. She seemed to be recovering smoothly, but sometimes appearances were deceptive. It wouldn't hurt just to check it. It would ease her mind—and perhaps mine, too. I found Kight's card in my wallet and dialed his cell phone. He answered promptly.

"Mr. Kight, this is Matt Rutherford…"

"How are you, Matt? Your uncle said that you and Lisa had gone to the beach for a few days. Everything okay?"

"I think so. I wanted to get an update on the investigation."

"We've about got it wrapped up, the domestic part, anyway. We've taken about a dozen people into custody in New York. Our European guys are still working a few leads, but it's just routine mopping up at this point."

"How about Habersham?"

"Still missing. Since we talked, we were able to confirm that he was the passenger on the charter out of Teterboro. We impounded the plane in Miami and interviewed the pilots. They said they dropped Habersham off at the airport in Cartagena, Colombia. They didn't seem to know much, but they overheard talk of a boat. We got word last week that he may have been spotted in Curaçao, off the Venezuelan coast. Our guys with the consulate down there are following up."

"How do you know it was him? Couldn't it have been someone that looked like him?"

Kight laughed. "Not a chance. We lifted his prints from half a dozen spots on the plane."

"No chance that the pilots were lying?"

"Why should they? They really hadn't broken any laws. It was a legitimate charter. There's no way they could have known at the time we were after the guy. We let 'em go after we talked with them."

I thanked him and hung up. Lisa was simply mistaken. There were no other explanations.

53

I TOLD LISA what Kight said. She seemed satisfied, but I wasn't sure. The longer I live, the more I realize that you can be close to someone and never really know what they're thinking.

A quick, warm rain shower blew through in late morning. By two, the late summer Bermuda high had pushed the clouds out of an otherwise perfect blue sky. We headed for the pool, Lisa with laptop in hand and me with a paperback spy novel. She plunged in, swam a few laps, then settled in on a chaise under an umbrella to chip away at Jarrard's puzzles. I ordered a beer and read. Neither of us mentioned Habersham.

After an hour, she said, "Did you look at these puzzles, the other four?"

"Not really."

"So you didn't see the clue asking for the last name of the sixth Postmaster General of the U.S.?"

"Are you kidding? No, of course not. Who would know that anyway?"

"Nobody. That's just it. The clue is so arcane that it's forced. Something shoehorned in just to give a certain answer. Look at 30-across." She handed me her laptop. A completed crossword puzzle grid filled the screen.

"I see. It says Habersham. But it's just a name. I mean, maybe he used it because it was the best word to fit in that spot in the puzzle." Apparently she hadn't gotten over the morning's events. "Don't you think you're obsessing over this? Lisa, I care about you so much, but you've been through a really rough time. Maybe you're trying to find a pattern when there's nothing there."

I could tell immediately that I'd said the wrong thing. Lisa took off her sunglasses and looked at me. "You may be right," she said, a touch of hardness in her voice, "but cut me some slack, okay? Habersham may be in South America or wherever, but this is something I want to do."

She put her shades back on and resumed studying the puzzle. After a moment she said without looking up, "Just because you're paranoid doesn't mean that they're not out to get you."

We lay by the pool in silence for another hour. I had another beer. Lisa continued fussing over her laptop until she said, "My battery's about dead." She looked toward the sun sinking lower in the afternoon sky. "Why don't we get the bikes and take a ride before it gets too late? I could use some exercise." She seemed to have forgotten my earlier comments.

We walked back to the room, pulled on shorts and T-shirts over our bathing suits and headed out for a leisurely ride around the island. Sea Island is a long narrow barrier island that owes its fame to The Cloister, an ultra-luxury hotel at the south end originally built in the 1920s. To the north of the hotel, private homes with large, manicured lawns line Sea Island Drive and its side streets. The island is a private place, accessible beyond the gatehouse only to homeowners, Cloister guests, and members of the Sea Island Club.

We pedaled north, shaded from the afternoon heat by a canopy of live oaks whose branches reached out and met at mid-street, forming a green tunnel illuminated by a patchwork of sunlight that filtered through openings to the blue sky above. I was happy.

Lisa led on her bike. I followed a few yards behind. At Sixteenth Street, we turned toward the beach, parked our rides, and spent a few minutes gazing out at the near-deserted ribbon of sand. A few blocks further on, Lisa took a sudden turn toward the marsh. I looked up to see a small sign that read *Twentieth Street*.

"Where are we heading?" I asked.

"Nowhere in particular," she yelled back. "Just curious." It was a short street with a house on each corner of the Drive, one on either side where the pavement ended in a patch of green grass overlooking the marsh, and one house between each, facing the street. Lisa brought her bike to a halt at the end and looked around. "He was driving out of the street, so he couldn't have come from either house on the corner. It must be one of these four." One of the houses facing the marsh was a huge Italianate monstrosity of stone and stucco with a tile roof and faux-Tuscan accents. The other three were substantial, but more conservative cottages whose style suggested they'd been built in the 1950s.

A teenager with longish hair and baggy pants was shooting baskets in the driveway of one of the homes facing the marsh. Lisa pedaled over and said hello. The kid nodded and continued dribbling his ball. "Does someone that lives on this street drive a big black car—I think it's an Audi?" she asked.

"I don't know. This is my grandpa's place, and we're just visiting. My folks are over at the beach if you want to ask." He pointed toward the other end of the street. Lisa said thanks, looked at me and shrugged.

A lawn service truck carrying mowers pulled up at one of the middle houses facing the street. Four workers got out and began unloading. An older man who appeared to be in charge stood by barking orders. Lisa walked her bike over, smiled, and said, "Do you know if the man who lives in this house drives a black Audi?"

"Mr. Harvill? Yeah, I think he does—or I maybe should say that's what I think he was driving when I spoke with him the other day. I'm not sure what kind it was—it's one of them big fancy foreign cars, I do know that."

"Oh, do you know Mr. Harvill?" Lisa asked as if they'd been old friends. "He's a friend of the family. My mother told me I should look him up when we were here."

"Yep. I've been doing his landscape maintenance about six years now—ever since he's had the house. He doesn't stay down here too much—just drops in for a few days every now and then. I've talked with him a bunch of times on the phone, but truth is, this is the first time I've met him in person."

"My mother knew him years ago."

"She from England?"

"No, why?"

"Well, Mr. Harvill lives in London, I think," the man said. "Or somewhere over there. Doesn't get over here that often." I could see Lisa stiffen.

"You say he lives in London?"

"I think so. One of them foreign countries. He has an accent is all I know."

"My mother knew him when they worked together in New York." Lisa was fabricating a story. She paused. "I'll bet it takes a long time to get paid, having to send your checks all the way from England."

"Oh, no. I get paid out of New York. There's a law firm up there that handles Mr. Harvill's business here in the United States. They pay right on time every month."

"Do you remember the law firm's name?"

"Sure. My wife's a librarian. When I first met her she was going to school to learn how to classify books. They call it the Dewey Decimal System. That's the firm: Dewey, Naughton, Pierce, and so on."

54

"**THIS TIME YOU CAN'T** deny it," Lisa said angrily. We were back at our room at the hotel. "I see someone who I *know* is Habersham. The landscape guy says the man's from London— and that he has an accent, just like Habersham. And he says that he gets paid by Jarrard's old law firm. I mean, look at the odds. What are the chances…"

"You may be right," I said, "but what are we going to do? Call the local cops and have him arrested? What if you're wrong? How much proof do we need?"

"I'm not saying that we have to do anything ourselves. We call Kight. Tell him that we've found Habersham and let the FBI handle it. This guy's a murderer—he put a contract on Jarrard and was going to have us killed, too. All I want to know is that he's safely behind bars. I'm not going to be able to relax until I do." I couldn't argue with her, but I still wasn't convinced. Lisa's whole argument was based on a random encounter that lasted a few seconds. It would be too easy for her eyes to be playing tricks on her.

I said, "Okay. Let's call him right now." I found Kight's card and dialed the number on my cell phone, handing it to Lisa when he answered. She spent five minutes explaining to him what she'd seen and heard.

I saw a look of frustration come across her face. "I know you've got other leads and…" She stopped. Kight was saying something on the other end. "But what if they're wrong? Is a sighting in Aruba from someone you don't know more accurate than one that comes from someone who's actually met the guy?'"

Lisa shook her head. "That may be too late. What if he makes a run for it?" Then, "No, we're not leaving. We're staying here until someone proves to me that I'm wrong. So you can tell your guys in the Jacksonville office that we'll be expecting them to call." She slammed the phone down.

"He doesn't believe me. Says they've got reliable information that Habersham was in Aruba, then Curaçao, and is headed for Isla Margarita, just south of Trinidad. Called it 'specific and reliable.' That's bullshit. Says he's going to get one of the Agents in the Jacksonville office to set up an appointment with us, but then he also said that they had several hundred other leads that they were following up. Basically, he's hoping we'll go away."

"Okay," I said slowly. "What do you want to do?"

Lisa took a deep breath and pursed her lips. "Nothing. We'll just stay here until they call. Kight said he had your cell phone number. He promised that we'd hear something within forty-eight hours." She flopped down in the chair and rested her chin on her elbow, thinking. After a moment, she said, "Where can we find a set of property records for Sea Island?"

"Lisa, it's private property. I'm not sure that…"

"Georgia does have property taxes, right?"

□□□

AT 9:15 THE NEXT MORNING, we were standing in front of the W. Harold Pate Courthouse Annex in downtown Brunswick. The Tax Appraiser's office was on the second floor, accessed off a lobby that overlooked the Brunswick River and commercial docks in the distance. It took us only minutes to find the aerial maps that covered the coastal islands. Lisa traced her finger down Sea Island Drive to Twentieth Street, then copied down the block and parcel number. With a few quick instructions from Lynn and Andrea, the Appraisers' clerks, we found the owner of record for the house on the computer work station next to the map rack.

"It says 'The Harvill Trust,'" Lisa said. "Let me see if there's an address." She typed in a search command. A new screen flashed before her. She smiled. "Will wonders never cease? You'll never guess the name of the contact person at Dewey Naughton. Our old friend Douglas Eaton."

"You're kidding."

She pointed at the screen.

We thanked the staff and walked out of the building into the bright sunlight of the parking lot. "Okay. We've confirmed what the lawn guy said. Now what?" I asked.

"I'm thinking," Lisa replied, and she was quiet for a moment. "I want you to call Douglas Eaton. We need to know how he got in the picture."

"For God's sake, why? What's that going to tell us?"

"We'll see. This is what you need to say…"

□□□

I CALLED DIRECTORY ASSISTANCE and got the Dewey Naughton firm's number. Two minutes later, Douglas Eaton's assistant answered, "Mr. Eaton's office."

"This is Matt Rutherford from Walkerville, Georgia. I met with Mr. Eaton not too long ago on business. I was calling back to talk with him about some things."

"Of course, Mr. Rutherford. Let me see if Mr. Eaton is available."

Eaton picked up the phone almost immediately. "Mr. Rutherford. So glad to hear from you. Are you ready to let us help you with that inheritance?"

"Yes, I think so, but that's not exactly why I'm calling."

"Oh?"

"Lisa and I decided that we wanted to buy a beach house, and we've been down here at the Georgia coast looking around. We found one that we both thought was just perfect, but it wasn't listed as being for sale. So we went to the tax office to get the owner's name so we could contact him to see if he'd consider selling it. You can imagine our surprise when we found out that it was owned by something called the Harvill Trust, and that your law firm is responsible for the taxes and other bills. We wanted to know if you could see if the house is for sale or, if not, they'd let us make an offer."

"The Harvill Trust. I think… let me check on that. Hold on a second." I could hear him in the background asking his assistant to bring him a file. Papers rustled on his desk. "The Harvill Trust,"

Eaton said again. "Yes, I remember now. That is owned by a United Kingdom entity that we administer for the principles in… uh… here it is, London. It's a private trust and… uh," I could hear more paper shuffling, "our contact is a group of solicitors there. I'm really not terribly familiar with it. To be honest, Matt—you don't mind my calling you Matt, I hope—this is one of the accounts I inherited from Stewart Jarrard. This firm sets up and manages literally hundreds of trusts yearly—that's how we make most of our income. I see now, looking at the statements, that the trust has an account here in New York that gets regular wire transfers from…" He stopped. "But you don't want to know all that—just if the house is for sale, right?"

"You got it, Mr. Eaton. And let me tell you, if you can pull this off for me and get me that house, it'll go a long way toward getting the ball rolling on letting y'all manage those trusts." Eaton said he'd get back to me right away. I gave him my cell phone number.

Lisa said, "You do so good with that fake southern accent."

"It's not fake. I just turn it on or off—on, in this case, when I'm trying to scam a Yankee lawyer."

"What'd he say?"

"That Jarrard apparently set up the trust when he was with Dewey Naughton. Eaton didn't seem to know much about it. I expect his paralegals handle the routine stuff."

"One more nail in the coffin," Lisa said. "Now we just wait for the damned FBI to call. Give me your phone. I want to call Kight again."

"Why don't you wait? I don't think it's going to make him move any faster."

We drove back over the causeway across the marshes to St. Simons and turned left on Sea Island Road. Traffic slowed as we approached Frederica Road, with the stoplight turning yellow just as we reached the busy intersection. Sea Island causeway and The Cloister were directly ahead of us. I'd leaned over to adjust the radio when Lisa grabbed my right hand. "He's there!" she said in an urgent whisper. "There!"

I looked up. "Where? Who? What are you talking about? Why are you whispering?"

"There. Straight ahead. Across the street coming from Sea

Island." She held her head down and pointed. A large black Audi sedan was stopped for the light, signaling to turn onto Frederica Road. I could make out a dark-haired man behind the wheel, but he was too far away to see the details of his features.

"Are you sure?" I asked.

"I think so. It looks like the car I saw yesterday. Follow him, Matt. See where he goes."

The directional arrows for the turning lanes flashed green. The Audi turned left, pulling in front of us. I saw the silhouette of the driver's head. It could have been Habersham, but I wasn't sure. I flipped on the BMW's right turn signal and followed after him down Frederica Road. "Where does this street lead?" Lisa asked.

"To the airport, and then it dead ends into Kings Way. If you turn left, you'll end up at the Village—that's what passes for downtown in St. Simons. If you go right, you head to the mainland." We followed at a discreet distance, keeping several cars between us and the Audi. At the first large intersection, he turned left on Demere toward the airport terminal, but passed it and kept on down the oak-covered street.

"Where's he heading now?" Lisa asked again.

"The street goes through a residential area. Lots of houses, vacation cottages, condos—that sort of thing. If you follow it far enough you end up back in the Village, or if you turn to the east, you'll be at the beach." The Audi passed the Bloody Marsh battle site, then flashed a red blinker to turn left. "He's heading toward the old Coast Guard Station and East Beach," I said. We followed him across a short causeway through a marsh, again keeping several cars between us.

At the end of the causeway, the Audi turned right on Ocean Boulevard, passing between jam-packed "beach villas" on the left and the marsh on the right. I could see a yellow caution light ahead. The car's left blinker flashed to turn into a small street in a residential neighborhood next to the beach.

"I wonder where..." Lisa started, then said, "Oh, my God." I glanced at her. She was pointing at a yellow and black sign with an arrow in the direction that the Audi was turning.

"What's..."

"That sign. It says *The King and Prince*."

"Yeah, it's an old beachfront hotel."

"Unbelievable," Lisa said with amazement in her voice. "It's also the answer to one of the clues in Jarrard's crosswords."

55

THE STREET APPEARED to dead-end into the gated courtyard of a small hotel. "I haven't been here in years," I said, slowing the BMW to a crawl. "That used to be the main entrance up ahead." The driver of the Audi tapped his breaks and turned right down another small street along the side of the building. I eased forward just in time to see him turn into a parking lot directly in front of what must have been the new main entrance of The King and Prince. I pulled over into a parking place with a good view of the street and main door of the hotel.

A figure emerged from the parking lot and strode confidently toward the hotel. He was thin with medium brown hair, wearing a dark green blazer over a white open-necked shirt. There was something familiar about him. I silently admitted to myself that Lisa could be right. The man approached the entrance where he was greeted warmly by the doorman. They exchanged a few words and parted smiling as the hotel employee held the door open for his guest.

"Ideas?" I said. "It could be Habersham, but I'm not sure that I'd recognize him from a distance."

Lisa turned around and rummaged in the small storage area behind the seats, coming up with a floppy hat. She held it out to me, commanding, "Try this on."

"Are you kidding?"

"Nope," she said, wrapping her head in a scarf and grabbing a small disposable camera out of the glove box. "Just be sure to

268

keep your sunglasses on."

"I look ridiculous."

"You look like a tourist—you're supposed to look ridiculous. Pretend you're an accountant from Atlanta on vacation." She opened the door and stood by the car. "Are you coming?"

I reluctantly followed.

Lisa ambled down the sidewalk toward the parking lot. She stopped, reached out, and grabbed my hand. "Look happy," she said. The Audi was parked just in front of us, its Florida tag clearly visible. "That's it," she confirmed.

She turned and surveyed the building. It was an ugly shade of ochre-yellow with brick-red roof tiles. The architectural style was "added-on modern"—an ill-fitting conglomeration of boxy Palladian next to Dutch-topped facades juxtaposed with short Byzantine towers, all painted the same color in hopes that the details would be lost to the casual observer. Grabbing my hand once more, she pulled me toward the fake Moorish arches of the hotel entrance following the path of the Audi's driver.

The doorman saw us coming and held the door open. Lisa asked him, "That man who just came in, I think I recognized him. Isn't that Sir Laurence Fishburne, the famous British actor?" I winced behind my sunglasses.

"No, ma'm," he replied. "That's Mr. Peter Harvill. He's British, all right, but I don't think he's no actor."

"Well, I could swear he looked so familiar. He *must* be famous then. I know I've seen him somewhere."

The doorman laughed. "Maybe. He's got a house over at Sea Island, but he's been staying here for the past two weeks while he's remodeling and adding on an extra room. They've got his house all tore up, he says. I know he's had painters and plasterers parading in and out of here about every day, consulting with him about this or that. I can just imagine what it's like at his house with workmen swarming all over the place. He's a nice fellow, though. I've gotten to know him pretty well."

"He's not in the textile business by any chance, is he?" I had no idea where Lisa came up with that.

"No, no. I'm pretty sure he's retired…"

"But he looks so young," she protested.

"Looks can be deceiving, young lady." Then glancing around

and lowering his voice said, "He's older than he looks. I think he dyes his hair."

"Thanks," she smiled, and we walked in the hotel. "Peter Harvill. Pendleton Habersham. At least he kept the initials the same," Lisa said, speaking softly.

The cavernous lobby was humid and reeked of chlorine from an indoor pool half-concealed behind a row of low greenery. Lisa looked around and sniffed. "This is a big jump down from Sea Island. Why is he staying here? And what was all that about renovations on his house? There's nothing going on over there."

"I don't know," I said, starting to remove my sunglasses. She motioned for me to keep them on.

Lisa pointed to a couple of chairs in the lobby. We sat down while she examined the hotel's reception area near the front door. The short length of counter was manned by one overweight receptionist who was constantly being interrupted to answer the phone. "They look understaffed. I've got an idea." Spying a house phone on the far wall, she said, "I'm going to call the front desk and ask them to connect me to Harvill's room. Go over and make conversation with the clerk. When she answers my call, see if you can see what number she punches to forward it. I'll hang up once it starts ringing."

I strolled over and pretended to study a hotel brochure that I found in a clear plastic stand on the counter. I felt silly in the floppy hat and sunglasses. The receptionist asked if she could help me. "Perhaps," I said. "My wife and I are planning a romantic getaway for our anniversary and I was wondering if you could..." The desk phone buzzed softly.

"Could you excuse me just a sec?" the girl asked. "I apologize, but one of the staff had to go home sick and we're a little short-handed." Without waiting for my response, she pressed a button and picked up the receiver, saying "Front desk." A pause, then, "Certainly." She looked at a printout next to the phone, running her finger down a list. I couldn't read the name but could see the figure *200*. I watched her press 7-2-0-0, then hang up.

Looking back up at me, she continued, "I'm sorry. You were asking about anniversary packages?" I nodded. "We have several in various price categories, ranging from ordinary rooms on up to our oceanfront suites. What did you have in mind?"

"Something nice. A suite maybe."

"Well, if you're really interested, I'd advise you to book far in advance. The hotel's been here since the 1930s, and a lot of couples who honeymooned here come back at the same time every year. Our best room is the Governor's Suite. It's in the historic part of the building, looks out on the ocean, and has two levels. It's $389 a night. Then there's the…"

"Could I see one?"

"I'm afraid all of our suites are occupied at the moment. They do stay full. In fact, we're even having to move one guest out of our Governor's Suite to another room tomorrow morning because we've got a couple coming in to celebrate their fiftieth wedding anniversary. They stay here every year…"

I could see Lisa motioning to me. The desk phone buzzed. I said, "I know you're busy. Let me take your brochure. I'll study it and give you a call later." I headed toward the front door without giving her a chance to respond.

"He's in room 200. I have no idea where that is. What now?"

"Back to Sea Island. We need to call Kight. Then I'm getting back on my laptop. Jarrard uses the term *King and Prince* as the answer to a crossword puzzle clue and we find the man responsible for his death staying in a hotel by that name. This is getting to be Alice in Wonderland."

"How so?"

"Curiouser and curiouser."

56

I CALLED KIGHT and told him what we'd done and seen. He listened quietly, asking an occasional question, until I'd finished. He then said, "Matt, you two are survivors. In the last couple of months, you've been through more trauma—both physical and mental—than most people go through in a lifetime. I appreciate that. I understand it. But let me explain something to you. I've been in law enforcement all of my life. I've seen a lot of people in your situation. I want you to know that it's hard sometimes.

"The worst part for me is seeing what crime does to its victims. Take you and Lisa, for example. You both had very narrow escapes—you're lucky to be alive. Things *should* be fine now. To most objective observers you *should* be doing well. We've busted this case. We've got the bad guys. Yeah, Habersham's still on the run, but we're virtually certain of his general whereabouts in the southern Caribbean. You get the idea.

"Matt, I don't want to sound unsympathetic, but this is the third phone call I've gotten from you in the last twenty-four hours. I got your message. I promised you that we'd be in touch just as soon as possible. So *please*, hang in there for a while. We know what we're doing. Trust us." The line went dead.

Lisa had been listening from her perch in the chair, her feet propped on the bed. "What'd he say?"

"He gave me the old Jimmy Carter line—Trust me."

"So…"

"So, we wait. He said they'd call." I flopped on the bed and

272

propped myself up on a couple of pillows. "And he's probably right. I've got to admit that Harvill looks like Habersham with darker hair, and I can't deny that there are just too many coincidental connections, but what can you and I do?"

Lisa thought briefly, then looked at her watch and smiled. "It's nearly lunch time. I'll give you a choice: room service or sex."

An hour later, we drifted over to the Beach Club for lunch.

□□□

WE SPENT A SECOND AFTERNOON at the pool, Lisa with her laptop and me with my novel. I'd drifted off to sleep under the shade of an umbrella when I felt her shaking me. "I cannot figure it out," she said, sounding frustrated. "I know there's a message in there somewhere, but no matter how I approach it, I don't know where Jarrard was going with this. The two answers, *Habersham* and *King and Prince,* have to mean something. They have to be part of a pattern that I just can't…"

"Lisa," I said, rubbing my eyes. "Why don't you put it to bed for a while? Kight had a point. Maybe it's time for us to focus on other things. He said they'd call us, and all we can do is wait. Do you want to think about going back to Walkerville?"

She looked hurt. She took a deep breath and exhaled a little too loudly.

"Okay. I know you're right." She paused. "I don't think I want to leave here until we talk with the FBI and settle this Harvill-Habersham thing once and for all. What is it they say? The dust will settle, the loose ends will fall into place, the ducks will come home to roost…"

"Chickens."

"Whatever. I need to back off, don't I?"

I nodded. She smiled. "You remember when we first met in Savannah? I liked the city. Why don't we ride up there and have dinner? It's only an hour up I-95."

"Sounds wonderful to me. I know some great restaurants around River Street."

Lisa flipped her laptop shut with a sharp click and stuffed it in her beach bag. "I need to learn to relax, don't I?"

When a woman asks a rhetorical question, you learn not to answer it. I leaned over and gave her a kiss on the cheek.

□□□

I HIRED A CAR AND DRIVER through the hotel. I thought that a little alcohol might help the situation. We sat in the back of a dark green Town Car sipping champagne and holding hands. We dined on pan-seared *fois gras* followed by lobster and poached artichoke hearts washed down by good white burgundy. We got back to The Cloister by midnight, slightly drunk, but very happy. Or so I thought.

An hour or so before dawn, something awakened me. I reached out for Lisa, but the bed was empty. I could see light shining from under the bathroom door. All was quiet. I glanced at the clock. 4:40 a.m. I adjusted my pillows and turned over to go back to sleep, but ten minutes later, the bathroom door was still closed with the light on and Lisa hadn't come back to bed. I thought perhaps she was ill. "Lisa?" I called. "Are you all right?"

"I'm fine," she called back, cracking the bathroom door and peeking out. "I didn't mean to wake you up."

"You didn't. Are you all right? You're not sick, are you?"

"No, I'm fine," she said, opening the door fully and standing silhouetted in the light. "Last night was wonderful. The last two weeks have been wonderful. You're wonderful." I spied her laptop open on the counter behind her.

"Are you working on the crosswords?"

"Yeah," she replied, sounding a bit ashamed. "I wasn't going to—honest—but I woke up about half an hour ago and had an idea. I'm just checking it out. I think I'm on to something." She walked over and sat on the bed next to me, putting her hand on my cheek. "You know that I won't be satisfied until I unravel all the knots Jarrard hid in these puzzles."

"I know, but can't it wait until morning?"

"Sure it can. Just let me do one more thing and I'll be back to bed." She went back into the bathroom and shut the door.

□□□

I AWOKE AT EIGHT to find Lisa sound asleep next to me. She'd missed her morning run. She rolled over and smiled, "Sorry to wake you up, but you went right back to sleep."

"What time did you come back to bed?"

"About five-thirty. I'm making progress. I think the answer has to do with Jarrard's numbering of the grid matrix."

"Huh?"

"Never mind. I'll show you when I finish."

□□□

WE ATE A LATE BREAKFAST, took a long walk on the beach, then I headed back to the Shooting School for more practice with a Benelli 12-gauge. Lisa reclined on a chaise on the balcony, laptop before her and a yellow legal pad filled with numbers and copious notes at her side. We met for lunch at the Beach Club. I had the cold buffet while she had a Caesar Salad with blackened shrimp. I didn't ask her about the crosswords. She didn't volunteer anything. We talked about Savannah and Walkerville and her high school days in California. I told a funny story about something that had happened when I was living on the West Coast before moving back to Walkerville. Afterwards, I suggested touring some local art galleries. Lisa said she'd rather stay in the room for a while. "I'm almost there," she explained. We agreed to meet back at four for a late afternoon swim.

When I got back to the hotel at 3:45, she was in her bathing suit waiting for me. "Did you solve them?" I asked.

"I think so. There's one more little thing that I need to do, and I'd like your help with it."

"Do you want to go over it with me now?"

"Not really. Why don't I run it all past you after dinner tonight?" She came over and put her arms around me. "Matt, I know I've been distracted—I guess it's like the tale of the scorpion and the frog—it's just my nature. I finally realized what Jarrard was doing with the puzzles, and once I did that, things began to fall into place. I'm really sort of burned out on all this. Let's take a swim, dress up, and have cocktails, then have a good dinner over at The Lodge on St. Simons—I've already made reservations."

"Sounds wonderful."

We swam laps and had drinks with little umbrellas in them and napped by the pool in the soft afternoon light. For a change, the sun and the moon seemed to have resumed their usual orbits.

57

DINNER WAS, TO USE LISA'S NEW FAVORITE WORD,
wonderful. We ate in the Terrace Room. I had the filet with
Béarnaise sauce, Lisa had roast duck with mango chutney. We
got back to the hotel about 11:00, relaxed and very mellow after
a bottle of côte du Rhône and two glasses of a sweet Australian
botrytis sémillon with our dessert soufflé.

"Okay," Lisa said after I'd taken off my tie, "I promised to
show you the puzzles that I've been working on. I've come up with
a solution, but honestly, Matt, I'm not at all sure what Jarrard was
getting at. A pattern emerges, but it doesn't seem to make much
sense. I'm certain that he wasn't finished. He probably intended
to write some more clues or hints or something else that would
allow some of his friends in the puzzle community to decipher
his code."

She took four sheets of paper out of a folder and laid them on
the desk. I recognized them as printouts we'd made in Walkerville
from Jarrard's flash drive. "You remember that there were seven
puzzles in all, right?" I nodded. "Jarrard apparently intended to
send the first two to Bonifay and Cordy—they're the ones with
the artists' names and the bank information. I had to use the third
puzzle to solve the first two.

"Okay," she said pointing at the puzzles. "These were the ones
left over—the supposedly unimportant ones. Jarrard had named
them Puzzle 4, and so on, but I've decided that the name or order
is not important. Look at them. What do you see?"

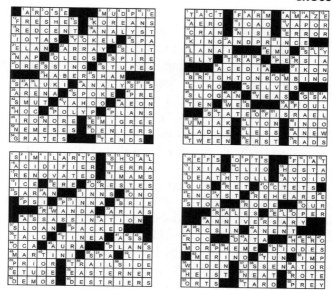

"Four completed crossword puzzle grids."

"Yes, but look at the longer words in each puzzle. We know about *Habersham* and *King and Prince,* but how about this one here, *Brighton Bombing*, or here, *State of Israel*? Those answers just look weird—sort of out of place. And two of them, *Habersham and King and Prince*, simply can't be coincidental. So, starting with those two, I tried to find a pattern. That's what I've been working on so hard.

"Last night, I was dreaming—I don't remember what about—when I woke up and realized that I'd been ignoring one thing. Remember that the bank account information was hidden in Puzzle 2, the unfinished one, and that the key to decoding it was in Puzzle 3?" She pulled another sheet out of her folder. "This is the clue list for Puzzle 2:"

Puzzle 3 Clues
1-26. Crazy bankers
27-41. Where it's at, baby.
42-52. = 53-59
59-70. 13D, 43A, 52D

93, 21, 152, 40, 70, 12, 136, 150, 91, 76, 88, 40, 1, 87

"See the list of numbers at the bottom? We—I—just forgot about them. Ignored 'em. That was my big mistake. They were there, just screaming at me, but I assumed that they were… well, I don't know what I was thinking. Last night it came to me that the key to whatever's in these four puzzles might be hidden in those numbers. That was what I was working on at 4:30 this morning. I needed to find a way to connect one of those numbers to *Habersham* and *King and Prince*.

"I tried everything. The puzzle grids are numbered, so the first thing, of course, was to try to link them to the grid numbers. I came up with nothing, *nada*. Next, I tried mathematical variations, relationships to prime numbers, Fibonacci sequences, you name it. Still nothing. Then, this afternoon after lunch, it hit me. What if I renumbered the grid?

"The puzzles are in fifteen by fifteen squares in size, so there are 225 spaces for letters inside the whole thing. I tired renumbering from left to right, with the first square being '1,' the second '2,' and so on. Nothing. I tried numbering backward starting with '225,' '224,' and that way. Again, nothing. Instead of horizontal numbering, I tried going from top to bottom. I did that sort of thing for an hour and came up with absolutely zip. Suddenly, I knew what I was doing wrong. I renumbered the grids while ignoring the filled-in black squares. It worked. Look at this."

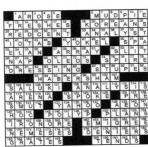 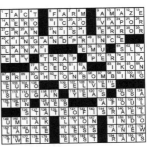

"See, *Habersham* starts with square number 93, and *King and Prince* starts with square number 40—both are numbers that are in the clue list for Puzzle 3."

"Lisa, that's great," I said. "So what's the solution?"

"That's where I need your help. I assumed that the numbers corresponded to a box that starts a word, but the grid numbers repeat themselves in each puzzle. Plus, there's no way of knowing if the word is across or down. So, for example, in this puzzle number '1' could mean either *arose*, which is 1 Across, or *areolar*, which is 1 Down. In the next puzzle, '1' could mean *tact* or *tackle*. And there's no hint as to *which* of the four puzzles the number refers to. Fortunately, a lot of the numbers fell in the middle of words in some or all of the puzzles, so that narrowed the options. Anyway, this is what I came up with. I want you to help me interpret it."

Lisa took a piece of yellow legal paper out of the folder and handed it to me. "This is a list of the words that correspond to the numbers. They're in their original order. Study it and tell me what you think." She motioned for me to sit down in the chair.

Number	Words Corresponding to Numbers
93	Habersham
21	Hate, Hosta
152	Prior, U.S. Senator
40	Iotas, King and Prince, Gus
70	Piney, Rode
12	Freshes, Friend, Zoo, Oratorio, A tissue
136	State of Israel
150	Plans, Maw
91	Assassination
76	Bridal, Brie
88	Rule, Anniversary, Accredit
40	Iotas, King and Prince, Gus
1	Arose, Areolar, Tact, Tackle, Similar to, Saris, Refs, Ridges
87	Stupes, Shako, Brighton Bombing, Best

I looked over the list, trying to make sense of it. Suddenly, it hit me like the blast of my exploding truck. "Holy shit," I nearly screamed, throwing the paper on the bed. I leaped across the room searching for the morning's *Brunswick News,* which I'd tossed in the trashcan after reading it.

"What are you saying?" Lisa demanded, her voice trembling.

I grabbed the paper and tore through it until I found the section I was looking for. "I'm talking about another murder. Habersham's going to kill Gus Rode."

"Who is Gus Rode?" Lisa asked as I fumbled for my phone to call Agent Kight.

58

"YOU'VE NEVER HEARD of Augustus Caesar Rode?" I asked, tossing the paper to her. Lisa stared at the article and photograph on the front of the Community Life section. The 40-point headline screamed, *Senator Returns To Golden Isles For Golden Anniversary.* The text below it read:

> St. Simons Island—Georgia's senior Senator Augustus "Gus" Rode and his wife Myrtle arrived today to celebrate their wedding anniversary in the historic King and Prince Hotel on St. Simons.
> "I was barely out of high school and in the Navy, stationed here in Brunswick, when Myrt and I decided to get married," the silver-tongued orator explained in his twangy north Georgia mountain drawl. "The most I could get was a 3-day pass, so we couldn't take a proper honeymoon. We headed for the best place I couldn't afford at the time, the King and Prince."
> In what has now become a yearly pilgrimage, Senator Rode and his wife return once more for a week's stay in the same room they occupied on their wedding night half a century ago.
> "A lot has changed over the years," the Senator reflected, "but this is one tradition we've both come to love and enjoy."

"What makes you think Habersham is planning to kill Rode?" Lisa asked. "I don't get the connection…"

"Hang on a second," I said as I punched Kight's number into my cell phone. The phone rang five times, followed by a click and, "You've reached the voice mail of Special Agent Andrew Kight. Please leave a message." I looked at my watch. 11:18. He must have cut his phone off for the night. Or did he recognize my number on caller-ID and refuse to answer? I said, "This is Matt Rutherford. If you get this message call me. I need to talk to you right away. No matter what you want to believe, I think that Habersham is going to try to kill Senator Gus Rode. Call me on my cell phone. Please. This is important."

Lisa demanded, "Matt! Explain this to me, please. You've lost me."

I held the sheet in front of her. "Look at the list of words. Think of them not as individual clues, but as part of a sentence. If you choose only one word for each number and string them together, it makes sense. Watch." I took a pen and began scratching through words in the list. I handed it back to Lisa. "Now read it."

Number	Words Corresponding to Numbers
93	Habersham
21	Hate, Hosta
152	Prior, U.S. Senator,
40	Iotas, King and Prince, Gus
70	Piney, Rode
12	Freshes, Friend, Zoo, Oratorio, A tissue
136	State Israel
150	Plans, Maw
91	Assassination
76	Bridal, Brie
88	Rule, Anniversary, Accredit
40	Iotas, King and Prince, Gus
1	Arose, Areolar, Tact, Tackle, Similar to, Saris, Refs, Ridges
87	Stupes, Shako, Brighton Bombing, Best

She read slowly, "Habersham-Hate-US Senator-Gus-Rode-Friend-State of Israel-Plans-Assassination-Bridal-Anniversary-King and Prince-Similar To-Brighton Bombing." She looked up. "Oh, my God. We've got to get word to the police. We've got to stop him." Then, "What does 'Brighton Bombing' mean?"

"I don't know, but based on what he tried to do to me, I have an idea that it involves explosives." I looked at my watch. "Let's go."

"Where?"

"To the King and Prince. We can call them on the way. Tell them to call the cops and get the senator and his wife out of there." I grabbed the cell phone and the BMW's keys and we ran toward the car. "What's the number for the King and Prince?" I yelled.

"How should I know?" Lisa yelled back.

I punched 4-1-1 into the phone and tossed her the keys. "You drive. I'll call." The phone rang and rang and rang, finally answering. "Welcome to Verizon Wireless 411 Connect. For English, press one. *Para español, marque numero dos.*" I pressed '1' as we cleared the Sea Island gatehouse. I could hear ringing again. Finally, a human voice said, "City, state and listing, please."

"The King and Prince."

"Is that a city?"

"No, no. I'm sorry. St. Simons Island in Georgia."

"Is that the listing?"

"No. I want the phone number for the King and Prince on St. Simons Island, in Georgia."

"One moment, please."

Lisa barely made the stoplight at the intersection of the Sea Island Causeway and Frederica Road. We took the turn doing sixty. The operator came back on to say, "I don't have a listing for a King Prince on St. Simons Island. Do you have a street address?"

"No, dammit. It's 'King and Prince.' That's spelled K-I-N-G-A-N-D-P-R-I-N-C-E."

There was a moment of silence, then, "How do you spell that middle name?" We were doing sixty-five down Frederica Road.

"There's not a middle name. It's a hotel. I said 'and.' It's a word."

"Sorry, sir. I guess I didn't understand you. So do you think it might be listed under the last name 'Prince' or the first name 'King'?

"It's not a person's name. It's a business, dammit."

"Sir, you don't need to curse at me."

"I'm sorry. I'm trying to stop a murder."

"Oh. Of course. You must have thought you were dialing 9-1-1. You dialed 4-1-1. This is Directory Assistance. You want Emergency Services. People make the mistake all the time."

"No, goddammit. I want the phone number of the King and Prince hotel so I can stop a murder."

"Sir, I'm going to hang up now. Abusive language over the telephone is never appropriate, and furthermore, you may be in violation of Federal law with such speech. I'd advise you to dial 9-1-1." The line went dead. We zipped though two lights and came to a screeching halt at the Frederica-Demere intersection.

"You get the number?" Lisa asked.

"No, and we're so close now that it doesn't matter, anyway. Forget calling. We'll be there in less than five minutes."

The left turn arrow flashed green. Lisa gunned the car around the corner, barely missing an obviously drunk college student who was trying to jaywalk while carrying a load of Domino's Pizza boxes. The airport flew by on our right. As we zoomed past a small side street, I saw a car flip on its lights and pull out into the road behind us. Our pursuer closed the gap rapidly. I looked over my shoulder and said, "Oh, shit," just as the cop cut on his blue lights and siren.

"What do you want me to do?" Lisa asked. I glanced at the speedometer. We were doing sixty-five.

"Stop, I guess. We don't have much choice."

Lisa pulled over under a huge live oak tree whose branches reached out across the road. I watched in the rear view mirror as the patrolman got out and cautiously approached the car, beaming his flashlight inside to blind us. "Ma'am, I clocked you at sixty-eight in a twenty-five zone. May I see your license and proof of insurance, please?"

Lisa instinctively reached between the seats, then murmured, "Damn," before turning to the cop and saying, "It's an emergency. I left it at the hotel."

The policeman leaned closer. "Ma'am, do I smell alcohol on your breath? Have you been drinking?"

"We had wine with dinner. I'm not drunk."

He stood up and took a deep breath, saying, "That's what they all say." Then, "I'm going to have to ask you to get out of the car and stand facing the vehicle with your hands on the roof and your legs spread apart."

I said, "We don't have time for this."

"It's your call," Lisa said, pressing the BMW's accelerator to the floor. I looked back to see the cop speaking into his lapel mike calling for backup. "I've got a little headway. Maybe I can lose him…" She was doing nearly seventy as she braked and made a sliding turn onto the East Beach Causeway toward the hotel. We'd reached the turn-off before the patrol car rounded the curve behind us, so I reasoned that we might have gotten away. Looking to our rear, I saw him fly past down Demere toward the Village. We were just turning on Ocean Boulevard when I looked back again to see flashing blue lights heading our way down the causeway.

59

THE YELLOW CAUTION LIGHT indicating the turn for the King and Prince flashed like a beacon in front of us. A huge delivery truck emblazoned with Monarch Institutional Food Services was waiting to pull out onto Ocean Boulevard, effectively blocking our turn into the street. Lisa said, "What do I do?"

"Go on down a ways. We can turn down one of the side streets and work our way back." We flew through the light and around a small curve before Lisa slowed and pulled into a small, barely paved lane lined with small, brightly painted wood-frame beach houses. An occasional street light bathed the scene in a yellow sodium vapor glow. We weaved our way back and forth through the maze of small streets, eventually emerging next to the glowing ochre hulk of the King and Prince. The cop was nowhere to be seen.

Lisa grabbed the same floppy hat and scarf that I'd worn on our earlier visit. "Put this on," she directed. This time, I didn't argue. She locked the car. We'd started toward the hotel when I saw a police car round the corner at the end of the street, driving slowly with only his parking lights on. I was sure he couldn't see us; we were between street lights. I pulled Lisa out of sight into an overgrown laurel hedge marking the border of one of the small yards. We were fifty feet away from the car.

The cop slowed, then stopped, turning on his headlights first, then turning on a spotlight over the car. I could see him talking into his radio microphone. He got out slowly, hand on his gun, and approached the BMW from the rear. He circled it, cautiously, playing his high intensity flashlight beam on the interior. Satisfied that no one was inside, he walked to the rear and copied down the tag number on a pad before returning to his patrol car.

Lisa whispered, "We've got to get out of here." Before we could move, I heard the muffled ringing of a cell phone from the direction of our car. "Where is your phone?" she asked.

"Locked in the car. And yours?"

"At the hotel." I couldn't see her expression in the darkness.

I said, "I hope that was Kight calling back. Let's head for the hotel."

We pushed our way though the hedge, cut through two back yards, and climbed a small fence to avoid a barking dog before we emerged on the far side of the King and Prince's parking lot. Two police cars rounded the corner ahead, blue lights flashing. I put my arm around Lisa while she leaned her head on my shoulder. We walked slowly toward the hotel. One car headed our way, slowed slightly as it passed us, then turned up the small lane toward the abandoned BMW. The other car parked on the entrance ramp of the hotel. "That's great," I said. "I guess now they'll be checking everyone entering the hotel." I turned to Lisa. "Suggestions?"

"I don't know..." she started, then said, "Look." A figure carrying two small duffel bags was walking across the hotel parking lot toward Habersham's Audi. "Is that..." The man walked under a streetlight in and out of a pool of illumination. It was Habersham. Or Harvill. We stood embracing in the shadows. A casual observer would have thought we were lovers out for a romantic evening.

Habersham pressed a remote control on his keychain. The Audi's parking lights flashed and the trunk popped open. He threw in his luggage, looked back at the hotel, then at his watch. Turning quickly, he walked back in the direction from which he'd come.

"Let's follow him," Lisa said.

Moving rapidly, we kept him in sight as he stepped into the open foyer of a building labeled King and Prince Beach Villas. He paused, looked around, then turned and pressed the elevator button. The door opened and he stepped in. We ran up the short steps to the foyer, watching the light on the lift as it blinked on and off for the second floor, third floor, and then stopped and remained lit for the fourth. Lisa pulled on my sleeve and nodded toward the parking lot. A patrolman with a flashlight was walking in our direction. We both saw the stairs at the same time and bounded up them, stopping when we reached level four.

The Beach Villas appeared to be condominiums, each with a separate door joining to an open common walkway. "Where did he go?" Lisa whispered.

"I don't know," I said, looking over the railing to see the cop prowling around the parking lot below with his flashlight. Three other policemen were searching between and under the cars in front of the hotel. "I think we're trapped for the moment. There's only one way down. If they catch us, it'll be jail first and explanations later."

"Why don't we knock on one of these doors? We'll explain the situation—tell them that we need to use the phone to warn the hotel."

I peered over the railing again. The cop was moving toward the elevator foyer. "We don't have much to lose." I walked up to the door in front of us and pressed the bell. I heard a "ding-dong" on the inside. We waited. Nothing happened.

Lisa whispered, "The cop is checking the second floor. I think he's working his way up." I peeked over the rail to see him walking along the second level walkway below. "You want to try taking the elevator down and bypass him?"

"Too risky. The others would spot us." I walked to a second door and pressed the bell, following it this time with a soft rapping. I heard another "ding-dong" then stirring behind the door. The light in the door's peephole went dark and then light. "Somebody's in there," I whispered. "I think they just looked out to see us."

I heard the scratching of a chain being removed from the door, then the solid click of a deadbolt being turned back. The handle turned. The door eased opened a crack. A male voice said, "Yes?"

"We need to use your phone. We need to call the police. May we come in—I need to explain things."

"In that case, of course," the voice said as the door swung open. Before us stood Pendleton Brewster Habersham, a.k.a. Peter Harvill, a.k.a. Yasir bin Hamid al-Aziz. He was holding a large caliber automatic pointed at my heart. "What a pleasant surprise,

Mr. Rutherford. Please, do come in."

60

WE SAT ON THE SOFA. Habersham sat across from us in a comfortable chair, slowly waving his gun back and forth between us. "It's strange, you know. Yesterday, when I was staying over in the main building, I got a call from the front desk, but they hung up just as I answered. I called the desk back, and the girl said that a woman had called for me from one of the house phones. She said she could see her from the desk, and that it appeared to be a young oriental accompanied by a man with a southern accent who wore dark glasses and a strange hat. Then, as I was leaving, the doorman told me the same thing—that you'd been asking about me, thought you'd seen me somewhere before. It crossed my mind that it might be you two, but I said, no, that's impossible."

"You're planning to kill Gus Rode, aren't you?"

"How clever you are. I have to assume my ex-son-in-law did leave you his secrets. But he must have bequeathed them to you two only; I haven't seen the FBI breaking down the door trying to stop me."

"But why?" Lisa asked. "He's a United States senator. You'll never get away with it."

"You must be terribly naïve about politics, young lady. Do you know who Mr. Augustus Caesar Rode really is? Perhaps you see him as a silver-haired, honey-tongued, pork barrel-delivering supporter of your great state, but I see him as the Chairman of the Senate Foreign Relations Committee and Israel's own man in Congress. He's a Bible-thumping religious bigot who has openly admitted that his support for Israel and the Jews is nothing short of some imagined religious mandate—based, of course, on his own perverted interpretation of the Holy Book.

"Do you know what is happening in Palestine? Do you know about the genocidal policies of the State of Israel? Do you realize the level of suffering and starvation that has been visited upon the Palestinian people in their so-called refugee camps—camps that have been there since before your dear Senator Rode first bedded his repulsive wife in yonder building? I fully suspect that you don't. I'm an old man. I'm past seventy. I've lived a full and successful life and now I want to give something back to my people."

"By more killing?" Lisa asked.

"Now what's so wrong with that? It's an official state policy of Israel. Targeted assassination. You've seen the news reports. And it works. History has been changed many times by the untimely elimination of a prominent man or two. The loss of Rode will mean the loss of Israel's mouthpiece in Washington, which will mean fewer dollars flowing to Tel Aviv, which will mean fewer bombs and rockets to rain down on the Gaza Strip. You're so young, so idealistic. It's Bismarck's *realpolitik*.

"So," Habersham continued, looking at his watch, "in about twenty-five minutes, the good Senator and his wife will become two more statistics in the global war against terror. In this case, the war against the Zionist terrorists and their allies. President Bush would approve—it's a preemptive strike."

"What are you going to do?" I asked.

"I'm going to blow him up, of course. Didn't you know that? Stewart did. That's why we had the big break. He had no problems with finding ways to send support money for suicide martyrs, but he drew the line at killing a U.S. citizen. I never really understood that. He threatened to expose our little plot."

"Our?"

"It was McKenna's idea, really. In fact he—not I—was supposed to be here to pull this off. Right now, I should be settling into a life of luxury and anonymity with a new identity somewhere in the Middle East, but… it didn't work out that way. So I became the pinch hitter, as you Americans say. You *do* know McKenna was an operative with the Irish Republican Army? He was one of the planners of that spectacular blow at the Conservative Party

Congress in 1984 in Brighton. He..."

"The Brighton Bombing," Lisa gasped.

"Yes. I'm glad you know your international history even if you don't know who Gus Rode is..." he looked at his watch again, "I can say 'was' shortly. A simple political killing is certainly important. A tragedy or a success depending on which side you're on. But a *spectacular* killing is so much more—a *statement*, as it were—not unlike those overpriced baubles that I've spent years selling to the world's *nouveau riche* and social climbers. Look at September 11, for example—how many times a day do you still see images of the Trade Center towers falling? I don't approve of that, of course, it was mass murder. But, oh, what a statement.

"In Brighton, an IRA man checked into the same hotel that was due to host Margaret Thatcher and associates a few weeks later at their party convention. He hid a bomb in the wall and walked away. In the middle of the night, when all should be asleep, boom! Unfortunately, the Prime Minister was up practicing her speech for the next day and avoided certain death. I don't believe that the Senator is going to be so lucky. He's too predictable. He's spent every anniversary here in the same room in this hotel for the last fifty years. McKenna and I have been planning this for a couple of years. I've been the occupant of the Rode Honeymoon Suite for the last two weeks while the house at Sea Island is supposedly being remodeled. All the workmen that have been coming back and forth to 'consult' with me have done an excellent job of patching and painting the hole in the wall where the bomb's hidden. And no one's the wiser."

"The FBI is. I called them on the way here," I said.

"As if they could change things now. In less than fifteen minutes, I want us all to stand on that balcony out there and watch the blast. The view won't be great, but we'll miss getting hit by flying debris. I'd actually planned to watch it from the beach, but since I have you two as unexpected guests..." He didn't finish, instead getting up to open the sliding glass door onto the balcony. He sat back down. "And then I've got a plane to catch."

"The FBI..." I started.

"Forget the bloody FBI. They're convinced that I'm somewhere in the Caribbean. They keep a long roster of so-called 'sources' down there, gathering information on the drug trade. A group of scumbags. I knew the day would come when I'd have to leave. I've been planning for years. Hence this Peter Harvill identity. He's a tax-paying British subject with a legitimate passport. And there're others. All I had to do was make a phone call or two to get the ball rolling. The government is going to believe that they're one step behind me for the next five years."

"What about the flight to Mexico? Your fingerprints were in the plane."

"A clever touch, eh? We stopped in Jacksonville to refuel. I deplaned. The pilots were well paid to say that they dropped me off in Cartagena. Money talks, Mr. Rutherford." Habersham looked at his watch again. "Why don't we step out on the balcony? We don't want to miss the fireworks."

61

HABERSHAM MOTIONED WITH HIS PISTOL for us to get up, then pointed toward the open door to the balcony. "I don't mean to be morbid, but the extra sound of a couple of gunshots should be quite well lost in the roar of the blast. I hope so, anyway." There was a glass-topped table with two chairs next to it. "Sit down, please." He leaned against the wall at the opposite end, his gun pointed at us. "We just wait now."

I looked out to see a patrolman walking below across the grass between the building and the rock seawall. He paused to shine his light into the shrubbery. "Don't get any ideas," Habersham said.

Lisa screamed at the top of her lungs, "Rape!"

Habersham raised his gun, then slid down into the shadow as the cop's light panned across the front of the building looking for the source of the sound. "Down!" he ordered in a loud whisper.

I knelt down next to the chair, out of site from the lawn. "Who's there?" the cop yelled. Bracing my knees, I placed my hand under the table's edge and heaved. It flew over with a crash, the top splintering in a hundred pieces. Habersham held his arm over his face to protect himself and fired wildly in our direction. The bullets smacked into the concrete above our head. Grabbing one of the chairs, I flung it at him just as he fired again. I felt a searing pain in my left shoulder.

The chair hit Habersham squarely in the face, opening an ugly gash in his forehead. The gun flew from his hand, bounced off the wall behind him, and slid onto the sparkling pile of shattered glass. He grinned, blood running down his face, and lunged for it. I caught him with a swift kick in his chest. He staggered back against the rail, a look of pain in his eyes. I started to ease closer, fists ready.

Habersham gasped, "I won't let you win. Not this time. See you in Hell." With unexpected agility, he dived over the railing, landing with a sickening thud on a concrete walkway four stories below.

Half a dozen flashlight beams instantly painted the balcony an eerie white. I raised my hands and yelled, "It's all right. We're okay."

A voice below yelled back. "Throw down your gun. Put your hands in the air and don't move."

I looked at Lisa. She nodded and kicked Habersham's pistol under the rail and off the balcony. We both raised our hands. "You're bleeding," she said. I looked down. The left shoulder of my coat sported a deep red stain.

"I think it's just a flesh wound," I said and placed my right hand over the spot.

The voice below boomed, "Keep both of your hands up where we can see them." I raised my right hand again. There was a pounding at the condo door. "Open up. Police." I turned to open it, but the voice below commanded, "Don't move. Keep your hands up."

A crashing sound from inside the condo heralded the arrival of four Glynn County policemen, their guns drawn. Two of them held us at gunpoint while the other two cautiously checked for hidden assailants. "There's a bomb in the King and Prince. It's going to explode in less than fifteen minutes. Someone is trying to kill Gus Rode."

One of the cops said, "Nice try, sucker. The old ticking bomb line. I haven't heard that one in years."

The other one asked, "Who is Gus Rode?"

Lisa screamed, "He means it. There's a bomb in the hotel. You've got to get everyone out."

The first cop gave her a hard look and lowered his gun slightly. "You're serious, aren't you?"

"Yes, goddammit. The guy who jumped off the balcony, he planted a bomb in Senator Rode's room."

The cops backed up slightly and looked at each other, still holding us firmly at gunpoint. "What do you think?" one asked.

The other one pointed at me and said, "You. Are you putting us on?"

"No. It's part of a plan to assassinate Senator Gus Rode. He and his wife are staying in the Governor's Suite."

"How do you know about it?"

"We're with the FBI," Lisa answered. "Anti-terrorism unit. Undercover." The two guns lowered a notch.

"Show me your badge," the first patrolman said.

"We're undercover, dammit." Lisa was nearly screaming.

"I don't know…" the first cop said, while the second asked, "Do you know a sign? A password that will let us know that you're for real?"

"Of course," Lisa replied. "Pi to the sixth decimal place is 3.141593." I stared at her, wide-eyed. The cops slowly lowered their guns. "Good," she said. "We don't have much time." She sprinted past them to the stairs. I followed behind her with the cops behind me, their guns still drawn.

Reaching the ground floor, she sprinted the hundred yards to the hotel's main entrance. The lobby was deserted except for a patrolman chatting with the night desk clerk. Lisa yelled, "There's a bomb in the hotel. I think it's hidden in Senator Rode's room. You've got to get the guests out of here."

The desk clerk stared at her. The cop placed his hand on his gun, but quickly withdrew it as the remainder of the policeman crowded in the door behind us. "I mean it," Lisa screamed. "It's going to go off in less than ten minutes."

"But we've got eighty-six rooms full tonight. We can't just…"

"Forget it," Lisa said. She walked over and jerked down a fire alarm lever. The lobby was instantly filled with the whooping wail of sirens, accompanied by flashing halogen strobe lights. Almost immediately, the front desk phone began to ring. Guests cautiously poked their heads out of rooms. Lisa screamed at the top of her lungs, "Fire! This is not a joke. The hotel's on fire! Get out now!"

Turning back to the clerk, she said, "Where is the Governor's Suite? Room 200?"

The woman pointed across the lobby to a second-level mezzanine balcony. "There, down that hall a little ways."

"Call them. Tell them to get out *now*." Turning to me, she said, "Let's go."

A strong hand gripped my shoulder. "Not so fast, buster." It was the cop who'd tried to pull us over on Demere. "You and the woman here are under arrest." He motioned to another cop who grabbed Lisa. He twisted my arms behind me and slapped on handcuffs while his partner did the same to Lisa.

One of the patrolmen who'd been in the condo said, "Hold on, Randy. The girl says they're undercover FBI."

"Bullshit. I clocked them at nearly seventy down Demere. They ran for it and lost me over near Myrtle Street."

"These are the two…"

"Yep."

"Look," I said, "You can arrest us if you want to. We'll sort it out later—but you've got to get Senator Rode out of that room. I promise you, there's a bomb inside that's going to blow any minute."

The cops looked at one another. The one named Randy said, "I'll take 'em to the car. You guys go check that room—what was it?"

"Room 200," Lisa said.

"You shut up," Randy said. "You are looking at multiple felonies." We were hustled unceremoniously out the door and thrown in the back of the patrol car parked on the entrance ramp.

"You all right?" I asked.

"Just dandy," Lisa said.

"What was that crap about pi to the sixth decimal place?"

"I don't know. It was just the first thing that came to mind. It worked, didn't it? It got us over here."

Throngs of guests, most in nightgowns, T-shirts, and robes, streamed through the doors and out into the street. I recognized a very agitated Senator Rode and wife being half-carried through the doors toward the parking lot. He said something to the officer tugging at his arm. I couldn't make out the words, but they seemed to be exchanging threats. The cop looked our way, then pointed toward our cage in the back of the patrol car. Rode broke away, stomped over, and pulled open the car's front door.

He stared at us for a moment through the wire mesh then said, "I don't know who you are or what communist radical pro-choice eco-terrorist group you represent, but let me tell you right now, you're not only going to be in jail, you're going to be *under* the jail. Tonight is my golden wedding anniversary. Come tomorrow morning, I'm going to…" The rest of his sentence—if he finished it—was lost in the muffled roar of the explosion.

E P I L O G U E

THE DAMAGE TO THE HOTEL was surprisingly light and mainly limited to the Governor's Suite. The only injuries among the guests were an odd assortment of sprained ankles and bruised egos, most of the latter in middle-aged women forced to emerge from their nighttime activities *sans* makeup. The gunshot wound to my left shoulder turned out to be minor. It was cleaned and dressed by an EMT who decided that I didn't require a visit to the hospital Emergency Room, probably because the county would be responsible for the bill since I was in their custody.

A series of phone calls to the FBI got Lisa and me released from a holding cell at the St. Simons substation of the Glynn County Police Department. Agents from both the Savannah and Jacksonville offices of the FBI, plus an assortment of law enforcement officials and Homeland Security types from Brunswick's Federal Law Enforcement Training Center, spent most of the night "debriefing" us before allowing us to return to our room at The Cloister.

After calling my uncle to warn him that the morning papers might allude to some trouble that we were involved in and promising to tell him all about it when we returned, both Lisa and I cut off our cell phones and told Sea Island security to block all of our calls. Despite this, both CNN and Fox News had in-depth stories about the attempted murder of a senator, complete with copies of mug-shot photos of Lisa and me taken when we were booked by Glynn County law enforcement. Lisa was horrified at the way she looked, but we were informed the photos were subject to Georgia's open-records law, despite the fact that all charges were hastily dropped.

The one person who did manage to talk his way past our security cordon was Senator Rode. He arrived with his wife by chauffeured limo and insisted on buying us dinner in The Cloister's main dining room. The food, as usual, was superb, and would have been better if he'd allowed us to order wine. During the course of the meal, we learned from the good Senator that alcohol in all forms promoted godlessness, and that his mother had been a prominent member of the Women's Christian Temperance Union.

Special Agent Kight dropped by a few days later to apologize and to say that the FBI would be picking up the expenses of our stay at The Cloister.

"You've been granted *ex post facto* undercover operative status," he explained.

We decided that he simply felt guilty for all their missteps, but didn't argue with the offer. They'd managed to round up all of the suspects associated with Habersham, both locally and in New York. "They weren't really terrorists, just thugs-for-hire," he said. Retrospectively, he added, it seemed that Habersham was the only ideologue in the group. The others were simply in it for the money.

As for Lisa and me, we went back to Walkerville for a few days to tie up loose ends and pack. It was early spring in New Zealand, and we both decided that we needed to get away for a while.

| A | U | T | H | O | R | ' | S | | N | O | T | E |

WHILE I HOPE THAT READERS enjoy *Crossword* as a "Southern" novel, I have to admit that the first words were written in a villa in the south of France overlooking Cannes and the Mediterranean, and further polished in view of rice patties and the Sea of Japan some weeks later. Inspiration comes from where the heart is, and, for me, that will always be the rural South.

My other admission is that I am a fanatical cruciverbalist, or so my wife often reminds me as I dig into the Friday *Wall Street Journal* puzzle. It's a nasty little habit that I picked up years ago, and is a regular source of joy and frustration. While riddles and wordplay are as old as spoken language, crossword puzzles as we know them are relatively new. It's generally accepted that the first crossword was written by Arthur Wynne and appeared in the New York *World* in December 1913. The craze spread rapidly on both sides of the Atlantic, and by the 1920s, they were a popular feature in many newspapers. The *New York Times*, whose puzzles are today among the most popular, was one of the last major papers to feature crosswords on a regular basis.

There are a number of excellent books that review the development of the modern crossword puzzle. A good example is *Crossword Puzzles: Their History and Their Cult* by Roger Millington (Thomas Nelson, 1975, with later paperback edition). A more current source of information is the internet, where there are multiple Web sites for puzzlers. I recommend www.cruciverb. com. Excellent information and strategy for all levels of play can be found, as well as a number of links to other information sources.

If one person should be given credit for popularizing crosswords and puzzles in general, it's Will Shortz, puzzle editor of the *New York Times* since 1993, as well as NPR's Weekend Edition puzzle master. I interviewed him while doing background research for this book. He is most gracious, and a nice guy. I am in awe of his wit, and much indebted to him for his input. His biography is available online through Wikipedia and other readily accessible Web sites.

Finally, I can't simply say that I'm a crossword puzzle fan and leave it at that. So, here's a little challenge. The crossword puzzle that follows is one of my own design. It's not easy, and neither is it terribly difficult. Read the clues carefully and solve it if you can. Photocopy the completed puzzle page and fax it to me at 478-552-5613, or mail it to Post Office Box 737, Sandersville, GA 31082. I will put all the puzzles in a jar, and randomly draw one out on December 31, 2006. The "winner" (if I'm allowed to use that term) and a guest will be invited to join me and my wife for dinner at one of the restaurants mentioned in this book—your choice. (The puzzle and clues are also posted on my Web site at www.williamrawlings.com.)

Thanks for reading the book. I welcome feedback, and will promptly answer e-mail and other correspondence. My mailing address is the post office box listed above, and my e-mail address is rawlings@pascuamangement.com. I am available and enjoy speaking to civic clubs, seminars, writers' groups, and the like.

The *Crossword* Crossword

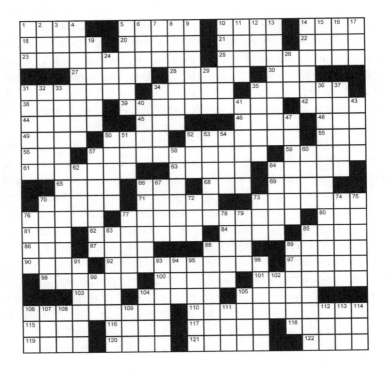

Name of Solver_____

Phone Number_____

E-mail Contact_____

When completed:
      1. Photocopy and Fax to 478-552-5613, or
      2. Photocopy and Mail to PO Box 737,
         Sandersville, GA 31082

The *Crossword* Crossword Clues

Across

1. Defect
5. The destroyer, to many in New Delhi
10. What he does after a raise, if he wants to stay in
14. Replica
18. Houston player
20. Michigan Senator
21. You can turn wood on it
22. Sounds like what a bank robber might be after, or he could play it
23. The state of being filled
25. 12-Downs written out
27. Avoids (stays away from)
28. The whale constellation
30. "So that's it!"
31. What paves the road to Hell (Michigan)
34. Spartan serf
35. One of the trailers
38. Fakes
39. Source of ambergris
42. Green-inducing
44. Isaac's mother
45. A single stranded helix, with uracil instead of thymine (abbr.)
46. They do it to you in bars
48. Keyboard key
49. An Australian wine grape is a city in the southern part of this country
50. A chieftain in the Middle East
52. The national game of India
55. Direction from Atlanta to Athens (Georgia, of course!!)
56. Hornswoggle
57. What the student did when he copped his essay off the web
59. Drang's partner, or play that thing
61. An indigenous Mexican (one of)
63. When they aired the old movie for the fourth time they _____ the rerun.
64. It holds your pack on
65. European eagle
66. The rt. hand dial on a Ford F-250 instrument panel gives you this information
68. Choler
69. Referring to the secular
70. Depressing (adjective)
71. Wipe out
73. A plaid weave textile
76. Short for the device used in external beam radiation treatments
77. Cleome hassleriana
80. You better hope you have a big one for your old age
81. Eggs, to Caesar
82. Matt Rutherford's housekeeper
84. Zwieback
85. Scalp sebaceous cysts
86. ___ Aviv
87. Central American cuckoo cousins
88. You can champ at it
89. Jesus does this, they say
90. Wife of Osiris
92. A 1924 opera by Richard Strauss or a 1936 film with Ingrid Bergman
97. Home of Minos
98. North Atlantic food fish
100. Elvis's shoes were made of this
101. Supermodel Brinkley
103. Add a "d" and you can spend it in Pretoria
104. Crackheads
105. What Lady MacBeth called a spot
106. Sounds like the Atlanta Zoo's late Willie B.
110. Chile part
115. You can sail there, or add a letter and walk it
116. Like antics of the Keystone Cops
117. A writer who thinks he can make a living at this
118. What a lawyer would think to do when he wanted to quit it.
119. How wild duck tastes
120. Newly hatched hawk
121. Where newly hatched hawks hang out
122. What labs test

Down

1. Against's opposite
2. Your place on the 10th
3. You can climb it, or add an "o" and Fido will eat it
4. Richard Burton or Dylan Thomas
5. When it rains it pours. When it turns to ice it _____
6. Fundamental players in the chicken or egg conundrum
7. In my possession, shortened
8. Guts
9. Benedictine monk and Archbishop of Canterbury
10. Dupin or Holmes, e.g.